Sweet Betsy

A FEMALE LAWMAN IN THE
NEW MEXICO TERRITORY

Michael R. Zomber

Cover Photo Credit: The Huntington Library

ISBN: 0615868444
ISBN 13: 9780615868448
Library of Congress Control Number: 2013915584
Renascent Films LLC, Devon, PA

Chapter 1
BETSY

Using great care, Betsy Johnson fitted the small, flat blade of her round, oak-handled screwdriver, into the slot of the single screw on the front of the frame of her Colt Single Action Army. It was just underneath the cylindrical base-pin with its concentric grasping grooves. The end of the base-pin protruded a good half an inch forward of the frame, itself. The blade of the screwdriver was hollow ground to begin with and Betsy had spent fifteen minutes with an Arkansas stone making certain the blade fit the slot snugly, for to her way of thinking there were few things more unsightly or more unnecessary than a badly marred screw. Betsy ordered three complete sets of extra screws from Colt's on Huyshope Street in Hartford just in case she ever slipped and peeled some steel from the screw. She felt the end of the blade bottom firmly in the slot. With a decisive counter clockwise twist she felt the screw break loose. She put the screwdriver down on the inch thick, smooth pine top of her small worktable and used her thumb and forefinger to remove it completely. Her nails were healthy looking but cut short and square. She placed the screw in a small, round metal tin and splayed out the fingers of her right hand. There were a few women in town with long, red painted fingernails. Their hands were soft and white, the backs so pale you could almost see the blood coursing through the blue veins, as delicate as a porcelain dinner plate. Betsy's were brown from exposure to the New Mexico Territory sun. Her fingers were long and shapely, but the pads were calloused from drawing well water, roping horses, chopping fire and stove-wood, and the hundred other tasks that she needed to do to keep her small spread running smoothly.

"Someday, I'll let them grow, file 'em, and then I'll have hands as pretty as Lorena Hutchinson's," she said to herself. Betsy transferred the long barreled Colt revolver from her left hand to her right hand and thumbed the hammer back to half cock. Her Peacemaker Colt was an older one, chambered for the .45 long Colt cartridge. Colt's had just come out with a 44-40 or 44 Winchester center fire caliber, the same cartridge Winchester used in their Model 1873 rifles and carbines.

"Wouldn't it be nice to have a rifle and pistol using the same ammunition? Someday, I'll order a Winchester saddle ring carbine and a new Single Action Army, both in 44-40."

She opened the loading gate and holding the pistol by the grip with barrel upright, she allowed the cartridges to drop out as she turned the cylinder through six distinctly audible clicks. She placed the five heavy cartridges upright on their bases.

Although her Colt had a safety notch or half cock, Betsy never bet hers or anyone else's life on it. She only ever loaded five of the six chambers. The firing pin on the hammer was a long piece of sharply pointed hardened steel that fell through a hole in the frame when the hammer was cocked and the pistol fired. Not that it had ever happened to her, but if the pistol dropped from waist level or higher, just right on a hard surface, a rock for instance, the revolver would fire, safety notch notwithstanding. The only really safe way to carry the handgun was with the hammer down on an empty chamber. When Betsy was a little girl, her father, Josiah, told her, "You either treat weapons with the respect they deserve, or they have a bad habit of teaching you themselves. You don't want them to teach you. When a gun teaches you, the first lesson is often your last one."

Where Betsy grew up in Western Kentucky, farmers, hunters, and children were often shot through carelessness. She knew the story of one man who died while he was out hunting. It was in the early spring and the ground was soggy from a recent thaw. He climbed over a fallen tree in search of a flock of wild turkeys and wasn't paying attention to the muzzle end of his double barrel shotgun. The barrels filled with mud like a cookie cutter with dough. Moments later, he flushed the turkeys. The birds lived but the man died.

After setting the fifth cartridge down, Betsy removed the base-pin, opened the loading gate and rolled out the cylinder. She put the pistol down, and carefully inspected the chambers, holding the cylinder up to the sunlight that streamed through the small window. Betsy was proud of her window because it was real glass, courtesy of John W. Tunstall, mayor of Early. Only the better shops and the saloon on the main street had glass in their front windows.

The other windows in Early had wooden shutters. Even Marcie Cabot's dry-goods store, which featured a dress that came all the way from Paris, France, had wooden shutters in the back. It was a mystery why a prudish, wealthy woman like Mrs. Cabot who almost single handedly funded the Church of Early and habitually campaigned to close the saloon as a "cesspit of moral turpitude" referring to both the liquor sold there and the so-called 'sporting women' who plied their trade, would display such a risque garment in her front window. The women in Early, Betsy included, would gaze at its flounces and lace as if they were having a religious experience. All over town it was referred to in hushed, reverent tones, as 'the dress'. The dress was without whalebone or any other stiffening and given the decolletage, it would require a very daring woman or one of dubious reputation to expose that much of her bosom to Early's public eye.

"I'll buy it for you, if you'll wear it," said Tunstall to Betsy one evening as he and Betsy were passing by. Betsy squeezed his hand tight.

"J.W., you know better than to dare me to do something. If you've got the ready, I'll wear it to the saloon tomorrow evening. I'll walk right in and order a beer." Betsy grinned at him, showing her even, white teeth, which were attractively set off between a pair of medium full lips.

"Of course," said Betsy, "I can think of much better ways to spend fifty dollars." Betsy knew that Tunstall kept his feminine qualities hidden behind a rather solemn, sarcastic exterior demeanor. Tunstall drank quite heavily, but was the rule in the New Mexico Territory, and unlike Marcie Cabot, the mayor was no exception.

With some disappointment in his tone, he said, "I suppose you're right. You could buy one hell of a good horse for what that dress costs."

"That's assuming you want to make love to a horse," said Betsy.

"If you want that dress, I'll buy it for you next month. I've got a check coming in from Mexico."

"Save your money. I need that dress like a moose needs a hat-rack. I'm just playin'. Why do you always have to be so darn serious?"

"Betsy Johnson," he said as playfully as he was able, "Do you actually think I was going to pay fifty dollars to Marcie Cabot, a woman who would be delighted to piss on my grave."

Now it was Betsy's turn to be disappointed. "No, I don't suppose you would at that." They walked to the end of the rough sawn, wooden plank sidewalk, which didn't take long at all, then walked back to the saloon. About midway, Betsy let go of his hand.

"You never were going to buy me that dress were you?"

The sidewalk wasn't well lit, but between the oil lamps burning in the stores that remained open and the light of the half moon hanging low in the Eastern sky, there was enough for Betsy to see Tunstall's face. His sandy hair was thinning somewhat, but his blue eyes were fairly clear despite the drink, and the skin of his face, though sun creased in the corners of his eyes, was relatively unlined for a man in his forties. It was an honest face, one you could trust.

Her father Josiah always told her, "Abraham Lincoln said he could tell everything he needed to know about a man by his face."

The night before the catastrophe that sent Betsy and her young daughter West as fugitives, Betsy was reading Macbeth. She told her father, "You always quote Lincoln saying he could tell all he needed to know about a man by his face, but Shakespeare says, 'There's no art to find the mind's construction in the face'. Which is it?"

Josiah took his omnipresent corncob pipe from his mouth and pursed his thin lips together considering this disagreement between two of the greatest gods in his personal pantheon.

"Well, let's put it this way. You're in a life and death situation. Who would you want backing you **up,** Will Shakespeare or Abe Lincoln?"

Betsy thought for a long moment but there really wasn't much of a choice.

"Abe Lincoln."

"Exactly," said Josiah, "'Nuff said."

"Abe Lincoln would have liked John Tunstall," said Betsy to herself as she stood

Bathed in the moonlight. Tunstall was almost a head taller than she was, but he preferred to ride small Indian ponies, while Betsy favored larger quarter horses. Thus when they rode together she always sat eye to eye with him, which suited her just fine. Neither said another word about Marcie Cabot or the dress that night. Tunstall reached for Betsy's hand, and she gave it to him. By now, Betsy had pretty much forgiven him.

Betsy didn't get to town all that often and when she did, she and Tunstall always dined at the saloon. The fare was plain, usually consisting of a beefsteak and some roasted root vegetables or potatoes. The owner was a young woman from Sacramento and San Francisco by way of Charleston. For whatever reason she had chosen to exile herself to the Territory, Francine was a fair judge of meat, as well as the girls who helped her separate her drinking guests from their silver dollars.

The next month, Betsy rode to town, leaving her six year old, Sara, with Ben, the Pima Indian, who was unaccountably named after Benjamin Franklin. She tied her quarter horse, Abby, to the hitching rail outside the one story, wooden City Hall, Courthouse, Marshal's Office, and Mayor's Office. She walked into the small room that served as Tunstall's place of business. He was sitting back in his red leather covered wing back chair, feet propped up on his mahogany, roll top, Wooton desk, reading one of his seemingly endless supply of English novels. That afternoon, it was William Thackery's, Vanity Fair. The mayor was so engrossed in the story he didn't hear Betsy walk in. Betsy stepped forward as noiselessly as she could and when she was right behind him, she put her right index finger inside her cheek and made a loud popping sound that lifted his nearly two hundred pounds right out of the deep seated wingback chair. Thackery went flying up in the air and splashed with a wet sounding plop on the pine plank floor.

"Damn it, woman, you nearly gave me apoplexy!"

"Sorry, I was thinking of cocking my revolver, but that might have really scared you.

"It's a bad idea to play with guns."

"I know, my father drummed that into my head when I was still a baby."

"Wise man, your dad. I wish I'd met him."

Betsy's light green eyes filled with tears.

"Me too, Tunstall, me too."

"You still miss him, don't you?"

Betsy sniffed, "Not a day goes by, that I don't think about him, sitting there gut shot, with that brass frame Henry rifle across his lap, telling me to take Sara and get the Hell out of Kentucky."

Tunstall got up out of his chair, picked up the fallen Vanity Fair, and replaced it on the top of the Wooton desk. He went to Betsy and encircled her with his powerful arms, looked into her watering eyes and said, "I'm glad you listened to him."

Betsy relaxed into his embrace and she rested there for a long two minutes. He had a faint but spicy and exciting, masculine smell of tobacco. He smoked two cigars per day, one after lunch and one following the conclusion of his supper. He used toothpicks constantly and rinsed his mouth after eating with a wintergreen and alcohol concoction put up by the town apothecary touted as a sovereign remedy against tooth decay and gum disease.

Many of Early's residents consulted the druggist even before calling on Ike Hill, Early' s real, medical doctor. The apothecary, Enoch Swank, was a tall, almost painfully thin man, with weak eyes and thick spectacles. He had a nasally voice, and large shapely hands with long sinuous fingers, permanently stained in varying shades of dark red, yellow, and brown from his experiments with acids, bases, and diverse plant juices and extracts. He wore his long, thick, dark hair loose, and looked at times, very much like an unnaturally tall Indian. His skin was naturally pale, but long and frequent exposure to the Sonoran Desert sun while looking for efficacious herbs, had turned it tobacco brown. No one, not even his friend Tunstall, knew the exact details of what exactly had prompted Enoch to leave a thriving business in St. Louis and come to the Territory, but townsfolk said even money it was female trouble. Mr. Swank was not merely University educated, he was a Princeton man, and if he'd so chosen, he could have had a distinguished career as a chemist. If he had fled because of a woman, he'd come to the right place by moving to Early. Aside from Francine, the girls in her saloon, a few half-breeds, and two or three widows, there wasn't an unmarried woman his age for 50 miles around. Santa Fe was an entirely different story, but Enoch rarely left Early, except to forage out in the arroyos and on the mesas for medicinal plants.

His shop on the only real street in Early was long and narrow, barely ten feet wide. About half way towards the back there was a pine board divider with a counter and a hinge to allow him to pass through. The walls behind the counter were lined with pine shelves filled with an astonishing number of books from quartos to folios, many bound in full calf skin, with gilt lettering on the spines in Latin. The front featured a second counter, also hinged, and here the walls were lined with shelves as well filled with row upon row of amber, green, and clear glass bottles and vessels of various shapes and sizes, many labeled in black India ink letters in Swank's gothic style script. Some bottles were nameless, their contents known only to him.

Though Enoch probably knew as much about the human anatomy as Doc Hill, the two men did not compete for patients. For more mechanical malfunctions like sprains, broken bones, crushed digits, blood poisoning, knife and gunshot wounds, and the like, Doc Hill was the man to see. For internal complaints, Doc Hill usually referred patients to Enoch Swank. This resulted in Enoch being the recipient of most of the really mysterious ailments, which was much to his liking. He generally acted as an assistant to Doc Hill during surgery, administering nitrous oxide, ether, chloroform, and laudanum as needed to reduce the patient to the desired state of insensibility. **At** least once each month, Enoch participated in his own personal cleansing ritual during which he would go out alone into the desert, where he would eat the fruit of a certain cactus known as peyote to the Indians. After ingesting their fruits, he would vomit copiously, as he explained once to Betsy, who had come to him with a female complaint.

"I see God and talk with Him," said Swank in all seriousness. Betsy was fascinated. "What does He look like7"

Enoch fixed his watery blue eyes on her green ones as if to offer his guarantee that he was telling the truth. "You're not going to believe me but at the time **I** know exactly what God looks like, but as the effect of the plant wears thin, the image fades like a dream after you awaken. I remember a most dazzling, white light and feeling that a small part of that light was in me, like God was a mountain of light and I a speck of glowing dust."

Betsy smiled, "Is God always the same?"

"Yes, it's always the same feeling and vision."

"Then I think I'd like to go with you sometime."

Enoch looked at her. "It's not what you think. The principle in the cactus is hardly guaranteed to bridge the gap between man and God. Sane people fall off the bridge right into Hell where all the demons we have locked away in the hidden chambers of our souls will assault and torment them. It can lead to madness."

"So either I get to see God or I get to confront my demons. Looks like I win either way."

"Miss Johnson, I'm not so sure it's a good idea."

"Well, I am. Are you going to take me? I suppose I can just ask Ben." Enoch sighed. He genuinely liked women. He liked their voices, their shape, their bodies, their feet, their breasts, their private parts, and almost everything about them was more appealing to him than men. When he lived in St. Louis, he was married to a red headed, pure Irish girl, Margaret O'Flynn. **Her small perfect white teeth,** milk **white** skin, and fluty voice drove him practically crazy with desire. One morning less than two years after they celebrated their nuptials, Enoch rose before dawn to use the chamber pot. He and Margaret lived in a fine home overlooking the Mississippi as his apothecary trade was thriving. He was thinking just how fortunate he and Margaret were and he smiled to himself at the thought for their future looked bright indeed. He stood patiently waiting for his urine to come. His bladder told him it was long past time. When his stream finally did come it felt as if he were passing molten lava. The pain was so intense it brought tears to his eyes and made him want to defecate. When he finished, he looked in the porcelain bowl. The noxious stink and the sickly greenish color of the discharge in his urine left him in no doubt whatsoever as to the cause. He dressed without a word, and left his adulterous Irish vixen fast asleep, her glorious red hair covering the satin pillow, looking like a reflection of the morning sunrise he could see through the window. Now her beauty was nothing but the most bitter mockery to him, and he walked out of his home, blinded by tears that burnt nearly as hot as his infected urine. He walked the three miles to his shop in a daze, unlocked it, opened and completely emptied his safe, and filled a large leather covered wooden trunk with his most treasured books and medicaments. He hired a wagon to take him to the train depot. On the way he dosed himself with a concoction consisting of the greenish mold that grew on wheat bread, and extracts of lime and cranberry. Enoch boarded the first train West and unlike Orpheus and Lot's wife he never once looked back. Before the train pulled into the station at Santa Fe, Enoch asked the conductor if he knew of a town that needed an apothecary. The trainman looked at him and pulled at the right side of his bushy black moustache. At that time, the apothecary wore his hair cut short and he was so thin the conductor took him for a consumptive looking for a cure.

"There's always Early," he said in a jocular tone. "There's not much there. You'd be the only apothecary, that's for sure."

Tunstall buried his nose in Betsy's luxuriant hair. It was soft, the color of honey, and smelled of sage and something else he couldn't quite place. She washed it with a special liquid soap Swank made for her. Tunstall had no idea if there were any sage in it. The important thing was that had a fresh, clean odor. He whispered into the delicate shell of her left ear, "I've got three double eagles if you still want that dress. I would have bought it for you that night if it were anyone but Marcie Cabot that had it."

Betsy could see a spot of roughness in one of the chambers. More than likely it was a trace of black-powder residue. One couldn't be too careful as the primers of the cartridges were fulminate of mercury, which attacked steel like acid. Josiah was fanatical about cleaning his guns, especially his Henry rifle. After Chancellorsville and before Gettysburg, he'd made a trip while on leave all the way to New York City, to Schuyler, Hartley, and Graham on Maiden Lane, just to buy one. Most of his fellow soldiers complained about but contented themselves with their government issued, single shot, percussion rifled muskets, made at Springfield Arsenal, but not Sergeant Johnson, or was he only a corporal then, Betsy couldn't remember the precise dates of his promotions. Her father just had to have Oliver Winchester's sixteen shot, lever action repeater. He told her, "I figured I'd better do anything I could to give me an edge. I'd seen men kill each other with the bayonet at Marye's Heights and I never wanted the enemy that close to me."

Josiah credited his Henry rifle for saving his life at Cemetery Ridge. A Confederate bullet from a sharpshooter's English Whitworth Rifle smashed into his right leg just below the knee, taking him out of the action on that baking hot July day in Pennsylvania, but not before he saved his colonel's life. Convinced the sharpshooter's bullet was aimed at him and not Josiah, the regimental colonel put his sergeant in for President Lincoln's new award for gallantry in action, the Medal of Honor. The medal when it finally arrived wasn't much to look at. It was just a little copper star with no brilliants, gold, enamel, or even silver. It was special not in its own right as an object of material value, but it was a physical manifestation of the gratitude of the nation, and that was worth more than gold to Josiah.

"It's all too crazy," thought Betsy. "My daddy survives three years of combat,   fighting in some of the bloodiest battles of the Civil War only to be shot and killed in his hometown." She opened a small bottle of earth oil, and dipped a circular copper bristle brush on a thin steel wire into the oil and began swabbing out the chambers of the cylinder.

When she was satisfied, Betsy picked up a round piece of polished oak about two thirds the diameter of the chambers, threaded a piece of clean cotton rag through the eye slot in one end and pushed it through each of the holes. Holding the cylinder up to the sunlight, she scrutinized each chamber. Satisfied, Betsy reassembled the pistol, reloaded it, first clicking the cylinder on half cock, then bringing the hammer to the full cock position, she used the side of her right thumb to ride the hammer slowly down to rest on the one empty chamber.

The varnished, one piece walnut grip was comfortable. Whoever designed it understood the many shapes and sizes of the human hand and what would feel natural to all of them. Most pistols were not at all comfortable in the hand. Josiah's little Smith and Wesson .32 rimfire Old Army was a prime example. Even Josiah's government issue

Colt Model 1860 Army .44 percussion revolver was nothing like Colt's Model P. To large hands and small, long fingers or short, the grip of the Colt Single Action Army fit them all. Some folks likened it to a plow handle, but Betsy thought it was more like shaking hands with an old friend whose hand fit yours perfectly.

Betsy holstered her revolver, put the cork stopper back into the bottle of oil, and walked out of the room into the main section of her simple wood frame house.

"I really should go into town and see about some things," she said to herself. It was the very beginning of summer and the sun was still high. Betsy had a decent gold, Elgin pocket watch with a hunting case, but she rarely wore it, and the walnut cased regulator clock on the wall had quit working months ago. It wasn't as if she had appointments at any specific time except on very rare occasions, so Betsy generally depended on the position of the sun to measure out her days and plan her actions.

Betsy was wearing her habitual garb, consisting of a well worn pair of denim pants, a button down white shirt with a low un-starched collar, a buttery soft, tan leather vest with slit pockets, and her favorite calf length boots of undecorated natural leather with a medium heel. Betsy's dark blonde hair was cut fairly short and rested on her pleasingly broad shoulders. Her green eyes were sensitive to the strong desert sunlight, and consequently there was a pine wood coat tree in her house next to the door with no fewer than four Stetson hats hanging from its prongs. Betsy wasn't that particular about her clothes. As long as they were clean and dry, she was generally satisfied. Her hats were another story. She usually chose a hat to reflect either her mood or the time of day. Since it was early afternoon and she would almost certainly see Mayor Tunstall, Betsy chose a light gray, 10X Stetson, with a band of black silk. The color complimented her eyes, and the black band was sufficiently formal for supper at the saloon.

She'd just settled the hat on her head when her six year old soon to be seven, Sara burst in. Sara had her father's brown eyes, brown hair, and her skin coloring most of the year made her indistinguishable from the local Apache or Pueblo Indian children. Sara's long legs were scabby with bruises from exploring the nearby arroyos. Ben, the old Pima Indian helped Betsy with the agricultural chores, like planting the vegetable garden and making sure the corn didn't wither and die in the heat. He also looked after the few, scrawny longhorn cattle that roamed around pretty much at will, and made sure they didn't do too much damage. Ben lived in the adobe house he and some of his friends had built for Betsy when she and Sara first arrived in Early to claim the 160 acres Josiah was given upon his honorable discharge from the Union Army after taking his wound at Gettysburg.

There had been trouble back in Kentucky, very serious trouble. Betsy and her father ran afoul of a local chapter or klavern in their parlance, of the Ku Klux Klan. Within three years of Robert F. Lee's surrender at Appomattox Court House the Invisible Knights of the Ku Klux Klan were a potent force for the restoration of white rule in the Southern and Border States where cotton was still king and tobacco was queen. These highly profitable and labor-intensive crops had an economic imperative all their own. The Northern dominated Congress passed the Force Act in 1870 and the Ku Klux Act in 1871, but like any law, without the will to enforce it, neither did anything to substantially diminish the power of the Klan. Dressed in ghostly white sheets and robes to frighten superstitious Africans the Klan whipped, lynched, and murdered freedmen and their white supporters. If the influence of the Klan had waned in the late 1870's it wasn't due to its lack of popular support but the fact that it had largely achieved its goal of completely restoring white supremacy throughout the South.

Betsy and Josiah engaged in a pitched gun battle with the klansmen from their local klavern, the night after Betsy shot and killed a klan officer, known as a klexter, or 'watcher', who had murdered the minister of the local African Methodist Episcopal Church. The klexter was about to murder the minister's son as well, when Betsy happened on the scene and shot the Klansman dead. The very next day the entire klavern, well armed, descended on Josiah's isolated farmhouse on the banks of a tributary of the Tennessee River. Torches were thrown on the roof, and as the flames spread, Betsy and her father killed several white robed men. The Klan temporarily withdrew, and during the lull though Josiah was badly perhaps mortally wounded in the belly he insisted Betsy take Sara and run for her life. When she refused he said angrily, "Listen, we Johnsons are well known nigger lovers and it won't be long before Elizabeth Johnson is charged with willful murder for that boy you shot yesterday. Prison is a certainty and hanging or even lynching is a strong possibility. Face facts Betsy, you killed a white man to save a nigger boy. That isn't considered self-defense around here it's murder. Most people in Southwestern Kentucky weren't too fond of blacks even before the war. You're forgetting Kentucky was a slave state, still is as far as most of our neighbors are concerned. Now be a good girl and clear the Hell out!"

"Go with God and a father's blessing," were Josiah's final parting words. After the Civil War, black troops occupied large areas of Kentucky that were seen by Northerners as having supported the South. By 1876, feeling in Southwestern Kentucky was distinctly anti-federal and anti-colored.

Betsy disguised herself as a man, taking the name Joe Johnson so as not to confuse her young daughter too much, and with the help of the minister's son who was fleeing as well, bought tickets on the Union Pacific for herself, Sara, and her beloved mare and rode the train as far from Kentucky as she could. She briefly considered going even further south to Mexico or Argentina, but her inability to speak the language and complete lack of knowledge of either country, discouraged her. She had a deed to 160 acres in the New Mexico Territory and she thought that there she would surely be beyond the reach of Kentucky law.

She, Sara, and her mare, Abby, arrived in Early less than a week later. Betsy's hair was cut short like a man's and dyed jet black with bootblack, which seemed to be quite permanent. She, or rather he, almost immediately encountered more trouble of the exact kind she thought she'd left far behind. An entrepreneurial and unscrupulous Army Colonel together with a gang of renegade Mexicans and Indians, known as Coyoteros, were trying hard to promote an Indian war, which would profit any number of interests in the Territory. John Tunstall, no relation to the noted Scottish rancher in Lincoln County, the doctor, Ike Hill, aided by Ben and reservation Apaches only too familiar with the Army policy of Indian pacification through extermination, thwarted the plot and nipped the nascent conflict in the bud.

At a church service celebrating Early's deliverance from destruction, Betsy had little choice other than to reveal her true identity and sex, something Tunstall had known all along from a wanted poster but concealed from everyone else in the town, even Ike Hill. There was gratifyingly little interest in Betsy's past, probably due to the fact that many of Early's residents had come west to outrun their own personal histories. At Betsy's prompting Tunstall sent a telegraph message from Santa Fe to Kentucky requesting detailed information on the fugitive Elizabeth Johnson, but the reply was so vague, he assumed the good folks back in Kentucky weren't really all that interested in apprehending her. Tunstall got her to agree that she wasn't Elizabeth Johnson but Betsy Johnson and that they were two entirely separate people, which was fine with her.

"As long as I don't have to be Joe Johnson for the rest of my life, I'm fine."

After the phony Indian uprising failed and the Coyoteros were crushed, Betsy was elected as the marshal of Early using her proper name and despite her sex. There was very little crime in Early, mainly because there weren't all that many citizens, and those that there were spent most of their lives barely surviving. There had been the contentious issue of serving Indians liquor in the saloon. Duffy, the previous owner, had posted a prominent sign reading "No Dogs or Indians Allowed." In view of the fact that Duffy made most of his fortune selling the poorest quality, adulterated whiskey to Indians on the reservation, in flagrant violation of government policy, Mayor Tunstall and several other so—called Indian lovers, regarded Duffy's prohibition as hypocritical. One especially bad batch of whiskey had contained enough wood alcohol and turpentine to blind one of Deaf Charlie's brothers. Deaf Charlie and two other Indians confronted Duffy and in the ensuing altercation, Duffy was shot and one Indian killed. Doc Hill operated on Duffy's leg and tied off the femoral artery with a ligature. In the hours that followed, feelings in the town ran high against Deaf Charlie and his companion. A man came to see Duffy, Tunstall was convinced it was Colonel Jessup, and shortly thereafter Duffy bled to death. Most of the town's people blamed Deaf Charlie and a lynch mob formed quickly. Tunstall barricaded himself in City Hall and refused to surrender the Indians to the mob. Tunstall finally convinced his constituents that Deaf Charlie was not responsible for Duffy's untimely demise. Duffy was a most unpleasant Irishman, greedy, grasping, and vile in almost every way and cordially detested by everyone in Early, but his skin was white, and thus in death, he was magically invested with virtues and qualities, no one had ever accused him of possessing in life. The potent, prevailing local prejudice against Indians and Mexicans, remained.

The intolerance reminded Betsy of western Kentuckians' attitude toward Negroes and disgusted her just as much. She couldn't for the life of her, understand why is was people seemed to think it was their God given right and duty to look down on an entire group of their fellow human beings, simply because their hair and skin were another color or shade. True the Cheyenne Apaches led by their war chief Victorio could be dangerous, but their numbers were very small and most of their depredations were directed at Mexicans across the border in old Mexico. Indians did have problems with liquor but so did every white man and woman in the territory over the age of sixteen save for the few temperance teetotalers like Marcie Cabot and her sort.

Duffy had left the saloon to Francine. Her very first action as proprietor was to have the sweeper up paint out the "No Indians" part of the sign over the bar to read simply "No Dogs." The fare improved from soda crackers and little else and Francine elevated the general tone to the point where Betsy no longer objected to Sara having supper with her on the rare occasions when she was still in town come evening. Betsy looked at Sara, who was dressed like an Apache Indian girl, and she wondered if her daughter weren't spending too much time with Ben and Deaf Charlie's cousins. Sara was getting to the age when at least a modicum of formal education would be appropriate. She could have Ben bring Sara into town some mornings; however to expect her to sit still for hours in a one room schoolhouse with other children from six to sixteen, listening to Violet Barnes, the schoolmarm, wasn't very realistic.

Sara had lived through a lot in her seven years. Some might say a lifetime. Her father wanted nothing whatever to do with her. He was a blue blooded Beacon Hill Bostonian, who was being groomed for the Episcopal Bishopric of Massachusetts, when a torrid affair with a wealthy parishioner's daughter and a question of some missing diocese funds, caused his bishop to banish him to the wilds of Kentucky, until such time as passions cooled and he could be recalled. Handsome as a fairytale prince, with a scintillating wit and great intellect, Arthur was unlike anything even seen in Southwestern Kentucky. A thoroughly unconventional girl and raised by an equally idiosyncratic father, Betsy fell hard for the priest.

Arthur never had the slightest intention of marrying so far beneath his station though he did graciously offer to make Betsy his official mistress with a home in Louisville or Cincinnati, a position she indignantly refused. Thus, Sara never knew her father, and after Arthur contemptuously referred to baby Sara as a "whelp" at one stage during Betsy's final encounter with him she was just as happy Sara didn't. The night the Klan attacked Josiah's home was doubtless traumatic for the child, as she lost both her home and her Poppa forever. If that weren't enough within a few months of moving to Early, Sara was abducted by Coyoteros and held for ransom. Betsy and Ben, together with Tunstall, Doc Hill, and Deaf Charlie, rescued Sara, who seemed to think her abduction and captivity was one big lark. Betsy utterly failed to see how Sara could look at it that way at the time, but once Betsy recovered from the terror and the shock, she could see how a child might think the horrifying experience was an adventure. Sara was well treated by the Coyoteros although she thought they were "dirty" and their food "disgusting." Sara never understood or knew she was in any danger. The little girl would have brought a high price in Mexico City. Fortunately it never came to that.

Even through the sunburned skin and dusty hair, Betsy could see enough of the handsome priest in her daughter to send a thrill like a current of electricity through her solar plexus. John Tunstall was nearly twice Betsy's age, not quite Josiah's age but closer to his than to hers. Betsy's feelings for the mayor were strong. He was a mature man; a man of stature in every sense of the term, physically imposing and intellectually accomplished. However he was no Harvard Divinity School graduate, whose forebears were on the same ship as Plymouth Bay Colony, Governor Winthrop. Arthur was a fiery preacher, the legitimate heir of divines like Cotton and Increase Mather, as well as Jonathan Edwards, whom he adored. Once for entertainment, he treated her to a recitation of Edwards' sermon, "Sinners in the Hands of an Angry God." The two were alone in a local church and his performance was so powerful, he knew the sermon word for word, that Betsy fainted dead away before he finished.

Sara liked living in the desert. Ben taught her to avoid the rattlesnakes, coral snakes, scorpions, velvet ants, and the black widow or fiddle-back spiders that lived in the canyons, mesas, and dry riverbeds in that part of New Mexico Territory. The people who lived in Early were wary if not actually scared of the creatures. Betsy figured if the Indians weren't concerned, then the danger posed to humans by animals and insects, like the danger of the Apaches was wildly exaggerated. It took Betsy some time to get used to Sara picking up the large, hairy, reddish brown spiders called tarantulas with her bare hands.

To her sweetly encouraging, "Try it Mommy," Betsy allowed as how, "I don't really like spiders, honey." To which Sara replied with characteristic seven-year old enthusiasm, "They're nice and furry. Soft as a feather."

Betsy wanted to say something about not getting bitten but didn't want to appear frightened which she was. Her first experience with one of the oversize arachnids was when she rode out to her property with Ben and was exploring a squatter's shack. The sight of a hairy spider with a body as big as her thumb, and including its legs, as large as her hand, made her scream just like a silly city woman at the sight of a mouse. Mice and even rats were part of country living but a five-inch diameter spider was larger than any Kentucky mouse. Ben didn't know her at all at the time, having just met her by a fortuitous accident as her train deposited her, her horse, and her daughter at the siding miles from Early. After Betsy stopped screaming, Ben patiently explained that the spiders were harmless to humans. Some Indian children kept them as pets, though they could give a painful bite with their fangs if provoked or mistreated. It was like Josiah always told her, speaking of another instance of people worrying about God's creatures when the real danger came from humans. Folks are always worrying about creatures with four legs, six legs, eight legs, or no legs when it's the two legged ones that'll get you most every time."

That was something Sara would have to learn as she got older, but Betsy would not teach it to her until Sara was old enough to understand. To Betsy's mind, Sara spent too much time with Indians as it was and seemed uninterested in playing with the white children when she did go into town. Betsy, herself, preferred the company of Ben and Deaf Charley to that of the majority of the townspeople except for Tunstall, Enoch Swank, and Doc Hill. The preacher, Reverend Gilbert, feared and mistrusted the Indians, calling them idolaters and children of darkness. Ben objected to his characterization telling Betsy, "He says we worship idols. What is the Cross of Jesus? Do you not worship it? Is it not an idol?"

Betsy said, "The cross is not an idol, it's only a symbol." Ben scowled, "Do you not kneel to it and pray to it?"

"We don't pray to the cross, we pray to what it represents."

"Well, we don't pray to the sacred mountain either, but what it stands for."

"It's different?"

"How different?" Not for the first time did Betsy wish she had some of Arthur's theological brilliance. There had to be a difference.

"Listen," said Betsy. "I'm on your side. The Great Spirit, God, Jesus are all names for the Creator of all things. Love your neighbor as yourself is the whole of the law and the prophets." She became agitated. "It's just that I don't want Sara to grow up to be a freak like her mother!" Here she burst into tears, much to Ben's dismay. He'd inadvertently blundered into Betsy's unresolved feelings for Arthur. Ben didn't see Betsy as a freak. On the contrary, she was the most civilized white person he had ever met, more so than Mayor Tunstall, Doc Hill, or even medicine man Swank, who was all but an adopted member of the Apache nation.

Ben thought most white people were crazy savages who confused cleanliness with being civilized. There was little doubt that many of his people were less concerned with dirt than the whites. What concerned them was seeing their brothers and sisters had full bellies and secure lodgings, while the whites didn't appear to care at all for their less fortunate fellows, no matter what was written in the Bible they all loudly claimed loudly their guide in life. Whites treated each other with the same hatred and contempt with which they treated all life. They even took life by choking men to death with ropes and forcing their children to watch such disgraceful acts. Ben knew the God of the whites told them not to kill, but they were always ready to kill horse thieves, sheep thieves, cattle thieves, and Indians, when white people were the greatest thieves the Great Spirit ever created. Hadn't they stolen the whole country from the Indian and destroyed every tree, river, and mountain they could? Hadn't they exterminated the buffalo? Betsy stopped sobbing and looked at Ben with her limpid green eyes. "I'm sorry," she said. "It's hard being different."

Ben looked at her with his shining, deep, dark, black eyes. His voice was deep and resonant as he said, "I know. Believe me, I know." Ben knew many things. He knew the white attitude toward his people was much like General Sheridan's, "The only good Indians I ever saw were dead." Ben knew of the trade-blankets infected with smallpox, the maggoty beef, flour so thick with weevils it positively crawled, poisoned liquor, all the tainted, broken, rotten, third rate garbage the government allowed to be sold or rationed to his people, and yet despite it all, he remained cautiously cheerful about life in general, and even about white people. Ben knew all about being different and he wouldn't have had it any other way.

He said once more, this time softly, "I know, Betsy, believe me I know." Sara was in no condition to make an appearance in town. She would have to be scrubbed with well water, her hair brushed, and dressed properly.

"Oh to Hell with it," Betsy said under her breath. So Sara looked like a waif and she hadn't washed behind her ears. What was the great importance people attached to washing behind the ears anyway? As if anyone were going to look for dirt under Sara's hair and on the backs of her ears. Better she should wash under her arms and keep her private parts clean.

In Kentucky, Betsy had a river to draw from and both she and Josiah washed themselves quite thoroughly at least once a day, more in the torrid days during August and September. Others of her acquaintance contented themselves with a sponge bath above the waist during the week, saving the more extensive ablutions for Saturday and a heated bath in a metal tub. Arthur took complete baths in hot water daily and said the most terrible things about the women in town, unprintable things about the filth and stench of their untouched and unwashed feminine parts. He would even deride Betsy's friend, Lucille Van Griff in such lurid detail that Betsy would walk away or clap her hands over her ears. This only made him speak more graphically about the unsanitary conditions prevailing in the private parts of certain local women until his diatribe ended in a peal of demonic laughter.

At least in Kentucky wash water was abundantly available to all. In New Mexico Territory except for the Pecos and the Rio Grande, few rivers ran year round, especially in summer, when it was most necessary. Water was a luxury. Betsy would bet money Sara was cleaner in the important areas than any little girl in Early. Besides, Sara and she would be dining with the mayor, under the gentle eyes of the saloon's owner, Miss Francine.

"Sara, are you ready to go to town?"

Actually, Sara was less than thrilled, partially because she thought she might have to change into something stupid like the white gingham frock with the frilly lace around the collar, which made her look like some sissy town girl who went to the one room schoolhouse, and pretended to have tea parties with imaginary guests. They screamed as if they were going to die at the sight of a tiny wolf spider. They'd shrivel up if they ever saw a scorpion or a tarantula up close. Even the older white boys were nowhere near as brave as the three-year old Indian boys she knew at the reservation. They weren't afraid of anything, not thunder, not lightning, and not crawling creatures. She would have to sit like a little lady all through dinner, but then Francine would bring her a lovely piece of pie with sweet, fresh cream, further sweetened with a kiss, "For my little princess." Eating supper at the saloon made Sara's mother happy, and Sara wasn't averse to making Betsy happy because she loved her mother more than anything in the world, even Ben.

Sara liked Tunstall. He always paid attention to her and made her laugh by puffing out his cheeks and making funny faces until Betsy made him stop. He'd stop for a while then Sara would look at him when Betsy wasn't watching and pinch her nose as if there were a bad smell and Tunstall would pinch his nose and pretend to look for what was making the stink as her mother rolled her pretty green eyes to the high ceiling of the saloon's main room.

Ben knew Betsy was going out and had already saddled, groomed and picked Abigail's hooves. Betsy rode with an Indian bridle, which was nothing more than a noseband with reins. Her horse was quiet when she needed to be and spirited when required. When Abigail and Betsy first came to the Territory and rode into the desert, the mare took one look at a sidewinder and pitched Betsy into a cactus with one terrific buck. Though Ben picked all the spines out of her backside through her trousers, Betsy didn't hold a grudge. She and Abby were an inseparable team in Kentucky, and now that they were acclimated to the creatures of the Territory, the two got along famously. Betsy put her left foot in the stirrup and swung herself smoothly onto the saddle, her left hand full of long, coarse, black mane close to the horse's neck as she did so.

Sara rode behind her mother, seated on the mare's ample posterior. Even when she was a very little girl, Sara was able to balance herself on the mare's back with such grace she rarely if ever needed to hold on to Betsy's thick cowhide belt, or the cantle of the saddle with hands behind her back. Betsy was not at all averse to riding bareback and frequently did so, but Ben would always saddle the horse if Betsy were riding at night. Not that either of them expected any particular misadventure after dark, but a saddle did offer an extra measure of control in the event of a bad stumble. Sara was all ready to vault onto Abigail by herself, Indian style, as the boys on the reservation showed her how to do. Abigail stood at least two hands higher than the Indian ponies Sara was used to mounting. In addition the mare was considerably broader and while Sara was tall and rangy for her age, taking after Arthur who was quite tall, the height of Abby's rump was more than a bit daunting.

"Sara, I'm waiting on you," said Betsy. There wasn't a single note of annoyance in her voice, though Sara knew it would come soon enough if she continued dawdling. Ben stood silently, encouraging Sara with a flash from his inky black eyes. Sara took a few steps back, broke into a short run and launched herself into the air, barely clearing the root of Abigail's tail which hung almost to the ground. She grabbed the high broad cantle with both hands and scrambled to her seat behind Betsy, grinning from ear to ear with pride and joy. The mare shifted her weight from her left rear leg to her right rear leg, twitched a horse fly off her neck, and these two things aside didn't move. Both Betsy and Ben were near so the horse knew she was as secure as any herd animal could be away from the herd, and having forty five pounds of child flying over her rear end didn't spook her.

Ben was delighted by Sara's leap, then he'd been enchanted by her since she arrived at the railroad siding, hungry, tired, and still so full of life and innocent curiosity that Ben's old and double locked heart was taken by storm. Even the most terrible of the Coyoteros, El Gordo, had failed to intimidate Sara or her mother. Betsy had drawn her Colt Single Action Army revolver and put a .45 bullet right through the crown of the astonished outlaw's sombrero. From that very moment on, Ben knew he wanted to work for the handsome young man, green to the Territory, and if the man would let him, be a grandfather to the little girl. Betsy turned out to be Sara's mother, not her father, and after that, Ben was very much a substitute father, or at the least a very involved uncle. Unlike almost all the other white people Ben knew, that when Betsy looked at him, she saw a man. Not a white Indian with brown skin and long coal black hair, but Ben as a human being, complete with all his faults as well as his virtues. Betsy never judged a man by his skin color, the shape of his eyes, or the color and coarseness of his hair.

Ben liked women, but the woman he would have married died of pneumonia despite the best efforts of two great medicine men to save her with powdered willow bark and other remedies. The girl was quite frail even when she was in relatively good health, and Ben's mother warned him to choose someone else, a sturdier girl, who would bear him many sons, but Ben didn't listen. He fell in love with her hauntingly beautiful, oval face, the soft eyes that reminded him of a doe. When the fluid in her lungs finally drowned her and she succumbed, his mother offered no words of sympathy but only said coldly, "I warned you."

Ben said nothing to her. He carried all the wordless grief inside him to a stream he knew of high in the Sangre de Christo's east of Santa Fe. There was snow at the higher elevations. There, all alone except for the unseen elk and the hawk, Ben howled out his pain to the mountain like a wolf. He stood in the icy stream until his feet were numb and he couldn't feel them at all. He then sat down in the freezing cold water, mortifying his flesh up past his waist, and soon that part of his body too, was numb. He closed his eyes to the beauty surrounding him, opened his heart to experience his loss, and allowed the swift flowing water to carry away the unsupportable burden of his anguish. As he opened his eyes, a sleek healthy coyote bitch was standing on the bank of the stream within the reach of his right arm, not drinking, but just regarding him. Ben knew enough to understand this was no ordinary animal attracted by his mournful howling. It was a spirit creature, what the white men called an angel. The coyote's fur was lustrous as if it had just been bathed and brushed. Its bright yellow eyes were like freshly minted gold with coal black irises. The coyote opened its mouth revealing bright white teeth and a long pink tongue. It spoke Apache but not with its mouth but words inside Ben's mind.

"Why are you so sad?" it asked him.

Ben spoke with his mind as well, forming his thoughts, "My love is dead. I might as well kill myself and join her in the spirit world. Most of my people are already there."

"The spirit never dies, only the body. You knew this as a child. Have you forgotten?" The coyote turned away and trotted off toward the East, swishing its beautiful tail as it went. Ben was unable to stand, so he rolled his body over the sharp stones, using his hands, elbows, arms, and shoulders, until he was on the bank where the coyote had stood. Ben lay on his back staring up at the intensely blue sky, feeling the prickles as his body slowly regained sensation, warming in the thin but bright sunlight. He experienced an immense peace flowing into him through his back from the contact with the Earth, and the crushing sadness that had brought him to the point of wishing he were dead left him. His love for the girl wasn't dead after all. Anymore than the warmth of the sun which shone down on where he was yesterday was dead. The sun's warmth was absorbed and took on an infinite number of forms, from quick-ened seeds, green leaves, and all the living things that its rays shone down upon. His love was like the sun of another day. Its warmth would not die with the girl, but live on in a thousand forms he couldn't possibly imagine. The coyote wasn't just an animal. It was a luminous being and from this day forth, Ben's life would be forever marked and changed, not by the power of death, but by the spirit of life. Ben was taught from birth that all life was connected and that the life force was not limited to plants and animals. It was present in rocks, streams, rivers, and the Earth itself. Ben had believed this with his mind, and some-times he sensed the truth of it in his heart. Now, he knew it in his heart and he would keep it there come what may. Nothing that ever happened to him, not even death, would ever steal this truth away from him. He returned to the reservation the next day and told his mother he was going to live with the white men. He did this not from love for the white men. Ben knew that sooner or later his mother would say something ugly about his poor choice of a wife, how weak she was in body and spirit, and how fortunate he was that she died before he married her. This was something Ben knew he couldn't listen to without violence, so he spent his days either in Early or at the siding taking odd jobs until he met Joe and Sara Johnson. Ben lived in a shack and spent his spare time in the desert hoping for another encounter with an angel.

Ben had nearly died trying to prevent Sara from being taken hostage by El Gordo, and as he looked at her on Abigail's back, he knew he would sacrifice his life for the girl without a second's thought or a moment's regret. There was something about the child, almost as if she were of the same tribe as the luminous coyote, not that such a thing were possible, for the spirits were never known to abide in the body of a living child, but he thought there was certainly a light around her, He thought Betsy might have had it around her when she was a little girl, from the stories Betsy told him about her and Josiah in Kentucky.

The old Pima Indian was only partially correct. Betsy Johnson was to be sure, a sprightly, charming little girl, but Betsy knew the magic Ben responded to had come from Sara's father, son of a bitch that he was. Fortunately to Betsy's way of thinking, Arthur's fiery brilliance was slightly leavened in Sara by her own personality, which was quite sufficiently mercurial in its own right. Though all parent's think their children are special, that is assuming the child is wanted to begin with; Betsy knew for a fact that Sara was exceptional since she seemed to have inherited her father's intelligence, indeed all his considerable genius was distilled in Sara.

Chapter 2
THE EARLY SALOON

Betsy and Sara were seated at one of the round wooden tables in the middle of the rough pine, plank floor, which was strewn with coarse sawdust and shavings. The decor in the rather large room consisted primarily of the rather elaborate bar and mirror that Duffy had ordered and shipped from St. Louis in sections, and at considerable expense, in anticipation of a population boom driven by an Indian war, and the discovery of gold, silver, and copper in the nearby mountains. None of these eagerly anticipated events came to pass. The few gold mines there were in the vicinity barely covered the costs of production and soon closed. The streams that ran in winter yielded a few small nuggets from time to time to those die-hards with the time to spend panning. The one silver mine, opened to great initial excitement soon played out and was shuttered in four months while the copper ore in the nearby mountains was of such a low grade as to preclude commercial exploitation.

Then Betsy, Tunstall, and the others thwarted Duffy and Colonel Jessup's war leaving the Early Saloon with a bar suited to a much larger and more posh establishment. The mirror was lovely, more than twenty feet long, in six mahogany framed sections. The glass itself was beautifully beveled and etched and gilt at the corners with roses and scrolls. The bar top was mahogany as well, a full three inches thick, with a lipped rim attached to prevent glasses and mugs from sliding off onto patron's bellies. Duffy spent most of his ready cash on the bar, leaving comparatively little for furniture. Consequently a number of the bar stools were of local manufacture, which meant they were sturdy enough. The seats were of wood and therefore hard on the backside and the legs were not precisely cut and varied by a half an inch here and there, making the inebriated drinker feel seasick. These eccentricities made the stools more comfortable to sit on at an angle up on the back legs. This was hazardous and more than once, a patron found himself flat on his back in the damp sawdust. The round tables and splat back chairs were local make as well and suffered from the same defects as the stools.

Duffy may have been unpleasant, but this did not make him a fool. When the gold and silver in the ephemeral veins of the earth around Early proved to be a dream, the Irishman adapted by devoting himself to the single minded pursuit of the silver and gold in his fellow towns-men's pockets and supplying adulterated, illicit whiskey to the reserva-tion Indians who being deprived of their nomadic way of life by the government, drank out of sheer boredom and frustration. Duffy had three women, more girls than woman, to assist him in separating his customers from more of their gold than beer, whiskey, and cordials could do on their own. Duffy permitted one poker game on the prem-ises with twenty percent of all winnings going to the house. Naturally though this rule caused considerable resentment and ill-will Duffy was unmoved. He told the gamblers, "If you don't like it you can always play in the mayor's office."

Playing cards in the town hall without Francine, the oldest of the girls, who affected a realistic, by Early standards, French accent and Gypsy and Rose to serve whiskey and beer, wasn't much of an alterna-tive, so even the mayor reluctantly agreed to Duffy's terms. Francine, Gypsy, and Rose, not only served liquor, they shared their favors and charms in private rooms for a fee of which Duffy took half.

In the unlikely event anyone forgot the purpose of the three whores, there was a large and rather graphic oil painting by a San Francisco artist, depicting a concupiscent Venus and a very naughty baby Cupid with a bow and arrow. Venus was painted using a blonde haired model with an ample snowy white bosom. Each breast was tipped with an accurately rendered anatomically correct pink nipple. Defying Victorian convention, Venus did not have one hand discreetly over her sex but was as naked and erotic as the not untalented artist could make her. The canvas was large, four feet by six feet, the figures nearly life size, and it was the principal reason most of Early's female residents wouldn't be seen in the saloon.

After Duffy's death, conscious of her dignity as a proprietor, Francine no longer offered herself for sale, except when she found the man particularly attractive. She didn't demand half of Rose and Gypsy's earnings as Duffy had, but required them to pay her one fifth. She continued Duffy's prohibition on professional gamblers, faro, chuk-a-luck, and other games of chance, though, unlike Duffy, Francine levied no percentage on the poker table. Together with Gypsy and Rose, she completely redecorated the private rooms where the girls had their trysts, which Duffy had insisted on remaining fairly Spartan, with bed, washstand, chamber pot, a few towels and little else. Now the rooms featured thick, red velvet hangings, feather pillows, cranberry glass, oil lamps, and various other inexpensive personal feminine touches. By Territorial standards, the girls kept the rooms immaculately clean, and drawing on his own unfortunate personal experience, Enoch Swank schooled Gypsy and Rose on the signal importance of maintaining the highest standard of personal cleanliness and requiring patrons to wear the very latest lambskin as well as the newest rubber sheaths or 'male shields' to prevent diseases like the one his wife had given him.

Betsy was drinking a beer and Sara was nursing a glass of cool milk. It was still quite early in the evening, and the blued steel hands of the large wooden cased regulator clock with the white enameled face and black Roman numerals read twenty minutes past five. Francine had had to send Gypsy to a nearby rooming house for Sara's milk but she and Betsy were good friends and Francine was only too happy to oblige Sara. When Betsy first came to Early dressed and acting as if she were

Joe Johnson, Francine was smitten with her, thinking the smooth faced young man was as handsome as could be. It was love at first sight, the lightning strike of love, or so Francine told Betsy later. Now, Francine's former infatuation was a running joke between the two women.

"You know, mon petit," said Francine to Sara. Even though Francine had never been to France, and she was no more French than she was Chinese, her affected manner of speaking was so much a part of her, that she had difficulty speaking unaccented English even when she wanted to.

"When I first met your mother," or 'muzzer' as she pronounced it, "I fell in love," which she said as 'luff.'

Sara liked Miss Francine not only because she brought her sweets and made much of her, but because despite her broad accent and her small, but well displayed white bosoms, she was very genuine, and wore her heart of her sleeve so to speak, though she rarely wore dresses with sleeves preferring to show off her shapely, ivory skinned upper arms. Sara could well understand why Miss Francine loved Betsy. Betsy was very lovable as far as Sara was concerned.

Betsy sipped at her beer. It was thicker and maltier than she liked, but she didn't much care for whiskey, and the well water in Early tended to be slightly on the alkaline side. One of the things she liked best about Francine was that unlike many of Early's citizens, she did not regard Indians as inherently vicious, lazy, habitual drunks, inferior to white men in every way. White men were equally liable to overindulge in ardent spirits, and as marshal, Betsy knew better than most that drunkenness was usually responsible for an argument that should have by rights been settled by wrestling or fisticuffs, being settled by axe handle, Bowie knife, or revolver. In the event of a fatal outcome, the so-called winner would be jailed and sent to Santa Fe for trial. Such a thing had yet to happen during Betsy's tenure as marshal. Tunstall was Justice of the Peace as well as the mayor, but all serious cases of wrongdoing in and around Early would be tried in the territorial capital. There hadn't been a shooting involving serious bodily injury since Duffy shot-gunned Deaf Charley's companion. A pistol was a tool in the West, like a hammer or a knife, and most all holsters and gun belts reflected the utilitarian nature of handguns. It took a very deliberate effort to loosen the pistol otherwise guns would be constantly falling out of their holsters while their owners were riding, mending fences, and doing general ranch work.

"You're expecting ze mayor?" asked Francine.

"He'll be in big trouble if he doesn't show up." Something Betsy said triggered a reaction in Francine and a worried expression suddenly darkened her pretty face. Tunstall and Betsy often said that the San Francisco artist who painted the Venus could have used Francine's face as a model. Francine had large, puffy lips, framing a wide, sensuous mouth, and wore her abundant soft, light, brown hair up, never down.

"Francine," asked Betsy solicitously, "Are you alright?" Betsy went back over what she'd said though she couldn't imagine how an innocent and playful remark about Tunstall being in big trouble could be misinterpreted.

"Marshal," Francine liked to call Betsy Marshal. It pleased her immensely that the law in Early was in the hands, the small, very shapely and capable hands of a young woman. Francine had suffered indignities without number at the hands, lips, faces, thighs, tongues, and penises of men, and so for her to live in a town where the law was a woman, and the mayor was a man who favored women's rights over men's, was like being an Indian in a town run by Indians.

"Bottom rail on top," was how Rose referred to the situation. Every man in Early knew the surest way to be locked up for a day or two was to hit a woman, any woman without good cause, and Betsy and Tunstall would decide if the cause were, indeed, just, and the odds were heavily against them deciding in his favor.

Duffy, had railed for years to anyone who could stomach listening to his endless litanies, about the utter worthlessness of all his relatives, how when he was growing up back east they were always holding him back from the free exercise of what he called his 'Natural abilities,' by which he meant business acumen. His talents lay more in the line of swindling, blackmailing, extorting, lying and cheating all the while wearing an almost inscrutable, poker face. Also he was completely without remorse of any type, which gave his a distinct advantage over his competitors. Duffy left upstate New York with a small sack-full of gold eagles that came from an uncle's life insurance policy, money he was supposed to invest in railroad shares on behalf of his bereaved aunt.

Duffy was tending bar in Syracuse when his 'opportunity' as he referred to it arose. He had left the saloon to Francine in his last will and testament, less from any great fondness for her, than a sincere desire to thwart any possibility of any of his relatives deriving the slightest benefit from his decease. Like so many people he sought to distance himself as much as he could from the victims of his wickedness. Not that the sight of his impoverished aunt would have chastened him any more than the presence of an Indian blinded by his wood alcohol adulterated whiskey, but Duffy wanted to avoid their accusations on general principle. Betsy thought that maybe one of Duffy's relatives might have emerged from the woodwork to contest her ownership of the saloon.

Francine continued, "Marshal, I think I might be in trouble." Betsy smiled up at her. "Francine, whatever it is, if I can help you, I will."

Sara was listening intently. The troubles of big people were usually so much more interesting than her own. Big people were always shouting at each other, and sometimes they'd stop shouting and start fighting, not so much the Indians, but the white men would roll around in the dusty street in front of the saloon, kicking, punching, and sometimes biting. Usually they were too drunk to do much damage to each other, but Sara had witnessed black eyes, broken noses, bloody lips, and chipped teeth. Fighting inside the saloon was strictly forbidden, and when fighting words were exchanged, Francine, Gypsy, or Rose, or a combination of the three would remind the about to be warring factions that they had best take their issues outside. This policy notwithstanding and in spite of her watering the whiskey of chronic quarrelsome, over-indulgers, there were incidents. For those who persisted while on her premises, Francine had hardwood ice mallets, a single tap of which properly placed would sweeten the most irate drinker, and if the mallets failed, there were two very short barreled, ten gauge shotguns manufactured by William Greener of Birmingham, England on their own shelves under the mahogany bar in strategic places. They were hammer guns loaded with rock salt in the right chamber and buckshot in the left. As of yet, no one had dared to try his luck and stake his life on whether Francine or the girls would remember which chamber held the non-lethal charge.

Sara had milk on her upper lip and piped up brightly, "I'll help you Miss Francine."

Francine looked down at the little girl and knew she really meant what she said. Francine suddenly felt bereft and all alone in an uncaring world. She would have given up the saloon and a great deal more to have a little girl like Sara. Without further warning, Francine burst into tears, Sara was startled, and since Francine's sobbing began right after she offered to help her, she thought it must have been her fault. Being responsible for a big person's hysterics was very confusing. Sara looked at Betsy for a solution and her mother seemed equally at a loss for words, and before Sara knew what she was doing she was crying in sympathy with Miss Francine. The two men drinking at the bar turned their attention from the squat glass tumblers of dark brown rye to the scene at the table in the center of the saloon. Gypsy dropped her corn broom and ran across the sawdust floor to help Francine. In the meantime, Betsy pushed back her splat-back chair, stood up, and went to Francine and put her arms around the young woman who was shaking with emotion. The one ranch hand at the bar, a sun burnt old man with a stubbly beard and a face seamed from long exposure to the

Territorial sun, said to his companion, a younger man with Spanish blood in his ancestry that could be seen in the handsome Castilian face, "Francine's the most sensible woman I ever met, and here she's turning on the waterworks right here in the saloon. That just about says it all about women, No matter what they're always carrying on about something."

"What's yer point?" said the thin, dark complexioned young man in a pleasant tone.
"Nothin' important. Just if you live to be a hundred, you'll never understand 'em."

The young man hawked loudly and spat a glob of phlegm rather inexpertly at the highly polished brass spittoon, so that it fell almost a foot short. While Rose, the girl behind the bar was preoccupied with the drama unfolding at Betsy's table, she wasn't so engrossed that she failed to notice the shiny blob not making it to the spittoon. Rose looked with disdain at the young ranch hand. All, three women, Francine, Gypsy, and Rose, together with Deaf Charlie's uncle, really tried to keep the saloon relatively free from dirt and rubbish. The Indian came early in the morning to deep clean, sweep out the saw-dust, lay fresh dust and shavings, and polish the bar, mirrors, spittoons, and the other furniture. Patrons were expected to comport themselves decently and spitting on the sawdust floor was strictly prohibited and regarded as criminal. There was even a sign to that effect posted prominently on the wall next to the left end of the bar. Rose picked up a dry, clean cotton rag from under the bar and handed it to the boy who looked at it and sneered.

Rose said sweetly, "It's for cleaning up your spittle. If you can't spit accurately then I suggest you don't spit at all." The young man looked at Rose as if she were an insect instead of a very comely young woman. His upper lip curled back revealing a fine pair of white front teeth. "Yer' nothing but a two dollar whore and yer tellin' me what to do?"

36

The older man looked up from his tumbler at Rose who was beginning a slow burn and all the more dangerous for being slow.

"Don't mind Pete, here, he don't know any better."

Pete, or Pedro as his Mestizo parents had named him was on his third glass of rye and had just passed the stage of feeling a warm glow of good will toward men, and was entering the stage of irascibility and arrogance. As far as he was concerned, he might have some Indian blood, but his Spanish blood made him far superior to a gringa whore and he wasn't too pleased at being patronized by his avuncular companion, who was old enough to be his grandfather.

"Well Pete," said Rose as she gently shook the rag in front of him. Keeping silent Pete dropped his right hand down to the butt of his Smith and Wesson American .44 revolver and began the arduous process of loosening it from the tight fitting, thick cowhide holster, which covered most of the large pistol, leaving only the butt exposed. Pete hadn't really thought things through. He knew he'd figure that out once he had the big Smith and Wesson in his right hand. He was going to show the insolent whore he was no one to trifle with or insult, and certainly a man who didn't need to answer to some prostitute who had the effrontery to tell him to clean spit off a saloon floor.

Betsy could feel Francine's tears soaking through her thin cotton shirt, plastering the material to her right shoulder. Francine was still sobbing though less violently, and Betsy looked past her brown ringlets over to the bar and saw the young ranch hand trying to free his revolver from its holster without attracting any attention. Tunstall and she had discussed the possibility of doing as other towns had done, and requiring people to leave their firearms at City Hall, but it wasn't practical, seeing as most of the time, Betsy wasn't in her office. There was that and the fact that nearly every male over the age of sixteen usually wore a pistol of some sort. There were remarkable few shootings all things considered. Since Betsy was marshal, a few vicious dogs had been murdered, and several dozen rattlesnakes but no people.

"Francine." "Francine…" said Betsy softly into the hole of her shapely left ear. Francine sniffed forcefully. Betsy continued, "That young man at the bar is trying to pull his pistol." Francine, stiffened, stopped shaking and crying and stood still. Betsy gently but firmly pushed her away so she would have a clear shot, and said in a voice she hoped was firm and steady, "Mister, you'd best push that pistol back in your holster." Pete turned his head to Betsy, but left his right hand clasping the butt of the Smith and Wesson. Pete's partner began sliding his glass down the bar and he moved to the stool on his left, one removed from the boy with the big revolver. He said in a deep, slow bass voice, "Pete, this is gettin' serious. I'm dealing myself out." Pete threw down the rest of his whiskey using his left hand, while edging the pistol ever higher with his right, an action not lost on Betsy. The cylinder of the young man's pistol was almost free of the lips of the holster. The relatively slender seven and one half inch barrel would offer little or no resistance once the thick cylinder was freed.

"I might have to shoot this boy," thought Betsy and she felt sick to her stomach. He was only a few years younger than she was, a baby, barely out of boyhood. He hadn't even begun to live and here he was about to throw his life away for absolutely no reason at all because he had too much pride to take Rose's rag. The confrontation had blown up so fast, like a sudden squall and turned deadly serious so fast, and now there were only a few moments before it would be too late for talk. Betsy's mind was racing faster than a hawk diving for a ground squirrel. The whole scenario of what happened back in Kentucky was going through her head, every detail indelibly etched in her mind like the frost etched lettering on the mirror over the bar.

She could hear the klexter shouting at the old Negro minister, "Out of the way old wooly head, less'n you're in a hurry to see Jesus." Then he shot the harmless old man down like a dog. The klansman hadn't ridden off yet when Ephraim, the minister's son, ran to his father's side. Ephraim was an object of the liveliest hatred by the local klavern, because of his suspected relations with a young, white farm girl. The man was about to send Ephraim to join his father when Betsy rode up and shot the man from his saddle as he leveled his shotgun at her. She felt nauseated as she watched the light die out in his eyes almost as if there really was a soul that animated the body, for once he was dead, the white robed figure seemed to shrink before her eyes. Betsy had noticed a similar phenomenon in the ducks she shot on the river. They too seemed smaller once the life force left their bodies. She assumed she'd killed at least one more Klansman before she fled Kentucky, and she knew she'd shot and killed the fearsome coyotero, El Gordo, and though the shootings were necessary and purely in self-defense, she didn't feel good about these deaths either. Betsy would have been ecstatic if she never had to shoot another human being, and she wasn't all that keen on killing animals, although she liked to eat meat, so she regarded hunting as a necessary evil. Betsy was furious with the boy for allowing the possibility of her shooting him to arise. She had to say something, anything to prevent this from happening. Pete looked at Betsy and said in a voice slightly roughened by three shots of rye to which he was unaccustomed, "Do females run this town?" Pete had most of his Smith and Wesson freed from the holster though he was deliberately taking his time clearing it completely. Betsy's entry into the equation distracted him. Pete was raised in a home with a mother, four sisters and no brothers. Pete's father died when Pete was twelve, dragged to death when his horse bolted and his boot caught in the stirrup. He was eighteen now, and he'd had a belly-full of being bossed around and constantly told what he could and couldn't do by women. Not that he had anything against the fair sex in general. On the contrary, he admired and enjoyed their company. He just reacted badly to females giving him orders. The third tumbler of rye clouded his judgment more than would have been the case if he'd been a veteran toper. His intention had been to frighten Rose and punish her in return for treating him with less respect than he deserved. She might as well have shaken the dirty rag in his face. Rose had in fact, been careful not to shake the rag, which was clean, in his face though this didn't matter to Pete. He felt what he felt, which was the

39

accumulated frustration of years spent in a home with five women, all of whom were older than he was, and weren't afraid to remind him of this at every opportunity.

The long slender barrel of the American cleared the holster completely and Betsy needed to make a decision. Pete didn't believe either Rose or Betsy would draw a gun on him, and he didn't intend to harm anyone, only brandish his big pistol and scare the silly, insolent women. Rose ducked behind the bar, and Pete's partner swan dove, head first for the sawdust floor, sliding right over the shiny glob of spittle that sparked the whole sequence of events.

All Betsy could see was the big Smith and Wesson revolver and the look of terror on her daughter's face, as if the two images were superimposed on each other, She'd loosened her Colt .45 Single Action Army, just enough to make a fairly fast draw if need be, earlier, when she'd told Pete to push the American back into his holster. What Betsy didn't see was J.W. Tunstall, standing at the louvered, single, batwing, swinging door at the entrance of the saloon. Tunstall's Colt Single Action was an old one in .44 rim-fire that used the same cartridge as his deluxe model 1866 Winchester rifle with the gilded brass frame finely engraved and chiseled in relief with a nude figure of Justice and fancy piano varnish finished walnut stocks. Like Betsy, he was planning on someday owning a Colt 44-40 and a matching 1873 Winchester rifle. Though he was not a wealthy man and his delay in purchasing the more modern model was really due to a sentimental fondness for his 1866. Tunstall's Colt was cocked and aimed at Pete's back when Sara saw the mayor and her tongue, which had felt like it was stuck to the roof of her mouth, freed itself. The sight of Tunstall freed more than her tongue and she took off running for the door, shouting, "Mayor!" at the top of her high voice. Pete's body spun on the stool, away from the bar and toward Betsy and the running child and the gun in his hand made an unfortunate arc in Sara's direction.

Pete had not the slightest intention of shooting Sara or anyone else, but all Betsy saw was a very large revolver pointing in Sara's direction, and she drew her pistol, cocking it as it came up with the side of her right thumb. Tunstall saw Betsy's hand drop to her right side and he fired. With the roar of the explosion, she saw Pete clutch convulsively at his right shoulder, and she was miraculously able to pull her own shot at the ultimate moment, putting a bullet hole in one of Francine's nearly priceless mirrors, rather than Pete's heart which is where it would have gone. Pete swayed on his stool and then fell heavily to the sawdust floor like a duck shot with a 10 gauge shotgun.

Betsy rushed to help the prostrate Pete, as did Francine and Tunstall, who had Sara in his big bear-like arms. The big blue Smith And Wesson American lay in the sawdust. Pete's partner got up from the floor brushing particles of sawdust from his shirt and his trousers. Pete's phlegm was pressed into his right shoulder but the old man didn't notice. Pete was making low groaning noises.

Betsy spoke first and said angrily, "Of all the damn, fool, stupid stunts." She was shaking not with fear but with rage. Tunstall knew Betsy well enough to see she was beside herself. He picked up Pete's American and noticed it wasn't cocked. He half-cocked it and lifted the checkered hinge at the top of the frame and opened it and as he did the ejection star that automatically ejected empty cartridges rose. Unlike Colt's revolvers which were all solid frame now that the Rollin White patent on the bored through cylinder had expired and Colt was making revolvers specifically for metallic cartridges using solid frame construction, all Smith and Wessons, even the costly large frames, were hinged break-opens. They were faster and easier to load than the Colt but far less durable. A man could fire a Colt Single Action as long as he could line up the cylinder with the barrel, and the hammer was fixed on its screw pivot in the frame. The mainspring could be broken, the hand dysfunctional, and you could fire it using a rock to strike the hammer. Tunstall had never seen a Smith and Wesson that remained in time during hard use. The mayor's body was taking its time calming down after being keyed up to kill another human-being, which was the most heightened state of alert he could imagine. "Damn," he said as the ejection star snapped down empty. "Gun wasn't loaded." Blood was pooling under the groaning man's back. Francine forgot her own problems as she contemplated the ashen face of the barely conscious boy. "I'll get Doc Hill and Mr. Swank," said Gypsy. Betsy turned her attention from Pete to his older companion, "What the Hell was he thinking? An unloaded gun?" Betsy grabbed the startled man by his upper arms, and filled with emotion, she shook the old man like a rag-doll, until his head bobbed back and forth. The old man, whose name was Roy had come to Early to enjoy a nice friendly drink after a hard day's work. They were employed at a nearby ranch and they'd finished repairing a section of fence earlier than anticipated. Everything had happened so fast and now it was he who was the object of the marshal's wrath, He was stunned when Pete brandished the Smith and Wesson and the blast of Tunstall's .44 Colt still echoed in his ears. Tunstall was still holding Sara and he said in his habitual pleasant baritone, "Betsy, get a hold of yourself. You're rattling the poor man's eyeballs.

Thirty minutes later, Betsy, Sara, and Tunstall were dining on freshly barbecued beefsteak, The bar mirror bore a distinct hole and a star shaped fracture nearly two inches in diameter, but no radiating longitudinal cracks. Mr. Swank came in and walked up to Betsy's table. "Pull up a chair, Enoch," said Tunstall. The mayor continued, "If you're hungry, these steaks make fine eating. A trifle on the chewy side, but they're real flavorful."

"Thank you, mayor," said Swank pulling up a chair. He wasn't quite a vegetarian though his taste in meat ran more to quail and duck than bleeding, blackened chunks of steer, although the fare at the saloon was better than the boardinghouse he usually dined at, especially now that Francine was running it. Enoch folded his lanky six-foot plus frame into the low chair. Sara liked Mr. Swank because he was very fond of small creatures like horned toads, armadillos, tarantulas, and even snakes. In truth, only Ben and the other Indians knew the desert like Enoch Swank. Betsy liked him because he was far and away the most learned man in Early, which, strangely enough was actually saying something, because both Tunstall and Doc Hill were comparatively well read. Swank subscribed to most of the medical and scientific journals from New York, Boston, and even London, though the British publications could take months or as much as a year to reach Early. The mayor liked Enoch very well, although he was slightly intimidated by the apothecary's ability to speak and read Latin, French, and German. Swank read Balzac and Stendhal in the original language, something the mayor would have dearly loved to be able to do. Tunstall was convinced that much of the humor and many of the subtle nuances of tone in French novels were idiosyncratic and virtually impossible to translate perfectly.

Stendhal's Red and Black, Le Rouge et Noir, was one of Tunstall's favorite books. It chronicled the life of Julien Sorel, the peasant son of a tyrannical father, who detests his youngest son's literacy and effeminacy and does all in his power to make him work in the sawmill beside his loutish, brutish, unlettered brothers. Julien is determined to rise above his humble station and does so with tragic results to all concerned. Enoch Swank preferred Stendhal's other masterpiece, the Charterhouse of Parma, Le Chartreuse de Parme, and its hero, Frabrizio del Dongo, a youthful aristocrat to the parvenu, as he called him, Julien Sorel. Tunstall thought it was typical that Princeton educated Swank would identify with the aristocratic Italian, while he better understood the poor, relatively uneducated, autodidact Frenchman.

Tunstall had had a considerable amount of time to line up his sights before firing on the hapless Pete. - The distance wasn't more than thirty-five feet, and although the rear sight on his Colt Model P was little more than a narrow furrow in the top of the frame, if he took his time, Tunstall could put five shots into a circle he could cover with a silver dollar, usually without a "flyer". Swank anticipated their questions and reached into the pocket of his shirt, which used to be white; however through the decidedly ungentle ministrations of Early's only public laundry service and the owner's tendency to indiscriminately mix unstable dyed fabrics with whites, it was more of an unhealthy shade of blue with distinct undertone of yellow. Enoch drew out a flattened, dark piece of metal, resembling a misshapen coin. Tunstall took it from Enoch's right hand with his thumb and index finger and held it up for Sara and Betsy to see. Tunstall said, "Flattened out considerably. Must have his something hard." Swank nodded, "The boy was wearing a medal of the Virgin of Guadalupe. When he twisted on the stool, he must have moved it, so your bullet struck it on the side and flattened then it burrowed sideways into the right pectoral muscle coming to rest between the ribs and the skin."

"And all this means?" asked Betsy, who had already consumed two beers and several shots of Napoleon cognac, courtesy of the house, and Francine who poured two for herself as well. Swank smiled, "Assuming our Mr. Garza follows the good doctor's instructions, apart from some stiffness in the right shoulder that will take some months to disappear, thanks to the wonder working Virgin and our mayor's excellent aim, the boy should suffer no lasting ill effects from his short lived stint as a pistolero. Sara reached up a thin, brown arm. "Can I see?" Tunstall obligingly handed the .44 caliber bullet to her. Francine walked over carrying the bottle of cognac in her right hand. "Mr. Swank, would you care for a glass of Napoleon, compliments of the house?" Francine asked in her best faux French accent. Enoch almost replied in French. He caught himself at the last second and said in unaccented English, "Yes, I'd like that very much, thank you." He was attracted to Francine, but after his experience in St. Louis, he'd sworn off women altogether, and his continuing study of the causes and effects of venereal diseases only served to reinforce his commitment to celibacy. He sold flexible catheters to more than one man, who needed to clear a path through the scar tissue built up from repeated infections, or a single stubborn one just so they could urinate. Some men kept them inside their beaver hats.

The sheaths he sold, usually of the finest lambskin or the new vulcanized rubber, offered some measure of protection from pregnancy as well

44

as love's *fiery* darts, but the only sure cure for all of love's many unintended consequences was abstinence. Something about Francine, it wasn't her accent, but a certain look she had, a way of glancing over her habitually bare left shoulder, gave him a tingling feeling deep in his gut and groin, that might have made a mockery of his intentions had the opportunity arisen. If there were any way they could have a secret affair, Enoch would have leapt at the chance; however Early was such a small insular town, he didn't want his personal life to be the topic of public discussion. Perhaps someday if they happened to be in Santa Fe at the same time, but although Francine seemed to like him well enough, she had given no indication of harboring any special feelings for him. She was a regular purchaser of his own sovereign cure for monthly female complaints. The remedy consisted of a tolerable measure of laudanum and powdered willow bark, with various herbs and oil of clove to give the normally bitter mixture, a taste more agreeable to the palate, and an odor more acceptable to the nose.

He'd first concocted it when he was in St. Louis, for his wild Irish rose of a wife had trouble with her monthly and most of the popular specifics sold were ninety percent alcohol, containing either too much or too little opium and stank worse than an overflowing privy on a hot summer day. Swank's Sovereign Remedy for Female Complaint was in the process of earning quite a local reputation for itself and several St. Louis concerns offered to market it on a larger scale through newspaper advertisements and drummers.

As one enthusiastic husband said, "At least Loretta's breath don't smell like the backside of a mule, seven days a month." Regrettably just as Enoch had almost convinced himself to seek fame and fortune in the relief of, "Female cramps, gas, vapours, and headaches," he discovered the love of his life had poxed him, and he decided to bury himself far away in the New Mexico Territory.

Betsy suffered quite badly at least three days out of every month and when she first sought relief in Kentucky as a young girl, the doctor told her, "It's the curse the good Lord put upon all daughters of Eve for misleading Adam." Betsy wasn't feeling very charitable at the time. The cramps were so severe they drove her to seek help from the physician in the first place. She badly wanted to punch the doctor in the overly prominent Roman nose of which he was quite proud. "I came to you because I hurt. If I wanted to hear about Genesis, I'd have gone to see the preacher and saved my father's hard earned money. Of all the pious drivel I've heard in my life, yours is the worst. You should be ashamed of yourself."

Doctor James was a fairly learned man of slight stature in his late forties. He was used to being spoken to with a certain degree of deference, and liked to think he was all but a deity in this part of Western Kentucky.

It was Betsy's time of the month, and this was the primary reason she reacted so strongly to Pete's shooting and attacked Roy. An added factor was she took it personally. It was the first person to person shooting in Early since the affair with Jessup and the Coyoteros.

"Don't take it so hard," Tunstall told her after supper as the two of them were enjoying a cigar.

"I know, I know," she said. "It's just that I might have killed that boy. I probably would have if you hadn't shot first and then I would have murdered an unarmed boy. I think I should take this as a sign and give up my badge."

"I don't know about that. I kind of like a town with a female marshal and a female saloon owner," he gestured with his fragrant, black cheroot in Francine's direction.

"Speaking of Francine," said Betsy, "Before you made your dramatic entrance, she was in tears about something. She never got to tell me what it was about. It sounded really serious."

"Francine's no shrinking violet, best if we talked to her right away."
At that moment, Ben walked into the saloon, and Sara left her warm
apple pie to go running to him. Tunstall who tried his damnedest to get
Sara to like him said glumly, "If she only liked me half as much, I'd be
satisfied."

"Don't take it so personally," said Betsy. "Sometimes I think she
likes him better than she does me. She spends nearly every day
with him. It isn't as if she doesn't mind her manners."

Tunstall shrugged, "I just wish she'd talk to me like that," and he
pointed to Sara who was chattering away like a tree squirrel.

"She ran to you for protection when Pete pulled his pistol."

Tunstall smiled, "I guess she did at that. Funny, I didn't think of
it. Thank you. Betsy you just made my day."

Ben's timely arrival did give them a chance to meet with Francine in
her private office, a tiny room in back behind the bar.

Francine related her story as tears streamed down her face, "I
was fifteen living in San Francisco. I met this boy and he was so
fair and so fine, he threw me off my feet."

Tunstall was about to say 'swept' but stopped at a look from
Betsy.

Francine continued, "He was from old Mexico and his family had their
land grant from the King of Spain. Luis knew his parents would never
consent to him marrying beneath him and a gringa as well. My parents
were dead. My father died in the war from cholera and my mother soon
followed him to the grave from a broken heart. I was sent to live with
my aunt in California, but she had little time for me. Luis said my face
was all the fortune he'd ever need. Then his parents found out about us

and they called him home. He went because he had no other choice. My heart was broken, and I fell into very bad company. What did it matter? Luis was gone and with him my only chance for true love. I left my aunt's and went to Sacramento.

There I met a handsome man a few years older than I was and married him. I knew nothing of marriage. He and his friend were successful small time gamblers, living the fast life in the capitol. Somehow, he never had a chance to explain it to me properly; he was with a gang of men when they robbed a Wells Fargo stage. During the robbery one passenger and a guard were killed. It was carrying a large payroll. Two of the gang were captured and hanged but my husband and his friend escaped. One of the outlaws they hanged, knowing he was going to die, told the Wells Fargo detectives that they forced my husband and his partner to join them at gunpoint. I haven't heard from him since. Somehow, he met Colonel Jessup in Santa Fe and found out about Duffy leaving me the saloon. He and his friend, Jack Jones, are coming to Early to 'help' me run the saloon.

"You never did tell us his name," said Betsy.

Francine sniffed, "It's Hal, Hal Russell." Francine blinked back the tears that continued to pour from her eyes, "What am I to do?"

Betsy said matter of fact, "There's not much you can do. He's still your husband, isn't he?"

"Yes," Francine said in a small voice that made her sound about Sara's age. Tunstall was thinking, "There's not that much you can do." He looked significantly at Betsy. "Folks come to Early for a fresh start. Last thing any of us needs is the law digging up our past. As long as he causes no trouble here, whatever he's done years ago isn't my concern."

Francine burst into a fresh flood of tears, "What about me?"

Betsy tried to console her, "He's your lawfully wedded husband there's nothing we can do about him."

"I'd rather pick up sidewinders bare handed than interfere between husband and wife," said Tunstall. "It's safer."

None of this was what Francine wanted to hear, "I was fifteen! Fifteen! I was crazy with grief about Luis, so I threw myself at Hal Russell. Now he comes back after four years and takes my saloon? This is fair? This is justice?"

Tunstall said, "Wait a minute Francine. He can't exactly take the saloon, but he is your partner."

Betsy said, "More than likely Early will be too quiet for the likes of them. They'll move on to El Paso or Juarez soon enough."

"No Marshal, not soon enough believe me."

Tunstall said, "Alright Francine, what do you want me to do."

"Arrest him. Tell him he's not welcome."

Tunstall shook his leonine head, "Not all that many of us would stand up to close scrutiny. Until they break the law here in Early, they're as welcome as the next man.'

Chapter 3

HAL RUSSELL

Hal Russell and Jack Jones were well armed. Each carried a Colt Single Action Army in .44 Winchester Center Fire, with Winchester Model 1873 rifles in the same caliber with twenty-four inch octagonal barrels. They both liked knives and each carried a thick, clip point George Wostenholm IXL Bowie knife in his boot. Hal liked spirited horses so he rode a nearly fifteen hand grayish Arab mare, which was equally at home in the desert or in a mile race. Jones rode a powerful and large saddle mule bred in Missouri. They rode along an arroyo about ten miles north of Early. A buzzard was high over their heads soaring on the thermals rising from the desert.

Jones had sandy blonde hair, bleached almost white by the sun, though he was wearing a tan color sombrero. His sun-strained blue eyes looked up at the vulture. Without a word of warning to the man riding next to him, he drew his revolver and fired up at the large bird. Russell's Arab executed a short dance on her rear legs, then came down and stood still.

"Damn it, Jack. I hate it when you just start shooting like that out of nowhere. It makes me think you're going crazy. What's that buzzard done to you?"

"I hate scavengers," said Jack somewhat petulantly.

Still in the saddle, Hal leaned down to his right and pulled the butt of his rifle forward until it was half out of its heavy, tooled leather scabbard, jerked it free, brought it to his right shoulder, worked the lever, and aimed up into the sky. This time the Arab backed up two steps and twitched her ears forward, but didn't rear. He fired, and about one hundred yards off to their right, the buzzard fell heavily to the sandy desert soil with an audible plop. The mass of black feathers scarcely moved in the weak breeze.

"There," said Hal, as he replaced the Winchester in its scabbard, "Are you happy now?"

"No," said Jack, "But I'm one hell of a lot happier than that buzzard." He lit a thin black cheroot with a Lucifer match, scratching it on the side of his left boot heel. As soon as the cheroot was drawing well, he threw the match aside.

"I don't know about you, but I would like a nice, hot bath, and then one of those saloon virgins for company, but you already got one of those so all you need is the bath."

Hal hawked loudly and spat out a gobbet of phlegm, which mounded up on the sand, glistening in the burning sun.

"I don't know about that. Francine might not be all that happy to see me. We'll see soon enough. I may want a different saloon virgin, you don't know." Only a few weeks ago Hal asked Jack, "What are you going to do when you get old?"
"I won't know till I get there. I'll worry about it then. Maybe I'll just keep drifting along the shores of the Delta until I die."

Hal hated the Delta. The air was always so damp, even though it was usually warm. The moist air seeped into your clothes and rusted your knives, guns, and tools. There was frequent dense fog in winter, which depressed him. "It sounds like Hell to me."

"One man's ceiling is another man's floor," said Jack laconically."

"Listen, how much do you reckon you need to retire?"

Jack Jones had an entirely undeserved reputation as a desperado exclusively as a result of wholly erroneous stories in the Sacramento Union, which had greatly exaggerated both his and Hal's exploits in order to sell papers. True he was a wanted man but the charges against him wouldn't hold up in a court of law assuming he had a competent attorney to represent him. The same could be said of his partner, Harold, 'Hal' Russell.

Hal's idea of retirement was a hacienda and rancho near Monterrey. The railroad had just recently completed a connection from Laredo, and Hal thought there should be unlimited opportunities for a man of his talents in a boomtown south of the border. Both men were thoroughly tired of living a peripatetic existence in the saddle and had every intention of securing a grubstake from Hal's interest in Francine's saloon.

Jones took one more huge drag on his cheroot, exhaled twin tusks of smoke through the forest of wiry brown hairs growing from his nostrils, and flicked the wet stub between his long thick thumb and forefinger. The discarded cigar landed in some sagebrush where it continued to smolder. Jones thought for a moment and lit another. "Hal, what are you going to do about Francine? She might not take kindly to us selling her saloon."

"She can buy me out, if she wants to," said Hal. "That saloon's as much mine as it is hers according to the laws of the New Mexico Territory. And I'm ready for that bath."

Hal was more than ready he was overdue. A man in the West would let his drawers go unwashed until it was a sin. Winter was the worst. Hal knew men who didn't wash their privates from December through March, and he didn't blame them. The rivers and streams in the Sierra Nevada were mostly fed by runoff from snow melt and were cold as ice in July let alone a freezing January. A proper bath required one hell of a lot of firewood, a large metal washtub, and a goodly number of hours to heat the water. To a lot of men, it just wasn't worth all the trouble, women too for that matter.

Francine was different. During the incredibly brief romantic flowering of their marriage, she bathed almost every day and insisted he do the same. The first time she refused him her favors because he wasn't properly bathed, he slapped her so hard, he could see the imprint of the back of his right hand on her left cheek, glowing an angry red on her ivory skin. She blinked back tears, and her pretty face registered first surprise, then hurt, but she still refused to have carnal relations with him.

"You stink like a, a..."

"Goat," Hal added helpfully.

Hal knew men who liked to be rough with their women. Some needed to slap them around a bit just to function as a man. Hal would act rough with men if he had to, but women, any women, put him in mind of his mother. She died when he was a little boy, leaving Hal in the care of his drunk of a father, who was never one to spare the rod, the strap or his big, bony fist. One night when his father had drunk himself unconscious, Hal took everything he could find of any value, which at the time wasn't much, his father having already converted most of what had any cash value into whiskey. There were a few things, a silver picture frame here, a gold wedding ring there. A drop of hair oil on his father's ring finger sufficed to free up the ring. Hal heard his dad snort at his touch, and he stopped for a moment, as paralyzed with terror as if he were in a nightmare, but the moment passed, the death rattle snoring resumed unabated, and his heart and body unfroze.

There was enough swag to take the thirteen year old as far as Denver, where he was hired on as a bellhop by one of the distinctly less fashionable hotels. Because many of his errands were on behalf of the primarily male guests' weaknesses and vices, women, liquor, or necessaries he never knew existed from the local apothecary shops, Hal developed a rather jaundiced view of his fellow man at a tender age along with the impression that an honest day's work was for those with little imagination or ambition. Procuring the right, willing, young woman for a guest with a taste or craving for the unusual could easily yield a shining gold dollar for an hour's easy work.

Hal made it a point to befriend the bellhops at the really fashionable establishments, and quickly earned a name for himself as a reliable, discreet source of clean, willing women for well-heeled gentlemen with exotic sexual appetites, the more exotic, the better.

When he was barely eighteen, Hal left Denver for Sacramento with no definite plan in his mind other than a change of scenery. By practicing his specialty, Hal was making more money than the hotel manager, but he was spending most of what he made on a sparkling, young, brown haired girl from South Carolina, with an accent nearly as thick as her mane of hair. Her ice blue eyes reflected fathomless depths of desire that captivated him like a bird fascinated by a cobra. Mary left Denver without letting Hal know. He went to her boarding house one evening with an ardent heart and even more ardent groin only to be told she hadn't paid her last week's rent and he'd better pay it of they'd have the law on him. Feeling like the biggest mark in Colorado, since he of all people should have recognized her for who and what she was, Hal left for California. His absence resulted in no little sadness on the part of a number of bellhops, hotel managers, and regular visitors to Denver, not to mention certain young, and some not so young ladies with collections of fascinating sexual devices from France and the Orient.

Chapter 4
JACK AND HAL

Hal Russell and Jack Jones rode into Early that night shortly after the excitement caused by the shooting of Pete. The town glowed here and there in the darkness from the few well-tended oil lamps, but the arrival of two strangers, though noticed by at least three citizens, was sufficiently unremarkable as to attract little attention. Hal was unimpressed with the town which was nothing after Santa Fe, and Santa Fe wasn't much compared to San Francisco.

"This town looks like it died years ago and they forgot to let the people know," said Jones with contempt fairly dripping in his tone.

"Well it isn't exactly San Francisco," said Hal. "I'll grant you that." "Somehow I think that army colonel was making fun of us. He's probably still laughing about the two boys from California who thought they were going to run this fancy saloon in New Mexico Territory and get rich quick."

"Well no great loss if he is, but let's not jump to conclusions. There could be more gold here than you think."

"Well one thing for sure, the streets aren't paved with it."

"No, they're not paved with anything but dust and more dust."

Duffy's or rather Francine's saloon was easily the most imposing structure in Early, its grandeur eclipsing both City Hall and the tall, white steepled church, which was mostly steeple. By Sacramento standards the saloon might have been only slightly above average, here in the desert, by Territorial standards, it bespoke luxury, elegance, and class.

In comparison to the buildings on either side the saloon looked like a palace. Jones halted his mule by shifting his seat in the saddle and studied the saloon as best he could in the dark. "Well," he said with grudging complimentary tones, "At least it's the most impressive building in Early.

"That's damning it with very faint praise."

"No," said Jones. "It's just that I can almost hear the colonel laughing at us.

"Let him laugh all he wants. The way I see it," here Hal gestured at the saloon with a wave of his sinewy, left hand, "I own it and that's more than he can say." Hal hadn't been giving much thought to Francine, but now that he was right outside he thought about exercising his rights as a husband to more than just her real property. The idea of cupping her breasts in his hands, and parting her creamy thighs, as her nipples grew hard wasn't at all offensive to him. He knew she'd lost her virginal heart to some rich Mexican named Luis and she'd married him on the rebound as a result of a broken heart, but that never bothered him. On the contrary it gave him the perfect excuse to hit her whenever she refused his advances, and call her a cheat and a whore. Back in Sacramento, he'd been mortally sick of her and when he was forced to flee after the robbery, he was certain their paths would never cross again and gave her no more thought.

Then in Santa Fe, he and Jones were in a saloon when an army colonel in full dress cavalry uniform walked in and the owner, who was surly enough with them, acted as if President Grant had arrived. He greeted the officer so obsequiously that both of them wanted to vomit. Hal was a prepossessing figure even before he washed the trail dust from his face and clothes, and Colonel Jessup noticed him immediately. The colonel said in a sepulchral voice, "Do you gentlemen mind if I join you?"

Hal allowed as how they didn't mind and ordered a bottle of rye, but Jessup told the owner who waited on them, "No bring us a bottle of malted ambrosia from the bonnie, bonny banks of the Loch," and in moments a bottle of fine Scottish whiskey stood on the table.

"Try this," said the colonel, as he poured out three generous measures. Jones looked at his glass suspiciously, for the color of the liquor was a lighter than he was accustomed to, almost as light as corn liquor, which he was known to drink, but strictly in desperation when nothing else presented itself. He brought the heavy glass tumbler to his fleshy and somewhat bulbous nose, and sniffed. The liquid had a smoky aroma, not unpleasant, and taking this as a good omen, he downed the contents of the glass in two large swallows. He smiled broadly and said, "Colonel," for the shining silver eagles on his uniform jacket were not to be denied, and the altitude made wearing such a fine jacket tolerable if not comfortable even in summer. Jones said honestly, "This is the best whiskey I ever tasted."

Having received his partner's imprimatur, Hal downed his with alacrity, and found it equally to his liking. "Damn fine tipple, Colonel, much obliged."

"What brings a couple of California boys like you to the Territory? There's not all that much gold in these mountains and what there is, is buried deep." "How'd you know we were from California?" asked Jones with a hint of menace in his tone. Jessup instantly picked up on what was only one level below a snarl. "Well, one of you has gold quartz set in his belt buckle and you," he said to Jones. "You'll forgive me for saying so, have a California way about you in the way you speak, although I may be mistaken and I apologize if I am." Though all this was said as a smile played around the edges of his thin and cruel mouth, Jessup looked, no it was more that he transfixed both Hal Russell's and Jack Jones' eyes in turn, and his affability dropped off like the mask it was. Without the least vestige of his bonhomie of the pervious minute, the colonel said in a voice that would have chilled the blood of braver men than either of them, "I'll repeat my question a second and last time."

"Now wait a minute, colonel," said Hal, though he was sacred, "This is a free country."

Jessup curled up his upper lip in a sneer, revealing dazzling white teeth. "Oh, what have we here?" he said sarcastically, "A lawyer or a philosopher? In case you haven't heard, much of New Mexico Territory is under martial law. As the ranking army officer for hundreds of miles that makes me the Constitution, the Bill of Rights, the President, Congress, and the Supreme Court all rolled into one. Isn't that so?" Jessup addressed this last to the owner, who said with a mixture of respect and a healthy measure of fear. "Whatever you say, colonel is just fine with me, and the governor too."

Hal understood Jessup' s threat, which was not a threat but a guarantee, and he treated it as such.

"We're headed to Early," he said forthrightly, "My wife owns a saloon there. "There's only one saloon in Early, used to belong to an acquaintance of mine name of Duffy. Little Irishman, bantam rooster type, died last year. Saloon's not bad considering Early's a real one horse town. Not that there's much there to interest two California gentlemen, but seeing as your wife's a prominent citizen you might find it bearable," he added with a more authentic grin, "For a week."

The colonel's smile thawed the freeze that had prevailed between the three men and as Jack and Hal applied themselves with enthusiasm to Jessup's Scottish whiskey, the colonel told them as much as he deemed fit about Duffy's demise, the Coyoteros, and Early.

"You'll excuse me for saying so," said Jack, "But it seems to me you might have a grudge against the town, and maybe that influences your opinion."

Jessup threw his head back and laughed long and loud, but it was less hearty than mean. Though Jack and Hal could be hard men if circumstances demanded it, they were not inherently evil or malicious men and the colonel's mirth, sent a shiver down each of their spines, as if the officer were Lucifer, Himself, chortling at the agonized contortions of some damned soul in Hell. Jessup laughed until tears came, and he dried them carefully with a fine silk handkerchief.

"Hold a grudge against Early? Believe me if I did, there would be less of that town remaining than there was of Sodom after the God of the Jews finished with it. As for my opinion that any man of sensibility would want to leave after spending twenty four hours there, enough time for a shave, drink, and a bath, well, you'll soon see for yourselves. As for seeking your fortune there, Duffy made much of his selling bad liquor to the Indians, but the mayor there has a soft spot in his heart for heathen savages of all kinds, so the only way anyone will make any money there, is by removing him from office, if you catch my drift."

"I do," said Hal and he spoke truly.

Hal and Jack tied their respective animals to the hitching rail outside the saloon using hemp rope halters they took from their saddlebags. Jack was, as he'd said to Hal earlier in the day, keen on the prospect of female companionship so seeing Hal hesitate on the very threshold of the potential oasis in which to slake not only his thirst for liquid refreshment, but his desire for sexual release as well, Jack said, "I don't know about you but I'm hornier than a hoot owl, then again I didn't go wild in Santa Fe like you did. You can stay out here all night if you want to, I'm going in."

As Jack finished what was for him a moment of volubility, a large mosquito stung Hal just below his right earlobe, and he slapped at his neck, striking as fast as a rattlesnake. He looked at his palm and saw blood shining in the lamplight."

"No," he said as he contemplated the bloody mess on his hand. "I'd rather get this over with than stand here and be eaten alive."

Chapter 5
THE PRODIGAL HUSBAND
RETURNS

Betsy and Tunstall were finishing their cigars when Hal and Jack swung open the single bat's wing door. Francine was still seated calming her nerves with smaller and smaller shots of cognac. Francine looked over to the entrance when she heard the long, low, moan of the rusted door hinges. She specifically forbade the sweeper-up from oiling them, as they were every bit as effective as bells in announcing the arrival or departure of patrons. Betsy and Tunstall were looking at each other. Enoch Swank had left after one glass, pleading the necessity of his looking in on Pete, and administering a soothing draught to the wounded boy. Betsy was feeling the effects of Francine's liberal dispensing of the costly brandy and was hovering on the cusp of mild inebriation. Tunstall was only three glasses away from her state, owing to his substantially greater weight, and his closer acquaintance with distilled spirits.

"Oh, my God," said Francine without a trace of a French accent. "It's him," and she dropped her thin blown glass snifter, which did lose its foot in the fall, but cushioned by the sawdust, did not shatter into fragments. If Francine had not already drunk as much as she had to lesson the terrors of the shooting, seeing Hal and Jack would have caused her to faint dead away. As it was, buttressed by the good liquor, she turned ghostly pale and shivered, although the saloon was more than warm with the evening air.

Betsy appraised the two strangers, and she thought they were both a cut above the usual run of cow hands, gamblers, and settlers that drifted through Early seeking employment, enjoyment, or trouble. Though all three were to be had, trouble was the easiest to avoid and the most readily available. She thought Hal was more than likely the husband. He was tall and good-looking, not an Arthur to be sure, but somewhat prepossessing, enough so that Betsy said to herself that she might have found him attractive. His partner was not as handsome, however he had an air of independence about him that was interesting. Both carried walnut gripped Colt revolvers in tooled leather holsters that covered most of the pistol except for the butt. Betsy could see the glossy varnish of the stocks was worn away, on the edges of the butt, an indication that the guns were more than mere decorative, male finery, but had seen careful use, which was what she would have expected.

Tunstall viewed them as potential troublemakers. Between Enoch Swank and Doc Hill he had all the friends he needed. The rest of the townspeople were acquaintances, some better than others, and this state of affairs suited him. Hal took one look at Tunstall and sized him up in his black suit as a man of stature in the town, a doctor, a lawyer, or the mayor Jessup was talking about. Tunstall's suit may not have been up to San Francisco standards but was made of good quality broadcloth. The elephant ivory grip on his Colt Single Action might have indicated a tendency to the dandyish, but the fine checkering in the ivory showed he was interested in his weapon's utility as well as taking pleasure in its appearance. Betsy interested him more than the heavy-set man with the ivory gripped Colt. She was quite as good looking as Francine and she wore a large silver badge pinned to her man's shirt above her right breast. As he met her eyes he saw they were green, curious, and full of spirit.

Jack took one look at Rose, who was standing behind the bar polishing glasses and walked straight to the high stool nearest her and sat down, leaving Hal standing alone, just inside the door.

"What's your name, Beautiful?" he asked with unfeigned warmth. Rose was a good judge of men. In her line of work she had to be to survive. She knew he could be a rough customer if he were crossed, but was inclined to be generous if he were pleased.

"My name is Rose, but my friends sometimes call me Rosie," she said coyly. She smiled, revealing her chipped front teeth, which Jack thought endearing, as they lent her a girlishness she might not otherwise have had, for Rose was buxom and her skimpy dress only accentuated her womanly swell.

"And just how do I get to be your friend?"

"Treat me right, and give me five dollars," she answered sweetly.

"I can do that," said Jack as he reached into the right pocket of his brown leather vest and drew out a shining gold half eagle with Lady Liberty's head on the obverse and an eagle on the reverse, and laid it on the mahogany bar. Rose picked it up and placed it reverentially in one of the oak cash drawers that hung beneath the bar, with round wood coin holders and spring clips that pressed down on the flat spaces for paper money. Rose and Gypsy each had their own cash drawer to themselves separate from the saloon's general till.

"I like to call my friends by their proper names, what's yours?" asked Rose with a sexy look.

"Jones," he said. "Jack Jones. How about I buy us a drink?" Rose batted her eyes and said, "I thought you'd never ask. Bottle or glass?" Though his supply of gold was running low, and the half eagle he'd just parted with so cavalierly had only four remaining companions, Jack was conscious of the prosperity evidenced by the mahogany bar and the elaborate gilt, etched mirrors. He thought the odious colonel in Santa Fe must have overlooked some aspect of the otherwise impoverished look of Early. Only real money could have paid for such opulence in the middle of the desert, and from Jessup's conversation, Duffy may have met with misfortune, but the man knew how to make money. Throwing his habitual caution and conservatism to the winds, Jack said, "A bottle of your very best whiskey, Rosie."

As badly shocked as Francine was, she still had enough presence of mind to pay attention to the bottle Rose fetched from her private office. It was genuine Scottish whiskey, one that came in a six bottle wooden case that had been opened only once nearly two years before for Colonel Jessup when he and Duffy were the best of friends. Her husband's partner was a player, that was evident, but then again Jack Jones always had been Francine recalled. At least they hadn't come to town penniless, relying on her non-existent girlish romantic nostalgia to feed and lodge them.

The years had not carved unsightly lines in Hal's face, though the sun had bronzed it and bleached his luxuriant light brown hair until it was dark blonde. If he'd only learned to keep his hands off her, she might have stayed there and waited for him to return, or even joined him as he ran from the crime he was forced into committing. He hadn't and now he was in her saloon and Francine could almost feel her security against a poverty-stricken old age slip from her grasp.

Francine was horrified she'd dropped the brandy snifter. It was costly and one of only three she had. She picked up the foot and the bowl, thinking that Mr. Swank might be able to fuse them together somehow, for the apothecary had a way with glass and knew how to melt it, though in actuality anything beyond blowing misshapen bottles was beyond his abilities. Francine took a deep breath arid stood up, slightly woozy from the brandy and the rapid pumping of her heart.

"I may as well take the bull by the horns," she thought to herself. Then she looked at Hal and said as firmly as she was able, given the amazing awkwardness she felt at confronting him after nearly four years, "I can't exactly say I'm glad to see you, but I'm thankful you're above ground."

Hal as Jack reminded him before they entered, had partaken liberally of the pleasures offered in the bawdy houses of Santa Fe, and he knew Francine was most likely a whore before a quirk of fate made her mistress of this establishment, but he didn't hold that against her. Hal Russell wasn't a man to hold a grudge, and although he knew men who lived for revenge he never saw the percentage in it.

He wasn't quite the Sacramento Delta sage Jack was, but he'd seen men and women eat themselves up lamenting the need to redress wrongs long past, or recapture old glories cruelly taken from them at the height of their success. Even if they did shoot or stab the party or parties responsible, the result was usually prison or worse, a feud with the survivors. Hal firmly believed revenge was a dish best not served at all, but thrown out, before it poisoned your life.

Hal didn't even blame the men who made him rob the Wells Fargo stage. He could have ridden away on a number of occasions. True, he'd have been risking a charge of buckshot or a bullet in the back though that was not a certainty. Jack told him on one memorable occasion that he had a "laissez faire" attitude toward life.

"What's that mean," asked Hal.

"It's from Adam Smith's Wealth of Nations, and it's French for live and let live. Do not interfere."

"That's me," said Hal. "I'm not going to let bygones eat me up. Each dawn brings a new day offering new opportunities, some good and some not so good." Hal looked at his long, lost wife. No one could confuse her with the little slip of a thing he'd married back in Sacramento. She had filled out with womanly curves in the places they belonged, and her face was as alluring to him as ever. Francine was the epitome of a desirable female to most men, and though Hal had no intention of remaining in Early one hour more than was necessary to secure the wherewithal to establish a reasonable basis for his life in Monterrey, he saw no objection to enjoying the favors of a beautiful woman in the interim, even if that woman were his own wife and his woman in the eyes of the law.

"Yes, Francine," Hal said. "I'm above ground but you don't seem too happy about it."

"Any reason I should be?" Hal looked at Tunstall and Betsy.

"Is there someplace we can talk in private?"

"These are my friends," she said indicating them with a gesture of her nicely formed, naked left arm and hand. "Whatever it is you want to say, if you can't say it in front of them I'd just as soon not hear it."

This response kindled Hal's anger and Francine could see the blood which rose in a flush, further darkening his sun burnt neck, a danger sign with which she was all too familiar. His eyes reflected barely suppressed rage at being checked and left her in no doubt whatever that he hadn't changed, not that she ever heard of a wife-beater that did.

When the Founding Fathers wrote the Declaration of Independence they stated it was self-evident that the Creator endowed men with unalienable rights. Sadly to Betsy's and Francine's way of thinking there were no Founding Mothers and so when the sainted Jefferson and the others referred to men, they forgot all about half of the human race, not to mention male Negroes and Indians. Women, Negroes, and Indians had no rights. Even the great Civil War didn't change Negroes' lives that much except they could no longer be bought and sold like livestock. In most states Negroes were only able to vote if they dared to, though in the South the Klan saw to it they didn't. Not a single state in the Union allowed women to vote, which meant they were even lower on the social scale than Negroes.

Betsy stared hard at Hal. She had an excellent intuitive sense about people and it grew stronger and more accurate as she grew older. She saw that Hal was quite capable of hitting any woman who challenged what he thought were his masculine rights. Francine had told her enough to look for the signs, and the tightening of his facial muscles and the coloring of the skin above his collar, were as plain an indication to her as a horse with his ears pinned back.

Hal had no intention of allowing his temper to get the better of him in public. For all he knew the pretty girl with the shiny silver badge had seen a wanted flyer with his name on it, though he doubted it. The crime was an old one and he had only participated under duress. Still he thought it best to curry favor with the local authorities, at least for the time being, and make his position known. He glanced at the bar looking for Jack, who had taken Rose and the bottle of Scottish whiskey into her private room. Hal faced Betsy and Tunstall.

"Fine, have it your way, Francine, you always did anyway. I'm Hal Russell and Francine is my lawfully wedded wife. I understand she's the owner of this saloon and that makes me a full partner. Isn't that so marshal?"

"I wouldn't care to say, being as I'm no lawyer. But this here is Mr. Tunstall and he's the justice of the peace and the mayor, so he'll tell you true."

Chaffer 6
A BROKEN NOSE

Betsy, Sara, and Ben were breakfasting the next morning on eggs Ben fried in a thick cast iron pan with butter and ham. As usual the summer was a dry one, and the corn Betsy and Ben had planted was dying for lack of water, and the tiny ears were as yet inedible. The only water sources were rain or well water. Therefore every gallon had to be hoisted by hand using a heavy wooden bucket from the well, which was more than thirty feet deep. Tunstall offered to give her the money for a windmill pump, but Betsy was averse to accepting money from the mayor.

Tunstall had already proposed marriage to Betsy, not in some rough, haphazard Western way, but during supper in a plush dining establishment in El Paso del Norte on the Rio Grande River. The room was lit with more candles than a Catholic cathedral on All Saints Day. He'd dropped to his right knee during cigars and tequila, and asked her in an earnest tone, with the love he felt was clearly visible in his warm, brown eyes, and Betsy had accepted, but that was over a year ago and she'd never set a date.

"I'd rather be engaged than married any day," she'd tell him. "The way I see it is, after the wedding, the romance dies and the man and the woman don't try half as hard as they did before the 'I do's'. I know, I know, everyone thinks they'll be different, just like they think they invented love." She would continue with ever increasing passion, "I know you think we are extraordinary, that we'll be the exception to the rule, every couple does, and I've yet to meet a man and wife who really is. Routine takes over, it's just the way of the world, and the magic burns out like a candle flame. First it's so bright it hurts your eyes then it starts guttering, then dies. There's not a boy or girl since Adam and Eve that doesn't think they've discovered sex the first time they try it. As if their parents had had them through Immaculate Conception. What I mean is that once that ring goes on my finger, I'm your property, and I ask you as your lover and your friend, do you really want things to change between us, because they will sure as the sun is going to rise in the morning."

"What are we going to do about it?" he said as a plain invitation to romance. Before Betsy could reply, in walked Ben and Sara.

"So much for a romantic interlude at your house," said Betsy with enough disappointment evidenced in her voice to completely mollify and frustration on the mayor's part.

"Well, Mayor Tunstall?" said Hal in a confident tone.

Tunstall had studied case law concerning a man's position relative to his wife's acquisition of personal and real property while married, and although there were questions about the status of inherited real property, in most instances both American and English courts invariably sided with the husband. Much as his sympathies might lie with the woman who'd made good while her husband was away, or even deserted her, settled law seemed to be on the man's side. It might be unfair, but the law never did have anything to do with fairness, and all too frequently in his estimation, precious little to do with justice.

"I'm sorry, Francine, the law's quite unambiguous on this very point. Your husband is right. The saloon is half his."

Francine exploded and her French accent enjoyed a recrudescence. "Zen ze law, she is an ass!"

Tunstall nodded his head, "You are not the first nor will you be the last to make that observation."

"Good," said Hal with a wide grin. "In that case, drinks are on the house!" This proclamation was greeted with a cheer from the few patrons at the bar being served by Gypsy and a snort of disgust from Francine.

"All right, Hal," she said. "You ween ze first round. Come wiz me," and with a regal flounce of her dress, which very nearly shook her breasts from her bodice, she took Hal's right arm, tucked it under her left shoulder, and led the astonished man to her private office.

"What do you think?" asked Tunstall.

"He's trouble. Did you see his face when Francine confronted him? Supposedly he's a wanted man. I could arrest him.

"True enough, but according to Francine he's no killer and if he's guilty of murder in self-defense, well, neither one of us was there. Besides let he who is without sin among you cast the first stone and all that."

"I, of all people can understand that. What about his partner?"

"Until one of them casts a stone here in Early, I say we let them be."

"You're very poetic tonight, I like it when you show your softer side."

Betsy continued, "Rose seems to have hit it off with Hal's part-ner Jack. They left together Lord knows where they went, unless she sneaked him into that shack she rents from Mr. Wilson. There'll be Hell to pay if he catches them, because he rented it under the condition that Rose doesn't use it to enter-tain paying gentleman callers. He doesn't want a whorehouse on his property, and I can't rightly blame him."

The following morning Betsy and Sara were seated at breakfast. Betsy was finishing her third cup of strong black coffee, when Francine rushed through the open front door, startling all three of them. Betsy didn't recognize her at first. She'd never seen Francine with her hair down and it was long, reaching almost to her waist. She was in great distress or appeared to be, and as she brushed the hair from her face, the cause was obvious. The nostrils of her nose were black with crusted blood, and her lips were puffy and bruised.

"What the Hell happened to you?" asked Betsy.

With an animalistic snarl and without a trace of a Gallic accent, Francine said, "Like I told you and the mayor, he's an animal! But no! You said, 'He's your husband under the law.' So that gives him the right to backhand me as hard as he can whenever it suits his fancy?"

Betsy was sympathetic though her feelings were somewhat leavened by anger at Francine's implication that it was her fault.

"Now you just slow down a minute. I'm your friend, not Hal Russell's, but you can't tell, me you were sitting down, minding your own business, drinking tea, and he up and slugged you. So tell me what happened."

Sara got up from the table and with a child's unsullied instinct to comfort the injured, went to Francine and put her long slender arms around the swell of her well shaped derriere, and pressed her head into Francine's pelvis, at which point Francine broke down and sobbed. Sara stood silently until Francine's emotional squall passed. Then Francine loosened Sara's hands with her own. "Sara," said Betsy. "Ben could use some help with the garden." That was enough for Sara and without a word she shot out the front door.

Francine sniffed. "We were half undressed and kissing like we used to when we first met in the Delta when he suddenly stopped and stood up.

"Before things go any further why don't you go downstairs and bring us bottle of brandy and tonight's receipts."

I did fetch a bottle of brandy and went back up. He took the bottle and then looked at me and said real quiet-like, 'Am I talking to myself, or have you gone deaf? I told you to bring the receipts."

"I told him the cash drawer was locked and Gypsy took the key."

Hal just looked at me with his face kinda' funny. I'd seen that look before and I backed away a few steps. 'You never were a good liar,' he said.

"This saloon and everything in it is as much mine as yours. I'm asking you one more time to bring me the receipts."

"No," I said. "If you think you can just come in here after four years and help yourself to all I've worked for, I don't give a damn what the law says I'll burn it to the ground first."

I ran for one of the Greener's, but he was too fast for me. He hit me twice with his fist and threw me out of my own saloon. I was going to wake the mayor or Mr. Swank, but I didn't want them to see me like this, besides I was afraid they'd say I provoked him and I guess in a way I did."

"I believe Enoch Swank's sweet on you and Tunstall would have backed you, still I'm glad you came to me."

"I spent the night with Gypsy and rode out at first light."

"Well, we can ride into town and swear out an assault complaint. I'll have him before the justice of the peace before noon today. As you know the judge is a particular friend of mine. What would you say to two weeks in jail and a fifty dollar fine?"

"I think that'd just make him want to kill me."

"Francine, I'm sorry to say it, but you kind of did bring this on yourself. Not that any man ever has a right to hit a woman except in self-defense, but it's not like we can send him to Santa Fe for trial. A broken nose, assuming it is broken, and a split lip isn't a hanging offense. In any place but Early this wouldn't involve the law, or ever come in front of a judge, you know that.

"Betsy, you know me and I'm not one who cries wolf at every little thing. Hal Russell is a vicious wolf."

Betsy took Francine's two hands in hers and looked deeply into her eyes.

"Now let's us talk seriously, girl to girl. I take it you don't want to resume your marital relations and live with Hal Russell as husband and wife?"

Francine slowly shook her head from side to side. This non-verbal answer satisfied Betsy who then said, "So once he gets his share of the saloon, he'll more than likely move on."

"Yes, I think he said something about Mexico."

"Good," said Betsy. "Then give him the money and good riddance to bad rubbish."

"But I haven't got the money. It'll take time to raise it."

"You can raise it while he's in jail, and give it to him when he gets out." Francine savagely twisted her hands loose from Betsy's, backed up a full pace, and snarled, "Why should I go into debt to give money to an evil bastard who pops up like a bad penny to enjoy the fruits of my hard work? Do you know how many nights I had to hump filthy cow hands, smell their foul breath, endure their horny hands kneading my tits like they were milking a cow, being ridden like a saddle mule, forced to endure a thousand unspeakably disgusting sex acts, all the while Lord Russell gallivants from here to Sacramento, drinking, gambling, and fornicating, no, Betsy Johnson, you simply have no idea."

Though she sympathized with Francine from the bottom of her heart, Betsy had heard quite enough of this Jeremiad. Francine had married Hal for better or worse, for richer for poorer, in sickness and in health, till death did them part.

"Listen Francine, as Mayor Tunstall told you, the law is the law. It's not fair and it's not just, but it's the law. You'll either have to tolerate your husband and learn to run the saloon together with him or buy him out. Now do you want to swear out a complaint or not, because if you don't, I have things I need to be doing."

"I thought being a woman and my friend, you'd have more feelings for me."

Betsy cut her off with a snarl of her own, "Francine, don't you dare start with me! I've told you half a dozen times I'm on your side and so is Tunstall."

Francine let out a long, moaning sigh, "Alright, let's go see the mayor. I'll swear out the complaint. I'll be able to think one whole hell of a lot better knowing Hal's in jail."

Chapter 7
THE ARREST

Hal Russell spent the night sleeping in one of the private rooms, Gypsy's as a matter of fact. It was decorated with a plush upholstered wine red satin, an overstuffed horsehair sofa, a lovely four poster brass bed with white cambric canopy, a walnut washstand, and a large, carved, gilt-wood mirror. The mattress on the bed was neither hard nor soft, but to Hal's mind it beat the hell out of sleeping on a thin bedroll on the bare ground, which is how he'd spent all too many nights during the past four years. Sleeping out in the open was always an adventure; you never knew what you might have as a companion come morning, from a spider to a field mouse seeking a warm place for the night. The room was most certainly done up in classic whorehouse vibrant red colors, but Hal didn't mind at all. The floor, walls, bed linen, and even the mattress seemed clean and Hal checked thoroughly, as he did not want to take his rest lying in some other man's love leavings. After he satisfied himself the bed was clean, Hal stripped off his shirt and dungarees, and washed his face, arms, neck, and chest as thoroughly as possible and dried off using a fleecy cotton Turkish towel.

"I'll take a nice, long, hot bath in the morning, and a barber shave if this one horse town even has a barber."

Francine's or rather his saloon exceeded his expectations, while at the same time, and as much as it rankled him to admit it, Colonel Jessup had been correct about Early, which was even more pathetic than he's imagined. Nevertheless, he couldn't see how the saloon, its contents, and the opulent bar could possibly be worth less than two thousand dollars at a fire sale, and he'd be content to take his half share and split it with Jack, then ride south to Monterrey and his new life.

Francine was a voluptuous example of the female form and she was more to his liking physically than the lithe, lovely girl, he'd left behind. Unfortunately, she was as independent and to his thinking just as mouthy as she ever was, and he'd had to remind her with his fist just who was the master in his saloon, just as he had to frequently remind her in their home in Sacramento.

When Hal was a young child in Eire, Pennsylvania, his father, the lockmaster, was given over to drink, and to administering frequent reminders of his authority to Hal's mother in the form of black eyes and split lips. "Boy," he'd say to Hal in his whiskey roughened-voice, "Don't you ever let a woman wear the pants in your house, even once. It's a sure road to a lifetime of misery." Of course after Hal's mother finally ran off, Hal found himself the object of his father's 'corrections.'

Hal awoke early from a dream in which he was in Monterrey eating a delicious breakfast of fried eggs, beans, hot tortillas, and a beefsteak. When he opened his eyes he temporarily forgot exactly where he was for a few seconds and how he'd come to be in the room with the big brass bed. Then he remembered he was in his own saloon and smiled.

"There must be food somewhere around here," he thought and suddenly he was ravenously hungry for any one or all the things he was eating in his dream. He dressed quickly, combed his hair using his fingers, and walked out of the room to forage in the darkened saloon. He lit several candles using one of the Lucifer matches from a brass cup on the bar. Against the wall, behind the bar, Hal saw a squat oak icebox, opened one of the upper compartments, and found several beefsteaks that would make for a fine breakfast. He figured Jack was with Rose. He thought that was the girl's name, not that he was worried either way. Jack could take care of himself, and he was a good partner to have your back in a scrape as he'd proven more than once. Jack wanted to return to the Delta with enough cash to buy a houseboat and past that he wasn't bothered about anything. He and Jack would say, "Via con Dios," and move on with their respective lives. With luck, he and Francine would do the same after they divided up the saloon.

Hal went out the rear door and there was a mud brick area with a large iron stove under a well-constructed overhang to protect it from the elements, A neat stack of finely split hardwood, well seasoned, stood next to some gummy pine kindling beside the stove. Hal arranged the fuel, lit the kindling, and within a few minutes he could tell the hardwood had caught fire. He went back inside the saloon just as dawn was breaking over the foothills to the East. Hal walked quickly to the room where he'd spent the night, and picked up his gun belt and holster. He drew out his Colt with his right hand and threw the rig on the bed with his left. He cocked the revolver with his right thumb, thumbed open the loading gate, and used his left hand to revolve the cylinder, checking all six chambers. Hal did not subscribe to the practice of loading five cartridges and keeping one chamber empty for safety. He always loaded all six, having faith in his ability not to drop it. The cartridges were fresh. He's purchased a brand new box of 44 Winchester Center Fire rounds made by Marcellus Hartley's Union Metallic Cartridge Company and these and Winchester's were uniformly excellent. The porous light paper container would retain the stain of any water or moisture though the cartridges were almost waterproof. A man could stake his life on the fact that by using UMC or Winchester cartridges his gun would fire when the hammer was cocked and the trigger pulled.

Hal's Colt, like all the early Single Actions had a seven and one half inch barrel, which made it an awkward thing to carry in one's belt without a holster, but if a man took it to a gunsmith to have it shortened, as he'd seen people do, one sacrificed accuracy at any distance greater than ten or fifteen yards.

"To Hell with it," Hal said to himself, and picked up the gun-belt once more and belted it in place, even tying the leather tie-down that hung from the bottom of the holster, around his thigh. Hal pushed the revolver down into the supple yielding leather and walked back into the saloon.

Now the sun was high enough so Hal didn't need candles, so he snuffed them out and took three beefsteaks from the icebox, chose two, replaced the rejected one, and walked back outside to grill them. The birds were singing and chirping, and the clouds in the light aqua blue sky looked like shredded cotton. The well-marbled meat met the hot black iron with a satisfying hiss, and the rich aroma of roasting beef made Hal salivate. He thought, "If only Francine had some coffee hidden somewhere, but then again, a mug of beer will serve just as well, and it's easier to pump than grind beans, boil water, and brew coffee." Once Hal knew where everything was kept, he would have coffee with his breakfast, but for the time being, since Francine had left in a tearful huff, he'd drink his beer and be satisfied.

Hal cut into one of the steaks with his IXL Bowie, not too deeply, for he had no intention of dulling the razor keen edge on stove iron. The gash filled instantly with blood and meat juices, almost as if it were a wound made in a living thing. Hal liked the look of his incision, and the gently charred yellow fat. The aroma was as welcome to his senses as freshly bruised sage, or rosewater on the nape of a pretty girl's neck. He turned the beefsteaks one last time and they hissed sharply as they met the dull red glow of the thick cast iron.

There was a long two tined iron fork hanging by a leather thong from one of the uprights of the overhang, which Hal used to turn the meat. He's discovered a large, white China charger under the bar, and he brought it out to receive the beefsteaks. He wiped his Bowie on the right pant leg and re-sheathed it in his right boot. Hal then forked the sizzling meat onto the platter and walked back into the saloon holding it with one hand on either end. He brought the large iron fork in with him as well and taking it off the charger, placed it and the oversized plate on the same wood table where the mayor and Betsy had sat the previous evening.

Hal sat down and lifted one of the steaks with the fork and used his Bowie to trim the blackened fat then cut it into strips as easily as if he were slicing overripe melon. Impaling a succulent piece, he brought it to his lips, bit off a good third of it, and chewed with complete enjoyment. He laid down the fork and still chewing, walked to the bar, selected a clean looking, heavy glass with a swell to the top, pumped the keg several times and pulled the tap, filling his glass. Hal blew off the creamy head of foam, and filled it close to the rim.

Hal drank and thought the beer nearly as good as the beef. He was about to go back to refill the glass, when the swinging door opened with its eldritch cry and in walked Francine, looking like a raccoon, with two yellowish black eyes, accompanied by Betsy wearing her silver badge. Francine glared at him and if looks could kill, Hal would have dropped dead where he stood. As it was he completely ignored Francine and addressed Betsy.

"Good morning, ladies. The stove's still hot, and these beefsteaks are mighty delicious eating, if you'd care to join me."

Hal spoke in a tone of voice that promised such good will and comradeship, that Betsy actually felt guilty about disturbing the man's breakfast. Hal was evidently richly enjoying himself. "But," she thought, "That was how it always was with wife—beaters. After the abuse they were all smiles and apologies as if the man who had laid violent hands on his woman wasn't the same man at all, and this was the whole problem. Men who hit women, really didn't know themselves, and nine times out of ten, a lot of the blame could be put down to demon rum or John Barleycorn. Not that liquor could make a good man bad, but it sure could make a bad man worse, or a normally decent man do things he regretted when he was sober." There was the cowhand Tunstall had shot the previous afternoon. Hal could have just as easily killed Francine, instead of just breaking her nose, splitting her lips, and loosening a few teeth. Betsy remembered this and her resolve strengthened.

"Hal Russell, I have a complaint sworn out against you for assault, duly signed by a justice of the peace." Here Betsy held out a folded piece of white paper.

"Let me see it," said Hal. Betsy walked up keeping a weather eye on Hal's right shoulder, and placed it on the bar away from the man. Hal picked it up, unfolded it, and read it carefully, all of which took less than a minute by Betsy's reckoning on the regulator clock behind the bar. When he finished, Hal refolded the paper.

"This says I struck my wife repeatedly. I say we were both so drunk on brandy during our joyful reunion that she stumbled and fell and hit her face on the chair seat on the way down. I picked her up and then she started screaming that I hit her. That's the way I remember it and that's the way it happened." Hal said all this in a calm, eminently reasonable tone of voice.

"That's a lie and you damn well know it," hissed Francine. Betsy hated having to be involved in this ugly husband and wife confrontation, but she was convinced it was her sworn duty to defend the rights of the weak and dispossessed. This meant women, children, Negroes, Mexicans, and Indians but most of all women.

"Mr. Russell, you're under arrest. Now if you'll just remove your gun-belt, leave it on the bar and follow me we can dispense with handcuffs."

"He carries a Bowie knife in his right boot," said Francine.
"I'll trouble you for your Bowie as well, Mr. Russell," said Betsy.

Hal picked up his glass and drained the dregs. For a brief moment, Betsy thought he might throw it at her. Hal was in fact, considering doing just that. He refrained because he still cherished a hope of making Betsy see things his way, although in his experience with women, reason and logic were complete and utter strangers.

"Wait just a darn minute, marshal. You got two different versions of events from the only two people that were there. One's telling the truth and the other's either a liar, or was too drunk to recall things properly."

"That may well be," said Betsy, "But I'm sworn to uphold the law and that complaint is legal so give me your gun and knife and come with me."

"Marshal, answer me one thing. Since when does the law dictate how a husband treats his wife? Can you show me a Territorial statute where it says a man can't correct his wife or his son? Next thing you'll tell me a man can't take a willow switch to his boy's backside when the rascal's been stealing candy from the store."

Betsy could see where Hal's argument would make good sense to most people, just not to her.

"First you say Francine fell on a chair and now you're defending laying hands on her. Point is, no matter what, you crossed the line and you're going to jail. Now you can go easy or you can go hard. What'll it be?"

Hal didn't want to shoot anyone, much less a marshal and a female one at that. He was bone tired of having to look over his shoulder, and watch every word he said, and every move he made for fear of being taken into custody and returned to Sacramento. He and Jack had become less vigilant and more complacent with each year, and now they were more than a thousand miles away, but though the mail could take weeks, even months, the telegraph was quick as thought. Hal didn't want to go to jail on an off chance.

"Listen up marshal, can't we settle this some other way, like me paying a fine or something?"

Betsy looked at Francine, whose lips were set firmly, even grimly, bruised and puffy as they were.

"No, I'm afraid not, Mr. Russell. Now I'm asking you for the last time to take off your Colt, your Bowie, and any hideout guns like derringers or other weapons you have on you, and put them on the bar where I can see them."

To punctuate her instructions, Betsy loosened her own Colt in its holster. The very last thing Betsy wanted was a shooting, especially after yesterday, but she couldn't allow Hal to flout her authority either. Betsy's movement with her right hand wasn't lost on Hal. He had looked closely at the grip on Betsy's Single Action the previous night. A man who knew what he was looking for could read quite a bit in the grip of another man's gun. The varnish on Betsy's was worn in all the right places it should be if she practiced drawing and shooting on a regular basis. Just as the checkered ivory on Tunstall's Colt indicated he didn't wear it as decoration, Hal figured Betsy was handy with her revolver. But shooting inanimate objects was one thing and shooting another human being was another thing entirely as Hal knew from personal experience. Hal looked at Betsy and conning her face he thought she was resolute and not all that nervous.

Betsy was growing impatient. Did this man think because he was handsome and she was a woman, he could talk his way out of being arrested? Or that he wouldn't have to show her the same respect he would if Tunstall or some other man was facing him? Either way, the handsome stranger figured wrong.

"If your gun-belt isn't on the bar in the next thirty seconds, I'm going to assume you're resisting arrest which is another charge. If it makes you feel better you can keep your Bowie."

"Marshal, before this whole thing gets out of hand, how about if I just put my pistol on the bar the rig kinda' helps keep my trousers up?"

Betsy was considering Hal's request when she heard the unmistakable snick of a Colt Single Action being full cocked behind her. She heard three distinct clicks, although they were run together, the final click of the hammer was accompanied by the sound of the cylinder heavy with cartridges locking into place. It was the sound of precision, well-oiled machinery in motion, as distinctive and deadly as the buzz of a rattle-snake, something one ignored at his peril. Betsy froze, and Francine yelped like a small dog hit by a stone. Hal smiled, first at Betsy, then at Francine.

"Now," he said with confidence in his voice, "Marshal, put your gun on the table next to you and don't try any heroics."

Betsy carefully drew her revolver and placed it on the table as instructed.

"Good," said Hal. "Jack, get the marshal's pistol and unload it." Jack walked past Betsy from the entrance to the saloon. Having returned from Rose's place, on his way he saw Betsy and Francine enter the saloon. He'd mentioned the gruesome noise made by the swinging door to Rose who told him that if you pulled open the door rather then pushing it, one could make a relatively silent entrance. Jack had listened to most of the conversation between Betsy and Hal before he decided the time was fortuitous to pull open the batwing door, and announce himself with his Colt. Using his left hand, Jack deftly cocked Betsy's gun, opened the loading gate, and turned the cylinder with his left thumb with the pistol's muzzle pointed at the ceiling, until five of the chubby forty-five caliber cartridges fell on the table. One rolled off and smacked onto the floor, which was bare of sawdust and shavings at this early hour.

"Alright now Mr. Russell," said Betsy, without a trace of fear in her tone of voice. It was the same tone she used with Sara when her daughter would find herself in a situation of her own creation that she couldn't resolve by herself. At least now she wouldn't have to shoot Hal, and that came as a relief.

"What now?" Betsy asked.

Hal hadn't had time to think things through. He was minding his own business, thoroughly enjoying a really good breakfast when Betsy and Francine rudely interrupted him. The beer he'd drunk on an all but empty belly made him a mite light headed. Pulling guns on the town marshal didn't square at all with his intentions.

"Jack," Hal said. "I think you can un-cock and holster your pistol. I got this under control."

Jack obligingly raised the barrel of his Colt to the ceiling and allowed the hammer to fall slowly and harmlessly down to rest on the primer of the cartridge in the chamber by simultaneously pulling the trigger and using the right side of his thumb to ride the hammer down against the tension of the mainspring. He then drew the hammer back ever so slightly to the first notch and loosely holstered the handgun. Betsy now only had one pistol pointed in her general direction.

"Now, marshal," said Hal not unpleasantly. "There has to be a way we can work things out so nobody gets hurt. You're the law so you know this saloon's half mine. That makes me a property owner and a citizen. I got rights."

"So does your wife, and in her case your rights ended when your fist came in contact with her nose. And now you're threatening an officer of the law, interfering with the performance of my duties, resisting arrest, disturbing the peace, Lord knows what else."

"Francine, let's us make a deal. I figure this saloon's worth at least two thousand dollars, it's probably worth a lot more but I don't care. You give me a thousand. I'll give you a divorce and leave the Territory. I swear you'll never see my face again."

Hal's calm, matter of fact voice, and the size of the amount infuriated Francine. Her face flushed a fiery red, and the veins stood out like blue cords on her neck.

"Never," she said in her best French accent. "I'll see you in Hell first." Betsy was more convinced than ever of two things. One was that marriage, any marriage, was not the state of bliss celebrated by poets and novelists. The other was that being a marshal called for nearly as much ministration as being a preacher.

As Betsy contemplated her options, she heard the unmistakable ratcheting sound of someone working the lever on a Winchester rifle. It was quite different from the noise of a Colt revolver being cocked, more machine like. Hal and Jack heard it as did Jack and Francine.

A deep male voice intoned solemnly, "Drop your pistol Russell." Betsy turned toward the door and saw Tunstall in the prone position on the wood floor just behind the swinging- door, with his fancy engraved, gilt brass frame Winchester pointed at Hal Russell.

> "You might be able to shoot me, but is it worth taking a chance with the marshal? There's only seven pounds of trigger pull between her and half an ounce of lead and a man tends to twitch his hand after he's shot."

Tunstall was confident he could hit Russell's revolver, but it was pointed at Betsy and though there was only a one in one thousand chance of her being hit by Hal's fire, it wasn't worth taking a chance. Jack took advantage of the mayor's hesitation and now there were two guns pointed at Betsy, though Jack hadn't cocked his revolver for fear of being shot. Now Jack used his right thumb to draw the hammer to full cock and the three clicks resounded in the empty saloon like the strokes of a sledge-hammer on an anvil.

> "Russell," said Tunstall. "It looks like we have a Mexican standoff."
> "No sir," said Hal. "It looks like I hold the high ground."

> "How exactly do you figure that? Five minutes ago you were looking at two weeks in jail. Now with luck you're looking at ten years in the Territorial Prison and hanging if you kill your wife, or the marshal."

"He's right," said Jack. "This is crazy. We didn't come here for this!" Tunstall used his elbows and rose to his knees, holding the rifle on Hal with his right hand by pressing the sharp, crescent butt-plate into his shoulder, and pushing the swinging door open with his left hand. The door shrieked as he opened it. Tunstall's moves were extremely awkward and uncomfortable, then within moments he was inside the saloon with the Winchester still pointed at Hal's heart.

Tunstall addressed himself to Hal, "I don't think you want to murder anyone. I'll tell you what. You two boys put your guns away and I'll put down my rifle, and maybe the five of us can have a drink and talk this out." Hal looked at Tunstall and he believed the older man was speaking the truth.

"Alright, Mayor, I'll trust you this once." Hal took his Colt and un-cocked it, then holstered it and Jack followed suit. Tunstall carefully rode the hammer of his rifle down with using his thumb and the knurl-ing of the hammer spur.

"That's one beautiful rifle," said Jack as he admired the brightly gilded frame and the highly figured, piano varnished walnut stock and forearm. Tunstall smiled thinly and shrugged. Betsy immediately picked up her revolver, bent to retrieve the cartridge that had fallen on the floor, blew the dust off it, loaded the five rounds, and holstered the pistol.

Betsy wanted to go back to the ranch and see to her new project, which was washing the tailings of the abandoned gold mine on her property. Ben had already accumulated nearly fifty dollars worth of tiny nuggets and dust, over the past three months. The mine itself was too dangerous for amateurs and neither she nor Ben had any intention of trying to re-open it. If only there were a stream nearby they might really strike gold by washing the tailings, then again if Betsy were going to wish for things, she'd think of something more substantial like a good school on the reservation so Sara wouldn't be forced to go into Early for her education.

Betsy, Francine, and Jack all declined to indulge in spirits so early in the day, so Hal and Tunstall each drank a beer. Hal agreed to a one hundred dollar fine to be applied to the one thousand dollars Francine agreed to pay him for his share of the saloon and a divorce. The hun-dred dollars was twenty times as much as Francine used to receive for her sexual favors and her anger at Hal and the whole situation was slightly mollified by this rather substantial fine, the more so as it was going to her.

As they were preparing to go their separate ways, Tunstall put his right hand on Hal's shoulder and said, "Now that we understand each other, let me say this. If you feel the urge to beat your wife, or any other woman in Early, and you give in to it, I promise you I will personally break your arms behind your back, and your face will frighten small children for the rest of your miserable life."

Betsy knew Tunstall was in deadly earnest and meant every word. Even Hal who was no coward acknowledged the menace in the mayor's tone, though his voice he never rose above the one he used in normal conversation. Francine was reassured by this declaration and knew it was something she could literally stake her life on.

Chapter 7
FRANCINE

Early was too small a town to have more than one bank, and the bank it did have had only one teller and somewhat irregular business hours. It was a branch of a larger bank in Santa Fe, and although it had a vault, many of Early's residents kept what little money they put by in Mason jars buried in secret places. Tunstall had a decent size floor-safe in his office that might or might not be fireproof. The day after the encounter with Hal and Jack, Francine came to the mayor's office. Her nose and lips looked one hundred percent better; however the skin under her eyes had a yellowish brown tint that looked most unhealthy, and this was after she applied make-up.

She had a tale of woe for Tunstall. "I went to the bank. Would you believe that teller, Mr. Green, and he's one of Rose's steady clients, refused to lend me more than five hundred dollars on the whole saloon?"

"Banks aren't known for taking risks. Banks like sure things," said Tunstall as sympathetically as he could.

"I don't suppose you have four hundred dollars you could lend me for about two years?"

"Sorry, Francine, I don't have four hundred dollars I could loan you for two minutes besides."

"Besides what?"

"I have a policy of never lending money to friends. I'll give them money if I have it to give, but loans, I don't like them. It seems the borrower always feels some resentment at having to pay it back. Doesn't matter what they say. Lending money has killed more friendships than politics and that's saying something. It just never works out, trust me on this. I can give you fifty dollars if it does you any good."

"Why, thank you mayor. I knew I could count on you. I'll take you up on it and give you credit at the saloon."

Tunstall frowned, "Francine, I appreciate your generous heart, but if you give me credit, then you're diminishing your income, which you'll need to pay your bank loan. If you give credit, next thing you know, you're behind in your payments and in foreclosure. Banks have about as much sympathy for debtors' sob stories as prostitutes, if you'll forgive the comparison."

Tunstall didn't think the bank loan was a good idea. He knew from his position as justice of the peace that the Territorial Bank of New Mexico was quick to foreclose, usually within days of non-payment, and did not as a policy lend more than fifty percent of a property's land value offering nothing for improvements like the saloon. The land itself, they appraised at what it would be worth to someone who didn't want it in the first place, but couldn't resist such a bargain.

Tunstall really valued what he considered the congenial atmosphere Francine gave to the saloon. Early was certainly the only town in New Mexico with a female marshal and a female saloon owner, and Tunstall was pleased at this notoriety. The heavy fine he levied against Hal Russell did not go unnoticed by the husbands in Early, and there would be more than one who would think twice about knocking his wife around after overindulging in rye on a Saturday night because of it. Several women had already threatened their spouses with the law if they slapped them around using Hal's fine as a precedent.

"Don't you touch me 'less you got a hundred dollars you can do without," said one long-suffering wife to her liquor befuddled husband. As most households in Early didn't have five dollars to spare, much less a hundred, the threat was effective.

Francine took the mayor's fifty, and Rose and Gypsy each put up twenty-five. She knew better than to ask Betsy, who was chronically short of money herself, largely as a result of numerous, spontaneous acts of charity to Indians on the reservation in need of warm clothing for their children. Francine was at the end of her list of possible lenders and donors except for Enoch Swank.

She hesitated to approach him, primarily because she had a notion that he was sweet on her, and whore that she may have been in Duffy's day, she was never one to take advantage of a man who was not a paying customer. Francine was attracted to Swank, not because of his tall, rangy, even ungainly body, but because she found his good manners charming. She liked his gentle expertise in treating female complaints, and his voluminous scientific knowledge. He was far and away the most educated man Francine had ever known, and this made him more physically desirable than she would have thought possible.

Rose was deliriously happy living with Hal's partner, Jack, and incredible as it seemed, in less than two days following his forced agreement with Francine, Hal had taken up with young Gypsy. How this came about was a mystery to Francine. Though she couldn't help but feel a twinge of jealousy, one look in the mirror at her fading, but clearly visible black eyes, instantly blunted the feeling. She warned Gypsy in no uncertain terms.

"Hal Russell may be good looking. There were those in California that called him Handsome Hal, but once a wife beater, always a woman beater. He's like all the rest. He'll smack you around, then cry real tears and tell you how sorry he is. He didn't mean it. You pushed him into doing it and all the while you're feeling your loose front teeth with your tongue. His remorse is real. That's the really scary part. He'll cry, scream and carry on, telling you it hurt him more than it hurt you. Then he'll swear by his God and his mother's grave, it'll never happen again. It was the whiskey's doing, or the devil's, or yours, but never his."

Francine stopped for a long moment to make certain Gypsy understood her perfectly. "Let me tell you one thing and you can count on it as sure as death that Hal, or any other man afflicted by that disease will do it again. They can't help themselves, but that don't help us. That's all I have to say, except you're on your own, and don't come to me with a broken wrist, or a sore backside from his boot toe, and say you weren't warned. Oh, and one more thing. A lot of women think this about the previous victim, 'He hit her because she rubbed him the wrong way, but I don't so we'll get along'. It's true a new romance has its own compulsions and distractions, but give it time and the old pattern will return just as sure as God made little green apples, and all of us, crooked or straight. If Hal had stayed with me in Sacramento I'd be crippled for life or in the grave by now. You're younger than I am and probably think I'm full of horse-crap. You might think Hal will be different with you, trust me I used to think he'd change too, fool that I was. Wishful thinking is all it was. The truth is he can't anymore keep from beating a woman than he can flap his arms and fly like an eagle. That's all I've got to say. Don't say I didn't warn you."

Later on some time after Francine had left her in search of more funds Gypsy related the conversation and warning that Francine had given her about Hal to Rose. Both girls agreed Hal was quite the catch, and that their boss was suffering from a classic case of sour grapes.

"Hal told me Francine married him and never told him about the rich, young Mexican boy, whose parents refused to let him marry her. She was still madly in love with him when she met Hal. No man likes to be a substitute for a lost lover, at least when he marries the girl. That'd make any man hostile after he takes the vows."

"No wonder he beat her," said Rose. "I'd have tanned her hide but good if she'd done that to me."

Francine stood for a long minute at the side of Swank's Apothecary. The small, narrow shop had a projecting sign painted a dark shade of green with elaborate, gilt letters of block capitals spelling out the name and next to them a silver colored, realistic rendition of a pestle inside a mortar. Like the man and the shop, itself, the sign was understated, bespeaking substance and quality to anyone with an eye trained to look for them. Francine didn't really want to ask him for three dollars much less three hundred, but she had no one else to turn to and she wanted Hal Russell and Jack Jones out of her life and out of Early as soon as possible.

She took a very deep breath and then walked the two paces to the door. Francine had dressed specifically for the occasion in a relatively new and very becoming light grey dress, whose bodice set off her plump, breasts to advantage without prostituting them. She wore a pair of soft black, suede leather half boots and her luxuriant brown hair was up as always with a few selected ringlets framing her well shaped ears. She deliberately wore no make-up or rouge as she thought the still visible but fading signs of her recent beating might elicit a more sympathetic response to her request. Francine's lips naturally tended to be full and the added swelling given by Hal's backhand benefitted further from a light coating of sperm oil. Francine was blessed with long, thick eyelashes, so her lovely brown eyes required no artificial emphasis. She did indulge in a touch of genuine

French perfume behind each of her earlobes, more for her own enjoyment than to please Enoch Swank.

Enoch Swank was compounding a jalap for a stubborn case of heat rash, that was making the life of Lorena Crick's two year old boy a misery, and through him, the whole Crick family. Enoch added a generous pinch of powdered willow tree bark, which he rightfully prized for its analgesic properties, though it wasn't nearly as effective on skin as it was on mucous membranes or taken internally. He looked up from his mortar and its contents, and was happy to see Francine though it gave him butterflies just to look at her and he thought it ridiculous in the extreme that a man of his maturity, learning, and experience could be rendered as giddy as a schoolboy by the mere sight of her.

If Enoch were nervous at Francine's approach, so much so he unthinkingly ground his left thumb against the side of the bronze mortar, which sent a thrill of sharp pain through the digit, his hand and up his arm, Francine was almost beside herself with nerves. On her way from the saloon, where she'd made her toilette, she went through at least a dozen imaginary conversations, most of which were similar to, "Mr. Swank how nice to see you. You haven't been to the saloon in ages," when in fact he'd been there two days ago. Then she'd say in response to his compliment about her dress, "This dress, why it's nothing, just an old one I thought I'd wear today for some odd reason. Why thank you, you look nice yourself."

There would be more small talk and polite badinage and then, "I am in need of three hundred dollars. Would you have an idea where I could borrow it?"

Francine said to herself, No, no, no," and then she was inside Enoch's shop. The air inside was redolent with exotic odors of camphor, menthol, peppermint, spearmint, sage, and other scents Francine couldn't identify.

"Francine," Enoch said with a smile on his face that she could hear in his voice as well, as he wiped his hands on his heave canvas apron, and held out his right one. Francine took it in both of hers and was struck by his long, shapely fingers.

"To what do I owe this entirely unexpected pleasure? No disorders with the girls, I hope? They're using the sheaths I sold to you are they not?"

"Yes and no," said Francine with a smile of her own. She was always amazed that a man could casually discuss the most intimate anatomical functions and dysfunctions of the female reproductive anatomy without the slightest embarrassment. Doc Hill was more squeamish about such matters than Mr. Swank and Hill was a real physician, a distinction that Swank never hesitated to point out. Francine had never spoken to Enoch about money, there was never a reason to, and she had no idea if he were rich, or like most of Early's residents just scraping along one month or one week ahead of being busted. Although she was no bibliophile or antiquarian bookseller, the richly bound volumes on his bookshelves looked like they cost at least five or ten dollars a piece and there were more than a hundred of them by her cursory estimate. Their actual value would have staggered her. Enoch had bought them with proceeds from his patent medicine sales in and around St. Louis, thinking they were not only useful in his profession, but a good long term investment.

"Gypsy and Rose are just fine, thank you for asking about them. They are both grateful to you for all you've done for them, Mr. Swank."

"Let's dispense with this formality, please call me Enoch. You called me Enoch only the other night, so are we grown so distant over the past two days that I am once again Mr. Swank to you? Mr. Swank was my father, may he rest in peace."

"Alright let it be Enoch then," said Francine prettily as she batted her long lashes at him a flutter that was echoed in the apothecary's heart.

"I have a problem you see. My husband has appeared from the past out of nowhere and he claims a half interest in the saloon. Mayor Tunstall says he is within his rights to do so. I'm trying to buy him out and he's agreed to terms and a divorce.

The bank will lend me five hundred. Tunstall gave me fifty. Rose and Gypsy, bless their tender hearts, each gave me twenty five, and I need another three hundred." All this information came out in a rush, as if some dam burst inside Francine's mind, and all her thoughts flowed out through her speech. Enoch arched his bushy eyebrows in a quizzical gesture. His brows were thick, glossy and brown, meeting just above the bridge of his nose.

"And where is this phoenix among husbands living now?"

"He's living with Gypsy and his partner's living with Rose."

"How extremely convenient for them both," said Enoch with a delicately nuanced note of sarcasm in his tone that was entirely lost on Francine, but as he said it more for his own pleasure than out of meanness, which was notably absent from his nature, the rusticated Princeton apothecary was not in the least put off by his missing the mark.

"Francine, there is no need for friends, and I sincerely hope you consider me to be among those you call one, to indulge in elaborate pretensions about money. If you need three hundred to send the man packing, I believe I can spare such a sum for so noble a purpose."

Francine's eyes grew big and her heart full. The small, narrow shop was close and the cacophony of strange fragrances, overwhelming. Gripped by powerful emotions, all the blood left Francine's head, and her skin was clammy and cold. She thought she might become sick to her stomach. Seeing her thus, Swank, who really was a first class diagnostician, raced to give her a vial of smelling salts and within a few moments her cheeks resumed their customary look of health.

"I'm so sorry," she said, setting the glass vial down on the wood counter. "All this came up so suddenly. I feel like I'm dazed or something."

Enoch was close enough to examine her fading black eyes, now a faint rainbow of bruised blood vessels, but diplomatically refrained from mentioning them. He attributed their origin to the husband, who in all likelihood was unworthy of any woman, much less fair Francine. She had obviously married as badly or even worse than he had. In his mind, this gave them a shared experience, which could only serve to enhance and enrich their relationship should they begin one. A closer friendship with Francine was a possibility that had a distinct place in Enoch's fantasies whenever they lighted upon females, as she and Betsy Johnson were the only women in Early he was attracted to.

"Listen Francine, has it occurred to you to sell your interest in the saloon to your husband? One thousand dollars is a great deal of money, enough to pay for a fine home in Paris for a year, two years in Boston or Philadelphia, all kinds of things. Is ownership of the saloon that important to you? If it is, that's all well and good, but you'll be beholden to the bank for months if not years. Turn the tables on the bastard. Tell him he can buy you out. Let him, his partner, Rose, and Gypsy run the saloon. They'll go broke inside of six months if they last that long and the bank will come begging to you to take it off their hands."

"Where would Hal get the money?"

"What do you care?"

"But I agreed to buy it for one thousand dollars."

"If you don't have the money, then the deal's off, isn't it?" Listen. I'm not telling you not to buy it. I am saying why would you bid against yourself? Tell him he can buy you out for nine hundred. The price will come down. Of course maybe you really don't want to run the saloon. A girl like you with a competence has so many opportunities. You could even go to college."

Francine had spent countless nights daydreaming about owning the saloon. When Duffy left it to her, it was a dream come true. The reality was a great deal of hard work and without the illicit profits from sales of poisonous whiskey to the reservation Indians, the income, while steady, barely covered the expenses. Once Duffy's stock of quality spirits was exhausted, and that time was fast approaching, replenishing them would be very expensive. Francine was already wracking her brain trying to figure out how to raise the money to restock such costly liquors. Even if she sold drinks at fifty percent over cost, the cognacs, cordials, and wines were far too expensive for the pocketbooks of her steady customers. It cost a fortune to ship cognac or champagne from France by steamship to San Francisco or New York and then by Adams, Wells Fargo, or some other express company to the New Mexico Territory. Duffy could afford to sell his patrons fine liquor at near cost or even below as the profits from his smuggling operations were enormous, even though a large percentage went to Colonel Jessup for turning an official blind eye. Francine didn't take a share from the poker table so the money had to come from beer, rye, and the twenty five percent of Rose and Gypsy's earnings that accrued to her. Food wasn't profitable and Francine served it more to please her customers than to profit from its sale.

She carefully weighed Enoch's words. The shooting of Pete, the young ranch hand, together with Hal's mysterious appearance, and his hitting her, had unnerved Francine more than she realized. She knew it in her mind that liquor and firearms were always a potentially lethal combination, having been the witness to several stabbings and more than one shooting when she worked for Duffy. She and the other girls could always see trouble brewing, like the gathering of dark clouds on the horizon before a thunderstorm cleared the humid, overheated air on a late August afternoon in the Sacramento Delta. They would dive for protection behind the essentially bulletproof, mahogany bar, laughing as two men would roll around on the damp sawdust covered floor, trying desperately to inflict harm on each other. Usually they were so drunk their whiskey-numbed fingers had difficulty holding a weapon, and Duffy, the originator of the rock-salt/buckshot Greener shotguns, would only take matters into his own hands if his precious gilt etched mirrors were in danger. Gunshots were a rarity in the Early Saloon, though fights were not infrequent. More often than not the arguments that lead to threats and then to blows were over nothing. In fact, Francine couldn't recall a single one that had as a basis anything remotely worth a broken nose, split knuckles, let along more serious injuries like puncture wounds to the belly or lung.

Francine thought the most idiotic thing of all was the number of punch-ups between friends who would enter sober, arm in arm like beloved brothers, only to become bitter enemies after three or four drinks over who would enjoy the company of which girl, or jealousy over a bonus being paid to one and not the other, or who kept whom awake by his snoring in the bunkhouse Wednesday night. Back in Sacramento there were several Temperance Societies that tried to point out the dangers of "Demon Rum," and Francine together with other citizens used to mock and scorn their highly visible and noisy marches. Now, she saw there were good reasons behind their attitude, though she had yet to see any man force another man to drink too much whiskey at gunpoint. In her experience, herself included, most people drank to relax, and file off life's sharp edges, escape unpleasant thoughts, drown the blue devils, that and in the dog days of summer, when Sirius the Dog Star stood high in the sky, few things were as thirst quenching as a cool, malty, glass of beer.

In Sacramento, ice was plentiful, even in summer as wagons brought it down through the Donner Pass and the high Sierras. Summer ice was non-existent in Early, and though there were high mountains in New Mexico Territory, some as high as in California, the roads were poor, many little more than trails, and what little ice that lasted past April was worth its weight in silver. Duffy had dug a small but well insulated icehouse under the saloon. It was more like a mineshaft than a house, but it served the purpose and was cool in summer.

"Why, am I so desperate to own the saloon?" Francine asked herself. "Is it because I need something substantial I can work, live, and sleep in that belongs to me and can't be taken from me?" She pondered. "They took Luis away from me and I hated that more than leaving home, more than my parent's death, more than anything. Then I became Hal's wife and his excuse for everything that went wrong in his life. I ran away and became a whore because all men were pigs, or so I was convinced, and I might as well be paid for what I gave Hal for free and then being beaten for it. Duffy left me the saloon and now I'm a person of importance in Early, and I take care of my friends Rose and Gypsy who are living with Hal and Jack who I have to give a thousand dollars to so I can own what I already own. Now, Enoch Swank offers to lend me the money I need but he wants me to think about it, what I'm doing and why."

Enoch untied his apron and hung it up on a wooden peg. Split lips, rainbow bruised eyes notwithstanding, Francine was as desirable a specimen of feminine pulchritude as Enoch had ever beheld. Added to this was his certainty that she had a kind heart. Like the Fountain of Youth, the Philosopher's Stone, or the Holy Grail, the whore with the golden heart was a fable, a legend, a will-o-the-wisp men had sought in vain ever since King David took Bathsheeba from Uriah the Hittite, and the Hebrew king may have been the only man in all history to have found the living, breathing, incarnation of the legend.

"But, then," thought Enoch, "Louis XV had Madame de Pompadour and Napoleon his Josephine."

Despite his marital misfortune, Enoch did not despise women. On the contrary, he enjoyed being on intimate terms with them and just not sexually.

"Francine," he said brightly. "What do you say you ride with me out into the foothills of the Sangre de Christos? I know a meadow there that would not look wholly out of place in Eden. There is a plant there that grows by a spring. I've been meaning to harvest some for the past month. We can talk further on our way."

A good long ride would offer plenty of opportunities to canter and nothing cleared Francine's head like a good long lope on horseback. She liked the idea of turning the tables on Hal, making him either put up the money, which he probably couldn't, or shut up and take much less. Though she'd agreed to the deal in front of Betsy and Tunstall, if Enoch didn't give her the money, six hundred was all she could raise and at six hundred Francine could live with it. She'd use Enoch's money to pay back most of her loan from the bank.

She said sweetly, "Enoch," and the apothecary was thrilled far more than he thought he could be by hearing his name pronounced by her lush lips. "I'd love to go with you. Give me time to change into my riding clothes, wake up the girls and tell them they need to open the saloon, and have my mare saddled. I can put up some cold beef sandwiches and a some beer in a bottle if you like."

"The sandwiches sound wonderful, but I assure you the water from the spring is cooler and sweeter than any champagne. It is truly an elixir worthy of the gods, pure nectar, I promise you."

"I can hardly bear to wait. I only asked about the beer because I'm used to being around drinking men."

"Don't mistake me, I have nothing against wine or brandy, and beer has its charms, it's only that there's nothing quite as refreshing as fine mineral water, icy cold from deep inside the living rock, unsullied by earth or air."

Chapter 8
THE SPRING

Neither Enoch nor Francine spurred their horses into the first canter just west of town, because neither of them wore spurs. Unless a man was cutting cows and needed to communicate signals to his horse amid the confusion of half-ton beasts, milling around in a herd, a good rider really has no need of them. Both Francine's quarter horse and Enoch's Paso Fino were well-trained, well-mannered mounts. They responded to leg pressure and the slightest shift of their rider's weight in the saddle. Francine was adept at sitting the trot and she was amazed at the smoothness of Enoch's gaited horse. The stallion's front legs seemed to fly out to the sides in different directions in an incredibly awkward appearing inside out motion, almost like a flurry, but Enoch sat virtually motionless, without having to expend any effort to counterbalance himself as if he were floating in the saddle. She couldn't help commenting and he replied,

"There's nothing like a gaited horse for trotting. The running walk of a Tennessee walker or Paso Fino allows the rider to cover great distances at a decent speed without exhausting the animal, and unlike most horse's trots, it's extremely comfortable. Would you like to try him?"

"I would, but my mare had a trainer she didn't get along with. She's skittish and she isn't willing to suffer rough handling or what she feels is rough treatment. She's not fond of men and that's an understatement."

"I guess it's no accident, the two of you get along so well, then."

"No," said Francine with a small laugh. "When the hostler told me her story, I saw her try to take a bite out of his backside when he wasn't looking, and she tore off the pocket of his trousers, I knew then that Dawn and I were made for each other."

"She's unusual being gray."

"That's so. Listen, Enoch, if you're game to try, I'll switch with you." She brought Dawn to a halt and gracefully dismounted, swinging a shapely right leg effortlessly over the high cantle of her saddle. Francine had donned a pair of moleskin breeches with leather patches sewn into the thighs in imitation of chaps, which she rarely wore.

They were light gray and admirably matched Dawn's thin summer coat. Enoch was dressed in a cream colored suit that contrasted nicely with the rich, chestnut hue of his Paso Fino. Enoch dismounted and handed the reins to Francine, who handed Dawn's reins to him. The stallion looked at Enoch as if seeking approval for the hand over. He nickered plaintively and Enoch smiled into his large, limpid, brown eyes, as Francine put out her right hand, palm up, so he could nuzzle it and see she meant him no harm. At no time during the get acquainted period did he pin back his ears or give any sign of displeasure. Francine put the toe of her left boot into the stirrup, and using a left hand full of rein and thick black mane, lifted herself and lightly took an almost perfect seat in the saddle. Though Enoch was considerably taller than she, he rode with short stirrups and Francine didn't think they needed to be shortened for her.

"Where'd you learn so much about horses?" said Enoch with genuine admiration.

"My father, God rest his soul, bought me a pony when I was a little girl and for years, we were inseparable. Sometimes when the weather was warm, I'd fall asleep next to him in his stall."

"What was his name?"

"He came with the name Danny Boy, but I named him Angel, because he was an angel."
"I won't ask what became of him."

"Don't," she said. "It's a short, sad story of colic."

"For such powerful, useful, and intelligent animals, they are prone to a veritable host of deadly maladies, especially of the digestive tract, any one of which can prove fatal."

Francine winced. "I'm sorry," said Enoch, abashed. "I won't say another word on the subject, but Angel taught you a great deal. Simon seems as comfortable with you as he is with me, although for a stone horse he's remarkably good natured." "Why Simon?"

"For Simon Bolivar, the great liberator of Peru and Columbia, founder of Bolivia, which was originally called Bolivar. He and his men rode thousands of miles through the Andes Mountains, which are much higher than the Rockies on their sturdy Paso Finos. The horse you are riding is supposed to be of the same bloodline as the Liberator's own stallion, although this may simply be a good story it's one I choose to believe as it gives me pleasure to be connected however remotely to a man so instrumental in furthering the cause of human liberty."

Enoch looked at Dawn and saw from the position of her ears that she was not taking his custody of her with the sang-froid and aplomb of Simon. He advanced toward her slowly and deliberately so the mare could see exactly what he was doing, until his head rested against the side of her neck. She couldn't see him though she knew he was there. She twitched her muscles as though his face were a fly but made no effort to turn and bite.

"There, there, sweet girl," he said in a soft, deep, bass voice. Francine could see her horse's ears rise up about thirty degrees from horizontal. Enoch continued to talk to her in his soothing voice, gently caressing her shoulder in long sweeping strokes. Enoch loved the scent of a clean horse. It was a unique odor, strong but not acrid, with a very faint ammoniac tang that awakened his senses like no other smell he knew, at once familiar, yet always exotic, a whisper of places unseen, of great power under restraint, potential energy waiting to be released. Enoch thought the smell of a horse unequalled in his wide experience of sniffing exotic scents as an apothecary though ambergris the real stuff formed in the intestine of the great sperm whale came a close second. Soft and black possessing a decidedly disagreeable odor when fresh, after exposure to air, sun or salt water, ambergris hardens and develops a most remarkably pleasant odor that is so persistent, it forms the foundation for perfumes. Enoch supposed a part of ambergris' romance for him was that it figures prominently in Melville's Moby Dick, though as an apothecary of rare brilliance, Enoch had occasion to treat his olfactory senses to an unusual array of rare smells on a regular basis, and Dawn's neck was equal to the very best.

When Enoch thought he'd gained a portion of the mare's confidence, he raised his head and contemplated her ears. They were not yet vertical only slightly past forty-five degrees but not pricked forward in pleasurable anticipation like his stallion.

"Maybe this isn't such a good idea," said Francine. "I'd hate to see all your hard work making friends end in her biting you or worse, throwing you." "Has she ever thrown anyone?"

"She threw the man who sold her to me three times and bit him more times than that."

"Let me try one more thing and if it doesn't work, just trot Simon over to that rise so you can feel the action of his running walk."

Enoch reached into the pocket of his coat and took out what looked like a piece of very light, white wood. He held it near Dawn's left nostril and instantly the ears went to ninety degrees like a flag at full staff, and even pricked forward. He presented the substance to her on the flat of his palm. The horse pulled back her soft black lips, not in anger but desire, and her big pink tongue licked it and then she began to chew it vigorously.

Enoch quickly placed his left boot toe in the stirrup and using a left hand full of rein and mane, swung himself up in the saddle with nearly as much deftness and grace as Francine had used in mounting Simon. Dawn's ears went to forty-five degrees, but she showed no inclination to bite, buck, rear, or bolt. Francine watched her anxiously for signs of an impending explosion. Enoch's bribe, whatever it was, seemed to have worked.

Francine trotted off on Simon and Enoch eased Dawn into a trot using gentle leg pressure and a click of his tongue. They rode side by side and Francine was nearly helpless with laughter for the first mile or so at the bizarre action of Simon's front legs. They looked as if the stallion were flinging them out, beating furiously at some imaginary insects. The motion was the most frantic, graceless action Francine had ever seen from a horse, the more incongruous as it was coming from such a beautiful animal, but the ride was incredibly smooth, as if she were sitting in a comfortable chair, not trotting in a well oiled stock saddle.

"I can't believe it," she said with tears of mirth in her eyes. "Simon's amazing." The trail was fairly even with few rocks so Francine changed her seat, shifting her weight forward and simultaneously moving the heel of her right boot behind the stallion's ribs and into the soft, yielding belly, signaling by collecting the reins she wanted to canter. The butter churning movement gave way to the familiar three beat gait of the lope, in which one foreleg and the two hind legs lead practically together followed by the other foreleg, and a moment of complete suspension with all four legs in the air,

Simon and Dawn's gaits at the canter were virtually indistinguishable.

"The Paso only distinguishes himself at the trot."

"Does he ever," said Francine. "I see why you like Pasos."

"Still," said Enoch, "There's much to be said for quarter-horses." The trail was now more sandstone than sand and to protect their horse's legs from possible injury, Enoch and Francine slowed them by sitting back in the saddles deep against the cantles. They came to a confluence of several arroyos, dry now, though it was evident that they were swift running streams during one of the infrequent heavy rains.

"When the snow pack melts in the Sangre de Christo, these dry beds are free flowing creeks, and even now if you were to dig down three or four feet into the sand, you'd find some damp mud, or if you were fortunate, the mud would be damp enough to leave a trace of water at the bottom of your excavation. In February the arroyo on the left has trout in it, tiny ones to be sure, but trout nevertheless."

"Where do they come from?" she asked. She could see from the rocks and sand, where there had been water at some time in the past, but under the hot sun, it seemed impossible that only a few months ago, fish had been swimming here.

"I don't really know," said Enoch. "Somehow their eggs, fish lay eggs like chickens only thousands at a time. Frogs do the same. The eggs must lie dormant during the dry months, and hatch out when water finds them."

"But then if it rained, wouldn't that hatch them too?"

"I wish I could tell you, but I don't really know. I do know that of all forces on earth, the life force is the most powerful. Using a microscope we can see an entire world in a drop of water, tiny animalcules, invisible to the human eye, living, reproducing, and dying, all blissfully unaware of us observing them, and that their universe is so tiny and fragile. I see it all as relative. The rains come, the snow melts and this seemingly lifeless arroyo becomes a lush world of green grass, sage, mesquite, yucca, fish, frogs, salamanders, tadpoles, newts, countless varieties of insects, arachnids in, on, and outside the water, then summer comes and the world dries out, everything dies or goes underground, and the desert dwellers, the scorpion, centipede, velvet ant, gecko, tarantula, and rattlesnake rule, where months before frogs croaked and fish swam. The entire cycle repeats itself year after year, worlds come into existence, flourish for a time, die, then come again. Is it any wonder the Buddhists and the Hindus see life as a wheel?"

Francine was deeply moved by Enoch's evocation of worlds within worlds. "Here I am," she thought, "Worrying myself sick about a saloon, when for all I know, everything I see as so permanent and important, might be nothing more than the contents of a water drop under the lens of some unimaginable being's microscope, and a million years, but a second to him."

Francine shivered at the idea.

"Francine," said Enoch. "Are you feeling well?"

111

"Yes. It's just when I think of all the worlds around us, like you made me do, I can't help thinking that the one we humans see as so limitless and so important, perhaps isn't that at all, and it could be no more lasting than the winter stream is to the trout. It makes me feel like I might faint. I'm sorry."

"No, no, don't be sorry. Trust me Francine, sometimes I frighten myself so much, I need a glass of something or a cigarillo to bring down my heartbeat and regularize my breathing. Sometimes it's like falling endlessly in a dream only I am aware that I'm wide awake."

Enoch's frank admission of frailty astonished Francine. In her experience, men, even Luis, rarely admitted to any vulnerability. Usually they made an extraordinary effort to appear superior to ordinary human weaknesses. Luis, though not much more than a boy, possessed an unusual measure of insight into his own nature and character. He told Francine that being Spanish, he couldn't help but display his macho nature, scorning danger as if it were nothing, disdaining to show fear, when all the time, part of him was every bit as uneasy as the next man or woman for that matter.

Hal lacked Luis' self-knowledge, and hid his fears under a facade of reckless bravado, which led to his involvement in the robbery. All anyone had to do to use Hal like a tool was to dare him or somehow imply he was lacking in courage. Hal's fragile sense of what it meant to be a man made him an easy mark for any unscrupulous confidence man or low life. Clearly Enoch not only had Luis' self-knowledge, but the courage to display his emotions, even though they were commonly thought of as more womanly than manly, and this, to Francine, made his admission courageous.

Enoch was physically far from her ideal. He was too tall and spare; however his mind was remarkable, and his wisdom captivating. He freely admitted to bribing Dawn with a stick of dried sugarcane, rather than concealing it and pretending the mare's taking to him was due solely to his superior knowledge of horses as Hal most certainly would have done. Enoch's brown eyes were warm and above all, kind. He was easy to talk to, even about personal, embarrassing, female complaints.

They exchanged horses without incident and Enoch led the way up into the foothills, through creosote bushes, sage, soap-weed, and yucca. Sometimes they rode in the arroyos and at other times along the banks, where the swift water of winter had cut channels in the sandstone too dangerous for the horses to negotiate. At times they were forced to dismount and walk through the narrow ravines. As the flanks of their horses brushed past the sage, their passage bruised the leaves and berries, releasing the delicious fragrance that made them both smile for the sheer joy of being alive to enjoy such pleasures. A solitary thrush, braved the mid-day sun to warble his song. Apart from that, even the locusts were silent. Hawks soared high above them, floating on the thermals, looking for prairie dogs, or an immature, unwary jackrabbit.

"Have you ever seen a bear?" asked Francine.

"I've seen several black bears, and mountain lions as well though only at a distance and once Simon saw the lion before I did and he reared, snorted, and prepared to fight the cat. I had the very devil of a time calming him down. He must have some ancestral memory of a time when his forbears had to defend themselves against jaguars or the instinct might go even further back to the era when horses were eaten by lions in Arabia.

"I would like to see a mountain lion," said Francine.

"You might but Dawn wouldn't. I guarantee you that."

"Don't they come out at night?"

"All the larger animals, deer, elk, pronghorns, coyotes, bear, and panthers are nocturnal, though they are sometimes seen during daylight, especially if they're hungry. On a hot day like this, you'll rarely see anything moving but prairie dogs and jackrabbits. I'm sorry, I forgot. Buffalo are diurnal, not that anyone will see a herd this far south anymore."

"The creatures have their own world, one we don't see, just like we were talking about."

"Yes, the desert comes alive after the sun sets." Trudging through the white and purple sage, creosote, and soap-weed, Francine was concerned about snakes.

"There aren't any snakes in these bushes, are there?"

"There are two kinds of snakes in the Territory that can harm you, rattlesnakes and coral snakes. It's too hot for them right now. The rattlesnakes are either in their burrows or under rocks, and I've yet to see a coral snake in the wild, although an Indian brujo, a holy man, showed me his. They're really beautiful, with brilliant red, yellow, and black bands from head to tail, like a piece of jewelry in serpent form. They're small, less than two feet long, with tiny heads. They're deadly, but shy and retiring. As I said, I've never seen one and I've looked."

This reassured Francine.

"Oh, look at him," said Enoch, who dropped Simon's reins over a nearly mesquite bush, and bent over a large red-legged tarantula.

"What a big fellow," he said admiringly.

It was a large wolf spider with a two-inch long body and a five-inch leg span. Enoch would have picked up the spider to admire it more fully; however he was mindful of Francine, and didn't want to appear too eccentric. Francine evidenced polite interest and stayed at what she considered a safe distance.

"Don't worry," said Enoch anticipating her trepidation. "Tarantulas don't jump.

They're pretty sluggish. They too, eat mainly at night, mostly insects, though a stout fellow like him might assay a frog or toad from time to time, or even the odd mouse."

"Does he live in a web?"

"No. He might have a burrow nearby but he mostly catches his prey by pursuit." "Well," said Francine. "I'm glad he's too slow to pursue me."

"I think we're both old enough to know it's not the four legged, six legged, or eight legged creatures we have to look out for. It's the two-legged animals that are our concern. Their bites are the most likely to be fatal."

Francine thought this was hilarious and laughed loudly. Enoch thought that if someone took a celestial tuning fork and struck it upon the brightest star in the northern night sky, the sound might be something like an approximation of the loveliness of her laugh. No nightingale's song ever sounded half as sweet to him as the music of Francine's mirth, and the apothecary was dumbfounded to find that despite the heavy armor he'd donned after his wife infected him to fend it off, Cupid's arrow had pierced his heart. Francine hadn't eaten any breakfast and she was getting hungry and thirsty. In addition, she had been resisting a call of nature that was becoming more and more insistent.

"How much longer till we reach the spring?"

Enoch looked off up the increasingly steep canyon.

"I'd say another hour should see us there. Don't worry, it's not going to be much more difficult than it has been for the past two miles or so."

It hadn't been safe to ride for quite some time, as the dry wash was a maze of loose rock and two and three foot high drop-offs. Francine could see some creosote bushes up ahead where the canyon seemed to widen, and she thought they would provide sufficient cover for her to relieve herself. Francine had used a chamber pot any number of times in front of clients, but she wanted to be demure for Enoch, believing this is what a respectable man expected of a woman.

"Enoch," she said sweetly. "If you don't mind, I'd like to walk up to those bushes and answer nature's call."

Enoch was charmed by her way of asking. "If you can wait there are a number of places near the spring."

"Honestly," said Francine, "I've been holding it for sometime already."

"I understand. Give me Dawn's reins and we'll wait here until you call us." Francine handed the reins to Enoch and she walked forward, her boots scraping on the sandstone. She reached the bushes, which weren't nearly as concealing as she'd thought they'd be, though when she looked back at Enoch and the horses, he was facing away like the gentleman he was. She quickly bared her privates and squatted carefully, directing the hissing stream away from her breeches using her index and middle fingers. As always, the sensation of relief was exquisite, particularly after she'd been holding it. The air was still with almost no breeze, and despite the altitude, the sun was hot as well as bright. No insects not even a grasshopper, buzzed or chirped as if nature were unwilling to disturb the profound silence. She and Enoch were wrapped in solitude so intense they might as well be the last man and woman on earth.

She played with this idea for a few seconds, then there was a crunching noise on **the** other side of the clump of bushes, not ten feet away, which scared her so much, she was paralyzed. She clenched her teeth hard enough to hurt, and stood, lock-legged as in a nightmare, taking infinite care not to make the slightest sound, for that might mean whatever it was would knew she was there, and the unknown horror would spring upon her and kill her. Francine's heart was hammering in her chest and her blood sang in her ears like a million locusts. She was unarmed, bereft of her Remington .41 rim-fire derringer with the mother of pearl scales, and her small folding IXL Bowie with the pretty scrimshawed, ivory grip. Not that either one was a formidable weapon, though either was more effective than her hands, teeth, and feet. She really wanted to scream her lungs out; however that might bring out the author of the noise out of the brush and on top of her. Predators, even dogs, could smell fear on another animal, and Francine was sure a bear or a lion would be attracted by her scream.

Enoch was waiting patiently with the horses wondering what was taking Francine so long. Yes, she was a woman who paid close attention to her personal appearance but an elaborate, or even a rudimentary toilette wasn't possible among the creosote bushes. It was possible that one of the handful of Jicarilla Apaches who stubbornly refused to be confined on the reservation, preferring a cave high in the Sangre de Chris to, shunning all contact with the corrupting influences of European civilization save for firearms, and living alone in close communication with the Great Spirit, might be hunting in the foothills. Such independent Apaches were even less commonly encountered than the elusive coral snake, though Enoch had been told both existed and he believed it. Although they might be interested in his activities in the mountains, Enoch doubted he would ever see another man unless the Apache wanted to show himself.

He turned to look at the bushes and couldn't see Francine.

"Better she should be angry with me than take a chance on something being amiss." It wasn't as if he hadn't seen her undressed before, though that was in a professional capacity to treat a discharge and a persistent bladder infection on several different occasions, months apart.

"To Hell with modesty," he said to himself and draped Simon's reins over the saddle horn and did the same for Dawn. He loosened the straps of his right side saddlebag and took out his Smith and Wesson Schofield. Holding it in his right hand, he walked as stealthily as he could up the narrow arroyo.

Francine was terrified. She didn't dare look into the five-foot high creosote bush from whose branches, the crunching sound emanated. Then to her indescribable relief, she saw Enoch advancing, big blue steel revolver in hand. When he was within twenty paces, he stumbled as his left foot stepped on a loose rock, and nearly fell then regained his footing. Francine held her breath as she looked into the heart of the bush. It was enormous, thick with old growth shoots. Then the quiet was rent asunder by an ear-splitting snarl that echoed off the canyon walls, chilling Francine's blood to the marrow of her bones, and made her involuntarily release what little urine remained in her bladder, not that she noticed at the time. Enoch broke into a dead run and bounded the last ten feet in a single leap, as a dun coated mountain lion emerged at a lope, away from Enoch, and up the steep face of the canyon with as little effort as if it were level ground. Francine threw herself into his arms, trembling all over, though not crying.

"There, there." He said this in a tone nearly as soothing as one of his better herbal anodynes. "The cry of the catamount is truly frightening, like the worst scream a human can conjure. And at such close quarters. I believe I would have soiled my drawers had I been in your place."

"Oh, Enoch," she said breathlessly. Her heart was beating as fast as if she'd run a mile being chased by a man dagger hand. She could feel Enoch's long lanky arms, and the heavy Smith and Wesson he was carrying, pressing into her belly, as she stood plastered against him, and found both extremely reassuring.

"It's so quiet here, when I heard the crunch and snap of dry twigs, I knew whatever it was that made the sound was no jack rabbit. You saved my life."

"I wish I could claim such an honor, but in truth, as terrifying as your position was, you were in no danger. I do not know of a single instance of a lion attacking a man or woman. If you happened to startle one in a cave where she was guarding her cubs, then perhaps, but even then unless she thought you were threatening her, she wouldn't spring on you."

"You still saved my life, you brave, wonderful man."

Enoch had slightly misjudged the distance they had to travel, for it had been some months since he'd made a journey into these mountains. Most of the efficacious plants, roots, herbs, and trees, grew either in the low desert or in the Pecos River Valley. Ben, the Pima Indian, had told Enoch of the marvelous spring, shortly after the apothecary came to Early, and as he had more time on his hands then than now, he made his first trip only a few weeks later.

The rugged landscape of the steep arroyo hid the entrance to the canyon leading to the spring from all but a handful of men who had been told of its existence. There was a granite outcropping among the sandstone formations of whitish gray rock, almost a miniature butte, so rich with mica that it mirrored the sun and split it into an infinite multitude of tiny stars or diamond chips.

"We're almost there," said Enoch. He led Simon through a passageway in the canyon wall so narrow, the well-fed stallion squeezed through with barely six inches to spare on each side of his belly. Dawn passed through with plenty of room.

"If you keep feeding that horse so generously, in a year or two you'll have to leave him out here by himself."

Enoch laughed. "Simon is too fond of his bran mash." He turned to look at Simon's profile wrinkled up his large, beaky nose and said, "I see what you're talking about. I've been spending too much of my time in the shop and not enough in the saddle. It's my fault, not his. I'm going to make it a point to ride more and work less." Once through the stone passageway, Francine could see they had entered a hidden valley, one that looked as if it had been lifted from an entirely different part of the country, like the green hills north of San Francisco. There was long, bright green, grass, and a substantial copse of cottonwood trees growing on the fringes of a crystal clear limestone bottom pool of water, perhaps twenty feet in diameter with a depth varying from a few inches at the margins to as much as five feet in the deepest part. The spring that fed the pool flowed as Enoch said, from deep in the earth, issuing from a black basalt ledge at the height of Enoch's head, not ten feet from the pool. At their approach, a covey of quail flushed through the grass into the thick sage that grew behind the pool.

"This canyon has only one entrance," said Enoch. He loosened the throatlatch on Simon's headstall and lifted it bit and all over the horse's head. Thus freed, the stallion moved quickly to the succulent, emerald green grass, tearing off a long mouthful. Francine liberated Dawn, who walked up next to Simon and began to feed. The rock walls of the canyon rose nearly vertical from the level floor of the valley soaring hundreds of feet into the air. The entire valley wasn't more than a hundred yards long and thirty yards wide at its widest point. Francine saw a cottontail rabbit duck away to join the quail scared off by the horses.

The sun was nearly overhead and even so, she imagined the air in the valley was cooler than in the arroyo they had just left.

"This is far and away the most beautiful place I've ever seen in the Territory. It's like finding Eden in the desert," said Francine reverently. "It's enchanting

"I just love it."

"I know what you mean," said Enoch. "The Indians call it the waters of the moon flower. The story has it that long ago a lovely Indian girl walked too far from her pueblo and was captured by an enemy warrior. She was a remarkable beauty, an Indian version of Helen of Troy. She escaped from the enemy village with the warrior and all his braves in hot pursuit. She was swift as an antelope, but the warrior was a peerless tracker and determined to recapture his prize. As they were closing in on her, she found this hidden canyon, and waded into the pool, where she prayed to the Great Spirit to deliver her. It was dark when the warriors finally found the entrance to the valley and this meadow. The moon was shining and there were two moccasins at the edge of the pool but no tracks coming out. It is said the Great Spirit heard the maiden's plea and changed her into a flower that grows in the moonlight."

"Is there such a flower?"

"In the late spring, after the snow melts, the yucca sends up its tower of blossoms and they are white as ivory. Perhaps this is what they meant."

"But yucca's bloom all over the Territory."

"Then perhaps they were thinking of this," and Enoch bent down and plucked a small pure white blossom from a stalk that grew amid the grass, like a white buttercup. He presented to Francine with a flourish of his right hand as if she were a queen. She took the flower and brought it to her finely chiseled nose. The exquisitely shaped bloom had a faint scent she couldn't place exactly though it was reminiscent of night blooming jasmine.

"The moon princess must have been truly beautiful if this is what she became." Enoch looked at her and his heart overruled his brain as he said, "However lovely she may have been, she would have paled in comparison with you."

Francine hadn't intended for Enoch to fall in love with her, though she knew for a fact that intentions and love rarely had much to do with each other in real life. In novels, women and men, girls and boys, planned the most elaborate schemes to ensure that someone would fall in love with them or whoever they wanted them to fall in love with. Real life wasn't a Dickens' novel, and even in Dickens, love, like death, came when it would, heedless of the ideal or the most favorable circumstances. By her own calculations, Francine's predisposition to being in love at this time were somewhere between unlikely and impossible, and closer to the latter.

"But," she supposed, "That's typical," and she decided if it had been Enoch's intention in bringing her to this magical, enchanted meadow to sweep her off her feet, she would not swim against the tide, she would allow herself to be swept away. Enoch knew the spring was a place of power and had been so long before the Spanish Conquistadores ranged all over the Sangre de Christo in search of the fabled Seven Cities of Cibola and the treasure of gold and silver rumored to rival that of Montezuma. The leather soldiers of Spain, the Soldados de Quera never found the cities though they gave the mountains their name.

Enoch had spent a good deal of time with Apache medicine men and though they didn't tell him of the spring one of them had taken him to a place of power near the reservation and there they ate the fruit of a certain sacred cactus. For the first half hour, by his gold Waltham pocket watch, Enoch experienced nothing but a growing nausea until it was so overpowering, like a powerful emetic, and he vomited up the well- masticated plant fibers. As the sickness passed, Enoch noticed an intensification of colors like nothing he had ever known. The reds and oranges of the rock were wet, as if they were painted on with a heavily laden brush, and the air assumed a distinct texture. The blue of the sky began to ripple and breath like the waves of the Pacific above his head. In the hours that followed, Enoch saw the inner workings of the universe, the lines of energy lying like white fibers of light in an enormous grid over the entire surface of the earth, and at the intersections of the grid were places of unusual power. The old Indian explained that a good healer knew how to tap into this energy to cure the sick. Enoch confirmed the existence of this energy with other Apaches, Ben the Pima, and with an old Yaqui Indian sorcerer, or brujo, he met on one of his herb gathering journeys, southwest into the Sonoran Desert north of Hermasillo.

The spring literally vibrated with energy fields. Enoch hadn't consciously brought Francine here to manipulate her feelings, if anything, the spring, itself, had drawn them of its own accord. Why else would this of all places be the first one where he was really alone with her, other than in his shop, or in the private office in the back that served as a consulting and examining room? He gestured to the clear stream of water that issued from the jet-black basalt. "Cup your hands and drink. You must be perishing of thirst after such a long and tiring journey under the hot sun. I know I am. It's safe to drink I assure you."

Francine was more than thirsty, she was dehydrated from perspiring, and her meeting with the catamount only added to her need for water. She cupped her hands together under the rill, closed her eyes and drank. As the icy water filled her mouth, her ears opened and Francine heard the quail calling to each other with their melodious, liquid cries. She always took the taste of water for granted. Sometimes it was cool, other times cold, warm or tepid. Regardless of the temperature, it didn't register as a flavor like beer, wine, or champagne. She never considered it to have gradations of taste. One drink of water was like all drinks of water. The deliciousness of water to the thirsty is proverbial and the water of Enoch's spring was no exception in that regard, but it was infinitely more to Francine that afternoon. It wasn't only her body that responded to the liquid like a desert plant that blooms only after the first soaking rain, it was as if her spirit had been thirsting for something it knew not what, and now it too drank. The water was perhaps not so very cold though it seemed icy following their hot and dry quest to reach the meadow. The soluble minerals in the granite through which the water passed on its way to the surface were blended in perfect proportion and lent to the water a delicate effervescence that only added to its remarkable taste that Francine thought far surpassed any champagne. To be fair the champagne Francine was familiar with, spent months in the dank hold of a ship sailing around Cape Horn, or weeks crossing America on the Union Pacific Railroad, jostling and bouncing as it was transferred to the Santa Fe Line, so her experience with the precious liquor may have been tarnished by the damage done during difficult and lengthy shipping.

Francine drank long and deeply, not stopping until she had drunk her fill and when she was through, she opened her eyes and the sun dazzled her, making the air in the meadow shine and dance. The spring, the meadow, the encounter with the lion, and the magic of the moment combined, kindling a joyous recklessness that set all her inhibitions at naught. She walked up to Enoch and placed her lips, still chilled from the spring, on his sun warmed ones, and kissed him with the full effect of the passion she'd been holding in reserve since she had kissed Luis before making love to him for the last time.

"Gypsy," Hal called out in a sleep-roughened voice for Hal wasn't yet fully awake. He wouldn't be until his second cup of strong black coffee chased away the last remnants of the whiskey spun cobwebs left by the previous night's overindulgence. The spirits were courtesy of Gypsy and the few remaining wooden cases left from Duffy's stockpile, which had been larger than that of many larger establishments in California, owing to the Irishman's purchasing it as a basis for the adulterated filth he sold to the Indians.

"Bring me the chamber-pot." Hal wasn't the least bit shy or embarrassed at relieving himself in front of women or men for that matter. Gypsy handed him the brightly painted slop basin of soft paste porcelain decorated with red, rose blossoms. Hal sat on the edge of the firm corn silk stuffed mattress. Then he stood sleepily with his bare feet on the cold pine board floor, with the pot in his right hand and his manhood in his left. Gypsy looked at his toenails. They were much too long and the one on the middle toe of his left foot had given her a long and unsightly red scratch on the soft back of her right calf. When she offered to cut them for him, Hal snapped, "I don't like anyone messing with my feet. I'll pare it down myself one of these days when I think of it."

"You'll wear holes in your stockings leaving them long like that."

"Like I said," he spoke impatiently, "I'll take care of it. You know, when you rag me like that you sound like a wife, always at me about something. In case you forgot, I already got a wife. What I need is a lady friend who isn't judging every damn thing about me, morning, noon, and night."

Gypsy allowed as how she was sorry, because Hal rarely criticized her, even when she thought he should have, like the time she inadvertently unhitched his gun belt and holster from the bedpost during a transport of sexual ecstasy and the Colt fell butt first on the floor, taking a chunk out of the right side of the varnished grip.

Hal picked up the rig, drew the revolver and ruefully contemplated the damage. Gypsy had held her breath expecting a tantrum. Instead, Hal smiled and said, "Gypsy, if that's the price of pleasure, you can drop my pistol till there's nothing left of the handle but the back-strap and trigger-guard. It'll still do what I need it to do, so don't you give it a second thought."

This was not the only instance of Hal's forbearance, and at such times Gypsy thought Francine was crazy for letting go of such a handsome, personable man.

Hal waited patiently for his urine to come, longer than he could ever remember waiting. He could tell his bladder had released the stream, but for some reason it wasn't flowing, and Hal Russell normally pissed as he, himself described it, "like a racehorse." Gypsy had returned to her brushing and was on the forty-first brushstroke of the second fifty, completely absorbed in her task, when she heard Hal scream. She turned her head to face him, and his sun-browned face was as white as the skin on the back of her ivory hands and she could see sweat beading his forehead. Hal's scream was loud and Gypsy was startled as well as frightened, because men simply didn't make such sounds unless they were either horrified out of their wits, or in mortal agony from some outside force like a doctor touching a blood poisoned arm or foot. Gypsy had seen ranch hands with septic wounds, and the lightest pressure on an infected finger or toe could make the toughest, most hardened man scream like Hal just did.

Hal likened what he'd just done to pissing out molten lead. His penis felt like someone had just pulled about ten cruelly barbed fishhooks down its entire length, all the way from the root near his anus to the tip. Either that or filled the entire passage with broken glass, then squeezed it hard, driving the jagged splinters into the exquisitely sensitive tissue.

The pain was so intense it literally took his breath away, leaving him gasping for air. In the aftermath, which was still painful enough to make his sphincter twitch like a horse bitten by an especially vicious botfly, Hal had some relief from his bladder being somewhat empty, though not nearly the same empty feeling he'd had every other morning of his life.

The agony left him and in its place was a towering fury that rose from a wellspring deep within, seeking vengeance on whoever or whatever had hurt him so badly. His first thought and most convenient target was Gypsy, and he shied the heavy chamberpot at her head. Gypsy saw his arm move and anticipated the throw, which was made awkward by the size of the vessel and the shifting of its liquid contents. It smashed heavily against the plaster wall, showering Gypsy with shards of porcelain and droplets of its evil smelling contents.

Gypsy had seen any number of altercations in saloons and bawdy houses from El Paso to Early, and at the foundation of them all was whiskey. Hal wasn't drunk and this scared Gypsy more than anything.

"Are you crazy?" she asked him with her eyes wide open. Hal needed someone to suffer for what he'd just been through. He practically flew the two paces to the hassock Gypsy was sitting on and before she could react, he backhanded her on the right cheekbone with the full force of his right hand. Gypsy was hurled to the floor and lay there sobbing bitterly. Hal's blood was up and he kicked her, not with his toes, but his heel, and he heard a crunch as three of her ribs broke. Gypsy's chest was on fire, or so she thought as she tried to crawl away to the bedroom door. Hal's right boot was laying on its side, and despite the burning sensation in her chest that became unbearable each time she tried to breathe, Gypsy had the presence of mind to remember the razor keen, George Wostenholm and Sons Bowie knife Hal set such a store by, in its leather sheath, sewn to the inside of the high top leather boot. She pulled the knife out with her right hand, and as she did, Hal reached down and dragged her to her feet by her hair. Between the agonies in her face, scalp, and chest, Gypsy nearly fainted.

Hal no longer resembled a man to her or anything remotely like a man. He was a monster with a blood red face, and yellowish white bloodshot eyes, devoid of the slightest trace of humanity. As he held her hair in his left hand, positioning her head so he could smash her face in with his right fist. As he drew it back for a full stroke Gypsy drove seven inches of needle sharp Sheffield steel Bowie into Hal at a sixty-degree angle from the horizontal with all the strength of a woman fighting for her life. The blade entered just under the right curve of the lowest rib on the left side of Hal's chest, the keen clip point slicing through muscle and flesh as if it were so much soft butter. The point entered Hal's heart, which fluttered, then stopped, and Hal fell heavily to the floor. As he dropped, Gypsy could see the life force leave his body as clearly as if a candle flame were snuffed out. She was covered in blood from her belly down to her feet, though she'd tried to jump aside after she struck the blow. Hal wasn't by any means the first man she'd seen die a violent death but he was the first one who'd died by her hands.

Gypsy was less horrified at having killed her lover, than at her own condition. She had no idea how badly his kick had injured her only that each breath she took made her chest feel like it was being transfixed with the tines of a pitchfork. Gypsy knew Hal's hard bony heel had broken something inside her. It was not only a burning pain but a stabbing pain as well. Gypsy heard the bones break as clearly as if Hal had snapped some very dry twigs. Though her face throbbed as if it had a heartbeat, severe as her injuries might be they were not in any way even remotely equivalent to having seven inches of Wostenholm's best steel in one's chest. Gypsy's head was in a whirl with images of Jack Jone's shooting her or being dragged through the streets of Early by a howling lynch mob composed of the town's respectable men and women.

It wouldn't be the first time the town tired to lynch someone they thought was a murderer. Gypsy remembered all too well Reverend Gilbert leading a mob to lynch Deaf Charley and another Indian for Duffy's murder. If it weren't for Mayor Tunstall and Betsy, the mob would have succeeded and hanged two innocent men. Tunstall was a man and to Gypsy, that prevented him from being truly sympathetic to her present plight though he had, as justice of the peace, fined the holy Hell out of Hal for smacking Francine around.

"If only Francine were here," she thought. She couldn't ask Rose for help because Jack Jones would surely kill her. Betsy's ranch was too far away, besides there was no possibility of her riding a horse when she felt like an insect someone had stepped on and squashed.

Gypsy decided she'd better risk going to the mayor and the question was should she try to clean herself up before venturing out. It was past eight thirty by Hal's silver pocket watch, which lay on top of the cheap deal dresser. The people on Early's main street would surely take notice of her since she looked like she'd just slaughtered a pig or a steer. The final pulsing beats of Hal's heart had sprayed his gore all over her legs.

"If I wash I'll definitely look less guilty and I'll look better as well," she thought. Gypsy took the capacious ceramic water pitcher and poured the contents into the zinc-lined basin of the pine washstand. Using a cake of rose scented animal fat soap, Francine had given her for a birthday; Gypsy did her best to wash the blood from her face and her legs as well as the droplets of urine from her hair. There was an ugly, bluish bruise on her cheekbone, larger than a silver dollar and the swelling was affecting her eye. Not that temporary disfigurement would have a distinctly negative effect on her ability to attract clients. Gypsy, Rose, and Francine all had faces that were at the very least, pretty, though they were all convinced most ranch hands, herders, lawmen and the others that comprised their clientele were much more interested in their warm female bodies than in their good looks.

"Most of them are so randy they'd screw a woodpile if they thought there might be a snake in it," was how Francine put it one memorable evening and Gypsy couldn't disagree. When most of the blood was in the wash stand and not on her body, Gypsy donned a clean petticoat, a yellow gingham dress, a pair of short tan suede boots, brushed her hair only fourteen times, and with a shudder that made her knees buckle from the pain it caused her, looked down at Hal Russell's lifeless remains. She couldn't believe there was that much blood in a human being. Mercifully he had slumped forward on his chest, so his face wasn't staring up at her, though the handle of the Bowie knife propped up his corpse slightly higher on the left side. His hands were splayed wide not clutching at anything, lying like two brown islands in an ocean of blood, his fingers jutting out like five long peninsulas. Gypsy's stomach heaved at the sight and she vomited a stream of bile, which pooled on the blood like a yellowish pond. The sour sweet smell of Hal's blood mixed with the putrid stink of his urine, and heedless of the shooting pains the spasms were causing her, Gypsy vomited once more, and then gave a dry heave that nearly made her pass out.

Gypsy fought against the blackness that threatened to overcome her and stumbled to the door, smashing her right shoulder heavily into the doorframe. The effect of the collision on her broken ribs was instantaneous. Her bladder clenched and Gypsy pissed all over herself. The pain was like nothing she had ever known, as if a white-hot iron rod were driven from her chest directly into her brain. She grabbed the large brass doorknob and held on, gritting her teeth so hard they ached for days afterward. In a brief moment of lucidity, she turned the knob clockwise, opened the door and fell out, swinging it closed as she swung herself free of it. Gypsy would have fallen once more had she not grabbed the equally large knob on the outside of the thick wooden door. Sweat pouring from under her arms and off her face, wheezing for breath as if she had pneumonia, and heedless of the urine stain all over her pelvis, Gypsy staggered outside into the street.

Chapter 10
MAYOR TUNSTALL

The sun was hot on Gypsy's head, though in her distracted state she paid it scant attention. The only street in Early was a wide dusty avenue with rude board sidewalks. There were assiduous shopkeepers cleaning windows and sweeping the sidewalks, and a few passersby. Gypsy managed to walk to the mayor's house without drawing any notice, except for a cursory glance from the boy who worked at the livery stable. In addition to his work at the stable, he was paid by the town to remove horse turds from the street and dump them in a canyon outside the town limits. He had his own horse drawn wagon specifically for this purpose and as Gypsy passed by Swank's Apothecary, Billy thought Gypsy might need help. Billy was a good boy and the money he earned went for the most part, the odd piece of rock candy and plug of tobacco excepted, to his mother, who used it to supplement the meager pension she received from the War Department. Her husband, a cavalry corporal, had died of cholera in a filthy encampment during the course of one of the early Apache uprisings led by Cochise. Billy had three younger sisters and his hard earned dollars were put to good use. Mayor Tunstall had insisted he be hired out of the town's general fund, and not just because he wanted to assist the widow and her family. During the warmer months, the horse droppings were breeding grounds for myriads of flies and the steaming piles soon boiled and writhed from countless insects. Tunstall deemed the few dollars a month for Billy's services, money well spent and the program had the imprimatur of Doc Hill as well as Enoch

Swank, who as the self-appointed guardians of Early's public health, enthusiastically endorsed the expenditure.

Billy had a youthful crush on Gypsy and his boyish fantasies often featured Gypsy's golden hair and barely concealed, pert breasts. Though his overalls were spotted with flecks of dung, Billy wore calfskin gloves to keep his hands clean. He leaned his manure fork up against the split log hitching rail and summoning all his courage to address his inamorata, said in a voice that cracked slightly because it hadn't quite settled into the pleasant baritone it was destined to when Billy was fifteen, "Miss Gypsy, is there anything, anything at all I can do to help you?"

Now that he was only two paces from her Billy could see the big bruise on her face and the large damp spot on her gingham dress, which made the thin cloth of the dress and the petticoats cling to her private parts, leaving nothing to the imagination, revealing what they were meant to conceal. Billy was flooded with conflicting emotions, embarrassment at seeing what he'd only imagined, and a fierce desire to avenge the swelling on Gypsy's pretty face. Gypsy was in far too much pain to care what Billy saw between her legs. "Take my arm and help me get to the mayor's house," she said with each word costing her more discomfort than she'd had from the worst monthly female complaints she could recall. Billy heard her, and thought that this was without question, the very best day of his young life. He took Gypsy's right arm gently in his left, for he could see she was favoring her left side. The swell of her breast touched the skin of his upper arm and the contact gave him inexpressible joy. Later, Gypsy remembered very little of that walk, only that Billy took much of the weight off her feet, and she had an impression of floating down the sidewalk borne up by his arm. Then they were in front of the chest high wooden gate that opened to the red clay Mexican tiles that formed the walkway to Tunstall's hacienda with its authentic red Spanish roof tiles, of which he was very proud. His front door was Spanish as well, arch-shaped, studded with black painted wrought iron and made of four-inch thick pine planks stained to look like walnut.

"I'll be leaving you here, Miss Gypsy," said Billy once they reached the door. "Wait, Billy," she said in a soft voice. "I have something for you."

"Miss Gypsy," he said with total sincerity. "Please don't give me anything. I'd do anything for you, anything."

Gypsy hushed him then brushed the boy's lips and in that moment, Billy thought he'd died and gone to heaven.

Tunstall was pacing in what he called his sunroom, a room with a large glass window in the roof that could be raised or lowered and a wall that had larger glass windows than most. It wouldn't have passed as a sunroom in the strict French sense of the term though it was more exposed to the sun than any other room in the Spanish style adobe home. The room was really more of a library and the sturdy pine shelves featured Tunstall's fairly extensive collection of English novels by such luminaries as Dickens, Thackery, and Jane Austen, as well as the now more obscure practitioners of the art such as Fielding, Defoe, and Sterne, a few Americans, Hawthorne and Melville, and English translations of Balzac and Stendhal. There were two oil paintings of horses, fine copies of works by Stubbs, and a framed Matthew Brady photograph of Lincoln. The floor was of the same red tiles as the outdoor walkway. The mayor was dressed in his habitual black cotton suit, and was pacing back and forth as was his habit when agitated. Gypsy was seated in his large, soft, tanned leather armchair with a glass half filled of Napoleon brandy on the spindly-legged Hepplewhite table beside her.

"Damn it all," he said as his frustration brimmed over. "How do we make this mess into a simple, open and shut case of self defense?"

The mayor put his powerful left hand to his noble, but sun and age furrowed forehead, and there it remained as he said, "If he'd had his gun in his hand that would be one thing. I know, I know, he'd already stomped you, probably broke your ribs. We'll have Doc Hill look at you as soon as we figure this out and get our stories straight. He'd backhanded you, and thrown the chamber pot. I guess he thought you poxed him and he went crazy."

"But I couldn't have poxed him," said Gypsy who was feeling slightly better after a large glass of brandy and even more because it seemed Tunstall was taking her side. He was the most important man in Early. His imposing physical presence and the fact he was not at all afraid to stand, one man against the whole town as he'd done for Deaf Charlie were reassuring. The mayor had the courage of his convictions as surely as did the martyred president whose picture he so prominently displayed.

"I couldn't have poxed him. I always made him use one of Mr. Swank's sheaths, 'cause I don't want no pox or babies."

"I understand. Then he must have contracted it before he came to Early, perhaps in Santa Fe. I understand he and Jones were there. Swank is a mighty clever man, knows all kinds of things. You say he and Francine rode out together shortly after seven o'clock? That's good in one way and bad in another. If we're going to make up a story, it's best if it's just the two of us. You know the old saying that 'Three can keep a secret if two are dead.' Sorry." he said. "It's just that he was unarmed. I know you thought he was going to kill you and believe me I see it your way. Unfortunately that doesn't mean a jury will, and women can't serve on a jury in this great land of ours so it will be twelve men."

Tunstall didn't share his private thoughts, which were that on the face of it, Gypsy's actions looked like murder. She'd sneaked his Bowie out of his boot, and when he cocked his arm to hit her she stabbed him through the heart. Her status as a saloon girl and prostitute would not work in her favor. He could possibly persuade a jury she was in fear of her life, especially if Francine testified to Hal's involvement in the Wells Fargo hold-up and subsequent shooting of the guards, though that was years ago, and one of the outlaws practically exonerated Russell and Jones before he was hanged. Sure he'd beaten Francine; however wife beatings in the Territory were hardly a capital offense. They were no offense at all until broken bones were involved and even then smacking one's wife around was common, socially acceptable behavior. Black eyes and split lips on a wife were sufficiently frequent as to cause little comment. The prevailing view held by women as well as men was that the man was doubtlessly provoked and if anything were said it was usually, "She had it coming," or words to that effect. In Hal and Francine's case, one indignant matron was heard to remark: "The mayor should have fined her for being a whore not him for smacking the harlot around. Then again we all know he's got a soft heart for whores."

At the very least there would be a coroner's inquest with Doc Hill and him presiding to determine the cause of death. Russell could have fallen on his Bowie but this verdict would be one Hell of a stretch. As tractable as Doc Hill was under most circumstances, asking him to subscribe to a scenario in which a man slipped and somehow drove a seven-inch knife through his heart in a lady's bedroom was a bit much to expect. Tunstall brought his analytical mind once more to the idea of self-defense, one which almost always resonated with residents of the Territory and was usually the most effective way to address questionable shooting, bludgeoning, or stabbing deaths. Self- defense was the time honored and honorable means to close vexing inquiries into the causes of violent death.

"If only Mr. Russell had his cocked revolver in his hand that would solve the problem," he said to himself. Failing that it was quite likely Gypsy would have to stand trial for homicide and spend years in a territorial prison, an outcome that was manifestly unfair and unjust though inevitable.

"I've considered this from every aspect," he said in his distinctive bass voice, which sounded unnaturally authoritative to Gypsy, possibly because of all the glass in the sunroom, or because she was feeling so very small, sitting in his oversized chair.

"We'll go back to your room, and I'll put his revolver in his hand, bend his fingers around it and fire it into the wall."

Gypsy's eyes opened wide although the swollen one wasn't as wide as the other.

"Won't that make a lot of noise?"

"I'll muffle it with a pillow. I assume you have some nice thick pillows." "Yes I do."

"Don't worry, no one will hear anything louder than a pop. If no one came knocking after that chamber pot crashed into the wall, they're not going to hear a .45 smothered in pillows, now are they?"

"No, but," Gypsy took a shallow breath and though it scarcely moved her chest, it still felt like an arrow was piercing her left lung.

"Mayor, I can't let you do this."

"Gypsy, if I don't, you'll be lucky not to hang. The best you can hope for is a stretch in the Territorial Prison."

Gypsy had no intention of spending a month in prison much less years. She looked at Tunstall and said as resolutely as she was able, "Hal was going down to Monterrey as soon as Francine paid him the money. I could go there myself."

Tunstall considered this, although ultimately the decision wasn't his to make, the girl had come to him in her hour of need, and he was the type of man who took the plight of others as seriously as if it had been his own.

"I don't know about that Gypsy. If you do that everyone will assume you murdered him in cold blood and I can't very well say you came to me before you left and told me the story. I'll give you what money I have, but you'd be on your own. The telegraph moves faster than the fastest horse and you might be caught before you make it across the border."

"I could cut off all my hair and dye it black like Betsy did when she left Kentucky No one will know who I am."

"Betsy had a whole night to prepare, and with her father being fatally wounded and his house burnt down, there were questions and diversions, doubts as to what really happened. I don't think a man with a Bowie knife in his chest presents quite the same picture."

Gypsy was confused though even in the welter of her confusion, the image of Hal Russell's body lying face down in a veritable sea of blood conjured up nothing but murder. Tunstall would be unable to clear her name for fear of being accused of aiding and abetting her escape. He'd tell Betsy the truth, and she'd believe him but even Francine and Rose might think she'd killed him in cold blood. Then there was her son in El Paso. Gypsy had intended to make herself known to him once she was settled and respectable. That beautiful dream would perish in the wake of her flight. **At** the same time Gypsy hated to involve Tunstall in a crime. Then again the mayor was a powerful intelligent man who, together with Betsy and Ben, defeated the Coyoteros and fought the omnipotent Colonel Jessup to a draw. "Who am I to question the actions of such a man," thought Gypsy.

"If we're going to do anything you'd better make your mind up fast. Time is most certainly not on our side," said Tunstall.

"Let's go to my place," said Gypsy repressing a shudder."

'Don't worry, you won't even have to look at him." Tunstall had anticipated her understandable reluctance to see Hal's corpse. As they walked out of the sunroom, he said, "You're making the right decision, believe me you don't want to be on the run."

Jack Jones opened his eyes and the next thing he did was to carefully move Rose's arm, which she'd flung with dream induced abandon over his belly, just above the pelvic bone. Regardless of what he'd had to eat or drink the previous night and his assiduous use of toothpicks flavored with clove oil, with which he cleaned his teeth and gums after eating, he always woke with a gummy residue in his mouth and on his tongue in the morning. Rose had touted the virtues and wonders of Enoch Swank and Jack intended to consult the apothecary about his gummy mouth before he departed Early.

He turned his head on the goose down and satin pillow to look at Rose. He really didn't see what Hal found so attractive about Gypsy. She was so very young. Rose was only three years older and at twenty another three years represents nearly fifty percent more life as an adult, or so Jack figured it. Rose told him, her father and mother died of yellow fever in New Orleans when she was a little girl, and she was sent to live with her mother's brother and his wife, who lived on a farm near St. Paul. Rose hated the endless, cold winters, and as she grew older her aunt began to resent her "presuming on the charity of good Christians," as the older woman put it and she began to treat Rose more as a slave than a relation. Rose milked the cows, cleaned the henhouse, shoveled manure, and in the spring, summer, and autumn was put to weeding the fields and the garden from dawn to dusk, six days a week.

"Thank the good Lord for the Sabbath thy or that old battle-axe would have worked me seven days a week. By the time I was fourteen, I had a belly-full of her 'Christian charity', and was ready for all the sin I could get into with the neighbor's boy. When she found us in the hayloft one afternoon, she raised holy Hell. She said, "Satan had his hooks in me and I was going to Hell and I should have died with my momma and daddy. I had to leave because as a good Christian, she couldn't permit a 'spawn of Satan to dwell in her home'. She handed me five dollars and I'm sure it hurt her to the heart to give me that much the old bitch. I took her worn silver dollars and told her if Satan had his claws in anyone he had them in her. Then I hauled off and kicked her in the shinbone as hard as I could and left her right there and then there hopping and cursing an un-Christian blue streak. I felt kind of bad about my uncle, who worked real hard, himself, six days and even some on Sunday. Now that I think on it, he probably worked so hard just to get away from my aunt. I could tell by the looks he'd get on his face when she'd use her tongue or the strap on me, I think the tongue was worse, but they fed me good, I had my own room, and they dressed me tolerably well. I learned my letters as a little girl in New Orleans. My uncle had a few books and I read them pretty good. I walked into St. Paul, and this older man took me into his home. I learnt from the farm-boy exactly what a girl has that men want so bad they'll kill and die for it. There's this Englishman, named Shakespeare, and all he writes about is men killing each other over Juliet or Desdemona, or Queen Cleopatra. Long before Jesus' time, there were Greeks and Trojans killing each over Helen of Troy. One thing I learned better than anything else is that even preachers who say they aren't interested hanker after what women have between their legs and hanging off their chest. They say that sex is a sin but the ones who condemn it the hardest are the ones who pant after it like dogs after a bitch in heat. I call it the fire down below, and all men have it till they're too old to do anything about it, but generally it still burns in them even then. 'Course there's those that prefer boys and I can't help them," said Rose with a smile. Rose's honest analysis of the whole feminine mystique was so refreshing to Jack, who was used to women blowing smoke up his rectum, not to revive him after drowning, but to separate him from the contents of his purse, that he thought here in this God-forsaken town he might have pitched upon the legendary whore with the golden heart.

Hal was more than pleased to move in with Gypsy after his reconciliation with Francine foundered on the rocky shoals of abuse. Jack was positively delighted with Rose, so much so, he asked if she wouldn't consider leaving Early and traveling North with him. His glowing descriptions of life in the Sacramento Delta made California sound like heaven. Besides Rose was weary of the Territory.

"I don't know, Jack. Life here is pretty sweet to me. Francine is more of a friend than a boss, the split she gives me is fair, and Mr. Swank makes sure we don't have any unwanted little packages. Having Betsy Johnson as the law is a very good thing. Women are treated good here in Early. Too good according to your partner and he's not the only man who thinks so. The mayor's inclined to favor a woman over a man. This might just be the only town on earth where women get treated like they were as good as men, and in case you hadn't noticed I'm a woman."

Jack just smiled and gently squeezed her left breast in acknowledgement.

"I noticed. I can't help noticing all the time, believe me Rosie. Listen, I'm not telling you to come with me and go whoring. Once I get this robbery business straightened out, I'm going to buy a houseboat, do a little fishing, a little gambling, and some prospecting for gold on a claim I have near Grass Valley. I'll never be rich though it's unlikely I'll ever be poor either. I'd like you to come with me Rosie," he said and the earnestness he felt was in his voice. "I really like you. You're open and honest, well, I think we could make a go of it."

"I think I'd like to go with you too, but I can't just run out on Francine and Gypsy. They're like my sisters and I love them."

Jack seized the moment, "Talk to them then. As soon as Hal gives me my share, I'll tell you what, I'll split it with you. That way you'll be independent until you decide otherwise."

Rose didn't know or understand why Hal Russell was giving Jack half of the saloon money, since it was Francine who was Hal's wife. Rose assumed Hal must have his reasons. Jack Jones was sweet. He seemed to genuinely appreciate her and although he too was ruled by his 'little head'. It was a nice agreeable size, unlike the donkey-sized members she was required to accommodate from time to time. The money would be Francine's and twenty-five dollars of it was her own money she'd lent to her, so in a way it was partly her money. Hal and Francine were legally married and both Mayor Tunstall and Betsy Johnson said it was fair she should pay Hal, so it must have been legal and proper or they wouldn't have said it. After all, they were on Francine's side and not Hal's.

Rose was sick and tired of being 'ridden' as she called it by the filthy men, who came to the Early Saloon seeking respite and refreshment from a girl, in addition to the liquids served at the mahogany bar. Rose reserved the right to refuse any man for any reason she wanted. Even Duffy respected that right as long as it wasn't exercised too often or with an important guest. It was in theory, an inviolable right pertaining to all 'sporting women'. In practice, Rose, Gypsy, and Francine, when all three were working with Duffy, rarely turned any man down, though it was not uncommon for one of them to insist the prospective lover have a bath, and there was a large zinc tub in one of the private rooms for that purpose. The girls insisted on clients using one of an assortment of Mr. Swank's sheaths as well. This requirement did occasion some grumbling, though when given a choice of what was referred to as the "French" treatment or a sheath, most men opted for the sheath.

Rose didn't yet know if she could completely trust Jack. As she told him, "Early isn't much compared to Sacramento, still I'm relatively secure." She had a relatively lucrative calling, a goodly number of ardent and regular admirers, and the esteem of those she worked with. The idea of pulling up stakes and journeying to an unknown place where she knew no one was frightening. She'd be almost totally dependent on him and she wasn't used to being in the power of any man, since Duffy died. Then again, Jack had offered her a partnership of sorts with two hundred and fifty dollars and if worse came to worse, and they parted company, California men had the same fire down below as the men in the New Mexico Territory and Rose was a girl who knew just how best to quench it. Rose could satisfy clients from all walks of life. She knew how to please even the violent man and the just plain mean one, though she would not suffer any man to hit her, past a spanking for which she charged an extra two dollars. Rose made the spankings worthwhile, and the men received their two dollar's worth of crying and tears, all of which was an act, though so authentic, that the performance was as pleasing or perhaps even more so than if the whimpering and pleading were genuine.

Jack wanted to take Rose to California more than he'd wanted anything in his life. Jack knew Hal was impatient to leave for Monterrey, and he also knew him well enough to see he was infatuated with Gypsy. Hal had a wide streak of indolence in his nature and if a girl tapped into it by catering to him, he was content to spend entire days eating and sleeping without ever leaving a bedroom. These periods of idleness were always followed by a mania to get as far away from the girl as possible, a need to travel and seek new fields of endeavor, which was usually fine with Jack. He thought Hal might be beginning one of his lay-ins with Gypsy, and the delay in selling his half of the saloon was a by-product of the usual Harold Russell process, which Jack had seen played out over and over for the past seven years, since meeting him over a faro table in Sacramento.

Jack had no intention of cooling his heels in Early, waiting for Hal's affair with Gypsy to run its course. He was going to offer to take a discount of twenty percent for payment in cash now, which would appeal to Hal's avarice. Unfortunately, as Jack knew from experience, in a tug of war between Hal's greed and Hal's sloth, sloth was usually the victor, at least in the early stages.

"I'm going to see Hal this morning about the money."

"That's good," said Rose. "I've got some cleaning up at the saloon, Francine was by early to tell me I have to open up."

"So that's why you got up just after dawn, I was wondering."

"I thought you were sound asleep."

"I was just dozing, thinking about you and me on that houseboat."

"Was it good?" said Rose with a smile.

"It was real good," said Jack with a playful expression on his not particularly handsome though interesting face. He was no conventional Adonis like Hal. Jack's nose was large and fleshy with a slight bump at the bridge. His hair was longish and hung down past the tips of his ears, wavy and dark brown, as was the thin moustache that he sported on his upper lip. The lips, themselves, were tending toward thin, though they had a clearly discernable bow. His cheekbones were high and prominent, almost Indian-like, and his heavy beard made his tanned face look even darker than it was, though he was clean shaven other than the moustache, when he had access to hot water. His chin was relatively sharp with a cleft, and his teeth were white, for he took pains to keep them clean and didn't chew or smoke, other than a rare cigar now and then. His own mother wouldn't have called him a 'pretty boy'; however in its own way it was a compelling face, and there were certain women, Rose among them, that liked it better for having more of character than beauty in it.

Chapter 11
THE DISCOVERY

As Tunstall and Gypsy neared the arched, iron studded front door, there was a resounding smack of the heavy bronze doorknocker, which consisted of an eight-inch long, one-inch diameter pestle on a hinge that the visitor lifted and allowed to drop on a quarter inch thick bronze plate. Long use had flattened the rim of the pestle and battered a series of dents in the plate. Tunstall liked the booming sound it made, almost as if the heavy door were the skin of some huge drum. He opened the iron barred Judas hole and was astonished to see Rose, looking as if she'd seen a terrifying apparition. All the color was drained from her face.

"Mayor Tunstall," she said breathlessly. "Something terrible has happened! Hal Russell's been murdered and Gypsy's gone."

Tunstall was momentarily taken aback and his face reflected his shock, though it wasn't at Rose's news; however Rose didn't know that and assumed he was as horrified as she was. The mayor had to think quickly. His plan to make Hal Russell's death look like self-defense by placing Hal's revolver in his hand and firing it was destroyed. He had to hide Gypsy until he could think of a different strategy. The difficulty was with each minute of delay now that Rose and possibly others knew of Hal's death Gypsy's absence would be more and more awkward to explain. The worst thing was Rose, Gypsy's best friend, was already saying Hal had been murdered.

"Sorry, Rose, I'm in my drawers. Give me a few minutes and I'll be decent." With that, he closed the Judas hole. Rose sat down on a nearby wooden bench with the knuckle of her right index finger pressed firmly against her front teeth.

"Gypsy," said Tunstall. "We've got a problem."

Gypsy looked at the mayor and despite her precarious position, felt an outpouring of gratitude to have such a stalwart and imposing man on her side. Unlike any other man he'd said, "We have a problem." Anyone else in his place would have said, "You've got a problem." Tunstall paced around the large drawing room like a caged tiger. Gypsy could almost hear the thoughts in his leonine head being ruthlessly examined, evaluated, considered, and rejected. There was something awesome in having such a man defending her, and Gypsy had a child's faith in his ability to shield her from the consequences of Hal's death.

"You had best wait in the sunroom. I'll lock the door so no one can bother you." Tunstall hurried her into the room, locking it with a large iron key, and made his way back through his house, his bare feet slapping on the red tile floor.

Rose had spent the last few minutes chewing on her knuckle and leapt from the bench as soon as she heard the suck of the heavy door against the jamb. Tunstall beckoned her in without saying a word, and led her into the dining room dominated by a massive trestle table of two inch thick poplar boards, highly varnished, and six high back chairs with tooled leather seats and backs in keeping with the Spanish colonial theme the mayor favored. A sideboard that matched the table differed in that the doors were gaily painted with red, white, and yellow blossoms of some unknown flower. This added some bright color to what otherwise would have been a somber, masculine room. On top of the sideboard were colorfully painted Mexican platters of glazed and fired clay and two polished silver candlesticks, Tunstall had bought in the city of Taxco from one of the better silversmiths with a flair for the Baroque. The dining room opened on an atrium in the Roman style without a roof, tiled in the same red tiles as the rest of the house, and had a large, red terra cotta fountain in the middle. There was no water source so it was usually dry, except during festivals.

Rose had never been inside such a grand house, and between that and her agitation about Hal and Gypsy, she was quite beside herself. Hal wasn't the only stabbing death she'd seen, though his was by far the most spectacularly gory one. The mayor pulled out the chair at the North end of the table and Rose sat down gripping the tabletop.

"Can I get you coffee or maybe a glass of water?" asked Tunstall.

"No, not right now," said Rose in an uncharacteristically small, quiet voice. Even in the midst of her anxiety, Rose was looking at the furniture, the silver, and the other decorations, all lit by the indirect sunlight streaming in from the atrium, wondering what it would be like to live every day amid such luxury and beauty. In her mind Tunstall was as wealthy as Jay Gould and his house as splendid as Queen Victoria's Buckingham Palace. Tunstall took a seat in the chair at the south end of the table to give the distraught girl some space to tell her story as opposed to crowding her. He saw her eyes taking in the surroundings, and gave her a few more minutes to do so then said,

"So tell me what happened?"

"But I don't know what happened?" she said tearfully. "That's the problem." "Fine, just tell me what you know," said Tunstall.

"Alright, it was like this. Jack and me, that's Jack Jones, Hal's partner, we're kind of living together if you know what I mean."

Tunstall just nodded not wanting to interrupt Rose's train of thought."

"You know he's been waiting for Hal to get the money for the saloon. Then he's going back up to Sacramento." Here Rose debated about the advisability of telling Tunstall about Jack asking her to go north with him, and decided it might needlessly complicate her story.

"Anyway," said Rose, "See Jack's getting kinda' impatient waiting around so this morning. No, no no, wait, I forgot something," said Rose who was nervous and flustered. Tunstall consciously resisted a powerful urge to prompt her, knowing that if he gave in to his natural impulse, it might distract rather than guide a person as distracted as Rose.

"I forgot. Early this morning, Francine came to see me to tell me she was riding out with Mr. Swank and more than likely wouldn't return before nightfall. So me, Gypsy, and the Indian needed to open up the saloon without her. We've done it before without a problem so I thought nothing of it. After Hal and Francine decided to get a divorce. That was after Hal hit her in the face, but you remember that of course. Jack wasn't ever interested in Gypsy, she's much too young for him."

This nearly made Tunstall guffaw as Rose was at most three years older than Gypsy.

Ordinarily, the mayor would have had little time for listening to the intricacies of the love lives of whores, fascinating as they may have been, simply because he had a large number of official and personal responsibilities that required attention. Tunstall was nearly unique in the Territory for a number of reasons, one of which being that he really was a staunch advocate for the rights of women, Indians, and Mexicans.

He'd even proposed a law to allow women the right to vote in municipal elections. This proposal was vociferously denounced by Reverend Gilbert as, "Contrary to God's law as set forth in Genesis." There were a number of respectable matrons who opposed the change to Early's voting law as well on the grounds it would have enfranchised saloon girls as well as Mexicans.

Rose continued, "So me and Jack went to Gypsy's place this morning. I knocked on the door a couple of times but there was no answer. Jack said they might be sleeping it off and I said no, Francine had probably talked to her about opening like she'd talked to me. I should have asked Francine but I wasn't thinking. Anyway Jack said Hal was in one of his indolent periods, meaning he lies around in bed till all hours. So Jack pounded on the door until it was rattling on its hinges. Then he shouted, "Get up you lazy son-of-a-bitch!" Then Jack put his right hand on the doorknob and wrenched it to the right. It was open. He walked in and I followed him, then we saw Hal and all that blood. My God Almighty, there was a lot of blood, the flies came out of nowhere to eat it and the room stank like," here Rose struggled for an adequate description, "Like horse piss mixed with a rotten piece of meat. It was all I could do to keep from puking up the breakfast I'd just eaten. Jack rolled Hal over and there was this knife sticking out of his chest and his face smeared with so much blood it was a red mess. Only thing white was his eyes and they was wide open like he was surprised. Jack closed 'em and told me to fetch you. It stunk so bad because someone smashed the chamber-pot against the wall and the slops that was in it was everywhere. I don't know how Jack could stand the smell. I was so glad to get out of there. Anyway, Hal Russell's dead and Gypsy's nowhere, maybe they took her like they took the marshal's daughter. Either that or she's run off. Not that I'd blame her. Whoever killed Hal might have tried to kill her.""

Tunstall took full advantage of the pause in Rose's account to interject softly and firmly, "Hal Russell was a man who liked to hurt women. Isn't it possible he and Gypsy got into an argument and Hal pulled his Bowie, then went for Gypsy, tripped and fell on his own knife? This was after he threw the chamber-pot at her."

Rose thought about it then said, "But Hal's arms were stretched out and his hands were flat on the floor."

"That's perfectly consistent with falling flat on your face," said Tunstall, knowing perfectly well this wasn't the case still, he wanted to plant the scenario in Rose's mind. He was pleased to learn that Jack had turned the corpse over, and with any luck, after closing Hal's eyes, Jack had arranged the deceased's arms folding them over his chest rather than leaving them stretched at full length over his head. Rose was left wondering how Hal could have been holding the Bowie, and not at least tried to pull it out of his chest. If you tripped holding a knife, you would fling it as far away from you as you could, not clutch it to your heart.

"I don't know, mayor. Maybe Hal killed himself."

"If he'd killed himself, he'd have used his Colt. Men with revolvers don't commit suicide with Bowie knives." Tunstall said this automatically. Then it occurred to him that having Rose associate Hal's death with anything but murder was beneficial to Gypsy. Tunstall spoke in an unsure, tentative tone, "I guess it's possible Hal killed himself. Any man who attacks women, drunk or sober, is mentally unsound and that's a fact."

"Do you think Gypsy's been taken?" asked Rose giving voice to her greatest fear,

"People are taken hostage for a purpose, usually ransom, or to force someone to do something. Is there anyone who would benefit from killing Hal Russell, and taking Gypsy?"

154

Just then, Rose had a horrible thought which turned her stomach. "Francine won't have to pay Hal the money for the saloon."

"No," agreed the mayor, "The till death us do part has taken place. Still I don't see Francine killing him."

"No," said Rose. "But in a thing like this your mind goes off in all different directions at once. You know what I mean?"

Tunstall badly wanted to get Rose out of his house so he could talk with Gypsy. Other than Rose, Jack Jones and Gypsy, no one else was aware Hal was dead. If only it were Rose who knew he could easily convince her that Hal had accidentally stabbed himself after tripping during a blind rage, especially with Gypsy's eyewitness version backing Rose up. As justice of the peace, he could prevail on Enoch Swank and Doc Hill to agree, and their coroner's jury verdict finding of death by misadventure would effectively end all official inquiries into the demise of the late Harold Russell.

Hal's partner, Jack Jones, was the grand complication, the fly in the ointment, and the snake in the garden. If he were to cooperate there would be no problem. The life and death question was whether he would. First, he had to get Rose out of the way so he could talk to Gypsy, then he needed to speak with Jones before anyone else learned of Russell's murder.

"Rose," he said gently, "Do you think you could ride out to the marshal's farm and bring her to town? You can take my horse. I'll give you a card to take to Ernesto at the livery stable. The horse is only fourteen hands, gentle as a kitten and he'll canter for hours if he has to."

Tunstall forgot that Rose had never been to Betsy's ranch, taking it for granted that all the girls at the saloon knew where it was because Francine had been there several times.

"But I've never been to Betsy's place," said Rose who was intrigued with the idea of riding Tunstall's horse and bringing the marshal back. It was an important, even heroic task and Rose was ready to ride like the wind.

"It's not hard to find. If you think you can do it, I'll tell you how to get there, besides you can ask Ernesto to go with you. You'll be back in two hours and I'm sure the stable will survive that long without him. Wait here while I fetch a card."

Tunstall stood then walked to his bedroom. On the walnut dresser was a box of chased silver featuring scenes from Greek mythology, with the Judgment of Paris on the lid. He opened the hinged top and removed a carte-de-visite, more of a visiting card because although cards bearing the owner's portrait were immensely popular during the Civil War, now only hopelessly old-fashioned men and women gave out cards with their photograph on them. Tunstall's were of cream-laid card stock printed with his name, J.W. Tunstall and his title, Mayor, in gothic lettering using India ink. He ordered them from a printer in Santa Fe. The Territorial governor had given him a silver pen with a gold nib on one of his infrequent visits to the capital. There was a silver topped crystal bottle of India ink next to the card box.

"Where's my damned pen?" Tunstall muttered to himself. "Why is it that useful things like pens are never to be found and useless things like cuff-buttons are always near to hand?"

He misplaced the governor's pen at least once a week, necessitating a lengthy search. He opened the top drawer of his dresser and reached for the tray full of various English steel pens with assorted nibs none of which he liked. The pens were either too sharp and they cut into the paper, or the nibs were too broad and smeared the ink. He chose a fine nib, dipped the pen into the ink and wrote a brief note to Ernesto then he remembered Ernesto wouldn't be able to read his English so he did his best in schoolboy Spanish.

"Caballo," yes, that's it he thought. "Donde me caballo por Rosa, por favor, J.W. Tunstall."

He signed his name with a flourish and a blob of ink landed on the c in caballo, so he blotted it with a corner of his silk handkerchief. It wasn't perfect though it would suffice.

After seeing Rose safely out the front door, Tunstall returned to the sunroom. Gypsy was curled up in the leather armchair, trying hard not to take any deep breaths. Anything more than the most shallow intake of air resulted in pains worse than the most intense birth pangs, though these were much higher up, and therefore not from her very core like those of childbirth.

"Well," said Tunstall. "I planted the ideas of self-defense and accident. I told Rose Hal could have fallen on his Bowie while he was attacking you and I even suggested Hal might have killed himself."

"Hal wouldn't have killed himself, he wasn't the type."

"Oh no?" said Tunstall. "A man rejected by his wife after he beats her. A man reduced to waiting on his soon to be ex—wife for money. No job, no land, no prospects, drinking himself to sleep every night. Living with a saloon girl. No offense, it sounds pretty much like Hell to me."

Tunstall's words painted a portrait in Gypsy's thoughts of a pathetic life, one that might well make a man take his own life.

"You make Hal's life sound downright depressing."

The mayor's way with words encouraged Gypsy more than anything, more than his imposing physical presence, more than his indomitable courage, his lovely home, or even his mayoralty.

"Language is an amazing thing," said Tunstall, indicating the gilt stamped spines of the leather slipcases that help first editions of many of his favorite novels. He knew an older Mexican gentleman who'd learned the art of bookbinding from a master in Mexico City. The man worked in the governor's palace as a translator and bound books and made slipcases of pasteboard covered in soft calf leather in his spare time as a labor of love.

> "There are entire worlds within these volumes, with people as real in almost every way as you and I are. Though they are made of words, they eat, speak, make love, think, hope, suffer disappointment, and live and die much as do we creatures of flesh and blood, bone and sinew. There are times I think in ways they are more real than we are ourselves. For what is reality but persistence in time?"

Tunstall stopped himself in mid—career. He and Gypsy had an immediate, time-sensitive problem that needed a solution, and allowing his thoughts to roam realms of metaphysics was a mistake. Tunstall needed to find out from Gypsy just how Jack Jones might react to Hal's untimely and violent demise. He had wanted to ask Rose how Jack acted when he first saw the body, yet he didn't want to seem overly interested, so he had to be content with Rose's descriptions of how he rolled Hal over, and closed his wide, staring, blood-filled eyes, the traditional service of the living to the dead, as if a dead man's eyes could see. Tunstall thought it had much more to do with the live man or woman being made uncomfortable by the look on the face of the deceased than doing a favor to the corpse. Absurd as the gesture was when subjected to logical analysis Jack Jones obviously thought he needed to do it for Hal.

> The mayor had an inclination to go to Jones and suggest that Russell had tripped and stabbed himself in falling, and if Jones failed to buy that version, he'd have to go with either a third party with a grudge, who slipped into Early unnoticed by

anyone, killed Hal, left as mysteriously as he arrived, or fall back on self-defense. Tunstall hated the whole notion of using self-defense in Gypsy's case, because while he understood the girl thought her life was in mortal danger, there wasn't a jury in the Territory that would think; however badly Hal may have disfigured or maimed Gypsy, that such an injury regardless of how severe was worth a man's life. He most certainly felt Gypsy was entirely within her rights and Enoch Swank, and possibly Ike Hill would agree with him, but they were a distinct minority. A year had passed since the mayor saved Early from the Coyoteros and memories tend to be short at the best of times.

"Gypsy," said Tunstall. "I'm going to talk with Mr. Jones and see if we can come to a meeting of the minds about how Mr. Russell came to his untimely end. Is there anything, anything at all you can think of about Jones that might be helpful? For instance, is he the type of man whose silence can be bought? Or is he one of those men who believes in truth and justice above all, which I doubt given his being wanted in a hold-up and shoot-out. Then again one never knows how a man gets involved in certain situations."

Gypsy knew all too well how one gets involved in situations. When she awoke this morning, everything was fine. Hal was asleep, Francine came by for a moment, and she was looking forward to griddle cakes with maple syrup, and less than half an hour later, she was fighting for her life with the man who was supposed to be her lover. Now scarcely two hours later, she was in Mayor Tunstall's home trying to figure out how to escape from being hanged or imprisoned for murder. Gypsy was still so unnerved that all she wanted to do was sit curled up in the mayor's chair, where she knew she was safe.

"I don't know that much about Jack. All he talked about was how much he loved the Delta, how much he missed California, and how he was going back there, hire a lawyer, and clear his name as soon as he had his share of the money." Tunstall mulled this over. He would have preferred it if Jones were more of a criminal type, uninterested in his reputation.

"This shouldn't take too long," said Tunstall. "I'd like to have Doc Hill examine you. I think the cowardly sonofabitch broke your ribs, but until we get our story straight, if you don't mind, I'm going to lock you in the house until I return. If you get thirsty, there's water in the pantry in a jug, harder stuff too if you've a mind to relax or ease your pain."

"No," said Gypsy. "I'll just wait, thank you."

Though it was the last thing she wanted to do, using great care, she got up from the chair using her arms and hands to shift as much pressure from her chest as possible, stood with an audible gasp, she tried manfully to suppress, walked to Tunstall, though every step caused a new spasm of pain, and stood in front of him looking up into his brown eyes.

"I hope you know that whatever happens, I don't want you to suffer in any way for what I have done. You're doing more for me than anyone ever has including Francine, and no matter if I go free or end up swinging from a rope, as God is my witness, I'll never forget what you've done for me."

She stood on her toes and kissed his cheek. Tunstall knew there was neither art nor design in Gypsy's words or gesture, and this made them far more powerful and moving than they would have been had there been artifice behind them.

Tunstall had no children of his own, and whether it was his age, stature or a combination of the two, he thought of the petite, golden haired saloon girl as a child! Much to his discomfiture, his eyes filled with tears, and though he'd never burden Gypsy by telling her, he instantly knew he would sacrifice his home, his mayoral office, even his life to save the whore standing in front of him. It was this quality, his willingness to put his life in jeopardy to save another's that made Betsy Johnson love him as she did. Betsy had almost worshipped her father, a hero of Gettysburg, and there was much of Josiah Johnson in the mayor's make-up. Neither man was what anyone who knew them would call careless or reckless, which made their courageous deeds magnificent, and invested their very being with a degree of saintliness. Their heroism was of the deliberate kind, like Sidney Carton at the foot of the guillotine. Betsy saw the Sidney Carton in Tunstall, though unlike Carton, Tunstall was a success in the worldly sense, and she only loved him the better for it.

As Tunstall looked down on Gypsy, she could see the tears shining in his eyes. He wanted to reassure her with an embrace; however he didn't want to hurt her so he placed a large hand on the crown of her head.

"I'm not going to tell you everything's going to be alright. I would if I could but I don't have that power, only God does and I don't pretend to know His mind unlike all those who will tell you they do. But I will do anything and everything I can to see you safely through this."

Gypsy didn't doubt for a second that the mayor meant every word he said.

"God bless you, Mayor."

"And you too, Gypsy, and you."

He gave her a wistful smile, gently removed his hand, turned, and walked from the room, leaving Gypsy staring at his retreating form.

Chapter 11
ROSE'S JOURNEY

Rose was thoroughly lost. Ernesto's instructions were vague, and his fractured English only made them less intelligible. In truth, the directions were not faulty, the difficulty lay in the fact that Rose rarely rode very far from Early, and the few times she did, it was always with someone who knew exactly where they were going. The country immediately around Early was fairly level. There were very few trees, apart from a few mesquite bushes, so when Rose rode she was always in sight of the steeple of the church, or the copper arrow weathervane atop City Hall. The mayor's horse was every bit as biddable as he said it was; however she'd been in the saddle for over an hour by her reckoning using the position of the sun. She was supposed to ride due North, then turn East when she came to the arroyo, after following it she would come to a large cluster of creosote bushes, at which point she would see Betsy's frame house to the Northeast. It was supposed to be about six miles and take no more than three quarters of an hour at a slow trot. Rose had been cantering to what she thought was the North, and though she'd passed any number of dry washes, none she saw deserved the dignified title of arroyo. Rose had a feeling she'd come further than she should have, because she was able to see a hill that surely have been mentioned as a landmark if it were on the way to Betsy's house. Rose was already regretting not wearing a hat, and the sun was uncomfortably hot on her head. She carried a

> full canteen of water and she stopped the horse by shifting her weight like Ernesto told her to do, and opened the screw plug of the old U.S. Army canteen and drank. The water was tepid, tasting of wet metal with a slight tang of damp cloth from the dun colored canvas covering still stenciled with large black letters, U.S. Army. Rose capped it and hung it from the saddle horn.

Ernesto had helped her adjust the stirrup length and she enjoyed the ride out of Early. The reciprocating rocking motion of the lope relaxed her and the fresh air redolent with the spicy scent of sage as she and the horse bruised the berries, chased away the memory of the death-room and its stench. However, now that she knew she was lost her sense of well-being evaporated as tiny, prickles of panic broke out on the soft skin under her arm-pits, racing down the sides of her chest, prickling her breasts as they went on to roil her belly. Rose was all alone in the middle of a trackless, desolate wasteland and she was angry as well as frightened. Tunstall had made it sound as easy as riding down Main Street, and of course it was for him as many times as he'd been out there. Why was it that men assumed once they had done something, anyone else could do it easily? They never remembered or they glossed over all their own uncertainties from their first time.

> "Damn them!" she said aloud. "Damn them anyway. And that Ernesto! All smiles and 'Yes senhorita, the marshal's estancia, ee's no problema'. No problem for you. One big problem for me."

Rose imagined herself being captured and ravished by Coyoteros or Indians, though nothing like that had happened for a year that she knew of, though lone travelers in the Territory could disappear without a trace or anyone taking notice. After all Tunstall's horse was worth more money than most people earned in a year. More than some folks earned in their lifetime. Violence around Early was sufficiently rare that neither Tunstall nor Ernesto offered her a rifle to put in the saddle scabbard that was integral with the saddle. Rose was no gun-hand like Betsy, still she knew the muzzle end, and she would have felt a great deal safer if she had some kind of firearm. Not only was it possible there were desperate men in the mountains, there were bears and mountain lions.

Rose shielded her eyes with her left hand and looked up at the sun. She knew the sun rose in the East and set in the West. The tricky part was remembering whether it moved North or South before noon, because when it was more or less overhead it was of little use in determining direction. Rose decided to trot in one direction as parallel to the sun as she could, all the while counting to six hundred, which would mean ten minutes had passed.

"No gun, no watch. Why didn't I bring anything with me, not even a hat?" Rose was furiously angry with Tunstall, Ernesto, and Jack Jones, even with Hal Russell for getting himself killed and causing all her troubles. No, the whole thing was Gypsy's fault and now she'd run off, Rose was convinced of it.

"I'll ride for ten minutes in one direction, then I'll really panic." Rose pressed her heels into the horse's flanks, urging him into a trot. By the time she reached three hundred, she forgot if she were supposed to be on three hundred eleven or three hundred twenty one, and lost count totally as her horse brushed a creosote bush and spooked a large jack rabbit which exploded from the base of the plant, startling the horse, which took off at a full gallop for about fifty yards. Rose held on to the reins and saddle horn for dear life. After his mad dash, the animal seemed embarrassed and settled down to nibble tentatively at a sage brush. Rose's heart was thundering in her chest, and blood pounded in her head. Her plan had gone awry. Tunstall's horse had been well fed and watered at Ernesto's livery stable, even so the animal would need water before too long if she expected him to maintain a lope for any extended period.

"This is the stupidest thing I've done in a long time," said Rose aloud. She was thirsty and reeled up the canteen heedless of the warm temperature and unpleasant taste of the water. The canteen felt much lighter than when she'd last had recourse to it. She shook it and the screw—plug fell out of its own accord. She hadn't screwed it in tightly and most of the water remaining had leaked out when the canteen was canted at an obtuse angle relative to the ground after the horse shied from the rabbit.

"This is wonderful," she said in bitter acrimony. "Now my horse has no water and I don't either."

Rose was so frustrated she forgot all about her fear of being alone, miles from human habitation, unarmed, without water, food, shelter, or even a hat. Rose dismounted and loosened the straps on Tunstall's saddlebags. The leather was supple and well maintained as was all of the mayor's tack. The offside bag was empty and flat. The one on the right contained a colorful Mexican bandanna in reds and yellows. Rose didn't think Tunstall would mind if she wore it and didn't care if he did. She shook it out folded it into a triangle, then shrouded her hair and tied it under her chin like a headscarf. It would keep the sun from beating down on her head. There was something else at the very bottom of the bag. Rose picked it up. The object was in a black metal case with a folding cover that was hinged. She popped open the cover and to her inexpressible relief, saw it was a United States Army compass. In 1862, the first liquid compass used a float on the directional card and took the weight off the pivot. A system of internal bellows expanded and contracted with the liquid preventing most leaks. The blued, steel needle swung decisively to the black inked N on the white card when Rose held it level on her palm. Tunstall and those familiar with its use, knew that in the absence of familiar landmarks, if one wanted to ride West to reach a given destination, he merely had to line up the needle so its ends were over the North and South marks on the card and travel in the same direction ninety degrees to the left of the North end of the needle. Rose was unaware of this refined use, so she figured she could either travel North or South. Having the compass was like possessing a magic talisman and it made her think she at least had something other than the constantly shifting sun to guide her.

Tunstall's horse pricked his ears forward, aware of something in the distance that Rose couldn't see or hear. Though it might have been distortion caused by the heat, Rose thought she could see a small dust cloud silhouetted against the hill, and the dust appeared to be moving in her direction. She remounted as quickly as she was able, placing her left boot toe in the left stirrup, and tucking the compass in between her belt and the flesh of her belly, took a handful of mane and rein and vaulted gracelessly but safely into the saddle. The added few feet of height enabled her to see the cloud was no mirage. It was real, moving fast, and in her direction.

Rose fought down her panic. The odds were greatly in her favor that whoever it was would be not only harmless; he would help her find Betsy's ranch. Rose's terror stemmed from the very small chance that the dust might be someone with evil intent, a lone Apache, or worse, a coyotero, and for the moment this highly unlikely possibility outweighed all other considerations in her mind. Rose wanted to ride as fast as she could in the opposite direction, though she was so lost, she feared a headlong flight would only delay her having to face the pitiless sun and the lack of water.

The last thing Rose wanted to do was harm Tunstall's valuable and well-loved horse. The mayor's fondness for horses in general and his own in particular was a fact of life in Early. One had best not whip, mistreat, or exhaust a horse in Tunstall's presence. A serious tongue-lashing was the best a man could hope for and the mayor was known to confiscate a sick or mistreated animal without compensation to the astonished owner. If the objections grew too heated, Tunstall would arrest the offender. There were signs posted in front of the saloon, City Hall, the livery stable reading, "Mistreatment of horses is a crime in Early."

This town ordnance, like having a woman marshal, was another of the features that made Early unusual, some said downright weird. Enoch Swank, Doc Hill, and Tunstall conspire to ram the so-called 'horse law' down the throats of some residents who believed it was their God-given right, written in Genesis to lord it over 'dumb' animals. The three of them persuaded Reverend Gilbert that dominion in scripture wasn't the same as domination. Afterward, the Reverend even preached a sermon on the duty of men to be kind stewards to their beasts citing Jesus' assurance that God paid attention to the 'fall of a sparrow' and since that was true, God certainly paid more attention to how a man treated his horse.

One evening when Tunstall was having a whiskey at the bar, a drunken ranch hand was outside at the hitching rail, cursing his grey quarter horse gelding who wasn't letting him mount. The man started punishing the horse by whipping him across the face with the lead, swearing all the while. Tunstall heard the commotion, the horse's frantic whinnying, and the hand's loud imprecations. Tunstall was adept at fisticuffs; however he wasn't in the mood, and he wanted to return to his whiskey, so he walked outside, drew his Colt Single Action, and fired a shot off into the air, startling man and horse. The man stood still, while the horse bolted down the dusty street.

"What the Hell do you think you're doing?" shouted the man.

"You must have trouble reading," said Tunstall in a quiet voice. The mayor gestured with the seven and a half inch barrel of his .44 at the sign, which was clearly visible in the light cast by the oil lamps. The ranch hand read it, cleared his throat and launched a glob of spittle to show Tunstall just how much he thought of the sign.

The ranch hand's voice was dripping with scorn as he said, "It's my horse. I bought it with my money and if I want to beat it or kill it that's my affair."

Tunstall shook his head. "Not in Early. As justice of the peace I'm confiscating that horse."

The man was dumbfounded. "You can't do that!"

"I beg to differ. I already have."

Tunstall watched as the man passed through the stages of disbelief, astonishment, realization, and outrage, wondering if the man, who looked about twenty-five, and should know better, was sufficiently drink-befuddled to reach for his pistol. The young man's revolver had a grip shape that was more Smith and Wesson than Colt, possibly a Remington. It was set firmly, deep down in the holster and drawing it out would take time and effort, so Tunstall wasn't overly concerned. The ranch hand looked at Tunstall's revolver, pointed at his chest, the stony expression on the face of the black-suited man, and sobered up instantly.

"You're a justice of the peace and you'd shoot me for beating my horse? This is plumb crazy. What kind of a man are you?"

"I'd like to think I'm a just one. Your horse can't defend himself. Who knows he might even like you."

Tunstall was secretly relieved he wasn't going to have to hurt the boy. Though he never was going to shoot him, he had fully intended to slug him across the face with the barrel of his gun. The man looked at the faces of the saloon patrons who had gathered in the street and on the step, seeking sympathy from at least one or two of the faces and finding none. The powerful urge to fight gave way to the horrifying realization that without his horse, he'd have to walk back to the ranch where he was hired, a distance of some twenty miles, and all of his wages for some time would go to the owner for another, almost certainly inferior animal. Until the new horse was paid for, he'd be nothing more than a slave. It had never occurred to him just how essential his horse was to his life.

"Judge," he said in a sober and chastened voice. "Can we talk about this private like?"

Tunstall spun his Colt counter-clockwise in a blur around his index finger so dexterously that the revolver seemed to holster itself. The mayor practiced this for at least an hour a week, knowing it was vanity, though it amused him, notwithstanding. Like a good break-shot in billiards dexterity with a handgun could be useful in a variety of circumstances. Seeing Tunstall's skill with the Colt, the ranch hand was very grateful he hadn't tried to draw his Model 1875 Remington. The incident ended with the ranch hand being reunited with his horse and a heartfelt promise to behave better in the future. The recollection of this episode, played a role in Rose's decision not to go galloping off through the brush, heedless of holes and stones, and to stand her ground and await whatever fate was approaching, heralded by the dust cloud.

Rose was more and more frightened with each passing second, until she realized from the behavior of the horse, that he wasn't scared of what was coming toward him. His ears remained pricked forward, his soft dark nostrils flaring, and then he raised his head and gave out a long, loud neigh, whose whicker was answered by a similar call off in the distance.

"Horses aren't stupid," thought Rose. "He must know whoever is coming," and relief flowed through her body. The stallion pawed the dry, reddish, decomposed, sandstone soil, showing his impatience.

Rose heard a woman's voice, though she couldn't see that well through the sage, creosote, and mesquite bushes.

"I'm Marshal Johnson and you're riding Mayor Tunstall's horse. Stop where you are or I will shoot!"

If an angel from heaven had called to her, Rose wouldn't have been any more thrilled than she was to hear Betsy's voice. Betsy rode up on her big mare, which proceeded to nuzzle the stallion. Rose sighed, the longest sigh she'd given in years.

"Oh, Betsy," she said. "I've never been so scared in my like. I thought you were an Indian."

"The Mescaleros won't bother you and there aren't any bad men out here except for your friends, Russell and Jones."

"You saved my life!"

Betsy looked at Rose as if the girl lost her mind to the sun.

"Ben thought he saw someone on the mayor's horse about an hour ago, but it was too far to be sure, besides, Tunstall would no more ride by my place without stopping than the earth will stop turning. Then when I thought about it, it bothered me so I figured I'd see if I could catch up on the off chance Ben might have been right, and it seems he was."

"Thank God!" said Rose. "The mayor sent me to get you, see Hal Russell's dead and then I got lost. I thought I'd die out here."

Betsy raised her eyebrows at this. "Well, you must have ridden right by the place. I admit it's kind of hard to see, and we didn't light the stove this morning so there wouldn't have been any smoke. No, I see how you could have missed it."

Betsy didn't see it at all, though she saw no harm in agreeing with the girl. If Hal Russell were dead, he wasn't going anywhere. Tunstall would take care of things, so there wasn't any need for haste.

"Let's go to my place and get Abraham some water. He looks like he could use some, and you do too if you don't mind me saying so."

Seated on one of Betsy's plain but rugged pinion pine, splat backed chairs, and gulping as much cool well water as she could, Rose told her story of finding Hal Russell face down in Gypsy's bedroom, which looked like an abattoir. Betsy listened to her, all attention, and as Rose finished her narrative with Betsy's timely rescue, Betsy said, "Hal Russell is or rather was a handsome man I'll grant you that, an attractive man. But deep inside there was something very wrong with him. No matter what she said to him, there's no excuse for what he did to Francine. Men like him really hate women, and the worst part is they'll smack you around, then cry and say it was your fault. If you didn't make them angry, they wouldn't dream of hitting you. I know all about it from personal experience, only my man wasn't a sniveling coward about it. He never expressed any remorse at all. He let you know he thought he was your superior, and I guess in some ways he was. He was the Devil himself in the most pleasing shape you ever saw. But that's unimportant. Let's just say I know enough of the Hal Russell's of the world to say that sooner or later, he would have killed some woman, either inadvertently or on purpose. Men who beat up their women either end up in prison or the graveyard.

Betsy fixed her green eyes on Rose's grey ones, making sure she understood exactly what she intended to say. "And as much as I hate to say it, good riddance to him either way."

"What about Gypsy?"

"Well you can't blame her for hoofing it." Betsy assumed Hal either fell on the Bowie or Gypsy stabbed him in self-defense.

"You don't think she could have been kidnapped?"

"No, no more than I think Francine hired a gunman to kill him to avoid paying him."

This possibility had entirely escaped all of Rose's feverish speculations, though now that Betsy mentioned it, it made sense. Francine could hire a killer for a fraction of nine hundred dollars, and she did have a grudge against Hal, not that Rose blamed her. Rose didn't think Francine was so cold blooded and calculating, though she knew men and women too, had hidden wellsprings of all sorts of behaviors they kept concealed for years, or even their entire lives, up to the moment when they gushed to the surface making them act in ways no one including themselves could have imagined, and not just in evil ways, but good ones as well. The coward of the county could become a hero in an instant and vice versa.

Jack Jones had told her, "Never forget Rose. There's a little bit of the worst in the best men and a little bit of the best, even in the worst."

"You just never know everything about anyone," thought Rose. "Hal might have pushed Gypsy over the edge."

"Like I said," Betsy spoke more forcefully this time, "The chances are that Hal hurt Gypsy and she stabbed him. Then she got scared and ran."

Ben walked in and nodded politely to Rose.

"Where's Sara?" asked Betsy.

"She's playing with Deaf Charlie's sister's young ones near the gold mine."

"You think it's safe to leave them there alone?"

Ben looked at Betsy with much the same expression as Betsy had given Rose when Rose told her she'd saved her life, as if to question Betsy's sanity for asking such a foolish question. Betsy gave him a wry smile acknowledging the absurdity of even asking him. If Ben didn't think they were as safe by the mine as if they were in bed he wouldn't have left them there.

"Rose and I have some business in town. It shouldn't take more than three or four hours. If I'm not back here by late afternoon, you and Sara can either meet me in town or stay here, because I'll be eating with the mayor.

Ben crinkled his wise, wizened face in a smile. His skin was dark brown and sun-creased and there was an inherent nobility in the high brow, prominent cheekbones, and large scimitar shaped nose that reminded Betsy of certain pictures of busts of Julius Caesar and Marcus Aurelius, paintings of Solomon or King Saul. Ben could be evidence that the Indians actually were one of the lost tribes of Israel as some Easterners claimed.

As far as Betsy was concerned, Ben, who was the first Indian she ever knew, was as good a man as Enoch Swank or Mayor Tunstall, and was better to Sara than either of them. Ben was as tough as Tunstall when he needed to be and as childlike as Sara when he was with her. The most wonderful thing about his unique ability to be completely comfortable and natural in a man's or a child's world, was that Ben did so effortlessly and spontaneously. This was why Sara responded to him in ways she never would with Tunstall. There were times, Betsy found herself envying the rapport between Sara and Ben, though her predominate emotion was gratitude. There was the fractious and thorny issue of Sara's formal education, though Betsy hoped that soon her daughter would ask to go to school on her own.

"I can't recall the mayor ever letting someone borrow his horse," said Ben with respect and surprise.

"Come to think of it, I don't know if he's ever let me ride him," said Betsy. "Not that I've ever needed to," Betsy hastened to add.

"I guess he thought it was important to reach you as soon as possible and he couldn't come, himself, so he thought he'd take a chance. When I got lost, I think I was more worried about the horse than about me. I kept thinking what if he breaks a leg or runs away while I'm walking him? Or, what if somebody steals him and leaves me out there to die? All kinds of terrible things go through your mind."

"Especially after you saw what happened to Hal Russell?"

"What happened to Russell?" asked Ben. Rose looked at Betsy.

"We don't really know," said Betsy. "Only that he's dead."

"Dead," said Ben without any surprise evident in his low bass voice. "Who killed him?"

"We don't know it he was killed or died in an accident. That's why I'm going into town. To find out."

Ben was concerned and not because Hal was dead. Ben had only contempt for a man so craven as to hit women and a man who would take his wife's property was, in his estimation lower on the scale of values than a maggot.

Ben did have concern for Francine. Like Betsy, she treated Indians like human beings, not like mongrel dogs. Francine had altered Duffy's No Dogs and Indians sign by painting out Indians as soon as she took over the saloon. Her saloon was the only one in the New Mexico Territory and maybe all of America, where an Indian in native dress could sit at the long, beautiful mahogany bar, and be served a more or less cold beer, much colder in the winter, and if a white man objected, it was he and not the Indian who would be asked to take his custom else-where and in Early there was no other public drinking establishment. If the white man continued to complain there were either the wooden ice mallets or the sawn-off Greener double barreled shotguns to make him understand that if he wanted to continue drinking, he either accepted the Indian's right to do the same or left. On several occasions, Mr. Greener had to clarify the hazy concept in a drunken ranch hand's mind that Indians were human. There were obstinate white men who clung to the notion that they were too good to rub elbows with a 'red-skin'. They left thirsty. Francine was steadfast in her enforcement of Indian rights in her saloon and this engendered an unshakeable loyalty to her in the hearts of Ben, Deaf Charlie, and a number of other Indians who would have been only to happy to bury Hal Russell in an unmarked grave if she had asked them to.

Chapter 12
TROUBLE IN EARLY

Less than one hour later, Betsy and Rose rode into Early. It was past noon and the heat was a palpable force, almost like riding through an invisible cloud of scalding vapor as opposed to the cool dampness of a fog. The birds roosting in the eves of the buildings were too warm to sing, and the heated breeze was strong enough to kick up miniature dust devils in the middle of the principal and only street. Tunstall had instructed Rose to come directly to his house, bypassing Gypsy's. When they arrived, Rose was as astonished as Betsy to see Jack Jones with several other men, including Reverend Gilbert -, waiting in his front courtyard, under the fair sized cottonwood that was the largest tree in Early. The men looked at the two women, and the reverend walked up to Betsy. The preacher was a not ill-favored man of thirty and while not cleaving to any identifiable Christian denominations he was in the opinion of his flock, a reasonably good speaker of the Word. He had grown up in Houston and studied at a Catholic seminary for one year before determining that there were certain features of the Apostle's Creed that strained credibility, as did the Virgin Birth, and why an omnipotent and omniscient Deity would need to resort to such subterfuge to create Himself in human form. Besides, he reasoned, if Jesus were the Word made Flesh, why would God find it either necessary or desirable to die like a human being, and resurrect himself, to 'save' men from sin when He could do so with a single breath.

Seminarian Gilbert went so far as to ask the Father Superior, "Since Jesus did all these things for the Jews, why didn't God decide to die and resurrect Himself in Moses, David, or Daniel? What was so special about the reign of Caesar Augustus or Tiberius that suddenly the Almighty felt a compulsion to put Himself through the process at that time and never again either before or since?"

The Father Superior, genuinely liked Gilbert, though he thought the otherwise estimable young man would make a poor bridegroom for the Catholic church.

"My son," he intoned, resting his warm, kind, brown eyes, on Gilbert's restless blue ones, "You must accept these things on faith alone and not seek to question them. You have shown love for your fellow man and this is commendable. My advice to you is to find some isolated community and present yourself as a seminarian turned preacher. I will prepare a letter to this effect."

Armed with the Father Superior's letter of introduction, Gilbert made his way West, preaching at churches of various denominations as a guest to generally favorable reviews from the faithful. The deacon at the new Catholic Cathedral in Santa Fe took a liking to him and suggested that Early might be in need of a preacher. The deacon had visited the Mescalero Reservation nearby and had met Tunstall once or twice when the mayor came to Santa Fe. Though Tunstall was no Catholic, he liked stained glass windows and the architectural grandeur of the cathedral. He would sit in the cool silence under the soaring ceiling, which he found very conducive to maintaining a connection with the Divine.

"Marshal," said Gilbert, as Betsy dismounted and removed Abigail's headstall so the mare could take better advantage of the water trough under the hitching rail. The trough was kept half full of water by the same youth who assisted Gypsy and kept the one street free from horse manure. Similar water troughs were in front of the saloon, livery stable, and City Hall.

"Am I glad to see you," said Gilbert. "We have ourselves a situation here." From the look on the preacher's face, Betsy knew whatever he had to say wasn't good. Gilbert continued, "Hal Russell, Francine's husband, has been murdered. Gypsy killed him with his own knife."

Betsy looked at Rose, who looked down at her boots.

"Wait a minute, Reverend," said Betsy. "Rose here found the body this morning. She didn't say anything about murder."

"That may be. But you know Mrs. Cabot," Betsy groaned to herself.

Not only was Marcie Cabot a notorious busybody, she hated Tunstall and made no secret of her antipathy. As far as Marcie Cabot was concerned, all unmarried women of marriageable age were nothing more than undeclared whores while single men were satyrs, and J.W. Tunstall was the anti-Christ because as mayor he condoned whoredom by permitting Francine, Rose, and Gypsy to openly ply their trade, and he favored the rights of heathen savages over Christian, white men. Mr. Cabot had died of natural causes some years before, though Tunstall always said with a wife like Marcie, he must have greeted the Grim Reaper with open arms. The late, lamented Mr. Cabot left her quite well off thanks to his faith in the Santa Fe railroad and the Union Pacific. Marcie continued to operate his dry goods shop, more to have something to do and a meeting place for those who like herself, detested John Tunstall, than from financial necessity. Marcie was generally thought to be the richest person in town. It was she who contributed the bulk of the funds to erect the church. She was the leader of the Early temperance movement, such as it was, and the focus of

organized opposition to the mayor and all his 'peculiar' policies including the female marshal.

Nearing her fiftieth year, Marcie stood five foot five inches and as
ramrod straight as a first year West Point cadet on parade. She wore her
graying, curly blonde hair cut short. Her face was relatively unlined,
with pleasantly regular features, a well-sculpted nose, and icy blue
eyes. Her frame was spare and she carried little excess flesh, She had
large firm, round breasts of which she was proud, but kept them carefully concealed under dresses that came up to her throat as to not tempt
the weaker sex as she referred to men.

"She's an attractive woman," moaned Tunstall on many occasions. "If only she weren't such an intolerant, incorrigible, judg-
mental bitch."

At such times, Betsy who wasn't in Mrs. Cabot's good graces would sigh
and agree with him. "She'd like nothing better than to see you tarred,
feathered, and run out of town on a rail."

"And now," said Tunstall glumly. "With Rat Face and El Gordo
gone and Colonel Jessup busy frying other fish, people in Early
are complaisant. Mark my words Marcie will turn us out come
the next election sure as spring comes in March."

The Reverend Gilbert continued, "Mrs. Cabot passed by the death
house this morning. She heard a man screaming and throwing
things. Then she hid herself in a doorway and saw Gypsy walking
to the mayor's house with blood on her face and dress.

She followed the girl and saw the mayor open his door and let
her in. Then she returned to the death house."

"Reverend," said Betsy with some asperity. "Will you please
stop calling Gypsy's house the 'death house'? I know Gypsy's

just a whore, but according to accounts in that book you say is your life so was Mary Magdalene, and she was Jesus' best friend, so I'd appreciate it if you'd stop being so dramatic."

Gilbert didn't dislike Betsy at all. He liked her face and her strong character, which reminded him of the Biblical characters like Sara, Rebecca, Rachael, and Leah. If Marcie Cabot weren't so adamantly opposed to everything Betsy represented, he would have made an effort to know her better, but Marcie paid at least half of his salary, and she wasn't the sort of woman who'd allow him to forget it.

"Sorry, marshal," he said, and he meant it. Marcie had called it that primarily so she wouldn't have to sully her medium-full lips with Gypsy's name.

"By the time Mrs. Cabot returned, the door was open and she walked in and found Mr. Jones. She told him what she'd heard earlier and what she just witnessed. Mr. Jones showed her the room, and the body lying in a pool of blood, with his own Bowie knife jammed up to the hilt in his chest. Marcie and Mr. Jones came to the parsonage and we roused the town. We came here to demand that the mayor give up the murderer and take her to jail."

"Have you spoken with Mayor Tunstall?" asked Betsy.

"Mr. Jones and I went to the door and knocked but he didn't admit us. He opened the Judas Hole and told us to, 'Get the Hell off my property and mind your own damned business,' whereupon Mr. Jones demanded he give up the murderous," here Reverend Gilbert hesitated.

"It's alright Reverend, these ears of mine have heard worse, I'm sure. Don't pull any punches on my account."

The preacher smiled wanly, "Bitch," he said.

Then the mayor said, "Hal Russell fell on his own knife. Now get off my doorstep or I'll arrest you for trespass."

"You're shielding a cold blooded murderer," replied Mr. Jones.

As he finished saying this, I heard the sound of a Winchester being worked. Mr. Jones heard it as well and said, "You're not going to shoot us or intimidate us, besides the whole town's roused."

"Then to Hell with you and the whole town. Hal Russell was a vicious shit and he got what he deserved." Then he slammed the door in our faces. That was a few minutes before you and Rose rode up."

While Reverend Gilbert was talking to Betsy, Rose had gone to Jack Jones and was talking to him while Marcie Cabot was speaking with Doc Hill, and two other men, the owners of the livery stable and the general store.

"Gypsy's like my little sister," said Rose. "I couldn't bear for anything to happen to her."

"I understand," said Jack. "Listen to me. I've got nothing against the girl. She's always been real nice to me, but Hal was my partner and the way you feel about Gypsy I feel about Hal. If the quarrel ended with Hal stabbing Gypsy, if it were her body lying there buzzing with flies, a Bowie knife through her heart how would you feel? Now look me in the eye and tell me the truth."

Rose didn't want to think about it, Gypsy lying there instead of Hal. It was too sickening to comprehend or imagine.

"Picture the scene in your mind," said Hal his eyes boring into hers. "Makes you kinda' sick, doesn't it? So imagine how I feel."

He could'a tripped and stabbed himself."

"Who told you that?" he snorted with contempt. "Tunstall?"

"Well it's possible," Rose said hesitantly. "Isn't it?"

"It's possible Hal pulled a Juliet as in 'O' happy dagger this is thy sheath'," somehow I seriously doubt it. He wasn't even wearing boots and the throw rug wasn't mussed. You're telling me Hal rushed at Gypsy with his Bowie knife, holding it with the point facing him? That's the only way he could have fallen and driven it through his heart with his own knife in that impossible position? It's always point or edge away from the user, that's the rule, unless you're throwing your knife by the point, which I like to do. Hal wasn't as good with a blade as he was with his pistol, though he was no amateur, much less a clumsy man who'd fall on it."

Rose stood silently mulling over Jack's words. In her heart she knew Gypsy had killed Hal. Nevertheless, Gypsy was her friend, not Hal Russell, though if it were Gypsy lying dead, Rose would want nothing more than to see Hal Russell swing from the noose of a stout, hairy, hemp rope. Doc Hill excused himself, broke away from Marcie Cabot, and walked over to Reverend Gilbert and Betsy.

"Marshal," said the doctor, touching the brim of his fine dark brown Stetson hat with the sidewinder rattlesnake hatband by way of respectful greeting, "Am I glad to see you. If this goes on much longer things might get out of hand."

Betsy said sarcastically, "You mean like they did a little more than a year ago when the last town lynch mob tried to hang Deaf Charlie and his companion, both innocent? You, of all people, Reverend should remember the good Christian men and women of Early screaming for innocent blood."

Reverend Gilbert looked away from Betsy to the steeple of the church. He recalled the night all too vividly, and it was the lowest point in his life. He had led the mob. He was carrying a lantern. Behind him were most of the men and women of Early together with a number of girls and boys. The adults were armed with torches, shotguns, picks and shovels, all thirsty for godless, heathen Indian blood. They all saw Deaf Charlie as a rabid dog that needed to die. One man slung his lantern high so it would land on the wooden roof of City Hall, spilling its burning contents and hopefully burn it down while Mayor Tunstall and the Indians were inside. Betsy, or rather Joe Johnson as she was known then shot the lantern out of the sky before it struck the bone dry, sun-baked roof.

The reverend stopped looking at his church and looked directly at Betsy. "I can recall everything as if it were yesterday, and though a large part of me wants nothing more then to forget and erase all the details of my pusillanimous behavior, the 'better angels of my nature' to quote our martyred president, command me to keep my cowardly acquiescence before me as an exemplar of how not to act."

"No one wants to hang Gypsy," said Doc Hill. "Look around you. Do you see anyone ready to fire the mayor's house?"

Betsy looked around her at the faces and saw in them less of vengeance and more of curiosity as if the scene of the sidewalk was a public spectacle. All it needed was a few sellers of flags, patriotic red, white, and blue bunting, a few sparklers to make it into an election rally.

"Now I know you've sided with Tunstall in nearly every dispute and finding of the coroner's jury," said Doc Hill.

Betsy smiled, "So have you and you're on the jury, not I." "It's not that," said Doc Hill. "Jack Jones has a point when he says

Tunstall runs this town like it's his own private kingdom. He's an elected representative not an absolute monarch."

"He kept this town from lynching two innocent men. He risked, no it was more like he deliberately sacrificed his own life to save this town and for some reason the Good Lord chose not to take him. The two of you saw him come into church. I'd just confessed I was a woman though that wasn't all that important at the time. The real reason we were there was for a memorial service for John Tunstall. You saw with your own eyes when he walked in still bearing the marks of the explosion like Christ bore the stigmata. If Early ever has a patron saint it'll be Tunstall. No he's not a king but he'd make a damned good one."

"Alright," said Doc Hill. "Fine, Tunstall's a saint. You know as well as anyone that I love him as if he were my own brother, the one I left behind in Philadelphia."

He pointed with his right index finger at Jack Jones, who was listening intently to Rose. "That man there just lost his best friend and partner. Hal Russell's blood demands justice, not revenge. Notice I said justice."

"I noticed. Alright, let's you and me talk with his honor." Betsy addressed this specifically to Doc Hill and not to Reverend Gilbert, who looked slightly nettled at being excluded. Rose and Jack Jones walked over to where Betsy and the others were standing.

"Pardon me, Marshal," said Jones. "I know you and the mayor are close, just like Rose and Gypsy are close, and Hal and I were close. The question I have is given all these close relationships how am I going to get justice for Hal? All this stuff the mayor's been trying to convince Rose of like how Hal fell on his own knife, tripped on a bare plank floor in the morning when he was sober no less. Well it just doesn't wash or hold water. Somebody stuck that Wostenholm Bowie in Hal's chest, buried it up to its German silver knuckle-guard."

To illustrate his version of events, Jack reached down into his right boot and drew out the matching pair to Hal's Bowie. The blade was two inches across, a good eighth of an inch thick, keen as a razor with a needle sharp point. Jack indicated the stout German silver guard that protruded nearly half an inch on either side of the ricasso.

"You'll see, Marshal. The knife is buried at an angle up to the hilt. It couldn't have been an accident."

"Was he face down or face up when you found him?" asked Betsy.

"Face down," said Jack and Rose nodded her agreement.

"So falling down could have driven the blade in that deep. I mean the weight of a falling body and all, plus that knife looks really sharp. Probably shaves hair."

"Yes, it does, but the thing is both his arms were fully extended and the fingers were splayed out not clutching the knife."

"Did you do anything to the body?"

"I turned him over, closed his eyes, and folded his arms across his chest. That's the least I could do for him."

"Still, he could have fallen on the Bowie," said Betsy crisply."

"If the Bowie knife was sticking up, point first, out of the floor all by itself, and Hal tripped, he could have fallen on it, and it still wouldn't have been at an angle. The knife would have gone straight in, more or less, and even if all that had happened, Hal would probably have lived for a while. As it was, the blade went in just under the lowest rib directly into the heart. It had to be deliberate, couldn't be accidental. The Doc here will tell you just like he told me," said Jack.

Facing Betsy, the doctor hemmed and hawed for a moment, shuffling his black, patent leather shoe in the dust, betraying his uneasiness at having to tell Betsy what he'd told Jones. "The angle of the thrust would seem to militate against it being accidental, though it is possible, just highly unlikely. From the amount of blood on the floor, the point of the knife pierced the heart. I would not be surprised to find the body almost entirely exsanguinated."

"I wish you hadn't moved the body around," said Betsy. The worst I can see in it is a simple case of self—defense."

Jack's face turned bright red as he exploded, "Self-defense? You're telling me a man gets stabbed through the heart while still in his drawers, unarmed, and it's self-defense? We'll see how the circuit judge in Santa Fe thinks about it. You and Tunstall think you run this town, but we'll see!"

Jack finished his tirade, just as Marcie Cabot walked up.

"Marshal," she said in a commanding tone. "I demand that you go into that house and arrest that, that, girl for this most foul and heinous murder." Marcie's icy blue eyes were flashing daggers at Betsy. She added, "That silver badge you're wearing demands you uphold the law."

"Mrs. Cabot, begging your pardon ma'am, you're doing an awful lot of demanding here. You might recall the last time you and Reverend Gilbert were demanding justice from Judge Lynch."

This would have given pause to anyone other than Marcie Cabot who blamed Tunstall for everything she thought was wrong with the New Mexico Territory. She characterized him as an 'Indian loving, heathen degenerate' amongst other things. Betsy's reminder left Marcie unabashed. "If you don't arrest that girl, the town council will deputize as many men as we need to do the job."

This was complicated, as the council consisted of Reverend Gilbert. Enoch Swank, Doc Hill, and the owner of the general store Mr. Rindge. Tunstall could count on the support of Swank and Hill, while Gilbert was tied firmly to Marcie Cabot, and Rindge usually went along with the preacher. The result of the split was that except for the most innocuous issues, not much was ever decided by the council so Tunstall ruled by executive order.

Betsy sensed a change in Doc Hill. Somehow Marcie had gotten to him, although she didn't have a vague clue as to just how she'd done it. During the past year, Doc Hill had voted in lockstep with the apothecary, now with Hill supporting Jones, that state of affairs seemed to be changing. Betsy devoutly wished Enoch were in town, for it seemed that Marcie's threat to deputize the men needed to arrest Gypsy was no idle one and the council might vote three to zero in favor of the emergency deputies. If this were a card game it could be said that Marcie had called Betsy's bluff.

Chapter 13
THE MAYOR OF EARLY

"Child," said Doc Hill to Gypsy, "You have at least three broken ribs." The doctor's first concern upon being admitted to Tunstall's home was to examine Gypsy and make sure she didn't have any life-threatening internal injuries. As a consequence, he was abrupt with the mayor, greeting him with a nod and a brisk, "Where is she?" to which Tunstall replied, "In the sunroom."

"Are you sure you haven't coughed up any blood?" he asked her. "No," said Gypsy.

Doc Hill reached into his breast pocket and extracted a clean, white silk handkerchief.

"I want you to hawk as deeply as you can. Yes I know it hurts but there's no help for it right now, and spit into the cloth."

Gypsy couldn't put too much pressure on her ribs. Now that he mentioned it, they did feel broken, and she'd heard them crunch under Hal's heel. She did her best and spit into the silk. The physician unfolded it and held it up in the light, scrutinizing the wet spot minutely. There was a small blotch of gunny phlegm and a more amorphous stain of spittle tinged bright pink.

"See," he said, as if he'd just won an argument. "There's the blood. One of the ribs must have poked the lung and caused hemorrhaging. Fortunately there's no major damage or the sputum would be bright red. I say fortunate because aside from applying a compression bandage to keep the ribs in place while they heal since they can't really be set like an arm or a leg; they'll generally heal themselves in a month or two, especially being as you're young and strong the bones will knit together relatively quickly."

He bunched up the handkerchief, heedless of Gypsy's sputum, and stowed it in the capacious right pocket of his black, cotton-twill suit. He proceeded to bring his face close to Gypsy's and touched the ugly bruise on her cheekbone gently with his thumb and forefinger. His breath smelled of tobacco and peppermint, not altogether unpleasant, and Gypsy noticed his fingernails were filed short and unusually clean. Gypsy was quite particular about the hands of the men who touched her in the private rooms at the saloon. She always kept a cake of rose-scented soap near two boar bristle brushes with maple-wood backs and insisted on men using them before she took off her chemise and exposed her pert, pink nipples.

Her face was tender to the touch and she involuntarily pulled away from the doctor' fingers at first as he ever so tenderly palpated the bone beneath.

"That's good," he said. "I didn't think the cheekbone was fractured from looking at your eyes, but it's best to make sure. You may look like a raccoon for a week, but the bruising isn't as pronounced as it would be if the underlying bone were broken. Like the ribs, a cheekbone really can't be set. Best to avoid breaking the bones of the face other than a nose or a jaw. A jaw, I can wire into place, uncomfortable as all Hell for the patient, now a nose," here he smiled as if it were pleasing to him just to contemplate setting a fractured nose, "broken noses are a specialty of mine. Reset it with your fingers, pack a little cotton in the nostrils maybe a little sticking plaster and voila, good as new."

All the while he was examining Gypsy, Betsy and Tunstall were seated in the dining room catty corner from each other at the south end of the table.

"So you think Gypsy should be arrested and taken to Santa Fe to stand trial for murder? Betsy, I don't believe I'm hearing this from you."

Betsy fixed her green eyes on him, "If you have a better idea that won't bring the sheriff down from Santa Fe to take her I'd be happy to hear it. Better I should take her than she go in shackles and leg-irons with murderers and thieves in the sheriff's wagon, caged like an animal."

"Better if Early's coroner's jury finds Hal Russell died by misadventure or by self-defense and that ends it."

Betsy took Tunstall's large, warm right hand in hers and looked into his eyes even more earnestly than she had been doing. "Tunstall, I'm on your side, you know that. Hal Russell was a dirty, rotten son-of-a-bitch, we know that. He'd have beaten up or killed the wrong woman sooner or later and gotten his just deserts. It's a shame it had to be Gypsy instead of some senhorita or her caballero down in Monterrey. I love that you see women as human beings and not just some man's chattel to be abused as he sees fit. Unfortunately very few men are like you. In Early there's you and Enoch Swank, and maybe Doc Hill. Sure there's Ernesto and Deaf Charlie but they're the exceptions and Indians. If you and Enoch try to sweep this under the rug there'll Hell to pay. Jack Jones and Marcie Cabot, together with Reverend Gilbert will go straight to the governor and tell him how you fixed it so a murdering whore who stabbed her lover to death went free. It's the type of story that'll get in the papers. The question will be whether the governor believes you or them.

191

Tunstall sighed, "It's worse than that. Colonel Jessup has power-ful friends in the capital, and they would be only too happy to have me arrested and charged with malfeasance in office, conspiracy, and God only knows what else. Next thing you know it'll be one of Jessup's men, probably Stephen Willis who's appointed interim mayor until a special election. Damn-it-all! There must be some way out of this that doesn't burn down our house so to speak."

"You've had a whole morning to think of something."

"Do you think Gypsy's self-defense argument can hold water?"

Betsy thought about it and shook her head. "If Hal had cut up her face, slashed off one of her breasts, or better yet shot her twice and crippled her so the jury could see she was ruined for life, then maybe, just maybe, twelve men of the Territory might see her being justified in sticking him like a pig."

"But Russell was involved in that Wells Fargo hold-up. Two guards were killed."
"Rose told me all about it and one of the gang made a death-bed confession just before they hanged him saying Jack and Hal were less than willing parties, and you can be sure Jones has a copy he'll read to the jury. Besides, Jones is going back to California to clear his name. He's not some ignorant cow-puncher and robbery or no robbery he'll be a credible witness."

"Gypsy's all beaten-up. I'll have photographs taken."

"By the time she's tried, her bruises will be long gone. You can be sure Marcie will insist on photographs of Hal lying there in a room that according to Rose looks like a slaughterhouse. Those photographs will impress twelve men one Hell of a lot more than a whore with a shiner. Most men think a black eye is good for a woman once in a while. Keeps 'em in line. Point being is there anyone on that jury going to sympathize with a teen-age whore? A girl who had a bastard child, deserted it, left a good home in Houston? You and I know that's not the truth. You of all people know that the first casualty in a courtroom is the truth. No one cares about the truth. It's whoever has the prettiest case."

Tunstall put his left elbow on the table and cradled his forehead in the fingers and palm of his left hand. He hadn't eaten anything more than a bowl of oatmeal since the previous evening, though he had drunk two large Meissen cups full of coffee. He was hungry and would have liked nothing more than tucking into a half inch think slice of bone in ham, pan-fried in butter. He hated the claustrophobic, suffocating feeling of being checkmated in any given situation, and when he was younger the helplessness and frustration would erupt into a spectacular demonstration of physical violence directed at any physical objects within the reach of his powerful hands.

He took his hand back from Betsy's and laced his fingers together prefatory to cracking his knuckles, then stopped himself knowing that Betsy thought it was a disgusting habit. She saw him relax his fingers just as they reached the curve when the fluid in the joints would begin what was to her an obscene popping. She knew he'd refrained only for her sake and that otherwise he would have taken great solace in the cracking.

"I love you Tunstall," she said softly.

He brightened for a moment then relapsed into contemplation. "What if I offered to resign as mayor effective immediately? Do you think Marcie would agree to abide by the coroner's verdict?

"She might at that. Gypsy and Hal Russell aren't important to her."

"That leaves Jack Jones."

Betsy sighed, "It's not just Jack Jones, half of Early is in the street outside your gate, or in your front courtyard like it's July Fourth. The Jinni's out of the bottle, and you and Enoch are going to have the Devil of a time making him fit back in. If Gypsy's room is half as bloody as everyone says it is, all that gore is going to want some justice." Betsy waited a minute for this to sink in. "And it won't want Betsy Johnson, Enoch Swank, or **J.W.** Tunstall justice. To most men and women too our kind of justice looks like soft-heartedness and soft-headedness, like Indian-loving, nigger-loving, Mexican-loving, whore-loving, and everything else the white European men and women of the Territory look upon as Satan's handiwork. No, the kind of justice that blood demands is either to lock the little whore up until her blonde hair turns gray, her pretty face looks like a prune, her little tits droop, or better still, see her pretty neck stretched right now and send a message to every whore in the New Mexico Territory. Make 'em think twice about stabbing the man who knocks 'em around."

"You say my resignation will satisfy Marcie Cabot. What if I gave Jack Jones five hundred dollars? Do you think he'd go back to Sacramento and forget all about this?"

Betsy was shocked, "One where would you get five hundred dollars? Two there'd be folks in town who'd say you paid money to conceal a murder."

Tunstall flushed as his heart rate increased and he felt butter-flies in his belly. "Betsy Johnson, am I not hearing you correctly or am I looking at a woman I don't really know, or both? Gypsy is a young girl who's never had a break in her life that wasn't her neck, and you damn well know it. If Francine weren't Hal Russell's wife, I would have met him outside of town for a little duel for what he did to her, and if he declined I would have beaten him ten times as badly as he beat Francine. And you know good and Goddamned well I've never partaken of either girl's favors, not because I think I'm too good for them, but because I'm one of those fools that likes a little romance with my loving. Twenty-five years ago it wasn't as important when the sap was flowing in me that thick and strong I could hang a Turkish bathrobe from my member, like it was a coat peg. Your face and eyes are accusing me of condoning murder, when we both know it's a certainty he would have killed Gypsy if she hadn't stabbed him first!"

Two large tears formed at the inside corners of Betsy's green eyes and slowly detached themselves from her long, light brown eyelashes and made their way down each side of her slightly upturned nose.

"I'm sorry if you thought I was against you. I'm anything but. I love you and I don't want to see you stake everything you stand for and believe in so lightly on Gypsy's say-so. Don't get me wrong. I like Gypsy. She's my friend. She's also a very young girl, who has, as you say, spent a lot of time in the school of hard knocks. I've been to that school and so have you. The teachers are real pricks, but their lessons once learned stick with you. And if you fail and get expelled, you die and it's over. The price of tuition's high though classes are open to all. Men, women, children, Indians, Negroes, it's what you call open enrollment. Gypsy's an honor's graduate. What do you expect her to say? 'I was afraid Hal might kill me so I killed him first?' You know that's what happened. The question isn't whether Hal Russell was God's gift to women. We both know he wasn't. It's did he deserve to die not for what he did to Gypsy this morning or what he did to Francine a couple of weeks ago? Did he deserve to die for what he was going to do to her? You say you would have shot him dead in a duel for what he did to Francine. John Tunstall, you're a knight out of his time, just like my father. You two should have lived in King Arthur's time, Knights of the Round Table, rescuing damsels in distress from fire breathing dragons. Don't get me wrong. I loved my father for it like I've loved President Lincoln all my life, though he died when I was a little girl. We had a shrine to him, complete with candles that we lit every night in front of his picture."

Betsy had strong memories of Josiah and Lincoln, whom her father revered above all men, even more than Jesus, not that he ever told anyone. Josiah knew that Lincoln, like Jesus who took on the burden of sin for all men, assumed some measure of personal responsibility for each and every one of the hundreds of thousands of Union and Confederate soldiers killed and wounded, and only Abraham Lincoln did it without Divine assistance or certainty. Josiah had seen more than one of the personal letters, the president sometimes wrote to the widows of soldiers felled by disease or killed in action. The letters were always brief, but in those few lines Lincoln made it obvious that he felt the loss keenly, that his empathy was not spurious and that the loved one had not died in vain. When Josiah learned of the assassination two days after the tragedy which coincidentally occurred on Good Friday, April 14th 1865, he wept so hard and without stopping that Betsy feared her father might go mad. Betsy was just shy of ten at the time, her mother Sara having died in childbirth together with her stillborn brother almost a year to the day after Josiah came home from the Army hospital in Pennsylvania.

Betsy smiled as the tears continued to well up in her eyes and stream down her cheeks.

"Men like you, my father, and President Lincoln are too strong and too principled. There's always a klansman, a John Wilkes Booth, or a Colonel Jessup ready to take you down."

Tunstall was about to demur and say he was hardly in Lincoln's league when Doc Hill walked in, took one look at Betsy's tear swollen face and said, "I'm sorry, I didn't mean to intrude on a private conversation."

"No, no, please sit down," said Betsy in a more husky voice than usual.

"So, Ike, what did dear Mr. Russell do to the woman he loved?" The doctor looked first at Tunstall then at Betsy. "The girl has at least three broken ribs, a facial lacerations, edema, and pulmonary abrasions. She's also scared half to death."

"Do you think any of her injuries put her life in danger?" asked Betsy. He shook his head.

"Although broken ribs take time to heal." Tunstall said, "I have two questions. One is, could Hal Russell have tripped and fallen on his own knife? The second is are you willing to rule his death an accident?"

Ike Hill was a man who had just turned forty. He had practiced medicine in Chicago, after graduating from the University of Virginia. He was driven to the Midwest by his revulsion with the Southern attitude toward Negroes, which didn't change much in the wake of the Civil War and in some circumstances actually deteriorated. He liked Chicago; however after a few years the brutality of the winters and the blistering summer heat proved too much for him. After one February, which saw more than four feet of snow falling on the city he sold his practice and bought a ticket to Santa Fe.

The good doctor had suffered considerable abuse in Virginia for what one stalwart son of the South referred to as his "soft, nigger—loving heart." It was that 'soft' heart that led him to tend to the broken bones of Negro children gratis, much to the chagrin of his fellow students. He was mercilessly derided for his veneration of Lincoln by his fellows at school who thought John Wilkes Booth a hero.

In Santa Fe, he met any number of miserably impoverished Indians and these too he treated without regard to payment. He moved to Early in response to Mayor Tunstall's advertisement in the newspaper seeking a physician for Early. He accepted the position partly because of the town's proximity to the Mescalero Reservation. At least once a week, he would ride to the reservation and he and the Apache Indian medicine men would see the sick and minister to their needs. He and the Apache healers were in agreement that a well ventilated, clean, and properly situated permanent structure taking advantage of the sunlight would be of great benefit to the Indians as a lying in hospital. The Indian Department in Washington never replied directly to his repeated requests for funds, referring him to Colonel Jessup or in the alternative, the Bishop of Santa Fe.

Hearing of his failures in a heated denunciation of the administration of Rutherford B. Hayes, who was continuing the disastrous neglect of legitimate treaty obligations toward the Apaches, begun under the Grant Administration, Marcie Cabot, who had come to see him with a laceration of her left thumb that required two sutures, suggested she might be interested in funding the hospital, provided it was named for her late husband. Ike lunged at the bait like a starving perch. In the succeeding months, she led him on, asking him for drawings, cost of materials, and the like.

She had no objection to the hospital as long as it was part of a Christian chapel. She omitted this caveat when speaking with him, knowing as she did of the Apache's antagonism to white man's preaching in general and to Reverend Gilbert's in particular. The Apache would never forgive the reverend for leading a lynch mob and attempting to hang Deaf Charlie. It was excellent leverage on Doctor Hill, and Marcie took full advantage of it, making in clear he would have to choose between his loyalty to Mayor Tunstall and the hospital. The doctor was torn. Tunstall was his good friend, but the hospital meant more to him than anything and if he were forced to sacrifice their close friendship for the even greater good of the hospital then so be it. The mayor knew of his friend's temporary defection to the Cabot camp, the reasons behind it, and though his feelings were wounded by it, he had said nothing partly out of pride, and also the distinct possibility that Marcie would actually follow through with the money, which would significantly benefit people on the reservation, whom Tunstall wanted to help very badly as their need was desperate.

The doctor had nothing against Gypsy. To him, she was a young woman with an unfortunate past, a not to happy present, and a dismal future, even before Hal Russell's untimely demise. It was a rare prostitute that retired from a career as a 'sporting woman' to a normal life of being a wife and mother, though such transitions weren't unheard of. Usually as their looks faded and their bodies thickened, they continued to live lives on the fringes of society, easy prey to drink or opium, living with men who were truly the dregs of civilization, suffering physical and mental degradation until an early death usually from disease came as a blessed relief. He was sympathetic to Gypsy's plight, and thought she was good-hearted, though he believed she stabbed Hal Russell. Not that he questioned her about it. There was simply no other reasonable explanation other than a suicide in which Russell placed the tip of the Bowie just beneath the ribcage, and taking the hilt in both hands, thrust upward, burying seven inches of Sheffield steel in his chest, and piercing his heart in the process. He said as much to Tunstall and Betsy.

"You say it took tremendous strength to bury the blade so deeply in the chest cavity," said Tunstall. "Does Gypsy strike you as a tremendously strong girl?"

Doc Hill didn't hesitate, "No she doesn't. But in times of great stress a relatively frail woman, or even a child is capable of extraordinary feats of strength. I knew of a woman who would have had trouble lifting a twenty-pound sledgehammer, whose husband was pinned under a tree that must have weighed half a ton. She lifted one end, mind you it was nearly two feet in diameter, and he dragged himself free. Gypsy was undoubtedly terrified and in fear for her life, and yes she could have done it."

"Are you certain he couldn't have stumbled?" asked Betsy.

"Anything is possible including the suicide though it's equally unlikely given the fact the knife was buried up to the hilt and the angle of the thrust. There are only two people who could tell us the true story and one of them isn't talking "So," said Tunstall, "What you're telling me is that I couldn't persuade you to bring in a verdict of accidental death because of the circumstances." He paused and looked directly into the doctor's hazel eyes, "And because Marcie Cabot has a hatred of prostitutes."

If Tunstall had slapped him across the face it would have stung him less viciously. Betsy stood speechless and stared at the mayor. After Enoch Swank, Ike Hill was Tunstall's best friend, and after Hill, the list of friends not including Indians, Mexicans, and women became very short. Hill was held in esteem not only by the white citizens of Early who regardless of their poverty constituted the town's aristocracy such as it was, but by the outcasts as well. He stood there bereft of speech at Tunstall's impugning his integrity.

Completely unashamed, Tunstall continued, "If a poor, young, friendless whore has to be sacrificed to build the Henry Cabot Reservation Hospital, a building that will dispense less of healing and more of the Cabot, 'God is an elderly white man and all those who don't bow down and worship him and his white son will burn in Hell for all eternity' religion than so be it. I could understand it coming from someone else, but coming form you, Ike Hill, it's very hard, and sticks in my craw like a fishbone."

"I'll tell you what's hard," said the doctor reddening. "Being accused of selling out by my friend. Everyone in Early has put up with your arrogant, iconoclastic rule as mayor, because you saved the town from being wiped out." He nodded to Betsy, "Excuse me, you, the marshal here, Deaf Charlie, Ben, and some other Indians, but I'll grant that it was you who dropped the lantern and set off the nitroglycerin, or was it dynamite, with Rat Face's gun on you the whole time. Early is the most eccentric town in the entire Territory, not that I personally object to a woman marshal, whores owning saloons, Indians being served whiskey and beer like white men, wife-beaters being fined and jailed, and a hundred other unusual practices," He paused to gather his breath, "Nevertheless, even you must admit you run this town less like an elected official and more like a benevolent despot, making civic life reflect your own private notion of how life should be."

Tunstall smiled, "I admit I believe in the Declaration of Independence one Hell of a lot more than I believe in the Constitution. If the Declaration were the law of the land there wouldn't have been any slaves and the country would be much better off. Let's cut to the chase, shall we? If you're willing to rule Russell's death was self-defense, I'll resign my office as soon as you sign the death certificate. You'll get your hospital. And," he added without a trace of acrimony or sarcasm, "Early will no longer reflect my eccentric values like 'all men and women are created equal, endowed by the Creator with certain unalienable Rights, Life, Liberty, and the Pursuit of Happiness

"That's all well and good," said the doctor. "You left out the part about 'Governments deriving their powers from the consent of the governed.'"

"Fine," said Tunstall. "Say the word and Tunstall's Reign of Terror is ended."
"You're assuming Enoch will go along with my verdict. That's a trifle presumptuous wouldn't you say?"

"Alright, I'll go you one better. If you agree and Enoch doesn't, I'll still resign. I'll sit down and write it out now and sign it effective immediately if it makes a difference. You can take it outside to Marcie."

"I wish you'd stop talking as if I am Marcie Cabot's factotum."

"Well in a way you are," Tunstall walked to Doc Hill and stood in front of him. "Listen, you're completely misjudging me. I don't presume to judge you and if you can save one Indian child from cholera or blood poisoning, that's much more important than me being mayor, or my having to listen to Gilbert tell people I'm sliding down the slippery slope to eternal damnation. If Marcie Cabot can buy enough votes to elect a temperance man mayor, I'll just drink at home and to Hell with it. I don't care what she does. I would like to know why a prude and a prig like Marcie displays a Parisian dress that makes anything Rose or Gypsy ever wears look modest, in her shop window."

Doc Hill no longer felt as if he were under siege. Tunstall's comment about the dress, indicated better than anything he could have said that hostilities were at an end.

"Marcie Cabot isn't averse to making money. She knows that dress attracts business, and it's good advertising. As long as no one wears it in her mind it's not obscene, to her mind. It costs more than a good thoroughbred so it's not likely anyone's going to buy it."

"I suppose it shows that underneath that narrow-minded, Bible-thumping, tight-laced exterior, there might be a small kernel of human weakness."

The doctor smiled, "Just so."

Tunstall smiled back, "Ike if I didn't know better, I'd say you find her attractive."

Betsy spoke up, "You two are forgetting all about Gypsy. The poor girl's been alone for nearly an hour."

Both men hung their heads like guilty children. Doc Hill had no objection whatsoever to signing a verdict of self-defense, though he would never agree to accidental death. He didn't know if Marcie could stomach Gypsy going free even if Tunstall did step down,

"Before we go into see Gypsy," said Ike, "Let me see if I can talk Marcia into going along with the plan. Then even if she does there's still Jones."

"I think Jones might prefer a well-filled purse to the profitless pursuit of vengeance against Rose's best friend. I would if I were in his boots."

"You would not," said Betsy. "I've listened to enough of both of your sanctimonious driveling, quoting the Declaration and deciding Gypsy's fate like God Almighty. If Hal Russell were your best friend and partner, either of you would do your damnedest to see Gypsy punished to the fullest extent of the law. That being said I believe Gypsy was in fear for her life, I know I was when I was attacked. If I could have, I would have taken a Bowie and driven it through the bastard's heart."

As Betsy finished saying this, there was a depth of emotion in her voice and her manner that left neither man in the slightest doubt as to her utter sincerity, and then there was a thunderous knocking on Tunstall's massive front door that reverberated throughout the house.

Tunstall said, "I think we'd best see who is the author of that gentle rapping, rapping at my chamber door."

The booming began again, this time for a longer period.

"You two go attend to Gypsy for a moment, while I go see who's trying to break down my door."

"No," said Betsy. "I'm going with you."

"Me, too," said Ike.

As they made their way through the house, Tunstall picked up his gilt frame 1866 Winchester rifle from inside the doorway of his bedroom.

Chapier 13
ENOCH AND FRANCINE
RETURN

Francine and Enoch rode slowly toward Early with occasional glances over their shoulders at the fiery, orange ball of the summer desert sun as it began to set, tipping the summits of the mountains to the East with gold. The air was still reminiscent of a baking oven, and shimmering waves of heated air distorted their long range views of the sage brush and creosote and mesquite that filled the banks of the arroyos. Two hawks were circling on the afternoon thermals, searching for ground squirrels, and the hooves of their horses crunched the hard, dry-baked soil, an they walked side by side, close enough for Enoch to reach out and hold Francine's extended left one from time to time, in an unspoken communication, whose very silence perhaps rendered it more intimate and eloquent than any words could have done.

Enoch's long fingers were expressive and he had been entirely content to entwine them with Francine's as their naked bodies had on the thick, verdant, emerald green grass of the meadow. At first Francine did not respond to his lovemaking as unreservedly as he had to hers, Francine had apologized with tears in her eyes.

"I need time," she said as he kissed away her tears. "It's not you, it's me. Hal Russell, the years of being a whore, as much as I want to erase it all this afternoon for your sake, believe me I want to with all my heart, only it's not that easy."

"I understand," said Enoch. "I know for a fact I couldn't do it. I want you to be just who you are, beautiful, sensitive, and intelligent, you make it easy for me. Then, again, I suppose I've loved you from a distance for quite some time. And here I left St. Louis to busy myself in herb lore and Indian shamanism to escape women, only to meet the true love of my life. Without you I would have lived out my existence here content to learn the secrets of the Apache, Navajo, Hopi, and Pima healers, write a book or two, and bury my heart's desires in caring for the afflicted. Call it fate, destiny, or karma as the Hindu's and Buddhist's do, the patterns of life are wondrous, and the older I become the less I believe in chance, luck, or coincidence, and the more convinced I am that there is some purpose, some method to what happens to us, not just men, but all living things from locusts to whales."

Francine laughed and once again Enoch was awestruck by her unalloyed joy. He heard more enchanting music in her laughter than in most of the violin and piano recitals he'd attended in St. Louis, and he enjoyed Chopin and Beethoven very much.

"So what you're saying is that it wasn't chance that led me to your shop just after dawn."

"Have you ever walked by my shop at dawn?"

"I don't know, now that you mention it."

"I came in the shop early this morning for the first time in months. This is yet another reason I have almost completely erased the word accident from my vocabulary. I'm no Calvinist who believes everything we do is pre-destined from birth and there's no such thing as free will. I'm saying that very little in our lives, if anything, takes place by accident. All life is a tapestry and it's hard for one of us, being no more than a thread or a knot in the grand design, in the warp and woof of all existence to see the purpose responsible for your coming to my shop at dawn and finding me there for the first time in months with the door open."

Francine made the delicious discovery that Enoch's intellect was nearly as sexy as Luis' smooth skinned youthful muscular body. Either that or she'd matured enough to appreciate them both for the pleasures they offered. She lay on her back, naked, looking up at the puffy white clouds floating in a sky so blue it looked lacquered. The sun was too intense to lie naked and exposed for too long. Enoch didn't want Francine's breasts, her taut white belly, or her cream colored thighs to burn, so they both dressed after a half hour of passionate lovemaking and fondling. The meadow was high enough to take the edge of the heat, though Enoch told her the sun's rays would burn human skin more rapidly at a higher altitude, and though temperature had something to do with it just because it was cooler up in the meadow than down in the desert, that didn't mean they couldn't be sunburned.

"A little redness is one thing, but a real burn is painful. As you may see from my face and my arms, I spend a great deal of time in the sun."

Enoch's face was as tanned and brown and dark as Ben's or Deaf Charlie's. His chest and back were tanned to a dark golden color for he often went shirtless on his forays for desert plants. Francine was amused to notice that Enoch's rather small, tightly muscled buttocks were as milky white as her own more shapely rounded bottom.

They entered the town just before the onset of real twilight when moths and the other flying insects began their nightly dances of death in and around the newly lit oil lamps outside the saloon. Francine wasn't the least bit concerned about the saloon being able to survive perfectly well without her for the day. She hadn't mentioned it once except in passing during the entire day. Instead she talked about the meadow and how magical it was, the amazing water of the spring, and how she'd never in her wildest dreams, she'd ever again have a day as wonderful as the one she was having.

"Francine," said Enoch, shortly before they left the valley of the spring, "One of the things I really admire about you is your ability to live in the moment. Here you are, sole proprietor of the saloon and you act as if it doesn't exist."

"Why, are you worried about Swank's Apothecary?"

"No. If there's an emergency, I left a note saying I'd be back before dark or see Doc Hill."

"And I've got Rose and Gypsy to open the saloon which they've done before together and separately. See, we're both the same in this. Responsible, yet as you say, in the moment."

"As the philosopher once said, Carpe diem."

"What's that mean?" asked Francine.

"It means 'seize the day'. In other words recognize the truism learned the hard way by King Canute that 'time and tide wait for no man.'"

"Oh, Enoch, you know so much. How can an unschooled, ignorant girl like me possibly be of interest to a learned man like you?"

Enoch was about to answer that her beauty was so transcendent, the question of the difference in their respective educations was irrelevant as stated in the ancient Roman adage, "Amor vincere omnes"; however the sincerity with which Francine made her comment precluded such a facile reply.

"Francine," Enoch said gently. "The very fact you ask such a question reveals your intelligence. People commonly confuse education and book learning with wisdom and intellect. I have met many so-called learned men who were woefully ignorant and others who'd never seen the inside of a school, much less a college, who were very wise. The greatest medicine man on the reservation neither reads or writes more than a few words of English, yet he expresses himself with a wit and eloquence that makes him the nearly the equal of Lincoln, and though he can't read a dime novel, he can read the night sky as well or better as any Harvard astronomer. And unlike the Harvard doctor who would die in the mountains, the old Apache can follow a deer's trail or lead you to a she bear's den. More importantly he can do what few men can do and that is to show you the lines of power that crisscross the earth, and if he deems you worthy, he can show you how to tap into this power for the good, to find the plants that heal in their proper season. Is this dried up, nearly black man with six teeth in his head a Harvard man? No he isn't but I have learned more from him and hold him in higher esteem than the president of Princeton. Don't denigrate yourself on my account because you lack some artificially acquired qualities you imagine I admire in a woman. You are independent, with a genuine integrity most people only wish they had. And," he smiled, showing his even white teeth, "You're lovely as the sunrise."

Enoch and Francine passed the mayor's house, City Hall, the church, and the livery stable. They reached the saloon, dismounted, took of their horses' headstalls, put on their horsehair bridles, and tied the lead-ropes loosely enough to let the animals drink from the long lozenge shaped, wooden water-trough.

"Do you have any feed in the saloon?" asked Enoch.

"Yes," said Francine. "I'll have Ellen's Man bring them each a feed-bag."

"They deserve a good bran mash for all the work they did today."
"I couldn't agree more," said Francine.

Enoch could smell the tantalizing aroma of beef being cooked over a mesquite wood fire, and though the cold beef sandwiches they'd eaten at the spring were delicious, they'd ridden far and loved away the afternoon, and suddenly he was ravenously hungry.

He and Francine entered through the squeaking batwing door not hand in hand but nearly side by side. Betsy, Tunstall, Ben, and Sara were finishing with their supper. Rose was behind the bar polishing a glass with a clean, damp, cotton rag, prefatory to drawing a beer for one of Deaf Charlie's numerous cousins, who was seated on a stool all by himself, staring peacefully off into space as he waited. Betsy and the mayor got up from the table quickly though not as fast as Rose. Ben and Sara remained seated, the Indian over his beer, and Sara over a baked apple with cream and melted brown sugar courtesy of the neighboring boarding house, whose owner, the widow Page, was very fond of her.

Francine and Enoch stood a few paces inside the swinging door facing the four, who looked at each other, none of them really knowing just where to begin, though each one had given much thought to what he or she was going to say, when the two of them finally returned from their outing.

A chill ran down Francine's back and her stomach was uneasy. This was hardly the smiling, enthusiastic homecoming she'd anticipated coming in as she did, practically arm in arm with Enoch Swank, after spending the entire day alone with the popular apothecary. All of them looked deadly serious, as if she'd done something wrong.

"What's wrong?" Francine inquired of no one in particular. Betsy said quietly, "Francine, honey, I think you'd better sit down."

Though Betsy intended for her words to be comforting they were anything but. Francine thought, "One of Duffy's relations has claimed the saloon." Then she thought,

"There's a warrant out for my arrest," though she couldn't think of anything she'd done to be arrested for. Then it came to her, "It's Hal. He's killed Gypsy!" she screamed.

This last thought wasn't silent. It came out quite loud almost as a shriek.

"No," said Betsy calmly in a steady voice, "It's Hal who's dead."

Francine put her right fist up to her mouth as Enoch reached for the closest chair, which he slid around her back, and she sat down heavily. Francine was surprised at how miserable Betsy's news made her feel. Though she'd never loved Hal with the wild, frantic, all-consuming passion she shared with Luis, or the deep abiding affection she was beginning to develop with Enoch, she'd shared a marriage bed and a year of her life with Hal, and at age twenty-two, a year was a large portion of her adult life. Tears streamed down her face of their own volition as if her body and her mind were processing Hal's death in two entirely different ways. She was shivering though it was a warm evening and Enoch took off his jacket and draped it over her shoulders. She put it on, grateful for the warmth. Tunstall offered her a clean white silk handkerchief, and she took it with a trembling right hand and dabbed at her eyes.

"This is ridiculous," she thought. "Hal Russell nearly beat me to death more than once, and here I am crying over him like he was good to me. Damned sentimental bullshit! He was a dirty bastard and that's that."

"I'm sorry," she said in a voice choked by her swollen throat. "Rose, get me a shot of Kentucky whiskey, not the rye, the bourbon. And serve Deaf Charlie's cousin while you're up." This last was said in her usual tone. "Poor man shouldn't have to wait on me."

Francine reached up to Enoch who took the proffered hand in his own.

"Francine waited for Rose to return with four fingers of caramel colored Kentucky bourbon in a squat glass. Francine disengaged her hand from Enoch's, looked at the brownish liquid with an appraising eye, and downed half of it in one swallow. The fiery liquor burned its way down her esophagus and the chill that had gripped her since she heard of Hal's death vanished almost immediately as she'd hoped it would, and the cold was replaced by a warmth that centered in her belly and spread out up into her arms and down into her legs. She offered the rest of the glass to Enoch, whose initial impulse was to decline but then he took it with a smile and drained it at one go as a gesture of solidarity if nothing else, though he could easily have done without it. Francine took his hand once more and Enoch fancied it was indeed warmer.

Doc Hill, though by no means as gifted in medicine as Enoch was in pharmacy, was far from incompetent as a physician or an intellect. He'd spoken with Gypsy and examined the malodorous fragments of the shattered chamber pot and told Betsy and Tunstall that Hal Russell had gotten a dose of the clap, the pox, Venus' foul kiss, whatever one wanted to call it. He explained that women often carried it though they had no overt symptoms. It was men who suffered the tooth-grinding agony, the stench, and the urinary tract blockage, scarring, and if left untreated, eventual sterility.

"I have no doubt whatsoever that Hal Russell was thoroughly poxed," he told them after making his third trip to Gypsy's house and the bedroom where Hal's body lay to examine it in private. He had unbuttoned Hal's drawers and taking the penis of the dead man in his right hand he squeezed it carefully, beginning his constriction at the root and working up the shaft to the tip. His care was rewarded with a trickle of foul smelling greenish-yellow pus, lightly tinted with blood, which formed a viscous blob on the once pink but now grayish tip. The odor was sufficiently putrid to make his gorge rise, and he wiped the stinking blob into a thin-walled glass tube, which he stopped with a small tapered cork. Setting down the tube for the moment, he rearranged Hal's penis, re-buttoned his drawers, and picked up the tube, proceeded to wash his hands as thoroughly as he could using Gypsy's rose scented soap, and he washed the tube as well before stowing it carefully in his breast pocket. On his way back to Tunstall's house, he stopped at his office which was attached to his one story white painted wood frame home, and washed his hands once more, this time disinfecting them first with wood alcohol.

"It would seem that," he continued, "Mr. Russell first experienced the symptoms this morning. The burning sensation is said to be agonizing, quite a shock coming so early in the day, and could well make even a mild-mannered man furious and from what I understand Mr. Russell was a temperamental man to begin with. He blamed Gypsy for his infection and threw the chamberpot at her. I believe Gypsy and Francine have been assiduous about using Enoch's sheaths, otherwise they would be at risk of having been pierced by the same Cupid's dart that transfixed Mr. Russell."

Tunstall was greatly relieved to hear of Hal's condition, as scientific proof would be invaluable. His offer of resignation to Marcie and payment of five hundred dollars to Jack Jones in exchange for their endorsement of a coroner's verdict of self-defense was indignantly rejected by both parties.

Marcie Cabot told him to his face, "If you think I would agree to such a monstrous manipulation of the truth to spare that young Jezebel a trial in return for your resignation, you little know

Marcie Cabot. My sacred honor is not to be sold or bartered for anything in this world, much less your mayoral office. You should be ashamed for even thinking I would stoop to your level of chicanery. Your era of misrule is at an end anyway. No longer will the good, God fearing people of Early have to endure the spectacle of a house of ill fame in the very center of town, of drunken Indians reeling down Front Street, of men being fined and jailed for correcting their wives according to Scripture and the absurdity of having an unmarried woman with a fatherless child as marshal."

Tunstall was wondering what Indians Marcie was referring to, since most Indians couldn't afford to get drunk in Francine's saloon, as she didn't follow Duffy's practice of emptying all liquor glasses into a barrel and selling the dregs for a nickel a shot to the unfortunates who lacked the funds to buy anything else. Francine thought the time-honored practice revolting and disdained the few extra dollars such parsimony would have yielded.

"No Sir," continued Marcie. "My honor is not for sale to you or anyone else. You are not King of Early, much as you'd like to think so. Our Lord alone is King."

"Yes," interrupted Tunstall. "And no one knows His will better than you do. I'm sure. Well you and the Lord can run this town and good luck to the both of you!"

With that being said, Tunstall turned and stalked off to speak with Jack Jones who was talking to Doc Hill.

"Excuse me, Mr. Jones, Doc," said Tunstall. "Might I have a word in private?" Tunstall led Jones to the other side of the mesquite tree. The mayor didn't want anyone to see Jones enter his house because Marcie Cabot would take it for granted he was engaged in some nefarious conspiracy. The trunk of the tree wasn't more than two feet in diameter and offered little enough in the way of privacy though it allowed Marcie to visually monitor their meeting, whole remaining out of hearing range.

"Mr. Jones," Tunstall began. "We're men of the world, not dreamers. Is there the slightest doubt in your mind that Hal brought his fate upon himself by attacking Gypsy?"

Jack thought about this honestly and fairly and he shook his head. "No I don't. Hal had a way of getting under a woman's skin in a bad way."

"Good, then we're in agreement on that."

"Whatever he did, it didn't give Gypsy the right to kill him."

"She thought he was going to kill her. It was a classic case of self defense."

"Maybe so," Jack admitted, and he hawked loudly and spat. He didn't mean any offense by it; he was just clearing his throat. Tunstall scrutinized him as closely as he could without crossing the line into rudeness. Jones was not an entirely unprepossessing figure. Tunstall was still smarting from Marcie's stinging rebuff. He thought he'd be more successful with Jones though without Marcie's acquiescence, he had no real hope of avoiding having to send Gypsy to Santa Fe. Still if Jones could be made to see it as self-defense, with him being Hal's partner and best friend, his testimony would resonate with a jury.

"Would you be willing to sign an affidavit to that effect?"

"No," said Jack. "I don't think I would."

Since finding the body, Jack's greatest source of perturbation wasn't Hal's untimely demise. The real wonder of it all to his mind was that he hadn't been shot by some woman years before. What perturbed him was the loss of his four hundred and fifty dollar grubstake. Francine's money would have gone to paying a good lawyer to clear his name, and left enough for him to buy into a few poker games. He'd emptied Hal's pockets when Rose left the room for a few minutes to get some air. Jack had also taken Hal's Winchester and would have taken his Colt and gun-belt as well. It was hanging on the bedpost and Jack was concerned that its disappearance would be noticed. Jack wasn't completely without funds, though he was far from flush. Hal's horse was at the livery stable and he'd be sure to take it on his way out of town. Hal's Colt could pay for his funeral, the undertaker's services, and a rude pine coffin. Public sentiment would demand that he defray the expenses of interring his late partner.

Jack thought that with Hal having passed on, Francine was under no obligation to pay him, unless Jack claimed to be Hal's rightful heir, and even if he were, Jack had no proof. It wasn't like he and Hal were blood relations, or anything of the kind. As far as the four hundred fifty dollars went, Jack thought he was plumb out of luck as far as the money was concerned. Rose was a pretty and winsome girl and there were still a few isolated mining camps in the high Sierra outside Grass Valley, where she would no doubt receive a rousing reception, though gold wasn't nearly as plentiful as it was thirty years before. Jack hated the idea of sharing Rose's favors with other men, irrespective of the shining dust and nuggets such ephemeral liaisons would bring them, beside he promised her.

"I have no interest in selling Rose, or in her selling herself," he decided. "I'll take Hal's horse, what money he had, and the Winchester. Now, Rose 'll get her twenty five dollars back, we'll get by."

Jack's major worry was paying the lawyer. If he were at all fortunate with Lady Luck at the poker table on his way north-west and frugal as regards food and lodging, he was confident he'd have the necessary retainer upon arrival in Sacramento. It would mean sleeping out under the stars more often that not, something he hadn't discussed with Rose. Assuming the railroad in Santa Fe sold tickets to passengers, he could sell his guns and their horses, but then they'd arrive in the delta having to start all over. Good horses, Colt Single Actions, and Model 1873 Winchester rifles were in high demand in California, commanding a premium, so Jack discarded the train as a possibility.

Jack knew, or thought he knew what Tunstall was hinting at. Jack was already very tired of Hal Russell's company in Santa Fe. One night Hal had gotten so intoxicated he'd gone upstairs in the rather sleazy, decidedly second rate bawdy house they were drinking in, accompanied by a girl who looked to Jack to be in her early teens if that. She was flat chested as a board, though Jack was forced to admit she had the face of an angel, with long, shiny, straight hair, black as a raven's wing, teeth like small pearls, a diminutive, perfectly chiseled nose, full ruby—red lips, and startlingly wide, fathomless brown eyes. Jack thought she might be as old as fourteen, and before the two of them went up hand in hand, he asked Hal if he thought it was right to have sex with a girl young enough to be his daughter.

Hal replied slurring his words as he did. "If my daughter looked like this," here Hal put her lower jaw in his left hand and displayed her face as if she were livestock. "I'd screw her until her eyes bugged out. You know what they say, 'if they're old enough to bleed, they're old enough to butcher'."

It was ironic that this innocent appearing, angelic young girl was most likely the one who poxed him.

As Jack waited for the mayor to make his offer, he made up his mind that whatever it was, he wasn't going to take it. This was not because he had any moral scruples about bribery, or somehow sullying

Hal's memory. The sight of his lascivious leer as he stumbled up the bordello stairs, leading the child to the stained, sheeted pallet, left an indelible image in Jack's mind. Out of all the possible memories Hal might have left him, this nightmare was the one that persisted. When he saw Hal with Francine, all Jack could think about was the under-age prostitute's face super-imposed on Francine's. No action on Jack's part could stain Hal's reputation any darker than Hal had already done on his own.

Tunstall sensed that Jack was expecting him to make a monetary proposition, and the mayor had been intending on doing just that. Now Tunstall determined that without Marcie's imprimatur on the verdict, Jones was important though not crucial. The mayor would not mention money.

"Your partner gave Gypsy a good beating including broken ribs. You look like a decent man to me. Are you sure you won't sign a statement?"

Marcie Cabot had expressed her condolences to Jack, "about the terrible murder of an unarmed innocent man, struck down in the prime of life. It was probably what they call a crime of passion though it was murder, foul murder. The Good Book says an eye for an eye and tooth for tooth. I know you won't rest easy until justice is done, and that, that," Marcie was having difficulty finding exactly the right epithet. She wanted to say whore though that was off-color and prostitute was too technical sounding. Jezebel was over-used. Girl sounded much too pure and innocent, yet woman was too dignified, so she settled for, "Murderess hangs for her heinous crime."

Under ordinary circumstances Marcie Cabot would no more converse with the likes of a Hal Russell or a Jack Jones than she'd admit a stray dog to her bed. However, Hal's murder was the first since Duffy's, and as Tunstall was shielding Gypsy, Marcie thought it was a good opportunity to remove him from office.

Jack Jones was not a man who frightened easily, nevertheless he was wary of Marcie. Rose had told him enough of the Tunstall-Cabot rivalry in Early to make Jack certain he didn't want to take sides. If Rose would agree to leave that evening, Jack was inclined to take Hal's horse and Winchester and ride out of the whole situation. He saw a potential quagmire that could waste months of precious time, time he use to build a future in California.

"That's right," he'd said to Marcie, touching his right hand to the broad rim of his brown sombrero.

"I'll tell you what, Mr. Tunstall," said Jack brightening. "If you want me to sign a statement that Hal Russell was a violent man and this might have been one of those times, I can do that. But I wasn't there, I don't know anything for a fact, so I can't say more than that."

Tunstall took him to City Hall where Jack signed the statement with Betsy as a witness. Tunstall thanked him, and after the mayor re-read it, he confided in Betsy that while it did Gypsy's case no particular harm, the good it did on the face of it was negligible. If Jack appeared in person and read it in court it would have had much more value.

Jack made it abundantly clear he wasn't going to wait in Early or Santa Fe for weeks or months to testify at Gypsy's trial.

By the time Tunstall, Betsy, and Rose finished telling Enoch and Francine their versions of the days events, Francine had a splitting headache. She'd drunk too much bourbon, though she had cooked a beefsteak and par-boiled some potatoes while she was waiting to hear Rose.

"Marshal," she said to Betsy. "I want to go see Gypsy."

Betsy took Francine's right hand in hers. "When I left her, she was sound asleep. Doc Hill plastered her broken ribs then gave her a good dose of laudanum. He said between what she'd been through and the medicine, she'd sleep for eighteen hours or more."

Enoch broke in, "With three broken ribs, it's best to keep the patient calm and inactive for the first few days. No excitement, that's a good prescription."

"Do you have to take her to jail?" Francine asked Betsy.

Tunstall looked at Betsy. "Gypsy was in my home for most of the day. I intended to keep her there. Then I considered the seriousness of the charge and the intractable attitude of the good Reverend Gilbert and dear Mrs. Cabot. Therefore the marshal and I decided it was best for all concerned if Gypsy were in jail.

"Oh, the poor thing," said Francine and she broke down in tears. Betsy said, "Relax, Francine. Tunstall took a feather mattress, goose down pillows, satin sheets, a mahogany washstand with a painted porcelain jug and bowl to the jail. It's not as if she's sleeping on a wood plank or the brick floor."
"It's still a jail cell, with iron bars. And she's locked up, all alone, without a friend in the world to keep her company."

Tunstall had done his best to make the single cell in the jail as comfortable as possible. The bedding was from his own guestroom and better quality than Gypsy's own bed. The chamber pot and basin were Limoges porcelain, painted with roses by a skilled artist. He'd installed a thick Turkey carpet of fine wool, tightly woven with red and other earth colors forming the traditional geometric borders, and an undecorated solid pink center to accommodate the knees of the Muslim faithful and point them toward Mecca. He would have gone even further, but when he was about to take his only pair of Georgian silver candlesticks, Betsy asked him if he considered this the action of a rational person.

"Tunstall, no matter how we decorate it, it's still a jail cell. Although we've made it a gilded cage because we sympathize with Gypsy it's still a cage. There's a limit to everything and I think you've reached it."

Tunstall put the heavy cast and chased silver sticks down on the mahogany sideboard with the light fruitwood inlays of graceful Grecian urns on the doors.

The mayor blushed, "I know I get carried away. It's just that I feel responsible for Gypsy being in jail, and I'm trying my best to expiate that guilt by making her as comfortable as I can."

Betsy frowned. "Unless I'm mistaken, you didn't stab Hal Russell with a Bowie knife so unless you did, I don't see how you're responsible. Your mania to fix everything for everyone you love or even like is very much to your credit; however you need to recognize when it's not good for you or the person you're helping. I love you and I won't stand by and listen to how it's your fault Gypsy's in this mess."

Tunstall paid close attention to what Betsy was saying. He was aware of his tendency to shoulder other people's burdens. Some of this was doubtless due to the fact that it's always easier to perceive the problems of others than one's own, and the mayor had more than enough awareness and self-introspection in his nature to see this. While sometimes deploring Tunstall's propensity to solve other people's difficulties, she had to admit he was quite adept at it and more importantly he never reminded anyone that he had assisted them after the fact. His self-deprecation and his policy of giving aid without even letting the person know where the help was coming from, much less who, made his actions that much more commendable in Betsy's opinion.

"Well mayor," said Betsy with a grin, "You've done a man's job of it. When Gypsy finally wakes up, except for the wall of bars, and the bars on the window, she'll think she's still dreaming when she sees your carpet, the fancy French piss-pot, and the satin sheets, not to mention the loaf of fresh bread, crock of butter, and real silverware on the side-table."

Chapter 14
GYPSY'S DREAM

Doc Hill couldn't have been more solicitous of Gypsy if she had been his only daughter. Once he knew Tunstall wouldn't strong-arm him into finding Hal Russell had died by accident, he couldn't do enough for Gypsy. He made an elastic bandage of fine linen and sticking plaster, which held her ribs gently but firmly in place so she could breathe with less pain. He applied cold compresses to her cheekbone and gave her several drops of laudanum in fragrant Madeira wine that not only eased her pain but also lessened her anxiety. All the while he diverted her with fascinating tales of his days as a medical student, amusing and absurd escapades with cadavers, before, during, and after gross anatomy cases. Ike Hill thought of himself as quite the raconteur when he put his mind to it, and now that he didn't have to compromise either his Indian hospital or his relationship with Tunstall and Swank, he gave free rein to his abilities as a fabulist. As the light dose of laudanum took its full effect, it lifted Gypsy up to a place where there were no thoughts of Hal Russell lying pinned to the floor, no trial, and no prison.

Betsy and Tunstall were occupied with moving furniture from the mayor's home to the jail. Ike, having exhausted his anatomical tales moved on to medical student adventures in the bordellos to which they all repaired on Friday and Saturday nights, as soon as anyone of their merry band received his monthly stipend from home.

"Of course," said Doc Hill. "I rarely ventured beyond the reception rooms for I had a mortal fear of disease. Even with my manhood well-armored, I was so frightened I could hardly perform."

He regaled Gypsy with this and many similar ribald stories. After they had transformed Early's single jail cell into a lady's boudoir all three of them escorted Gypsy to the cell. The cell, itself, was quite clean to begin with. It hadn't had an occupant in several weeks, because what miscreants there were in Early consisted of either drunken ranch hands, who were released to their respective foremen or bosses, or Indians who were returned to the reservation for punishment. An overnight guest in the jail was a rarity and there hadn't been a lengthy stay since Betsy began her tenure as marshal.

Contrary to the lurid and wildly exaggerated accounts in the Eastern press, and the fantastic tales of murderous outlaws in the dime novels, the vast majority of small towns in the New Mexico Territory were peaceful to the point of suffocating dullness. Gunfire was reserved for rattlesnakes and hunting.

As soon as Gypsy walked into the cell, she sat on the walnut single bed, which was the final touch Tunstall installed, over Betsy's objections. She wanted nothing so much as to lie down on it and rest. Doc Hill had told Tunstall and Betsy that his patient needed rest and quiet. Gypsy had taken a thorough sponge bath at the mayor's house, though the full immersion in Tunstall's oversize zinc tub, which she longed for, was out of the question due to the bandages on her chest.

"Whatever you do, don't squeeze her," warned the doctor as they were leaving. Betsy hugged Gypsy delicately and kissed her on both cheeks, one at a time taking special care with the left one. Tunstall ever the gallant, took her right hand in his, brought it to his lips and kissed it as if she were a princess. Gypsy was too overcome with gratitude to say a word for fear of dissolving into tears. That was one consideration behind her silence. The other being she was literally swaying with fatigue. Doc Hill ushered them out of the cell, and taking an amber glass bottle from his black leather physician's bag, measured out a dose of laudanum into a silvery metal spoon.

"This will taste slightly bitter for it is a stronger tincture than the one I gave you earlier."

"I'm so tired, I don't know if I need it. I think I could sleep till next month." "That's what you think now. If you roll over on your chest you'll wish you'd listened to me. This will ensure that you will sleep in one position. After you fall asleep I'll arrange the pillows so you'll remain sleeping on your back."

Gypsy was concerned about the mayor's bed and sheets. "I won't piss or shit myself, or anything like that?"

He burst out laughing, "Goodness no. Opium is a sovereign soporific for bodily functions. Enoch Swank could tell you all about it's history from Biblical times. No, your bladder and bowels will sleep as soundly as you will."

He put the spoon up to Gypsy's lips and she opened her mouth and swallowed all of it, though it was so bitter she gagged.

"Uggggh," she said. "Stuff tastes worse than the castor oil my father used to give me when I had the colic as a child." Gypsy yawned. "If it's all the same to you, Doc, I think I'll lie down now. I want you to know, I'm grateful for all you've done for me; I really do feel much better." She added with a sleepy smile, "And sometime in the future, if you can get over your fear of the pox, I'd be honored to show you how grateful I am."

This sleepy smile was so childlike and unaffected that had Tunstall asked him at that moment to swear Hal Russell killed himself, he would have sworn to it, hospital or no hospital. There were tears in his eyes as he tucked the thick comforter around her body in such a way as to support her without covering her, as the cell was warm. When he was satisfied, the doctor blew the sleeping girl a kiss, closed his bag, picked it up, and left the cell, swinging the iron barred door behind him. The door was heavy though well hinged and its inertia nearly knocked him off his feet as he stopped it from banging against the iron frame.

He walked up the three stairs and into Tunstall's small office down a hall.
"Are you going to lock the door?" He asked Betsy.

Betsy looked at the mayor who shrugged his shoulders.

"Is there some reason I should," asked Betsy in a breezy tone of voice.

He shrugged, "I just thought I'd ask in case you thought I should. The key is in the door."

"If Gypsy wants to lock herself in for protection she can. Not that I think there's any danger from a mob or anything like that. It's not like it was after Duffy. As long as she's not seen in the saloon or living in her house like nothing's happened, I don't think Marcie Cabot or Jack Jones is going to raise a fuss about whether she can come and go as she pleases in City Hall," said Betsy. Gypsy sank into the feather mattress and despite the oppressive heat in the room the sense of security it gave was stronger than the discomfort of being hot. The second dose of laudanum was far stronger than the first. It was nothing short of overwhelming, as if she had drunk an entire bottle of whiskey in one spoonful and it swept her away. She didn't really hear Doc Hill's last words or remember her own before falling fast asleep.

Chapter 15
JACK'S DILEMMA

Jack Jones was happy, happier than he'd been at any time during the years after he'd allowed himself to be pressured into helping rob the Wells Fargo stagecoach. Rose had agreed to go California on the evening of Hal's death. She took the murder as a sign that it was time for her to move on. As much as she loved Francine, Rose did not think she was obligated to stay, and with Gypsy in jail, she would have to service Gypsy's clients as well as hers. Rose was weary of the sporting woman's life, bored to tears if the truth were known, and Jack, while hardly the prince of her twenty-two year old daydreams, was more considerate of her than any man she'd known, and his companionship was agreeable nearly all of the time, not just when they were both drunk, as was the case with men before Jack. Jack, for his part was sold on Rose's being a reformed prostitute. He knew a man in Vallejo who's married a whore from San Francisco's so-called Barbary Coast and she'd made him a damned good wife in the estimation of both her husband and Jack, and Rose was much younger and to Jack's eye better looking than the woman in Vallejo.

There was the question of Hal's burial and whether Jack needed to be present at the funeral. Jack opined to Rose that, "Funerals are for the living so they can join with other bereaved survivors and better understand and accept the death of a loved one. As for paying final respects, unless you believe a man's ghost stands around at his grave-side to see who's there, it's not as if a corpse cares who show up at a funeral. The way I figure it is Hal's spirit, soul, whatever you want to call it, left for wherever it was going right after that Bowie pierced his heart early this morning."

As much as Rose wanted to shake the dust of Early from her boots, there was no way she was leaving without seeing Gypsy, getting her twenty-five dollars back from Francine, and making the rounds, saying her farewells to Doc Hill, Enoch Swank, Tunstall, Betsy, Ben, and several others who had shown her kindness. Jack wanted to leave in the morning; however he could hardly tell Rose not to say her good-byes and her wanting to say them was only further proof, not that Jack needed any more, of Rose's innate decency and generosity of spirit. He reluctantly agreed to postpone their departure until the following morning, two days after Hal's death.

The funeral, it was more of an interment, was held in the Early cemetery behind the church. The churchyard, like most of Early was a piece of undistinguished, flat ground, with one mesquite bush in the south corner and another in the west accompanied by scraggy weeds adept at eking out their existence from the reddish, sandy soil without water. The few headstones standing were not marble or granite, but grey limestone about two inches thick with their tops arched and inscriptions of simple block capitals giving mostly just first and last names with the dates of birth and death. All the inscriptions were carved by the same hand, neat enough, though nothing like the elaborate flourishes and fine elaboration used on some of the tombstones in Santa Fe.

A number of graves bore nothing more than white painted wooden crosses with names and dates in black paint. Others were totally unmarked as if the body really were nothing more than an empty vessel, robbed by death of anything worth making an effort to celebrate, commemorate, or tell a life story. Though he did not countenance ungodliness in any form, Reverend Gilbert was uncharacteristically liberal in permitting believers as well as non-believers, those who never attended a single one of his services, to rest in the consecrated ground behind his church. He'd even dared to stand up to Marcie Cabot when an Apache woman, for some unaccountable reason, sought to have her infant boy, buried in the churchyard rather than in the traditional Mescalero way.

When Marcie heard of the woman's wish from Reverend Gilbert, she was outraged. "I hope you told the heathen idolater, the un-baptized, damned child will not be buried in consecrated earth."

Reverend Gilbert turned his slightly cherubic face, it would have been cherubic except for the heavy beard that gave his face a swarthy look, which try as he might with Sheffield's finest razors morning and afternoon, he could not effectively efface, so that he always looked as if he needed a shave. His eyes were such a light brown they were almost hazel and they met Marcie's ice blue ones without fear or deference.

"Marcie," he intoned in his most sincere baritone, verging on tenor, voice. As you know all too well, you are the Peter, the rock, upon which this church was founded, and I pretty well march in lock-step with you, not for this reason, as much as I believe our views on doctrine and scripture are in harmony." He held up a long thin index finger, not in Marcie's face, but high enough to give his next words the unmistakable emphasis he thought they merited.

"I want you to know my decision has nothing whatever to do with any desire on my part to expiate the guilt I feel each day over having lead a lynch mob intent on hanging two innocent Indians for Duffy's murder. Although I haven't entirely forgiven myself for my un-Christian behavior, I know the Good Lord has and that is the important thing. No, this has nothing to do with that I promise you. It is my firm, unalterable conviction that while it may well be necessary to live a Christ-like life to attain salvation, once death claims us, the body is no longer of any spiritual or theological significance except to the living.

Therefore the remains of a saint are no more holy or deserving of any more reverence than those of the most grievous sinner. As Lincoln said at Gettysburg, "It is for us the living, rather to be dedicated here to the unfinished work," and you must forgive me for saying that if it gives comfort to anyone, be he heathen idolater, Catholic, Lutheran, Jew, Mormon, or Musselman to have his loved one buried here in holy ground, then I say to him, welcome. I will not be the one to cast the first stone or behold the dust that is in my neighbor's eye."

The Apache infant was buried under the tenuous shelter of the mesquite bush in the west corner of the churchyard in the presence of the mother and Reverend Gilbert. Marcie Cabot and the infant's father refused to attend, though she had sent Reverend Gilbert a note informing him that in this particular instance only, she would remove her objections to the interment of the 'un-baptized heathen baby'.

Early on the morning of the second day, Jack and Rose were lolling in bed, Jack in his drawers and Rose in a sheer, silk nightgown Francine had given her as a parting gift in addition to returning her twenty-five dollars to which she generously added an additional twenty five. All told Rose had more than ninety-five dollars with which to begin her new life.

"I still don't see why you think I need to be there for the burial," said Jack. He was reconciled to the loss of the four hundred and fifty dollars he was to receive from Hal. Rose was going with him and to his mind that was worth far more than the money. For some reason he couldn't explain to Rose or himself, he really didn't want to see Hal Russell's plain, pine coffin lowered into the ground. Jack wasn't superstitious. He didn't think Hal's ghostly hand would snatch at his ankle and drag him down with him into the grave though that very thought did occur to him. It was more of an idle fantasy than a visceral fear of such a thing taking actually taking place.

Jack had seen Hal's body, rolled it over on its back, closed the eyes, and been in and out of the room a dozen times with Rose, Doc Hill, Marshal Johnson, and finally the undertaker, Mr. Aguilar, who managed the livery stable. He even wanted Hal's Wostenholm Bowie, though the marshal had kept it as evidence. Jack's philosophy held firm that a dead body was nothing more than that and Hal's corpse was no more significant than the vulture Hal had shot before they rose into Early for the first time. Now that he thought about it Jack said to himself, "Maybe shooting that buzzard wasn't a good idea after all."

Jack twined his forefinger in Rose's dark brown curls, absent mindedly, as he continued to think about the vulture. At the time, he'd wanted to kill it because he was irrationally angry that the bird could possibly regard him or his mule as a potential meal There was that, and it was added to the fact he thought being shadowed by the large, black scavenger was a mildly bad omen, capable of casting a pall over their future in some fashion. Also Jack never liked watching as buzzards circled a stricken steer, as if they couldn't wait to sink their cruel hooked beaks into the creature's soft belly and eyes. Hal had shot the vulture pretty much at Jack's request and now Hal was dead.

"Maybe killing that buzzard was a bad omen," Jack muttered aloud. "Jack, honey," said Rose prettily. "Whatever are you talking about?"

He told her all about the shooting of the vulture, and shared his thoughts about how he now saw this as a bad omen that might have brought about Hal's death. Rose took the hand he'd been twining in her hair in her own warm ones and brought it to her lips, kissing it back and palm.

"Those buzzards give me the creeps, flying over you when you're all alone out in the desert. There was one following me when I rode out to the marshal's place. It's like they're up there just praying and hoping your horse breaks a leg in a hole and you die of thirst, like you're nothing but supper."

"That's it exactly," said Jack, more convinced than ever that he and Rose were kindred souls, meant to be together. He took back his hand and placed it on her flat stomach in a caress. A possible solution to the problem of Hal's funeral came to him.

"I have the same feelings about the funeral as I have about the vulture. It's like a bad omen for our future and I don't want any bad memories to haunt us." Rose pondered this, aware of Jack's rough, warm hand on her belly, and how much she like the way it made her feel. Propriety and protocol virtually demanded Jack be present at Hal's burial, and she wanted to be there to support Francine, who had been both gracious and generous about her leaving the saloon without giving advance notice. Being that Jack was Hal's partner it just wouldn't look right if he wasn't there.

"Honey," she said. "I can't think of any excuse for you're not going. I don't think it's a bad omen at all. It'll close the chapter of our lives in Early and we'll move on to our new ones in the Delta."

Jack removed his hand and groaned, "I know you're right. I was his partner after all. Still I don't like it. As my father always told me, 'Son, there are times in life we have to do things we don't really like'. I suppose this is one of those times. I'll just gut it up. I'm sure it'll be short."

Rose assured him the service, if indeed there were any would be brief. Now she could take her leave of Mayor Tunstall and the others at the memorial. She'd spent last night until one o'clock in Gypsy's sumptuous jail cell, laughing, crying, and reminiscing about some of the absurdities they'd seen in their time at the saloon. Gypsy seemed to think

Jack's statement would carry more weight than Tunstall did initially. Now the mayor had changed his mind primarily because Francine had given a powerful and damning statement detailing Hal's previous attacks on her, including the recent one, swearing that Hal intended to kill her. Now the mayor was fairly confident Gypsy would be acquitted, although he strongly cautioned her not to believe it was a foregone conclusion. He told Gypsy, "No one can ever be sure of a jury's verdict unless it had been bought and paid for, and sometimes not even then."

Nevertheless, Gypsy was sanguine about her chances, and the sheriff's office in Santa Fe was only too happy with Betsy's offer to escort her, so at least Gypsy was assured of agreeable company along the way. Francine made certain Gypsy ate well while she wait and had sent a bottle of brandy for her and Rose.

At Rose's prompting, Jack reluctantly got up out of bed, walked to the washstand, poured a good measure of tepid water from the large white ceramic pitcher into the **basin** and commenced his morning ablutions by cleaning his teeth with a powder from Swank's Apothecary, using his index finger to apply it. When both he and Rose were finished washing up, they dressed for Hal's funeral, which in Jack's case meant a clean shirt and stockings and otherwise, the same denim trousers and thigh high boots he'd been wearing for the past several days. He did spend an entire minute running one of Rose's boar bristle brushes through his thatch of unruly hair though he decided to forgo a shave due to lack of hot water. He and Rose had a long distance to travel and he was not about to throw four bits to a barber. Besides Rose liked the seven days growth of brown beard he sported and had said as much the previous evening.

Rose didn't have anything like a mourning dress, and even if she had, Jack said it wouldn't have been right to wear it because, "It isn't like Hal was your kin or anything so she wore one of her tight fitting, revealing red satin dresses, with a black cotton shawl over her breasts in deference to the solemnity of the occasion.

Jack surveyed Rose approvingly, "If Hal had anything to say about it, believe me he'd ask you to take off the shawl so he could see your pretty tits before he went to Hell or wherever he's going."

"Do you think Hal's in Hell?" asked Rose in all seriousness. "No," said Jack. "As a matter of fact I don't."

"DO you believe in Hell?"

"Do I think Hell is a place like Early is a place, full of lakes of fire, devils, ruled by Satan, no I don't. Hell, if there is one is when a soul is not with whatever orders all things in the universe what people call God."

"So is Hal with God or not?" persisted Rose.

Jack smiled broadly, "God only knows." Rose laughed outright and then kissed Jack on the lips.

"Don't start with me," he said after returning her kiss. "I can think of a whole lot of things I'd rather do than see Hal's coffin and number one on my list is eating a good breakfast, then coming back here and loving you up good and proper." When Jack and Rose arrived at the churchyard, which was less than a five minute walk, Jack was surprised at the relatively large number of mourners. Francine was there of course, with long, lanky Enoch Swank. She was not dressed in black, which surprised him, but in a light brown, nearly tawny frock with no lace and half-arm length sleeves. Enoch was wearing his usual black suit. Betsy was there with Tunstall and he hadn't expected to see either of them. Ernesto had brought the simple pine coffin from its stall in the livery stable with two stout hemp ropes for lowering it into the freshly dug grave.

The pile of earth was reddish brown, degraded sandstone colored with some brownish white from limestone. Jack had enough experience as a prospector to know something of geology and soils. He wondered if the dirt had anything in common with the soils of Monterrey, where Hal had intended to go. Jack knew it had nothing in common with the rich, alluvial dirt of the Sacramento Delta.

"Not that it matters any more to Hal," he thought. "Nothing does."

Francine had had less than three days to come to terms with Hal's death. It was shocking because it happened in Early and Gypsy was the person who stabbed him. She always knew in her heart that Hal would meet with a violent end at the hands of some woman he'd beaten up, though she'd always imagined him being shot. Not in her wildest imaginings did she ever think he'd die in Early. The night of Hal's death was the first night she and Enoch were together. Enoch was unsure of how he should behave so out of an abundance of caution and sensitivity toward Francine, he was less demonstrative of his affections than he'd been out at the spring in the afternoon. Francine couldn't help but notice and as she'd decided before they even reached the spring that if she and Enoch were to be lovers, then she would make her feelings known and teach him to do the same, she decided this was a good time to begin.

"Enoch," she said softly. "You don't have to act as if I'm in mourning. Hal Russell may have been my husband as far as the law is concerned. My heart says he was something left over from my past, and not a very pleasant thing at that. If you want to kiss me, then kiss me. If you want to hold me, then hold me. And if you want to make love to me then do it. Don't be stand-offish on account of Hal Russell having gotten what I wanted to give him so many times and should have. Then Gypsy wouldn't have to suffer for my weakness."

It seemed to Enoch that every cell in his brain and his body that was capable of feeling any sensation was thrilled by Francine's words. When she spoke with him her faux French accent was scarcely perceptible, and what remained of it bespoke an exotic sensuality as if she were the queen of his very own one-woman seraglio. He looked at her and his penis hardened for the fourth time that day. Enoch thought of John Donne's poem about death and the line from For Whom The Bell Tolls, "Each man's death diminishes me".

"In Hal Russell's case the diminution was as minimal as it could be."

Francine was far more preoccupied with Gypsy than Hal. The worst thing about Hal's death was Francine's sense that Gypsy was paying the price for her failure to stop Hal from harming women years before. Of course even if she had gone to the sheriff in Sacramento with her split lips, loose teeth, broken nose, and black eyes to have Hal arrested, the deputies would have laughed and guffawed her out of the building, telling her "the next time just shut up and don't ask the man to give you what you deserve". Until she came to Early, Francine had never heard of a man being arrested for hitting his wife unless he practically killed her and then the few days in jail only made it that much more dangerous for the woman when he was released. The law would act only if the man killed the woman in which event, whether or not the man was hanged made no difference to the victim of his violence. When she mentioned her notion of being in some way responsible for Gypsy's having to deal with Hal Enoch shook his head emphatically side to side.

"Francine, while your taking any responsibility is in a way admirable, I fear it is mistaken. Though Gypsy may be very young, she is far from being naive or a fool. She knew Hal beat the Hell out of you. She saw your face with her own eyes. It's just that she saw Hal Russell's handsome face and thought, 'It won't happen to me. He has no history with me'. Life is a series of choices and Gypsy made a very self-indulgent one that turned out badly, though not nearly as badly as it might have. He could easily have killed her."

Enoch took Francine in his long sinuous arms and put his face close to hers. "You didn't kill Hal Russell for what he did to you. You knew him better than Gypsy so maybe you knew that at the last minute he wouldn't murder you. Or maybe the sickness and self-loathing that was behind his hatred of women had gotten worse over the years. Either way by sparing his life when you lived with him in Sacramento and the few days he was with you here, you did the right thing not the wrong thing. What he did to you in the saloon made it clear as the rattle on a snake that he was dangerous. You told the girls all about him, lectured them for fifteen minutes. Gypsy chose to ignore all the warnings you gave her and she did so knowing Hal was rank poison. I'm happy you didn't kill him."

"So am I," said Francine. "Enoch, bless you, you've put my mind at ease. Francine dropped her right hand down and gently felt between Enoch's legs.

"My, my, aren't we the stallion."

Enoch pulled her closer. "It's been a very long time for me, Francine."

"Good then we'll make up for all the time you lost."

Francine held onto Enoch's right hand and looked at the coffin lying on the dirt near the oblong hole in the earth. She no longer worried about her having in any way facilitated Gypsy's deed. Now she had no guilty feelings about her sense of relief! Never again would Hal Russell surface like a submerged snag in the river of her life to tear out the bottoms of her dreamboats. She was no longer married, and she didn't have to borrow money, mortgage the saloon, and plunge herself into debt. She had already paid back Rose and Tunstall. She would give Gypsy's money to Betsy so that Gypsy could draw on it in Santa Fe. Francine couldn't help feeling joy that the pall Hal had cast over her life was finally and irrevocably lifted. Her heart was relieved of a crushing burden. Though he lacked Hal's obvious good looks, Enoch had an inner beauty of intellect and soul that Hal couldn't even begin to aspire to and with each passing day, her delight in being in love with Enoch Swank increased more than she ever thought possible with any man even Luis.

Reverend Gilbert stood with Tunstall and Betsy.

"Do you think I should say words over the departed?" he asked the mayor. Tunstall was utterly indifferent. He was only there at all because Betsy wanted to support Francine, who seemed to be receiving all the encouragement she needed from Enoch Swank.

"Reverend," said Tunstall. "You need to ask Mr. Russell's partner or his widow, or just do whatever you think is fitting."

Gilbert walked over to Jack and Rose. He asked Jack who shrugged and told him to ask Francine. Now the reverend was discomfited. This was due to his rejection by Jack and Tunstall and the unseemly fact that Francine looked far more like a girl in love than a newly minted widow.

The weather was hot and the sky was clear. There were birds in the two stunted mesquite trees calling to one another in sweet, melodic trills. As the assembled mourners waited on Reverend Gilbert, a breeze kicked up from out of nowhere, blowing dust from the ground and the burial mound on everyone.

"Reverend," said Francine, impatiently dusting off the front of her dress. "Please do whatever you think is best. Hal was a man of few words." She added the last sentence in the hope the preacher would take the hint and be brief, and not give in to his tendency and drone on and on. On Sundays he would usually lose the attention of half his congregation after the first thirty minutes of the lesson.

In this instance, Reverend Gilbert had his own reasons to truncate his message, the most powerful being a foreign object in his left eye, courtesy of the sudden gust of wind. Normally a few blinks and the eye's natural tearing mechanism sufficed to wash out such annoyances; however this particular object, whether animal, vegetable, or mineral was more persistent. He turned from Francine and Enoch and as surreptitiously as he could, used his thumb and forefinger to grasp the eyelashes of the upper lid and pull it down over the lower in hopes of dislodging the offending speck. All the while, Reverend Gilbert was thinking about Christ's admonition not to "And why beholdest thou the mote that is in thy brother's eye, but considerest not the beam that is in thine own eye". He was not so much superstitious as he was somewhat deterministic in his beliefs, that things happened for a reason, and the prime mover behind the reasons was God. He thought if that particular piece of dust chose this out of all possible moments to manifest itself in his eye, then there was both a reason and a lesson in it having to do with Hal Russell. Specifically he must be vigilant not to pass judgment on either Hal's life or his immortal soul when he spoke.

Jack and Reverend Gilbert took each end of the rope near the head of the coffin and Enoch and the mayor took the foot end and the four together lowered the mortal remains of Hal Russell into the sandy soil of the New Mexico Territory without incident. When this was done the men returned to their female companions, and held their Stetsons and Jack, his sombrero, in their right hands as they waited for Reverend Gilbert to begin. The preacher was anxious to return to the parsonage where there was clean water and a mirror. His eye kept tearing. It was painful though not so much debilitating as aggravating. He blinked once again and this dislodged the piece of grit. He wiped it from the corner of his eye near the bridge of his rather prominent nose. He was so grateful for the immediate relief he felt that he uttered a prayer of thanksgiving for his deliverance in his mind, hoping the Deity would know how truly thankful he was for this small but nonetheless important mercy. Now he could concentrate on the soul of Harold Russell.

"Where's Doc Hill?" Tunstall asked Enoch.

"He had to ride out early this morning before sunrise to the reservation. He was summoned by the tribal elders about the location of his hospital."

"I can see where that's more important than being here to see a man off he never knew except as a corpse."

Reverend Gilbert cleared his throat. Tunstall was relieved to see the preacher wasn't going to use the Book of Common Prayer with its homilies about "the corruption of the body" and "in the sure hope that it will be like his glorious one" because he wanted no part of any service in which a bastard like Hal Russell was going to be compared to and resurrected like Jesus Christ. Not that the mayor thought he should burn in Hell for all eternity. He preferred that Russell's body rot and nourish worms and plants, the latter being badly in need of sustenance in the New Mexico desert, and that his soul, his name, and his memory would be swiftly forgotten by all who knew him. When Reverend Gilbert asked Jack about a limestone headstone, Hal's partner said, "I imagine a painted wooden cross will do Hal just fine."

Tunstall bought Hal's Colt revolver for the town, from town funds and the ten dollars paid for the pine boards and the labor to make the coffin. Ike Hill allowed as how he'd accept Hal's Wostenholm Bowie knife as compensation for his services, once the Territory had no further need of it and that left Ernesto Aguilar's time for laying Hal out and his workers who actually dug the grave in need of payment. Tunstall offered him Hal's gun-belt and holster but the stable manager wanted cash. Tunstall rather reluctantly gave him eight dollars in gold from his own pocket, hoping the town father's would reimburse him at some future date.

After he heard the hollow sound of the pine box landing on the stonier ground at the bottom of the six-foot deep hole, Jack panicked and stepped away so quickly he jumped, for this was the moment he had dreaded the most. The other men, Tunstall, Swank, and Reverend Gilbert couldn't help but take notice of Jack's ashen face, and his recoiling from the brink of the open grave, though they all refrained from making any comments. Jack was sure they would talk later, even ridicule him, but he didn't know them, and besides by that time he'd be long gone from Early, and he wouldn't care if the whole town laughed at him and mocked his fears. The important thing was that he was too quick for Hal's ghostly white hand to grab his right or left ankle in a skeletal grip of steel, and drag him down into the grave on top of the coffin until his heart stopped from sheer terror.

If only he could survive the service, then the two Mexicans, standing with their right feet on the blades of their iron shovels at a respectful distance would earth over the grave and pat it down in a nice, packed mound. Then Hal could rest easy and far more significantly Jack Jones would be safe. Jack had absolutely no idea how he'd constructed the elaborate system of checks and balances that determined precisely how Hal's death could affect him. He only believed in his interpretation and the edifice he'd created as surely as he believed the earth and the sun were real.

"If this dithering preacher would just get off his sorry ass and
be done with it, any danger from Hal will be past."

Rose took his right hand, though it was dusty from the thick hemp coffin rope and squeezed it tight. Rose knew how anxious Hal was and why, and though she thought his fears were not based on anything real, she understood intuitively that for Jack, they were as genuine as anything in the whole world, which meant that as she loved him, she would take them seriously, even though Rose thought they were no more substantial than shadow cast in his mind by the death of his partner.

Even after he cleared his throat, Reverend Gilbert hesitated before beginning. The principal stumbling block to commencing was his sense that the mourners weren't mournful at Mr. Russell's passing. No one had tears in his eyes and though Mr. Jones was pale as a corpse, himself, his face reflected terror not grief.

"Oh, well," he thought. "I'll do what I can."

"We are gathered here together to commit the body of Harold Russell to the earth. As we are created from the dust so must we, all of us, return to it." Jack shifted nervously from his right foot to his left and back again, and as he did, Rose tightened her hold on his hand.

"I was going to make," said the preacher, "The usual comforting remarks about the sure and certain hope that Hal Russell would be resurrected when he was called by Jesus Christ, our acknowledged lord and Savior, and though Hal's body must necessarily undergo physical corruption, it will nevertheless by like His glorious one on that day, however as I don't know if Mr. Russell accepted Our Lord in his heart, I fear the usual words might not be appropriate."

Tunstall rolled his eyes toward a cloud high overhead and Betsy knew what he was thinking. "Will this self—righteous, sanctimonious, narcissistic prig please get to the point." In all fairness to Reverend Gilbert, he was correct in saying he knew nothing of the man lying in the pine box at the bottom of the hole. Christianity or lack thereof, notwithstanding, Reverend Gilbert sincerely desired to invest the ceremony with at the very least a modicum dignity. As far as the preacher was concerned, regardless of who or what Hal Russell may have been in life, the awesome mystery of death invested him with as much majesty as a crowned king.

Jack Jones understood that death was the necessary end of life. He'd seen men and animals die, still he had an insurmountable problem coming to terms with the inevitability of his own mortality and Hal's untimely death thrust the whole frightening conundrum squarely to the forefront of his thinking.

All of Hal's ambitions, his dreams of beginning a new life in Monterrey, his energy, his very presence in the world were no more, vanished like a drop of dew in the fierce rays of the morning sun never to return. What was left of Hal was inside the long, narrow, pine box, lying at the bottom of the hole Jack thought he was standing much too close to. Reverend Gilbert quoted from Marc Antony's speech about the "evil men do liveth after them".

"As if that son-of-a-bitch were a Caesar," thought Tunstall. "Still it's better than the Common Prayer Book." He concluded with, "Let us bow our heads and pray the 23rd Psalm of King David. Reverend Gilbert's voice was overshadowed by the cawing of a large and vociferous raven, perched in the mesquite bush in the south corner. The three Mexicans, Mr. Aguilar and the two gravediggers all crossed themselves and Jack felt an icy chill, run down the length of his spine and back up into his solar plexus. Everyone looked at the black bird. Reverend Gilbert was annoyed that the creature dared to interrupt his service. The raven, persisted until Ernesto picked a stone up from the mound of earth and flung it at the bird, which flapped its ebony wings and flew off to the West, squawking indignantly. Immediately after Reverend Gilbert intoned the Amen after the Psalm, he encouraged each of those present to take a handful of earth and sprinkle it on the coffin with or without a short prayer. No one took him up on this suggestion, so he soldiered on by himself, taking a handful and speaking in a firm voice, "Earth to earth ashes to ashes, dust to dust."

Jack led Rose away so he could barely hear the patter of sandy soil on the coffin lid. The Mexicans began shoveling in the soil with a will, and as far as Jack was concerned, the excruciating ordeal was at a blessed end. He silently but fervently thanked Almighty God for that. Two days later, he and Rose were in Santa Fe, without a thought for Hal Russell, though Rose thought of Gypsy and prayed for her the first thing when she woke up in the morning and every night before she went to sleep.

On their first day in the capital, Jack was showing Rose the Palace of the Governors, built in 1610, by the Spanish governor, Don Pedro de Peralta, and the 17th century, Chapel of San Miguel, known to residents as the Oldest Church. The sight that enchanted Rose the most was the magnificent Cathedral of St. Francis, which was completed in 1869 by the Bishop of Santa Fe, John B. Lamy. Rose lit a candle at the altar and prayed for Gypsy while Jack stood by her side and enjoyed the architecture. They walked out into the sunshine, and as they descended the steps, Jack noticed a man in an army uniform shielding his eyes from the bright sunlight and looking at him intently. Rose saw the tall, statuesque soldier and said, "Jack, I think that soldier knows you.' Jack's heart sank. He thought it might be Colonel Jessup, and was intending to ignore him, but now because of Rose's comment he really couldn't.

Jessup had immediately recognized Jack as one of the two Californians who'd been on their way to Early perhaps a month ago. The colonel never forgot a face, and he was always keenly interested in anyone having any business in Early, as he had quite a large score to settle with the mayor, the marshal, and the whole town for that matter in addition to the nearby reservation. He was a patient man who was more than willing to bide his time and wait for the opportune moment, which he knew would arise as surely as tomorrow's sun,

"I see you're already back from Early," said Jessup with a razor thin smile. "I'm not surprised since ten minutes is all it takes to see all there is."

He bowed elegantly to Rose, who was flattered by the attention from the handsome, mustachioed officer, a colonel no less, with fearsome, shining, silver eagles on the shoulders of his well-tailored, fine wool jacket.

"Charmed, I'm sure," he said to Rose, then turned to Jack. "I seem to recall you were traveling with a man, your partner I believe, good looking fellow, but not nearly as agreeable to the eyes as your new companion."

The colonel looked at Jack expectantly. Jack had a strong urge to turn on his heel and walk away as fast as he could. This would have been rude and offensive, and Jack knew only a great fool would snub a full colonel, who was the most powerful man in the New Mexico Territory. Jessup was a practiced and skillful observer of human nature. He could read Jack's conflicting emotions in his facial expressions and body language with not quite the same ease as he read the Santa Fe Republican newspaper, but very close to it.

"Listen," said Jessup. "Why not join me for luncheon at my club? The food is excellent. Why the governor himself, dines there nearly every day. We can talk and you can tell me all about Early and your adventures there." Jessup's club was a sort of private saloon, with an outdoor courtyard in the Spanish manner, featuring beautifully painted and colorfully glazed tiles on the floor, plantings in wood boxes, and a large fountain in the center. The fare was Mexican and fiery with liberal use of green and red chili peppers, and was every bit as delicious as Jessup promised it would be. The beer was alcoholic and fragrant. As he began drinking his third large mug, Jack lost some of his visceral antipathy toward the colonel. Jessup had captured Rose's heart from the instant he bowed to her, for he was a fine figure of a man, with exquisite manners, who wore his power well. By the time Jessup called for cigar and brandy, Jack and Rose had told him the story of Hal Russell's death in elaborate detail. Jack drew on his dark, brown cigar with satisfaction, as it was as good as everything else at the club. The superb food and drink were especially welcome, as Rose and Jack were trying to conserve their money, and would have never indulged in such luxury on their own even if they had the opportunity.

Jessup blew out a large, well-shaped smoke ring, which hung in the sunlight. Then he smiled as he said, "This poor girl, this Gypsy is coming to Santa Fe for trial? That's a terrible injustice. It sounds like a classic case of self-defense to me."

"Yes," said Jack. "There're others who agree with you. Why Mayor Tunstall and Betsy Johnson, she's the marshal you know, are bringing her to Santa Fe by themselves."

"Is that so?" said Jessup.

Chapter 16
COLONEL JESSUP'S REVENGE

Colonel Jessup was a subscriber to the adage, "Revenge is a dish best served cold," however he would always qualify it by adding his own codicil of, "Best served cold only when you can't have it piping hot, rare, and bloody."

He left Jack and Rose at the thick iron studded oak, and otherwise anonymous entry door to his club, which was watched from opening until closing by a man in black and gold livery, the club colors. Jessup spoke to the man in livery after Jack and Rose thanked him profusely for his kindness and generosity, and then strolled arm in arm down the brick paved street, full of food, beer, and brandy.

"Manuel," said Jessup to the tall spare Mexican. "If anyone asks for me, tell them I had some urgent business that came up quite suddenly. I shall be away a day or two; however I don't want my absence to be noticed." The colonel paused, "If it's something really important," he stiffened his aristocratic nose as he considered his words. "No, on second thought, if you have to say anything, just say I was called away on a personal matter. Nothing more."

Manuel was used to confidences, and no one ever misplaced his trust by reposing it in him. He regarded each man's secrets as a sacred bond, and no bribe or threat could move him to reveal one. As his time in service to the club grew longer, so did the value men placed on this truly unusual man. Manuel had been the personal valet of Benito Juarez, the Oaxacan Indian, who left the priesthood, and earned a law degree from the Oaxacan Institute of Arts and Sciences, and in January of 1861 was elected president of Mexico. In October of 1870, Juarez suffered a stroke and three months later his wife of twenty-seven years, Margarita La Maze, died. Juarez, himself, died in 1872, and Manuel left Mexico City for the United States, settling in Santa Fe. Someone told him of the club and the owner interviewed him, and hired him that afternoon.

Manuel had set aside enough gold to retire and be comfortable but he was restless and the club offered him an outlet for his talents. For nearly four years, Manuel had stood guard in front of the heavy oak door. He was esteemed by all the club members from governors to judges for his courtesy, discretion, and ability to address the most intimate needs of men of power and influence. During Manuel's first year, Jessup, with his genius for recognizing talent, had offered him a princely sum and a lieutenant's bars to be his personal adjutant.

Manuel looked at the colonel with his fathomless, golden, brown eyes, "Colonel, I am honored almost beyond words by your confidence. But a man such as I am can never serve another man as faithfully as I served my president. And if I cannot do my best for you, I prefer not to do it at all. Here, in my present position, I can do my best because my duties are limited by their very nature and scope. I discharge them to the furthest limit of my powers."

The sincerity with which Manuel declined his offer touched Colonel Jessup in one of the very few secret and hermetically sealed reservoirs of humanity in his heart. He understood exactly what Manuel was telling him and respected him all the more for it. Jessup thought of those who personally served Robert E. Lee. He had once met one of the general's former aide-de-camps, who'd told him of his time in service with tears in his eyes. That aide, too, couldn't serve under another man although General William Tecumseh Sherman had offered him a major's rank on his staff.

Jessup was not normally the sort of man to be on familiar terms with servants; however Manuel was hardly an ordinary doorman. The colonel gave him a five dollar gold piece and offered him his hand, which the Mexican took in his own warm, dry hand and shook it firmly. Though another man might think it incongruous, somehow shaking Manuel's hand put the colonel in mind of what it would be like to touch a king or a president, the Mexican had that much dignity about him. The colonel always left the club feeling the world was a better place, not so much because of the fare or libations or even the fellowship of the wealthy and powerful when such was to his liking. No it was the touch of Manuel's long, lank, brown, and vein ribbed hand that always reassured him that there were extraordinary people in the world living among the myriads of weak and desperate men and women shuffling along in their dreary, banal existences.

Manuel took the shining coin with the deeply milled rim, regarded it for a moment then slipped it into the watch pocket of his trousers, just below his right hip.

"Thank you, colonel," he said in a beautiful baritone, further enriched by his Spanish accent.

"Thank you, Manuel," said Jessup and he meant every word.

"Via con Dios mi Colonel," said Manuel.

Jessup drew himself erect and snapped Manuel a salute as crisp as any he'd ever given to Major General Crook.

"And to you, Manuel, and you."

The colonel could hardly believe his good fortune. Two of the people he most needed to settle with, Tunstall and Johnson would be coming to Santa Fe within days. That left him very little time to arrange a suitable reception for them between Early and Santa Fe where the road ran alongside the Pecos River in the foothills of the Sangre de Christo Mountains before they gave way to the southernmost extension of the Rockies.

Jessup would have liked to use three of the scouts, who were under contract to the army, and would have if Tunstall were traveling with two men. However the mayor was escorting two young, attractive white women and this circumstance was a variable, which complicated things considerably. What he had in mind was too gruesome for the scouts to carry out. If Gypsy and the marshal had been squaws or Mexicans, then possibly the scouts might be able to overcome their squeamishness and sensibilities, but with two young white women involved, never.

There were a few men, peripheral hangers-on, leftovers from Rat Face and El Gordo's ruthless band of Coyoteros, who preyed on the unwary when they left the seamier brothels and saloons in the small hours of the morning, drunk and incapable. These men were sufficiently depraved and desperate to be sure, so much so that Jessup hesitated to use them because they lacked the requisite finesse and intellect to carry out his instructions. Clearly Tunstall and the woman marshal were redoubtable gunmen and would not be taken without a fight unless they encountered such a devastating ambush as to preclude their mounting a credible resistance.

Jessup had the ideal weapon. It was a Sharps .45-150 buffalo rifle with a long brass telescopic sight mounted on its heavy, blued octagonal barrel. Made to Jessup's order by the Sharps' Rifle Company in Bridgeport, Connecticut, the 'Old Reliable', weighed nearly sixteen pounds and fired a three hundred grain lead bullet with great velocity. The Sharps could kill a full grown bull buffalo at a distance of half a mile not that there were many of the great, shaggy beasts left in the

Territory or anywhere else in the West except for Northern Wyoming and Montana. Jessup hadn't ordered it for buffalo. He had it specially made with its set triggers for long range assassination of certain stubborn, disaffected Indians, who vehemently opposed the sale of adulterated whiskey, maggot infested beef, and publicly denounced the so-called Indian-Ring, which profited from the Bureau of Indian Affairs' monopoly on supplying all reservation Indians with second rate merchandise at first rate prices, all under the guise of fulfilling treaty obligations. The colonel had intended to use it frequently during the war that never came about thanks to Tunstall, and so far he'd used it only for deer, elk, and one hapless she-bear. The range on the bear had been nearly half a mile. Jessup had measured it by stepping off the distance.

The colonel went to his headquarters, which was a small brick building, near the Palace of the Governors rented by the War Department. Once past the uniformed private who was on continuous sentry duty with his Model 1873 trapdoor Springfield single shot, 45-70 caliber rifle on his shoulder, Jessup walked into his private office nodded to the she-bear whose glass eyed head and skin graced the red tile floor, and unlocked a large leather and wood trunk with a domed lid, using a long iron key which he took from the long thin drawer of his gilt stamped leather topped walnut desk. He removed several items from the recesses of the trunk, a Russell's Green River Works skinning knife in a colorful beaded scabbard he'd purchased from a Mescalero Apache, several pairs of well worn Apache moccasins, arrows, and a serviceable Apache war bow. Jessup laid these Indian artifacts on his desk, carefully so as not to mar the leather. He went back to the trunk and removed a fine beaded leather Apache war shirt, looked at it with a connoisseur's eye, shook his head, and put is back in the chest, arranging it so that it folded properly. He shut the trunk, re-locked it, and replaced the key in the desk drawer.

Colonel Jessup didn't hate Indians the way the Klan hated Negroes. The Apaches, Zunis, Pima, Navajos, Cheyenne, and the hundred other smaller, lesser-known tribes in the Southwest, represented a culture, that in his opinion, had no more place in the United States of America than the Aztecs in Mexico or the Inca in Peru. The red man's time had come and gone and their way of life would be cast into the dust heap of history like all bygone civilizations from the Babylonians, to the Vikings, to the French Empire of Napoleon. The United States Army was the primary means of advancing white European mastery over the primitive, nomadic red man as well as the brown skinned Mexicans, who the colonel regarded as a mixture of Spanish, an inferior type of Southern European, and Indians, and therefore much inferior to the Northern European. Jessup was a firm believer in the white Christian God and the doctrine of Manifest Destiny and if Indians and Mexicans had to die in order to fulfill the latter then their loss should not be of the least moment to the former.

Jessup collected Indian beadwork, weapons, and all manner of relics. He had a genuine interest in preserving a comprehensive record of the very culture and way of life he was methodically eradicating from the Territory. He hated the thought of losing the objects he had on his desk; however the end he had in mind, more than justified the loss to his collection. As painful as it was he had already reconciled himself to the sacrifice.

Jessup was fond of Napoleon's saying that. "Every omelet demands the breaking of eggs." If his retribution demanded he sacrifice an Apache moccasin or two, a finely beaded knife scabbard, a bow and a few arrows then he was willing to make it. The war shirt wasn't necessary and besides an Indian might leave a moccasin in haste, even a knife after a fight, but no warrior would dream of leaving a war shirt behind.

As he continued to think things through, he decided that the war shirt might be needed after all, though it would be have to be worn during the mission. If anything happened to it, even a minor sweat stain, he would make the wearer sorry he had ever been born.

The colonel thought he should have an independent witness and he had a perfect candidate, a credible and thoroughly naive private. The private was from Virginia, a Southern boy, a disgrace to the military tradition of Old Virginia and scared to death of Indians. He believed they were all bloodthirsty savages who drank the blood of white men, quaffed it like claret, as they danced around the bodies of their hapless victims. The sight of an ancient squaw, dressed in rags, practically made his knees knock together and his teeth chatter. At least he was able to ride a horse without falling off.

The private would play Ichabod Crane in Jessup's version of The Legend of Sleepy Hollow only in this one the headless horseman would leave three very real victims. The colonel retrieved the key, unlocked the trunk, lifted the lid, and picked up the war shirt. It really was magnificent, the beadwork all sinew sewn, made for an Apache warrior to go into battle, not to sell to white men. "No," he thought. "It's much too fine to entrust to a Coyotero. Though they were useful to his designs, the colonel held the Coyoteros in low regard, and the thought of one of them, unwashed as they generally were, sweating into the buttery soft, brain tanned deer leather, was repugnant to him, a defilement and a desecration of a garment meant to be worn by a chief like Cochise. He would wear it himself, briefly, just long enough for the Virginian to see it, and gallop all the way back to Santa Fe to raise the alarm.

He packed all the articles on the desk into a long white, cotton sack with a drawstring closure. He folded the shirt with great care sleeves first, until it was as compact as it could be without putting undue strain on the beadwork, and placed it in a soft, tanned leather sack.

Having packed everything he thought would be required, Jessup sat down in his comfortable high-back, oak desk chair, on its form fitted, one-inch thick leather cushion. The colonel found himself in a quandary, he never expected, one that struck him like a lightning bolt out of a clear blue sky. He looked over the top of the desk into the sightless, yellow, glass eyes of the bear, not that he expected an answer from their lifeless depths, though it did temporarily distract him from his conundrum. Usually, no more than usually, invariably, moving seamlessly from abstraction to reality was the hallmark of Jessup's success not just in the army but all aspects of his life. He liked to think he had taken Rene Descartes' maxim 'Cogito ergo sum' to the next logical level. His motto was 'I think therefore I act'.

The colonel could uncannily foresee every conceivable contingency in almost every situation and long before difficulties arose he already had an effective solution. The utter failure of his painstakingly planned Indian uprising, which Tunstall and Betsy had forestalled, was the one glaring blot on his perfect record of achievements. Now the opportunity to even this old score, presented itself and the blame for the atrocity might, no probably would ignite the very war with the Apaches Tunstall had fought so hard to prevent. It was poetic justice at its best, and with his Sharps' 'Old Reliable' sniper's rifle and the Indian articles in his cloth and leather sacks Jessup thought he had the means to dispense it.

Of all the characters in Shakespeare's major tragedies, which the colonel knew from their opening lines to their final soliloquies, the one with whom he had the least empathy was Hamlet, Prince of Denmark. Jessup would not have spent weeks and months equivocating whether or not to kill Claudius. He would not have hesitated to avenge his father's foul murder the moment he learned the identity of the guilty party. Now, as he sat in his chair, he understood for the first time how an otherwise resolute man might not simply take up sword and dagger, or in his own instance, a Sharps 45-150 rifle and strike down the offending party. Jessup had already dismissed the idea of using any of the scouts. "Damn it all!" he said aloud in an extremely rare excess of self-loathing. "What ever is the matter with me?" he asked himself.

The head of the black she-bear remained silent. His own state of mind made absolutely no sense to him. All they stood in the way of his war were the lives of three people. It wasn't as if the colonel had moral qualms about killing men. As a seventeen year old corporal at the Battle of the Wilderness near Fredericksburg, there in the dense thickets, he used his Spencer seven shot repeating rifle to kill or wound more than a dozen of Lee's men earning himself a field promotion to second lieutenant in the process.

Jessup had never had the slightest intention of scalping the bodies himself. Nothing less than such a mutilation, which the Apaches had learned from the Spanish, would have to take place in order to suitably outrage the inhabitants of the Territory, not that the colonel regarded the practice of scalping as any more barbaric than killing but he knew that others felt differently. Exactly why it was so much more horrific and reprehensible to remove the scalp from a human skull than to remove a man's head entirely with an artillery shell, or too great a drop from the scaffold, made no sense. Then again despite all the great philosophers protestations to the contrary over thousands of years and diverse civilizations, men were essentially irrational, creatures of emotion and acted from primitive visceral responses having little to do with thought.

Why would it make such a difference to a man whether he killed a man a woman or a child. On November 29, 1864 1200 Army volunteers under the command of Colonel John N. Chivington murdered more than 150 Cheyenne children and women in Southeastern Colorado Territory. When the nature and extent of the slaughter, many of the women were scalped, their breasts slashed off, privates cut out, babies brained with butt-strokes of muskets; Jessup and many of his fellow officers were appalled and disgusted. Chivington was universally condemned and soon disgraced.

Over the next sixteen years, Jessup rose through the ranks to his present exalted status, and in quiet moments he would reflect on why it was heinous to kill women and children, and virtuous and heroic to slay men, even when the men were civilian non-combatants. Life was either all equally precious or equally worthless. The development of an artificial hierarchy in which the life of a young woman was more sacred than that of an older man who had spent years gathering wisdom and knowledge so that he was a veritable repository of learning struck Jessup as absurd.

Part of his present discomfiture was that during their luncheon, Rose, who was no more than a pretty prostitute, spoke enough about her friend and fellow whore, Gypsy, to have inadvertently humanized her. So if he saw her blonde hair under her sombrero or Stetson, through the clear ten power lenses of the telescope mounted on his Sharps, he'd be putting three hundred grains of lead through the skull or heart, not of some anonymous distant thing like the she-bear on his office floor, but Gypsy, the pretty golden haired whore who killed Hal Russell, a man to whom he'd taken an instant strong dislike that would have been hatred if Russell had been a man of any status worth considering. Jessup had had no compunction about silencing Duffy by pulling the ligature off his femoral artery, any more than he thought twice about stepping on a scorpion outside his tent when he was camped out in the desert. Duffy had had his uses; however over the years he had become a liability, and worst of all he had come to the erroneous and ultimately fatal conclusion that he no longer needed Colonel Jessup, except to fight Apache's at his beck and call.

Tunstall on the other hand was someone the Colonel would most certainly welcome in the field of view offered by the telescope affixed to his Sharps, or so he thought. Here, Jessup looked at the gold French repeater by Breguet, given to him by his regiment, at Christmas two years earlier. The finely pierced and engraved gold hands on the flawless white enamel face pointed to one twenty three. He replaced the watch in the special pocket for it in his uniform coat. He put the palm of his left hand up to his forehead, wondering if he were feverish.

"What on earth is wrong with me?" he said aloud. "Here I am in a better position that I was a year ago. Then I was ready for

Rat Face and El Gordo to massacre every soul in Early. To put it to the torch, dynamite it, use a Gatling gun on the Apaches, do anything to foment an uprising. Now, I'm acting like Hamlet over two young women and an arrogant old man, whom I'd like to run through twice with a triangular bayonet."

Jessup grasped the burl walnut desk-top with both hands, pushed his chair back and stood, then he began pacing the longest possible path in his office, a diagonal about twenty feet long, past the pine shelves of colorful Zuni and Hopi Indian pottery, Apache ollas and smaller finely woven and decorated smaller baskets. He intended to leave his collection to the Smithsonian Institute in Washington, either that or to his children, *if* and when he had any. That was presupposing he ever married, a life decision he'd postponed until such time as he was promoted to general, and not brevet rank either but a permanent rank. Promotion in the drastically reduced Army was now a rare event and wholly unlike it was during the Civil War. The step from full colonel to brigadier general, a foregone conclusion during the war, was now nearly impossible without serious support in Congress.

Jessup stumbled over the she bear's head then kicked her black nose with the toe of his boot cracking it open and exposing the plaster of Paris under the paint. Jessup didn't kick the bear out of petulance or pique, he needed an outlet for his mounting frustration with the unfamiliar phenomenon of self-doubt and ambivalence and the bear's head was convenient. He had never really liked game trophies to begin with and only had this one courtesy of the lieutenant who was with him at the time who had insisted he take the skin as much as a trusted subordinate could insist on anything to a colonel. The bear looked as if it belonged in the room, otherwise lieutenant or no, it would have been rolled up and locked away in one of the many trunks that contained Indian relics.

Jessup knew there was excellent historical precedent for a victorious warrior collecting the artifacts of an earlier defeated civilization. The Romans were great connoisseurs and collectors of Etruscan and Greek sculpture, bronzes, and pottery and the English looted and hoarded art and relics from vanquished peoples in all corners of their worldwide empire. Jessup quickened his walk and in so doing reminding himself of Captain Ahab pacing the quarterdeck of the Pequod. In a final outburst of frustration he kicked the bear in the teeth, breaking off the two oversize canines, which lay like two small white bones on the reddish-orange Spanish tiles of the floor. The colonel let out a sigh and ceased his walk having found the sword with which to cut his personal Gordian knot.

Chapter 17
AMBUSH

Gypsy hadn't been further than a few miles outside of Early in more than two years. Despite a recurring nightmare she'd experienced in the past several weeks in which she was sentenced to hang by a stern—faced judge, dressed in black, after hearing the jury foreman intone in a sepulchral voice, "We find the defendant guilty of murder," she was actually looking forward to seeing Santa Fe. Tunstall had gone to the extent of personally guaranteeing her appearance in court, thereby sparing her imprisonment in the Santa Fe City jail, a relic from the days the city was a provincial Mexican capital, and constructed with the usual Spanish prison emphasis on security at the expense of comfort. The cells were cramped, dark, and dank, with ancient ponderous iron fetters anchored in the thick stone- walls, and canvas pallets, stuffed with straw as beds.

Instead, Tunstall had engaged the spacious, airy, hotel suite, he customarily occupied whenever he was in the capitol on official or personal business. The mayor's first task on arrival would be to meet with the judge, whom he knew slightly, show him Jack Jones', Doc Hill's, and Francine's sworn affidavits and make certain that the charge against Gypsy would be manslaughter rather than murder. He was as confident as he could be when dealing with the vicissitudes of the law that this could be done, and had explained it all to Gypsy.

For her part, Betsy was optimistic about Gypsy's chances for an acquittal, although she did not underestimate the salient fact that the jury would be composed of men a few of whom would identify with Hal Russell, regardless of whether or not he'd beaten her half to death, which he hadn't, and feel his blood cry out for justice. Most fortuitously, Jack Jones would not be testifying about what a good partner and friend he had in Hal Russell. A sorrowing Jones would have more influence over the jury, than Gypsy's face would, if Hal had carved it up with his Bowie. Betsy knew most men would close ranks against a woman irrespective of the merits in any given dispute, and the twelve men who would judge Gypsy would be no different. This was why she agreed with Tunstall's strategy of immediately reducing the charge, which took hanging or life imprisonment off the table entirely. There was a negative to this, as there always seemed to be when dealing with legal matters. The same men who might shrink at the prospect of dooming a pretty, young girl to hanging might not hesitate to convict her on the lesser charge. What little chivalry they possessed in their limited natures would not countenance death, but would rest easy knowing Gypsy would spend ten years in the Territorial prison.

"The way I see it," said Tunstall to the two women before they left Early, "*You* never know what a jury will do for sure until the verdict is read. So if there's a one in a hundred chance of hanging, well, I think that's one chance too many." Betsy and Gypsy agreed.

Tunstall let Gypsy ride his own pony, as Enoch Swank had kindly let the mayor borrow his beloved Paso Fino. There were a few towns on the road to Santa Fe, a few watering holes, and little else but mesquite, soap-weed, creosote, yucca, and sage, brush and bushes, and the occasional cottonwood. Animal life during the heat of the day was limited to jackrabbits, hawks, and vultures though once Betsy spied an eagle soaring on the thermals high above them. The road wasn't so much a road as a trail, a path that ran from Early roughly paralleling the narrow gage railroad tracks until the railroad veered west to Albuquerque through the Estancia Valley. Their trail then followed the Pecos River up into the foothills of the Sangre de Christos. Unless the traveler was content to sleep in a friendly rancher's barn, there were no formal lodgings between Santa Rosa and Santa Fe. Though the distance was slightly over a hundred miles, the trail was rough, and the altitude together with the torrid heat of late summer precluded a fast passage. The horses were content to trot for a mile or two, and even canter, as long as they could walk most of the time. They slept out under the vast magnificence of the Territorial night sky. Tunstall entertained them by identifying not just the common constellations like Ursa Major, whose seven brightest stars are the most characteristic features in the Northern sky, known as the Big Dipper or Clare's Wain, and Scorpio, but the more obscure like the Pleides. He showed them Betelguese, the brightest star in Orion, that forms the Eastern shoulder of the hunter and told them that the star's name comes from the Arabic, 'bat al dshuaza', meaning 'giant's shoulder'.

> "I'll tell you right now," he said. "The only reason I know about the Arabic is because Enoch told me one night and I thought it was interesting enough to remember. Somehow the Greeks saw their legendary giant and handsome hunter in the stars and the Arabs either saw it the same way, or inherited the Greek legend when Alexander of Macedon conquered the Persians."

Lying on her bedroll, her back and thighs warmed by the sandy soil that retained the sun's heat, for as the road climbed higher into the foot-hills, the thin air cooled quickly after the sun set, not yet sharply, but by the small hours, Gypsy knew she would be thankful for her thick wool blanket. Even though her future was more than merely uncertain, sometimes it seemed nothing short of terrifying, as she looked up at the sky, listening to Tunstall's sonorous voice, Gypsy saw, she really saw Orion, not as a series of bright, bluish, white lights, but as a celestial being, complete with club, lion's skin, sword, and girdle. Gypsy's eyes filled with tears and she tried to recall when she'd last felt so much joy.

Tunstall's mind was not entirely at peace, and wouldn't be until Gypsy was exculpated. Still he was enjoying the journey and Betsy's company, which was usually more limited than he would have liked, either by his affairs, or hers, meaning Sara. He was trying to think of the last time they were outside together all night and was having a hard time doing so. Like everything he did with Betsy, at the time he was doing it, he chastised himself for not doing it more frequently. Then another month would slip by as stealthily and unseen as a single day, and his questioning why they didn't spend more time together would resurface. Betsy's right hand was warm in his and he was reluctant to relinquish it. The night was so effulgently lovely it wanted only a capful of cognac from his silver traveling flask and a cheroot to render the moment perfection, itself.

He moved his hand and sat up on his bedroll.

"I'm going to have a nightcap and a smoke. Would either of you two ladies care to join me?"

They both answered affirmatively, and Tunstall took three thin, dark black cigars from his hard leather cigar case, carefully lit two in the glowing embers of the campfire, handing one to Betsy, the other to Gypsy, then lit his last. He then passed around the silver flask with the pebbled, maroon, Morocco, leather band. The flask had a silver cup that screwed on to the top of the flask, and a stopper of silver and cork attached by a silver chain.

Tunstall thought, "The English must take their spirits seriously to have designed such an excellent container to keep a half pint of liquor so neatly packaged for imbibing while hiking on foot or riding horseback."

The flask was made by Asprey's of Bond Street, London, silver smiths by appointment to Queen Victoria and bore the royal arms of the rampant lion and unicorn in consequence proudly engraved in a small cartouche as well as the usual hallmarks on the bottom. Tunstall had first seen one like it belonging to the previous governor while they shared a drink together sitting on a bench outside the municipal square. Tunstall had expressed his admiration for it at the time, and the governor allowed as how he'd give it to him only he'd just have to order another one and it took months.

"There's the delay and of course anything from Asprey's is 'bloody expensive' as the British say." Tunstall ordered his own and it was not only costly, it took the better part of six months to arrive; however he'd never regretted either the expense or the wait. At times like this one the Asprey flask was invaluable.

The smoke from their cheroots blended with the smoke from the mesquite fire and the sagebrush nearby in such a way that Betsy thought the spicy aroma was the perfume of the trail. She had told Sara and Ben she wouldn't be away for more than ten days at the longest, and as her presence wasn't strictly necessary at Gypsy's trial, that was assuming there would even be one after Tunstall presented the affidavits to the judge. Sara would have cried and carried on that she wanted to go to Santa Fe but for the fact that there was a ceremony being held for young girls who were being initiated into the mysteries of preparing the sacred mescal plant for festivals. One of the girls was a relation of Deaf Charley and she had invited Sara to attend. Ben told her it was an unprecedented honor for anyone but a full blooded Mescalero Apache girl to know the secrets of preparing mescal, the food that gave the Mescalero Apaches their name, and he told Betsy it was an indication of the high esteem the tribe in which the tribe held Sara.

Aside from Sara being a winsome, beautiful, and fearless little girl, her courage during her brief captivity by El Gordo and the Coyoteros, had awed Deaf Charley and his companions, to such a degree that they told nearly every Apache on the reservation of the little white girl who had the heart of an Apache warrior. Thanks to Ben and Charlie, Betsy had a reputation as a warrior among the Indians as well, though nothing like Sara's, whose bravery had assumed legendary proportions, so much so that even the young, restless Apache braves, who believed all whites were demons, accepted Sara's presence on the reservation without demur.

Sara liked nothing better than to be accepted by the Indians, so Betsy was easy in her mind about her daughter, as she sat smoking her cigar, warmed by the fine brandy in her belly, and Tunstall's limpid brown eyes on her face.

The night breeze strengthened momentarily, causing the cherry red embers to flare briefly into a yellow flame as a mesquite branch that wasn't utterly reduced to charcoal caught fire. They didn't hobble the horses, though they were tied loosely to a nearby mesquite bush. There were mountain lions and black bear in the foothills, though both would hunt wide of a campfire, and wanted nothing to do with humans or anything that smelled of man. There hadn't been an Indian attack on the trail in months and the few Jicarilla or Chirhuacahua Apaches who lived in the Sangre de Christo Mountains and refused to be confined on a reservation generally avoided white men like the smallpox. Prospectors were known to disappear from time to time, though no one knew whether they fell victim to accident or attack by man or beast.

As many times as Tunstall had made the trip from Early to the capitol and back, nothing really untoward had ever happened. There'd been the usual mishaps associated with travel on horseback. Once he'd had to walk from Glorietta to Santa Fe after Abraham picked up a stone in his left front hoof, and he'd often had to assist other travelers with water and other aid from time to time.

Using his right thumb and index finger, Tunstall flicked the butt of his cigar out into the high desert night. The trajectory described an arc, and it spun end for end, cart-wheeling like a miniature Catherine wheel, then it struck the stony ground, casting a few fiery fragments of burning tobacco then lay still, glowing orange red like the eye of some fantastic creature. Betsy and Gypsy had long since extinguished their smokes, tossing them into the campfire without fanfare, when they were half-finished and beginning to taste acrid.

Tunstall looked from his reluctantly discarded cheroot to Betsy, who had fallen asleep. He wished it were just he and Betsy, so he could snuggle up next to her, brush her cool lips with his, and if she weren't sound asleep, she would kiss him back, and explore his teeth with the hot, soft tip of her tongue, something she liked to do as a prelude to kissing deeply and passionately, which was her overture to lovemaking. Betsy was not shy and if Gypsy had had a lover with her, Betsy would have no compunction about loving Tunstall, or suppressing her sometimes quite loud moans when she achieved her climax. However as Gypsy had no one, Betsy wouldn't dream of making love with him, and he was content to wait until they had time alone in Santa Fe. Tunstall was weary from the trail, though Enoch's Paso Fino offered an incredibly smooth ride, especially the running walk, the Paso's version of the non-gaited horse's trot.

"Should I have another cigar?" He debated then decided to forgo the pleasure.

He had another cup-full of brandy instead and watched as a falling star flashed across Ursa Minor, the Little Bear, near Polaris, which Enoch had told him roughly marked the North celestial pole. He watched the point of blue light fade as it reached the Western horizon, then he lay down on his bedroll and closed his eyes. As an exercise and soporific, Tunstall tried to remember all that Enoch had told him about Ursa Major, the Big Dipper. That it was referred to twice in the Book of Job and once in Homer's Iliad. He thought it was something about the nymph Callisto being placed by Zeus in the heavens as a bear together with her son Arcos, as a 'bear-keeper', and Arcturus and the Greeks naming the constellation Arctos or the 'she-bear'. The scratching sound of lizard feet on the sand near his head made him open his eyes for a moment, then he closed them and remembered the Romans used the term, ursa, for bear, then his mind stepped lightly over the line separating drowsiness from light sleep, while the lizard sought to capture a black beetle before crawling under a small flat sandstone outcropping near the camp-site.

Tunstall's bladder woke him when the quarter moon was high in the Western sky. He didn't check his watch as the moon told him it was past three in the morning and his bladder confirmed it. The air was cool on his face, and his right shoulder ached slightly from supporting his weight as he slept on his right side. Tunstall was warm and comfortable under his wool blanket. Except for his insistent bladder, he would have rolled onto his left side and gone back to sleep.

He knew he'd been dreaming about an incident from his childhood, something about a neighbor boy, Daniel Brown, who grew up to be a lawyer, or at least he was when last Tunstall heard of him, more than ten years ago. In the dream they were exploring a riverbank, he thought it might have been the Potomac or the James. They'd come to a wide mud-flat and basking in the sun were hundreds of alligator snapping turtles, some the size of a silver dollar, others as big around as a dinner plate, and a few as large as wagon wheels with human size heads. Dan and he were both shoeless and all around the flat were stinging nettles as tall as hickory trees and thick as his leg. They knew the turtles saw them. As they stood there staring, the really massive ones swiveled their heads in their direction, looking at them with glistening, reptilian eyes filled with infinite malice.

"Either we cross now," said Daniel, "Or we better go back."

"That one over to the right looks like he wants to take our legs clean off," said Tunstall. Then he noticed the turtles were actually arranged in a geometric figure that left diagonal spaces of several feet between them, making it feasible to dash across to the other side if the animals didn't change position. He pointed this out to Daniel, who said, "We could dive into the river and swim around them."

The boys had shunned the river thus far as the water was brownish with silt and mud, and the deep channel was some distance from the bank. Then they were both running on two parallel diagonals, closest to each other, as fast as they could, their feet skinning over the warm mud, making sucking noises, as they fairly flew across the flat. Then one of the largest turtles, the size of a pony on its side, whipped its long snake-like head to the side, as snapping turtles are known to do, and Tunstall heard a stomach wrenching crunch as the razor-like crushing jaws closed on Daniel's left femur. After that the dream consisted of an increasingly bizarre series of disconnected confusing events Tunstall couldn't recall with any coherence or clarity.

Enoch Swank subscribed to the theory that dreams were anything but meaningless, random associations of the human brain.

"I must respectfully and completely disagree with Descartes' statement that, 'Memory can never connect our dreams one with the other, or with the whole course of our lives as it unites events which happen to us while we are awake'. Pardon me if I say the great Frenchman is full of 'merde'. Look at the divinatory dreams in the Bible, Joseph, Daniel, and the other patriarchs and kings. The Mormon patriarch, Joseph Smith Jr., claimed the angel Moroni appeared to him in a dream and directed him to the buried golden plates that described the Indians as one of the lost tribes of Israel, not that I'm a Mormon. I have a copy of Alfred Maury's work on dreams. Maury is a physician who studied more than 3000 reported recollections of dreams. Maury concludes that dreams arise from external stimuli that instantly accompany such impressions as they act on the sleeper. One night part of Maury's bed fell on the back of his neck, he gives no details of this most interesting mishap. To make his long story short, the bed falling on his neck, woke him and left him with the memory of being guillotined. Coleridge wrote 'Kublai Kahn' after composing it in a dream. I tell you," here Enoch waxed even more fervent, "From my own experiences I am convinced that dreaming is another dimension of multiple realities, one every bit as real as the world we live in when we're said to be waking."

267

The apothecary then commenced to relate a lengthy and detailed chronicle of his dreams and their remarkable similarity to his conscious actions and encounters he'd undergone after ingesting various medicinal plants in the company of Indian shamans.

> "We'd actually travel together to sacred places in the mountains and the desert using our dreams, and all this occurred while we were what you'd call awake. I tell you it's incredible, and as real as we're sitting here right now." As much as Tunstall respected Enoch's scientific and linguistic acumen, he didn't entirely accept Enoch's contention that dreams were real in the sense that daily life was, governed by the laws of Newtonian mathematics and physics, as well as the laws of chemistry. He expressed these doubts to Enoch who replied, "At first glance what you say about physical laws of this world might seem to be the case; however when a man with an open and inquiring mind delves into Sir Isaac's higher mathematics involving calculating the surface areas of spheres, mathematical certainty seems less of a concrete reality and more of a beautiful approximation. And Newton's greatest observation into the phenomenon of gravitation states that 'every particle in the universe attracts every other particle with a force proportional to the product of their masses and inversely proportional to the square of the distance between their centers'. All of us, including Newton must rely on pi, which is a most irrational number, to calculate the surface areas of spherical objects, rendering them an approximation rather than a certainty. It's wonderful when you think about it."

Tunstall thought of all these things as he was pissing on sagebrush at a discreet distance from the two sleeping women. He supposed Enoch would think that in some alternate or parallel reality, a monstrous turtle, the size of a water trough was feasting on Daniel's leg, thirty years or more in the past.

Tunstall rarely slept through the night without having to relieve himself at least once. His stream was strong and made a spattering sound as of a rain gutter emptying itself onto the ground as the urine displaced enough soil to create a small puddle. The quarter moon was brilliant enough to turn the arcing stream silver with its light. He thought about the snapping turtles and wished Enoch were there to talk about whatever it meant. One thing he was sure of as he shook his penis to make certain it was empty, for his had a nasty habit of withholding a drop or two particularly when it was cold outside, was that Hamlet was right when he told Horatio that 'There are more things in heaven and earth than are dreamt of in your philosophy'. "One Hell of a lot more," thought Tunstall as he re-buttoned his drawers.

Tunstall removed his boots before lying down and he'd gotten up wearing his stockings without going through the cumbersome process of re-booting himself. Walking in stocking feet in the high desert in the early hours of the morning, when the nocturnal dwellers such as rattlesnakes and scorpions are actively hunting their prey, their cold blood enjoying the re—radiated heat of the sun stored in the first few inches of the soil may not have been the best idea; however he was less concerned about stepping on a scorpion or sidewinder than he was about tracking sand or small pebbles into his bedroll. He sat down and carefully brushed the soles of his feet before lying back down under his blanket. He looked up at Ursa Major and as he did, he could see many of the fainter stars which made up the visible portion of the Milky Way. Like other men since time out of mind, Tunstall reflected on the sheer immensity of the cosmos, and the infinite reaches of space which would never see or know anything of man, and the folly of man thinking his individual life was of importance outside his own insignificant circle, even a Christ, a Buddha, Alexander, or a Lincoln.

"Tunstall," he thought, "You're just going to give yourself a sleepless night doing this to yourself. Think about a hot bath in your suite, and a naked Betsy Johnson in that big, four poster, mahogany bed with the goose down pillows and feather mattress."

He pictured Betsy in the altogether and this was not conducive to sleep either, so he changed his thinking and it lighted on the dream of Dan Brown and the turtles. Tunstall turned over for the third time within a space of five minutes, becoming progressively less comfortable and more annoyed with each oscillation. Giving up on the right side and left side altogether, he lay on his back and stared up at the blue-black sky, studded with countless stars, closed his eyes and listened to the night wind rattle the dry stalks of weeds, scattering their seeds, picking up the fine dust here and there and carrying it a few feet, as if it weren't very serious about blowing after all. The occasional chirring of the night birds, soothed rather than jarred Tunstall, and as he listened to the soft susurrations of Betsy and Gypsy, he smiled to himself. "If Judge Holborn is on the circuit, there will be no trial, only a modest fine for assault. This might not satisfy Marcie Cabot; however given Holborn's respected stature in the Territory, there won't be anything much she can do about it after the fact." It was late summer and if Gypsy's and his stars were in conjunction, the old gentleman should be presiding over the court. As he contemplated this pleasant prospect Tunstall finally fell asleep.

When Betsy first opened her eyes, the rays of the nascent sun had only just begun to illuminate the few long thin clouds overhead, turning them from steel grey to pink. A few quail were calling to each other, sweetening the air with their melodious calls. The air was not quite cool, though it had a hint of autumn in it, due more to the altitude than the advancing season. Betsy was comfortable and warm inside her bedroll. She lazed and luxuriated in it for a few minutes, inhaling the early morning air as if it were a rare fragrance. There was a scent of sage, which always put Betsy in mind of the first day she'd spent in the Territory, and Ben had rubbed some sage between his leathery hands and held them palms up for her to sniff.

"This," he said with a warm smile, "is the smell of the New Mexico Territory. Beautiful, isn't it?"

It was spicy, pungent, foreign, exciting, fresh, and clean. Betsy agreed with the Indian, and never failed to appreciate the exquisite aroma.

Betsy was by no means as sanguine about Gypsy's immediate future as the mayor. If Tunstall failed to nip it in the bud with Judge Holborn, she figured the twelve men would look at Gypsy and see, a young, pretty prostitute, who killed not just her lover, but another woman's husband. They would see her as a home-wrecker, a Jezebel and a murderer. True there were extenuating circumstances and those would save her from the hangman, still Betsy thought five years in prison was the best she could hope for. Tunstall concurred with her calculation and was pinning his hopes on a successful, pre-trial judicial ruling.

"Well," she thought, "We'll see if the judge is there. If he is, then fine. If he isn't we'll have to consider the alternatives. Meantime I have to piss."

Betsy finished easing herself in nearly the exact spot where Tunstall had relieved himself a few hours earlier. She arranged some dead mesquite branches for the morning fire to boil water and make coffee. Neither she nor Tunstall would consider beginning their day without coffee. The slightly noxious trail brew which demanded the grounds remain suspended in the brownish, near-boiling water, precipitated to the bottom of the metal cup by cooler water would have to suffice. Trail coffee looked and tasted similar to mud, but it was hot, strong, and far better than none at all. The aroma of coffee and frying ham slices quickly roused the two sleepers and following breakfast, the three mounted their horses and took the road northwest to Glorietta and Santa Fe.

They were in the foothills of the Sangre de Christo, having taken the fork away from the Pecos River with its headwaters near the foot of Truchas Peak. Close by the road were the ruins of the ancient Indian pueblo of Pecos as well as the remains of two Spanish missions constructed in the 17th and 18th centuries. Tunstall was riding on the outside, closest to the ruined missions when out of the corner of his eye he thought he saw movement on a mud brick wall, perhaps four feet high and four hundred yards off.

"I think we have company," he said to Betsy and Gypsy. "Don't look, but on the count of three I think we should get the Hell out of here as fast as we can." Betsy and Gypsy held their breath. They both wanted nothing so much as to look in the direction of the ruined missions. Instead they prepared to ask their horses to make the fastest transition possible from a walk to a canter or gallop. All three horses would take cues from changes in the rider's seat and leg pressure, and were collecting themselves for the run. The animals were fresh and well rested. Tunstall knew this and counted on it as he said, "One, two, three," and as the horses felt boot heels press their bellies, they broke into a lope, pushing off with their powerful rear legs, and then into the four beat gallop as the riders all brought their weight sharply forward in their saddles and stirrups. Tunstall's body was twisted to the right on his hips, keeping an eye on the reddish mud wall. He saw a bright orange flash and simultaneously heard a loud boom, like a single peal of thunder. He knew it was a heavy caliber rifle and before this thought had time to fully register, he was nearly lifted out of his saddle by a three hundred grain lead bullet traveling at slightly less than a quarter of a mile per second. The impact slammed him forward and if his hands hadn't gripped the high horn of Enoch's saddle, he would have fallen off and likely been dragged to death. As it was the Paso Fino felt the reins slacken and the complete lack of bit pressure against the soft yielding back part of the stallion's mouth, made him drop back into a walk lacking impulsion. Betsy and Gypsy heard the explosion and were already far ahead of Tunstall.

"You keep riding!" Betsy yelled at Gypsy. "I'm going back."

"I'm going with you," said Gypsy.

"Don't be a fool!" said Betsy at the top of her lungs. "Keep going!" Gypsy quickly slowed Tunstall's horse and turned him around at a fast trot, then urged him into a canter. Betsy was too overcome with fear, shock, and horror, to discourage Gypsy further, so she slowed Abby to a lope and turned her to the left using a gentle rein and left leg and loped after Gypsy.

Tunstall had been shot once before by a disgruntled litigant whose lawsuit naming a neighboring rancher, Tunstall had summarily dismissed as without merit. His ivory handled gavel had no sooner hit the small block of ebony he used to protect the marquetry inlay work of his desktop, when the rancher took one look at the grinning face of the man he sued, drew a Remington two shot .41 rim-fire caliber derringer from his vest pocket and shot Tunstall in the left shoulder. It was a flesh wound and it burned like a live coal. Doc Hill extracted the slug, disinfected the wound, and Tunstall went about his business an hour later. The rancher apologized for losing his temper and Tunstall fined him one hundred dollars for disturbing the peace. Tunstall's magnanimity greatly enhanced his reputation as a brave and generous man, not only in Early but in Santa Fe as well.

He knew that this time it was no derringer bullet and the boom was not from a .44 caliber Winchester either. The pain was actually less severe than the derringer slug though he knew the numbness in his chest and back was only temporary and that his entire body was in shock from the impact. He was stunned as a miner is when a ledge of rock weighing thousands of pounds caves in on him, leaving him crushed and conscious, but feeling little pain until death takes him.

Tunstall had often discussed death with Enoch Swank, usually over drinks and cigars. The two men were in agreement that man's fear of death was his ultimate expression of irrationality for death was a 'necessary end that will come when it will come', regardless of human action. Swank once summarized one of Count Tolstoy's novels, 'The Cossacks'. The hero, an aristocratic Muscovite, Dimitri Olenin, enlists as a cadet and is sent to serve among the Cossacks in the Caucasus. The city dweller and aesthete comes to an appreciation of life in the country and becomes conscious of the natural rhythm of life, something he never knew in Moscow. Olenin goes hunting and has a revelation that every living thing, even a mosquito, "Is just such a separate Dimitri Olenin as I am myself."

The area of numbness now encompassed most of Tunstall's back, radiating out from a locus, just under his left shoulder blade, or scalpula as Enoch would call it. He didn't know if the wound were mortal or not, though he was cold, so cold his teeth were chattering. He was shivering and wanted to lie down in his bedroll under his blanket. Though much of his body had lost sensation his mind was preternaturally alert. He remained bent over the saddle horn so he would present less of a profile to the shooter, that, and he was afraid of moving and jarring the bullet, causing more internal bleeding. He was worried that the shot was only a prelude to a concerted attack. It had to have come from a buffalo rifle, either a Sharps big 50 caliber or a Spencer single shot, though he supposed it was possible it could have been an 1876 Winchester 50-95 express. There were precious few buffalo in this part of the Territory before the coming of the white man. Except for the North, most of the New Mexico Territory was too arid to support the grass they needed to survive. The caliber was much too heavy for even the largest mule deer or elk, which were the largest game animals unless one counted black bear, and in either case a buffalo cartridge would spoil too much meat, and except for the Winchester the guns were too heavy for much use beyond hunting from a stand using shooting sticks.

Betsy wasn't thinking clearly as she and Abby quickly covered the last few hundred yards at a dead run. There was her over-reaching need to rescue her man, driven by both conscious terror and unconscious guilt about having left her father, when he was fatally wounded, all alone to face the fury of the Klan. She had had no choice for as Josiah said the authorities would have hanged her for murder, and that was predicated on her living long enough to be tried in a court of law, and not be taken out of the local jail and summarily lynched. For her own sake and Sara's she could not do anything but flee for her life. Now less than two years later, closer to one year than two, the agony of that decision was replaying itself. Betsy's thoughts were rushing through her mind on no fewer than three levels. There were Gypsy, Tunstall, and Sara to consider. Gypsy was in immediate danger from attack, as were Tunstall and her, and through her, Sara. If she died what would happen to Sara? Ideally Ben would raise her, but without Tunstall as mayor and justice of the peace, Marcie Cabot and Reverend Gilbert would never permit Sara to be raised by Indians. Sara would either be adopted by a family on Marcie's approved list, or God forbid sent to an orphanage from which Sara would doubtless escape at the first opportunity. Betsy's death would result in Sara continuing to suffer an unending sequence of terrible, dislocating moves.

"I never gave this a thought when I was trying to arrest Hal Russell for giving Francine a broken nose. He could have shot me. What a fool I was. What a complete and utter idiot," she thought. "Lord," she prayed, "If I get out of this alive, I'm turning in my badge for good. I'm going to be a mother, not a marshal, I promise. For Thine is the Kingdom, the power and the glory, forever and ever, Amen." Gypsy was scared and her heart was pounding, still she wasn't so full of the sort of fear that so overwhelms all other sensations, that all one knows is stark, sheer terror. She did not despise her life, and though she had no special love like Rose had with Jack, she took her pleasure in nature, a warm day, clean clothes, a good meal, and a greeting from a friend on her way to the saloon. These were enough to make her happy most of the time. She got the blues now and again, like everyone else, especially if she thought about her little boy in Houston growing up thinking she was dead or had deserted him or not knowing her at all, but Gypsy was young and she had faith in the goodness of God, who would see everything right in the end. If He wanted her boy to know her He would find the right way and time, and if He didn't than God had His reasons and who was she to question them? This same childlike faith made it possible for her to accept that the Lord had used her as His instrument in effecting Harold Russell's death, assuaging any pangs of guilt she might otherwise have felt. She was sorry for Hal, though her sorrow was far less powerful than her anger at him for making her stab him and now face going to prison. In the moments before she knifed him, his eyes were not those of a human, they were the eyes of a foul wild beast. They reflected an evil so monstrous that it had no rightful place on earth, a loathsome, unspeakably vile excrescence from the depths of Hell. Hal at that moment was like no human being Gypsy ever dreamt existed in her worst nightmares.

Gypsy was no horsewoman. However, it seemed to her that Abraham Lincoln could read her thoughts. She had no more than to think canter than she would be loping effortlessly, a sweet rocking sensation that delighted her much more than riding a man, almost any man.

Tunstall heard his horse, long before he saw him by turning his head. He heard two horses so he knew Betsy and Gypsy had come back, putting themselves in harm's way in a noble, heroic, though entirely futile effort to save him. Tunstall's head which only a second before was as heavy and difficult to turn as if the weight of the world were in it and on it, now seemed as light as a feather. He had every intention of excoriating Betsy for returning then he remembered how she'd left her father's side. It was supremely difficult for Tunstall, who believed in the signal importance of the beau gest, the grand gesture, whether wildly successful or no more than a magnificent failure, to allow the woman he loved more than all the others he'd known combined, the freedom to make one herself. He knew he owed this to Betsy and not only that she damned well deserved the chance to make the sacrifice. This was her opportunity to put things right in her mind after what happened back in Tennessee and if it cost her life, than that was her decision to make it, and he would just have to live with it or die with is as the case might be.

What astonished Tunstall the most, aside from the absence of excruciating pain, and the incredible lightness of his head, was the fact there were no more shots being fired from the ruins of the Spanish missions. He was so sure there would be more heavy caliber rifle fire, or a mounted attack he would have bet his life on it and lost. He couldn't imagine he'd made an enemy so deadly, he would lie in wait to assassinate him, unless it was one of Rat Face's Coyoteros who escaped the nitroglycerin. Regardless, whatever he'd done to incur such a degree of enmity was now expiated, and any karmic debts he might have owed would be stamped 'paid in full' by the mysterious, unknown and unknowable Power that some men called God, others the Great Spirit, and a thousand other names, all the hopelessly inadequate verbal expressions to describe something so vast no man with his limited capacities could even begin to define, anymore than a grain of sand could adequately represent the Sonoran Desert or a drop of rainwater, the Pacific Ocean.

Colonel Jessup watched Tunstall, Gypsy, and Betsy through the excellent lenses of his telescopic sight. After an intense internal debate, carefully weighing all positives and negatives, using his risk versus reward paradigm, he'd decided before he rode southeast from Santa Fe, not to employ the Coyoteros to attack Tunstall's party. Rat Face and El Gordo were real jefes, men who would not have fared well in a drawing room, or who bathed regularly, or even knew how to use a knife and fork; however their word once given, was good, and they would die rather than betray a confidence, which was all Jessup required to transact business with another man. Not that the colonel would have wanted either one as a brother-in-law, but to terrorize the Territory, dressed as Apaches, they were nothing short of ideal. The Coyoteros left behind in the capitol, were no more than pale imitations of their deceased commanders, and as the highest ranking soldier in the New Mexico Territory, excepting General George Crook, whose presence was only temporary, he had far too much to lose by trusting his affairs to such thin reeds.

The other consideration was that while the Navajo were peacefully settled on their huge reservation in the Western part of the Territory, the Eastern Apaches, the Lipan, and the Chirachuachua were mostly nomadic and aggressive. Although from 1871 until 1873, it appeared that the majority of the Apaches, the Mescaleros and the Jicarilla, as well as their more nomadic brothers, were resigned to life on a reservation, a substantial number of warriors refused to accept a life they saw as nothing more than imprisonment. Their refusal to walk the path the white man insisted they take was seen as a threat to the United States by the War Department and the Indian Bureau. Two leaders, Victorio and Goyathlay, known as Geronimo, were the legitimate heirs of the greatest of all Apache war chiefs, Cochise and Mangas Colorado. Lieutenant Colonel George F. Crook, brevet Brigadier General, was the commander of the Department of Arizona, and presently in Washington. The Apaches confined on the barren wasteland of the San Carlos Reservation in East-Central Arizona were both homesick and physically ill, even dying, from eating the maggoty beef, weevily flour, and the usual trash masquerading as rations for Native Americans foisted off by the government in fulfillment of their treaty obligations. Crook's fragile peace had already unraveled in the West and it was only a matter of time before the peaceful Mescalero and Jicarilla tribes in the New Mexico Territory became sufficiently restive for Jessup to exploit their discontent. A year ago more active and provocative measures were called for, hence Jessup's alliance with Rat Face and El Gordo. The Indian loving, meddling, mayor of Early had single handedly put paid to their well laid plans.

Thus, after due consideration, Jessup had put away the Apache moccasins, the bow and arrows, and the Green River Works skinning knife with the richly beaded sheath, eventually taking only the superb war shirt and the Sharps rifle. He carefully timed his departure so he would have to spend no more than one night in the ruins of the Spanish missions in Pecos.

Assuming the information he'd received during his lunch with Jack Jones and Rose, the mildly attractive prostitute he was traveling with, was accurate, he would only kill the two women as a last resort if they saw him after he settled with Tunstall. Colonel Jessup was not so much averse to shooting them; however mutilating their bodies by scalping them was for some reason abhorrent to him. The United States Army paid him, and paid him well to kill on receipt of orders, and unlike his brother officers, Jessup did not think a white woman was any more deserving of life or mercy, than an Indian woman, just because the one allegedly worshipped Jesus or God and the other, the Great Spirit. The colonel subscribed to the spirit of the Declaration of Independence. To him, all men and woman were equal, Indians, Negroes, whites, and Mexicans. None was any better or worse than the other by virtue of his having been born with certain sex organs, skin color, hair, or eyes. Jessup had respected and liked Rat Face and this liking was at the root of his vendetta with Tunstall. Jessup had absolutely no respect for General Philip Sheridan whose well—known prejudice against

Indians the colonel regarded as ignorant, repugnant, and unworthy of an American Army officer. Jessup really had no quarrel with Tunstall's love of Indians, except that this love had interfered with what was certain to be an unusually profitable enterprise.

The colonel intention was to make enough money to go to Central America and use his considerable military acumen and his fortune to overthrow a government, and establish his own republic, founded on the principles stated in the Declaration, with him as president. After the Civil War, a group of Confederate soldiers, who refused to swear allegiance to the Union they'd been fighting for nearly five years, had gone to South America and very nearly succeeded in doing just what he intended to do only he knew he would succeed. Colonel Jessup understood the limits of military force better than the Confederates; and that military might combined with a sufficient quantity of gold would prevail where force alone would fail.

Tunstall had broken this dream with quixotic courage and benighted meddling. Now, thanks to the Sharps Rifle Company it seemed to the colonel that Tunstall was finally paying the price for his interference. As Jessup continued to observe the large man in the black suit, bent over the saddle horn, with a great wet stain, soaking through the jacket, and covering the entire back, he was convinced that the mayor had discharged any debt he owed him in full.

Chapter 18
DEATH OF A MAYOR

Due to the altitude, the morning air was cool; however the sun was hot. Even so Tunstall was as cold as if it were mid-winter and not late summer. There was a tussock of dry grass near Enoch's horse, and after she dismounted, Betsy led the Paso to the tussock. Gypsy followed, also on foot, carrying their two bedrolls. The two women arranged the bedrolls on the grass so as to make as thick and soft a bed as possible. As she lead Tunstall's horse, she could hear his teeth chattering, and she saw his entire back was black and soaked with blood.

It seemed to Tunstall, that his head had divorced itself from the rest of his body. Though his hands and feet, even his legs and arms were functioning, his chest and trunk had little or no sensation. He knew this was due to shock otherwise the pain would be unbearable. He heard soldier's stories of men who lost legs to cannon shells and some had no pain whatever at the time they were hit. They were capable of rational speech, though they all complained of being cold even at Gettysburg where it was over 100 degrees in the shade, and he was cold, so very cold.

He was extremely reluctant to give up his hold on the saddle horn. It was as if that grip was the only connection he had to the land of the living, though the cold finally overcame his reluctance. At Betsy's urging, he loosened and repositioned his hands as the sight of the bed they'd arranged and more significantly the thick wool blankets proved stronger than his fear of letting go. Betsy pulled the stirrups from his boots and his legs hung loose. Tunstall tried to raise himself to a sitting position by pushing up on the horn with both hands, and only managed to rise a few inches. This weakness frightened him, even more than the numbness and the cold.

"I'm sorry, Betsy," he said in as strong a voice as he could manage, which was just above a husky whisper. "I'm as weak as a newborn kitten."

Hearing Tunstall's voice so reduced, struck Betsy like a hammer blow to her chest. It was more devastating than the red blood, which continued to soak through his black coat. In a way this was worse than seeing her father, for her father had never entirely recovered from the wound he'd taken at Gettysburg, while Tunstall was in the prime of life, and now he was reduced to a pitiable object.

Betsy couldn't help herself, and in the extremity of her distress and agony, her thoughts raged like tempestuous seas.

"What Lord? What? What? What have I possibly done to deserve this? Am I a Job that I should be so tormented? Why must my faith in Your ultimate goodness be so sorely tried? I tell you right now before You go any further that I am not that strong. To lose the two men I love most in the same way when there's not even a war? It's too much. Too much I tell you!"

She really wanted to tear her hair, and throw herself down full length in the dirt, pound her fists, and punish the very earth itself, for allowing such an outrage to take place on it. But Tunstall needed her, perhaps more than he ever had or would, so she would have to forgo the luxury of wallowing in mordant self-pity for the time being.

Tunstall fell the three inches back down on the horn, and used what little strength remained to interpose his hands on top of the horn between the leather and his chest, and curled the fingers of his right hand around the rim. He thought that if he sat up, which he could no more do on his own than fly, the blood in his lungs would choke him to death. For some reason, awkward as it was, the position of his body, slumped forward in the saddle, allowed him to breathe and speak. Enoch Swank or Doc Hill, God he wished to God one or both were with him. They would be able to explain his present condition in medical terms. All he knew was that any alteration in his position might result in the loss of one or both of these functions, and like Hamlet, Tunstall had things he needed to get off his chest before making his final journey to the land from whence no traveler returns. If he had to 'draw his breath in pain to tell his story', so be it.

"We're going to have to get you down," said Betsy, all but choking, herself. Her throat was swollen and tight with emotion, and it took all of her considerable will to keep from bawling like a baby. She was not only trying to meet all the challenges of the present situation, but quell the still potent memories of her father as well.

Tunstall's head was turned to the left facing the two women. As much as he hated to die with so much left undone, at least he had two beautiful women acting as ministering angels to smooth his path. If only he weren't so damned cold. Now, he was convinced beyond all doubt, that if there were a physical dimension to Hell, Dante and all the others were wrong about it being a place of fire, of boiling rocks, and heat. If Hell did exist, which Tunstall refused to believe, it was a place of darkness and cold like the grave. All this light, heat, and fire were more than likely a product of wishful thinking, for lurid and frightening as they might be, at least they were a sort, however horrible, of continuation of life and being. A frozen cold, non-being, a dimension of utter blackness, utterly devoid of light, a state diametrically opposed to the very concept of being, total annihilation, was in his opinion far more probable. This vision of Hell was infinitely more terrifying, a total antithesis to life.

If there were a First Principle; a Great Spirit, and Tunstall believed there had to be something that ordered things, for he saw a more convincing sermon in the perfection of a butterfly's wing than in all of scripture, then the highest aspiration of the soul would be to merge its energy with this Principle. Thus the spark, the soul, which no philosopher, scientist, or physician could either adequately define, much less locate, but which animated all living things, would at death, hasten to rejoin the divine entity or force from which it came. Depictions and images of God as a long haired, bearded white man, always a white man, Tunstall admired as art; however as religion, he found them absurd. Even Christ the Savior was doubtless more North African than white.

It was hard to believe that only last night he'd drunk cognac, smoked a cigar, and watched as a star fall near Ursa Minor. He'd been concerned about seeing Judge Holborne to try and avert Gypsy's trial. Though he wanted to make love to Betsy in the bright light of the quarter-moon, he was content to wait until they were alone in his usual suite of rooms in his favorite hotel in Santa Fe. That was less than ten hours ago and now it might as well have been his entire lifetime ago. He'd missed the last opportunity to physically unite with Betsy one last time, to draw close in the mystical act men value so highly they will lay down their lives for it, and even kill for. Choosing a partner with whom to make love occupies a large part of a man's life and often becomes his primary motivation for living. As much as Tunstall regretted the loss, at the same instant, he knew it was far less significant in his scheme of things, than the much more important fact that he truly loved Betsy and he thought she loved him as well.

He was still in Simon Bolivar's saddle, and Betsy and Gypsy were standing near him. He'd had the time to think all these things as if somehow time had elongated, like melted glass, pulling apart, stretching thin as he'd seen Enoch Swank do when he made glass rods and tubes. He responded to Betsy's statement about the need for him to dismount.

"Betsy, honey, I think I'd best stay right where I am. I am cold, cold as Hell, and if you could put those blankets over me right here I would be most grateful."

As he was speaking, Betsy and Gypsy put all three blankets over his back and tucked them around his neck leaving his head uncovered. The wool blankets were fairly thick and dense, their weight pressed on him pleasantly warming his shock-chilled body as the blessed numbness, which the mayor knew was the barrier between him and agony remained intact for the moment.

"Bless you," he said, "Bless you both. That's much better," and his teeth stopped chattering.

Betsy wanted to say so many things, the sum total of everything she'd ever left unsaid, though given her fearlessness and forthrightness in personal discourse, the sum was far less than it would have been with almost any other woman. As strong as she was, being an unmarried mother and rancher in the Territory and brought up by Josiah not only as his daughter but the son he'd yearned for and lost at birth together with Betsy's mother, Sara, Betsy was a sensitive woman. She was afraid once she began to say the things she wanted to so badly, she'd break down and be of no help to anyone. So she bit the inside of her lip until she tasted the salty blood, and even so the tears rolled down her cheeks unchecked.

More than he'd ever wanted anything, Tunstall wanted to hold Betsy, kiss away each precious tear, and tell her everything would be alright; however he thought the only thing holding his life together at the moment was his hands on the saddle horn, and if he reached out with his left hand to comfort Betsy, he'd simply fall apart and shatter into a million fragments. He could move his mouth and even wiggle his toes though he thought any other movement was fraught with danger.

"Betsy, it's been long enough since that first shot that I don't think there's going to be any more. They either changed their minds, or accomplished what they wanted to. It really doesn't matter. I want you to leave well enough alone. By that I mean don't you go off like Ate, goddess of revenge. Sara needs a mother not a martyr. Now, I know you so I want you to promise me you'll just let it go. Swear it on Josiah's name so I know you'll honor it."

Betsy had never seen Tunstall's tanned face look so pale and bloodless and so old. She'd expected more gunfire from the wall or even a mounted attack and she was eager to wreak vengeance on the cowards who shot her man in the back. Whoever had the heavy caliber rifle could have shot either her or Gypsy, before or after Tunstall, and even if for some unknown reason he couldn't shoot them, their horses would have been easy marks. Betsy thought this was looking more and more like an assassination and she had a good idea who had the resources and the motive for arranging such an attack. Jack Jones and Rose undoubtedly passed through Santa Fe, and the capitol was the center of Jessup's sphere of operations.

"I know what you're thinking," said Tunstall, "And that's why I want you to swear so do it!"

Tunstall's command not to seek revenge was costly in terms of expending what little life force remained to him. The mayor knew it and Betsy could see on his face how vitally important it was to him that she forswear violence.

"I swear by my father and Sara it will be as you wish. I will do nothing, much as it goes against my nature," said Betsy in a raspy voice. She was rewarded with a beatific smile that chased twenty years from Tunstall's face.

"Good," he said with a modicum of his old enthusiasm as if Betsy's swearing infusing him with energy.

"Now that we've settled that, I could really use a drink of water, I'm so thirsty I could drink a whole barrel."

Betsy took Tunstall's canteen and gently pressed the spout to Tunstall's lips and he tried to moisten his cracked and parched lips. She repeated the process four times and then the canteen was empty, most of the water having spilled, but Tunstall's burning thirst was slaked for the moment.

"Do you want more water?" asked Betsy in a flat monotone, for the situation was too painful for her mind to deal with and her body took over. It seemed to have its own coping mechanism in extreme crises and functioned independently when all the normal actions and reactions were rendered inoperable or inadequate. Tunstall noted her lack of affect and decided that given as little time as he had left, he was going to be selfish. He wanted Betsy with him, even at the risk of her breaking down completely. If this were a gunfight, he would never dream of trying to snap her out of her present state of mind, for such cold calculation meant the difference between survival and death.

He thought, "But I've got a right to want all of my Betsy just now, no matter how much pain her feelings and emotions cause her. This is my death, and I want her with me as I go."

"Gypsy," he said aloud. "What in Hell are you still doing here? Stop looking at me with those sad eyes and make tracks."

Gypsy had been doing some calculating of her own.

"Mayor," she said in a tight, squeaky voice. "I can't do this. I thought I could, but I can't and I won't. I ran out on my son because I thought it was the best thing I could do for his future. And maybe in one way it was. But another part of me says, 'No Gypsy, you took the coward's way out'. I'm sure Hal Russell meant to kill me, and I was so scared I killed him first. Maybe he

287

wouldn't have killed me after all, and I stabbed him because I was afraid of the look in his eyes. Now, I'm going to run because I'm scared I might have to go to prison. I know one thing. If I get to Trinidad and take that eastbound train, I'll never stop running and I'll spend the rest of my life in a prison inside my own mind, wondering what if I'd gone to Santa Fe, what if I went back to Houston to see my son? I know you're angry with me, and that's the last thing I want, because the good Lord Jesus himself wouldn't have been no better to me than you."

He looked at Gypsy, who was pushing her right fist into her front teeth to keep from crying, and then to Betsy.

"You know she doesn't have to go to Santa Fe, now. Our party was attacked, I'm proof of that, and Gypsy was captured, escaped, whatever story you decide on, it won't make much difference."

Betsy had already given Gypsy's immediate future some thought, and though it wouldn't enhance her reputation as a stalwart lawman to have Gypsy escape, given the circumstances, it wouldn't give rise to awkward questions either. If Gypsy detoured around Santa Fe and rode along the Canadian River almost due North, she'd reach Trinidad in Colorado on the Purgatoire River in the foothills. The town was named for Trinidad Baca, the daughter of an early settler. More importantly about six years ago, the Santa Fe Railway built a line through Raton Pass and once there, Gypsy could take a train back East. The way south was too dangerous between Coyoteros, discontented Apaches, and ranch hands who hadn't seen any women for months, a young, blonde haired, white woman riding three hundred miles alone wasn't just tempting fate, she was daring it.

The trail to Trinidad was clearly no walk in the park. It was more than two hundred miles unless she took the shorter route across the mountains following the Mora River. The road along the Canadian River was fairly well-marked and really only truly hazardous in winter due to snow in the foothills of the Sangre de Christo, though the accumulation of the Eastern slopes was usually less than on the Western side. Gypsy's safest course would be to backtrack along the Pecos to the junction of the Pecos and the Canadian just North of Santa Rosa. This would take her nearly seventy-five miles in the wrong direction and would add another sixty or so extra miles on the Canadian River trail, though there were watering places all along the Canadian.

"Once you reach Raton, you'll be fine," said Tunstall. "The Spanish named it after a nearby mountain that was home to a large number of rodents. The Santa Fe's building a line from Trinidad to Raton through the Raton Pass. It's Hell to travel in winter, not too bad now."

They discussed Gypsy's options and she adamantly refused to back-track along the Pecos.

"If I can't make the twenty five miles to the Mora. I'll turn back and backtrack, otherwise I'll be damned if I do!"

Gypsy was nearly out of her mind with grief. Tunstall had stood reso-lutely by her from the beginning, a mighty bulwark between her and the consequences of her stabbing Hal. The mayor unhesitatingly risked his reputation, and was willing to put his fortune and now his very life on the line, a mayor and a wealthy man doing all this for a young saloon girl, a whore, he only knew casually and never professionally. She thought, "If he would do all this for me, to what lengths would he go for Betsy?"

The enormity of what Betsy was about to lose hit her with greater impact than Hal's fist, and she grew so faint, she had to steady herself by grasping Betsy's shoulder.

"Gypsy," said Betsy, then she said nothing. She could see the girl was about to collapse.

"Gypsy," she began once more. "I need you to stand up. You can't be leaning or pulling on me right now."

Betsy spoke in exactly the same way she spoke to Sara when her daughter would start hanging on to her which was always when she needed to think clearly or do something that demanded her undivided attention.

"I need you to stand tall, now."

Gypsy immediately removed her hand and stopped leaning, and a hot flush of shame colored her previously ashen complexion.

"Sorry, She said. A thought occurred to her, "What about the horse and the saddle "Damn it you're right," said Betsy.

Tunstall's saddle was monogrammed JWT on both flaps, the rear of the cantle, as well as on the saddlebags. Abraham Lincoln was branded and even in, or especially in Trinidad no one would ride into town on a valuable horse and expensive personalized tack, abandon them at the livery stable, and board a train. Gypsy needed the cloak of anonymity and riding in on Tunstall's horse would capture the attention of whoever saw her, and was sure to make her arrival the subject of talk and speculation, and questions from anyone who she met with. She would create a sensation as great as Lady Godiva without removing a stitch of clothing.

Betsy couldn't in good conscience give her Enoch's Paso Fino. Not only didn't she have the right, though Betsy was certain Enoch would sacrifice Simon to save Gypsy, the Paso would attract at least as much unwanted attention as Tunstall's horse because of his gait. That left Betsy's Abby as the one remaining candidate. Abigail had accompanied Betsy west, and though she wasn't quite as much a part of her family as Sara, until this moment, it never occurred to Betsy that she might have to give up her mare. A chill like approaching doom raced up and down her backbone prickling like tiny cold mouse feet at the very idea

of Gypsy riding Abby across the escarpments and arroyos of the foothills to the Moro River. Gypsy was not a veteran horseman. She was an
amateur and wouldn't know when to dismount and go on foot, leading the horse to avoid a broken foreleg, or the sharp stones that would
bruise and even pierce her frogs.

"Lord," said Betsy silently, "I surely hope you hear me because it
seems to me you've been silent for a mighty long time. Whatever
you require of me, I'll give to you, even if I do have a choice. Just
leave me Sara, and please don't mind if I fuss and even curse a
bit. I'll live with it. Amen."

Betsy looked at Gypsy and was about to speak when Tunstall said in
a surprisingly and unexpectedly strong voice, "Gypsy, if you're going,
you'd better get started. Whoever shot me might just decide he doesn't
want any witnesses. Things are quiet right now, that doesn't mean
they're going to stay that way."

Tunstall could hardly believe his voice had any resonance. He'd
expected each word to begin with a wheeze or a croak. The blankets
helped with the cold, and all of a sudden he was desperately thirsty as if
he hadn't just drunk water minutes before.

"Betsy, could you hold my canteen up to my mouth?"

She took her own canvas covered metal canteen from her saddlebag,
unscrewed the white metal plug and held it up to the mayor's lips.
Tunstall pouched out his left cheek and allowed the warm water to
collect then he squeezed it down his throat by contracting his facial
muscles. The water spilled down the side of the saddle as Betsy
tilted it.

Gypsy's words had touched Betsy deeply, in a secret place where
she kept all her emotions about leaving Josiah treble locked away.
Tunstall, who was looking at Betsy all the while Gypsy was talking, saw

the animation return to her eyes and her well-loved face. It was almost as if for the past few minutes, Betsy had been like Pygmalion's ivory statue in Ovid's Metamorphoses, and Gypsy's words had brought her to life. He was incredibly thankful Betsy had come back on her own without him having to force her.

"Gypsy, I'm not only not angry with you. I'm as proud of you as if you were my own daughter. Now if you'll excuse us, Betsy and I have some private things we need to discuss."

Gypsy covered his stubble left cheek with her tears and her kisses.

"God bless you mayor. I'll pray for you day and night."

Betsy's face shone with tears as well, and Tunstall was tempted to tell her to save her prayers for the living, though he knew the Jews and many followers of the Eastern religions prayed for the repose of the dead. Given Gypsy's innocent heart, he supposed that given the efficacy of any human prayers for the benefit of the human soul after the death of the body, Gypsy's would be among the most likely to be of benefit, so he said nothing. Gypsy left Abraham standing next to Abby and Simon, and walked about twenty paces off along the road to Santa Fe, then knelt down on the earth, bowed her head in prayer and spoke the words of King David's twenty-third Psalm, which she'd committed to memory as a little girl.

Tunstall was a great devotee of the Bard from Stratford-on-Avon and had taken Shakespeare's musings about death in the great tragedies, King Lear, Hamlet, Macbeth, and Julius Caesar, and incorporated them into his own thinking on the subject. He and Enoch Swank had discussed death at some length on several occasions. Enoch believed one's death was a thing all men should contemplate, not only in the abstract as an objective phenomenon, but as the most personal and inevitable event in one's life.

"Birth," said Enoch. "Is the first important life event, though the mind of an infant remains as obscure to us as that of the elephant. All we know of the birth experience itself by one being born is from outside observation, and by the time a child can speak of it, he has entirely forgotten it. There are certain holy men, those whom Christians call charlatans and sorcerers who claim to be able to recount their births, though even I who try to maintain an open mind, have serious doubts about the accuracy and validity of their a-priori accounts, written decades after the fact. Truth is a strange thing. Those who actually knew the hidden truths, Christ and Buddha, the true philosophers, did not record them though doubtless both were extremely literate men better able to write than any of their disciples. They understood that truth cannot be collected like a butterfly, dried, and fixed to a specimen card for all to see. The difference between the live insect and the dead specimen is life, the Divine gift that only God can grant. I know I'm mixing metaphors here but bear with me. The butterfly once dead is no more than a pale image of its living self. Captain Ahab's statement that 'all physical objects are but as pasteboard masks', that is your written truth. Spoken truths retain enough of the life of the speaker to serve as a better approximation of the real thing. All the words ever written cannot begin to properly describe a single dawn. A painting or photograph can capture a goodly portion of the visual element, but without the human eye to experience the image and the universe of physical and emotional reactions based on memories, the finest oil painting ever painted means little. What ineffable, unfathomable joy to have heard the truth from Christ's own lips, or Buddha's, or Socrates', and have those words inscribed on one's heart by the Master."

Tunstall thought it was bizarre that he could recall that time with Enoch almost in its entirety, and that he had the time to do it. Betsy couldn't hold his hands. They were firmly attached to the saddle horn and Tunstall was more convinced than ever their grip was inextricably bound up with his hold on life. If he released just the left one, he was sure he'd die. He had no idea how long Betsy had been standing next to him with her hands on his left thigh.

"Now regarding death," continued Enoch, "As I'm sure you'll agree, death like birth is one of the two inescapable events in one's life. One begins, the other ends. Once more, man is wholly ignorant of the event, except for outside observation, which tells us nothing whatever of the person experiencing it. Yet more purely speculative accounts of death abound in literature, art, and poetry than of almost any subject except for love. Think of the Bible, John Donne, and Walt Whitman."

"How about me right now," thought Tunstall. Betsy was still standing beside him, and he marveled at not only her patience but also the patience of Simon Bolivar, Enoch's horse. It seemed to him that he, Betsy, and the horses had been motionless for at least half an hour.

In the days shortly before his father, Asa, died of pneumonia, when Tunstall was a boy of ten, the two of them talked about many things. Asa Tunstall was a marginally successful surveyor, well sinker, and real estate speculator, this last being both his passion and his nemesis. He rarely met with good fortune in his purchases, buying property that somehow always just missed being affected by whatever new road, or public works project, had prompted him to buy in the first place.

"Always a bridesmaid but never a bride," he'd say with a wry smile to his long-suffering wife who's tell him, "And if you'd stick to sinking wells, and measuring other folks property, instead of always looking to buy it, we'd have money in the bank, a new trap with a blooded horse to draw it, and John could look to Harvard or Yale instead of studying law with Matthew Pinkney."

While allowing her good natured chaffing about the trap and horse she coveted, to demonstrate to the world and those who actually were, that they were landed gentry, people who would never see the Tunstalls as anything other than over-educated tradesmen even if they'd had five traps and thoroughbreds to pull them. Asa vehemently objected to her denigrating Matthew Pinkney Esquire.

"Our son will learn more law from Matthew Pinkney, than any Harvard boy."

Asa's faith in lawyer Pinkney's virtues as a pedagogue was considerably greater than his wife's and had Asa lived, she may have persuaded him to send John to New England, but Asa took a cold from digging a well in late November, which progressed through bronchitis into galloping pneumonia within three weeks. The day before he drowned in his own sputum, Asa lectured his son about the value of time.

"Time," he said, "Is a constant. A minute is a minute and an hour is an hour. It' s our human perception of time that's inconstant - This is why one day can seem never- ending, and another can pass by in an instant. I think this has to do with our life spans as well, which is why I have never believed in trapping animals. The hour a squirrel spends in a trap may well seem like an eternity of ceaseless torment and agony to the little fellow. Even with a fatal shot to the head or heart, one never knows but it might take a year of his life to die in that instant."

Tunstall thought this perceived elongation of time might account for his thinking everything around him was standing still as if he were Joshua commanding the sun. He was surprised to find he had very few regrets. There were most certainly some but they seemed relatively unimportant. They were of the "What if I'd stayed with Mary Selkirk, memories like that, and if there hadn't been such a bitter fight over the widow Henderson's property rights, then he might never have gone West and settled in the New Mexico Territory.

The New Mexico chapter of his life was by far the most satisfactory, except of course for the ending. Had his father lived, Asa would have had the last laugh at his detractors, when a new state road was routed through forty acres of one of his properties, and the frontage was declared fit for an extension of the city limits. Tunstall's share made it possible for him to build his fine home in Early and set himself up as the principal man of the town, though it was his knowledge of law, courtesy of Lawyer Pinkney that won him the position of justice of the peace and mayor. He had enjoyed his hacienda, his books, furniture, and decorations, but now these things were of no significance whatever.

> "I am dying," he thought, 'under the sun' as is spoken of again Ecclesiastes, and the old Jew was right. It is all vanity and the day of death is better than the day of birth, but then he says in his next breath that it's better to be a live dog than a dead lion so which should I believe? I'll find out soon enough, I suppose." All this and much more played itself out in Tunstall's mind in a series of fast moving images.

Betsy was unaware of the frenzied processes of mentation taking place within the man on the horse beside her, bent over the saddle horn as if he would never rise again. She badly wanted him to lie down on the makeshift bed, at least then she could lie down next to him and hold his hand. He seemed so closed off up in the saddle, remote within himself.

> "It's as if he's excluding me, protecting me as he always does with everyone and now that's the very last thing I want. But this isn't about my feelings, this is his time and his moment."

Betsy remembered how she felt when she and the rest of the town thought Tunstall had perished along with Rat Face and the Coyoteros. In the days that followed she was like the dried husk of her former self, like one of the almost transparent shells one finds in the dirt after a locust molts. Betsy was somnambulating through each minute of the endless days, making an effort at being animated for Sara's sake and otherwise not really caring if it were night or day.

As Reverend Gilbert's congregation and the others gathered in the church finished eulogizing their martyred mayor, and were closing with the singing of Amazing Grace, Tunstall walked in the back, bloody, burnt, naked, looking like a man who just walked right out of Hell. Betsy knew that God, or the Force that ordered the universe, whatever inadequate name one gives it, was surely closer to her in that instant than He or It usually was, or so it seemed. This time, however there would be no miraculous resurrection, as least in the world she knew, and Betsy needed to accept the pain, just as she'd so willingly embraced the joy of seeing him in the church a little more than a year ago. Betsy had her attention fixed on Tunstall 's face, and she saw he was slipping away not only from her but releasing the cords that bound him to life. It was as if he were being swept out to sea not that Betsy had ever seen the ocean. She and Tunstall had talked about taking Sara by train to Galveston to see the Gulf of Mexico though now this and all their other dreams and plans would never come to pass. Tunstall blinked his eyes and left his reveries of Asa and he was once more seated on Enoch's Paso Fino with Betsy beside him.

"I'm sorry, Betsy. I drifted away there for a while."

"Where were you?" she asked softly and kindly.

"No need to speak so softly," he said. "I may be dying. That doesn't mean I'm so fragile you have to whisper."

This was the mayor's first direct reference to death, and he spoke kindly, out of concern for Betsy.

"I want to remember you as you are naturally, not as woman worried about me or my feelings. I've been with my father, Asa, and with Enoch talking about life and death, how you don't have one without the other, why we foolish mortals cry tears of joy over the one and tears of grief over the other. Enoch Swank is a learned man and he's been with Princeton professors and Apache sorcerers. There are sages that teach that this is not the only world, and why should it be? Now I see it more clearly. What sense does it make that we are born, live to our three score years and ten, and I at least won't have to endure the manifold indignities of infirmity, only to vanish without a trace, leaving little but a headstone and hopefully some memories? Christians talk about heaven and the eternal kingdom then why bother living in this world at all? So we can prove ourselves worthy? In that case **I'd** say heaven is an empty place and Hell's full. Gilbert and other sanctimonious preachers of his stripe say you're saved by the grace of Jesus alone when Jesus, himself, said quite clearly "many are called and few are chosen". Damned few I'd say. If creatures have a spark of the Divine in them, call it a soul if you will, then this imperishable soul lives on in some way. Why shouldn't it, as the Buddhists maintain, take on another life, be reborn in a different physical body? I say why limit the soul to this world? Why not an infinite number of worlds and universes After all there's a world and a universe in a drop of rainwater. I've seen one in Swank's microscope. The earth and all the stars in the Milky Way could be no more than a drop of water in some inconceivable dimension beyond all human understanding. Why not I ask you?"

Tunstall stopped his discourse abruptly. He thought, "I must sound like a madman. All I'm doing is frightening the woman I love, but I don't want to talk about love, sorry but I just don't. No, more than that I can't."

Tunstall looked at Betsy and smiled. "I'm on the threshold of shade and I can tell you that I believe that life and death function according to principles of such unimaginable complexity and profundity and in so many dimensions that we foolish mortals can't begin to comprehend them in our most sublime moments of genius. It's not that we wouldn't want to it's just that the human mind simply can't do it any more than we can fly like birds or breathe under water like fish. Man has physical limitations and mental ones as well. Therefore I say that when we, in our abysmal ignorance of the realities behind the realities that shape our lives, give in to despair even our loneliest extremity of suffering, doing so is a form of pathetic, petulant arrogance. Betsy, I tell you truly there are worlds undreamt of within us and outside of us. Yes. I'm sad to leave you, immeasurably sad. I love you."

At this Betsy's tears streamed out in a torrent, covering her face from her eyes to her chin, blinding her. With a supreme effort of his indomitable will, Tunstall froze the tidal wave of empathetic sorrow at all the things that were not to be for Betsy and him. The tide obeyed him as it was his own creation and he bade it to be gone. This was not the time for indulgence; however great a comfort it would be.

"Enoch Swank is my executor, and my will, is as you who know me as well as he does might imagine, eccentric and I make no apologies for it. I will not waste what little time we have left on details, only that I have left my home to you, on the condition you do not sell it for a year after my death."

"I don't want anything from you Tunstall," said Betsy choking on her tears and the hard, unyielding lump in her throat. The mayor pointedly ignored her heartfelt declaration.

"As Gypsy has elected, foolishly though nobly I might add, to face all the vicissitudes and uncertainties of a Santa Fe jury consisting of fools, idlers, and buffoons, and place her fate in their unwashed hands, this solves the problem of my horse, which I admit has been vexing me. You shall have him, or rather Sara shall have him whenever you judge the time to be fortuitous."

The thought that Sara Johnson would ride his well beloved horse gave the mayor an intense sensation of bliss.

Betsy was awestricken that in the greatest extremity of his life, Tunstall would shift from dwelling on the meaning and significance of

his own death, to thinking of a future life from which he would necessarily be excluded, and marry his horse, his dearly loved constant
companion of nearly ten years, to her seven year old daughter. All the
literary accounts, fiction, drama, and poetry that employed the con-
ceit of a heart broken by loss, whether of loved one or love, wrenching
and accurate as some were, paled in Betsy's opinion, compared to the
immediate enormity of the heart break she was enduring. As bad as it
was with Arthur and her father, this was worse, and as she fought to
force breath past the stone that seemed to be lodged in her windpipe,
Betsy wondered if a human heart really could just break like a glass
dropped on a stone floor. If so hers was close to breaking.

Tunstall had done this from the best intentions. Pairing the horse,
Betsy knew he loved, nearly as much as he loved her, with Sara, was too
poignant for Betsy to bear.

"Oh, Betsy," he said. "It is so good to look upon your face.
Better than the heavens the mountains. The sea in all its
vastness does not contain such depths of meaning. I always
thought Melville guilty of blasphemy when he has Captain
Ahab say to his first mate, Starbuck, "Let me look into a human
eye; it is better than to gaze into sea or sky; better than to gaze
upon God'. And now, I know he spoke truly for I would rather
look into your green eyes, Elizabeth Johnson, than anything
in all creation and if I must choose between God and you, I
choose you."

Tunstall's last breath must have shifted the Sharps' slug; either that or
the shock was wearing off. He had no intention of dying with a scream
in his mind. Unconsciousness was in a race with agony, and Tunstall
believed he could affect the outcome in his favor. He knew he'd lost a
great deal of blood and if the bullet had come out his chest, he would
have bled to death in the first few minutes. The distance from the ruins
of the Pecos missions was great enough to have vitiated some of the
energy and velocity of the Sharp's cartridge and this loss, combined

with Tunstall's muscular back, kept the nearly one ounce slug from blasting right on through his body.

Tunstall thought of Mercutio in Romeo and Juliet, "Marry, tis enough to make worms' meat of me."

He knew if nothing remarkable happened soon, any dignity remaining to his dying, would be buried under an avalanche of pain. It wasn't even that he feared the pain, it was that so far his death had been his own, a play in which he was not only the principal actor, but the director as well to a point, and he didn't want pain to usurp his role in the drama. He would exit the stage of his own free will before death, the ultimate manager of all men's fates, brought down the curtain.

His hadn't been the perfect death, though Tunstall's notion of a perfect end wasn't most men's. The general wish to die in one's sleep was not at all what he wanted for himself. Tunstall knew most men didn't dwell too much on death, except in the abstract, something inevitable yet always happening to someone else.

Tunstall allowed as how if he had his choice, he would meet death at the close of day as the sun was setting, painting the clouds in the eastern sky, orange and pink. He would not be in a bed indoors at his home. It would be one of those unnaturally warm afternoon in late autumn, when the evening breeze is beginning to whisper through the pinion pines in the foothills of the Sangre de Christo mountains, and his life would end as his heart gave out, painlessly, his eyes fixed on the glorious sunset, his ears filled with the melodious calls of birds. Enoch had agreed with him that this was a good death and the apothecary shared Tunstall's wish to 'shuffle off this mortal coil' outdoors in the vastness, as opposed to inside a room, which was little more than an a more expansive coffin.

"If I have my druthers," said Enoch, "I'd like a death similar to yours, only I'd be somewhere out in the Sonora desert in late spring at dawn, and pass on with the rising sun, my soul taken away on its rays, my nostrils filled with the fresh scents you get as the morning wind scours the desert for the oils being released by the fragrant desert flowers and herbs to attract bees so they might pollinate and reproduce. The ancient Egyptians believed the soul left the body through the nostrils, then it was off to the kingdom of the dead to be weighed in the Scales of Osiris, balanced against a pure white feather, and then directed by Horus either to the Western Lands or if weighed and found wanting, thrown to the jackal-headed Devourer."

Tunstall thought, "At least I'm outside in the foothills, on horseback, that's at least an approximation of my ideal death."

Both he and Enoch were in agreement that the Apaches had the right idea about putting their dead on a sort of Indian version of a catafalque, wrapped in appropriate cerements, not buried in the earth, but left open to the elements and nature. Tunstall observed at the time that the pine box or casket in the churchyard wasn't for the dead but the living so that they could pay all the respects they never had for the deceased in life and offer prayers for the soul of the departed. He left very specific instructions in his will that he be buried in the churchyard of the Cathedral of St. Francis in Santa Fe because,

"I'll be damned if I'll let Reverend Gilbert spit on my grave whenever he has a mind to. St. Francis had a deep sense of brotherhood under God and that's a good thing, although Lord knows I'm no Catholic."

The Bishop, John Lamy, had agreed to permit him to be buried in the churchyard despite his being a non-Catholic. Tunstall had thought it important in the unlikely event his younger brother or perhaps a nephew or niece would come to the New Mexico Territory and succumb to an urge to visit their relative's last resting place. Seated in Enoch's saddle the whole question was rendered both utterly trivial and completely irrelevant, and Tunstall regretted not simply telling Betsy to dispose of his earthly remains however she saw fit. Whether his body rested in Santa Fe, Gilbert's graveyard, somewhere on Betsy's ranch, or right here in the deserted ruins, made not the slightest bit of difference to him, much less the grand scheme of the universe. He supposed it was too late, though he could dictate a codicil to Betsy, and use his last strength to sign it; however it was an exercise in futility. Enoch would take Betsy's word for it and strike the section with the funeral arrangements if it came to that. It wasn't as if his brother would come to the Territory, contest the will, dig up his coffin, wherever it was, and take it back with him.

"Betsy," he said, "I think my time is nigh. I'm tired and all I want to do is close my eyes and sleep. The only regret I'll have is then I can't see you."

This statement was slightly disingenuous, and he regretted it as soon as the words were out of his mouth. What he meant to say was something entirely different, and if he couldn't speak the truth at the penultimate moment of his life, then the whole long and often painful exercise was little more than an elaborate tissue of convenient lies.

"No, forget what I just said. Betsy, you are the love of my life, and I owe you nothing but the truth. Hell, I owe myself nothing but the truth. I've got my foot in the stirrup and if I don't mount up and ride off, I'm in for a whole lot of pain. I don't want to go, screaming, gritting my teeth till they crack. I think if I sit up, I'll go before the pain gets me, maybe not with a smile, at least not with a groan. It's kind of like one of those dreams when you're running on the ground about to fly. I know I can fly if I sit up, but my body won't balance and I'll fall off and I didn't want you to see that. Hell, I might surprise myself and fall backwards. So I'm telling you, don't scream when I do it, because if I don't do it soon, things are going to get ugly. I'm going now, my love. Give Sara a kiss from the president."

This last reference was to the time when Sara first met the mayor, and she thought since he was dressed in a fine black suit and looked official, that Tunstall was the president or 'pres'dent' as she put it.

Betsy looked up for a moment, as the sun was hot on her head, and she wanted to have some idea of the time, as if time had any relevance. There were three buzzards making their habitual graceful loops, round and round, doubtless confusing the lack of motion from the horses as distress prefatory to the prostration preceding death. Betsy had seen buzzards feasting on the bloated, rotting carcass of a steer that had fallen down a steep ravine. The dead steer's hide was stretched over the ribs, though there were enough putrescent fluids remaining in the belly to interest the six, large red—headed turkey vultures, who tore at the tough hide, their white-tipped hooked beaks slashing like knives, their naked heads scarcely taking the time to turn away from their feast to look disparagingly at Betsy and Abigail as if to say, "the living are of no interest at all, we will come for you too after you're dead."

Betsy was fascinated and repelled by the two and a half foot tall birds. Tunstall turned his head to the right, looked up as best he could and saw the three buzzards.

Chapter 19
PRESIDENT

Betsy watched her daughter sit the trot bareback, using nothing more than a rope halter with the lead tied to make a pair of reins to guide the horse. Sara was really depending almost entirely on leg pressure, which given her forty or so pounds was more in the realm of magic than skill. Betsy had ridden Abigail bareback in Kentucky when she was twelve with a snaffle bit and a regular leather headstall. Sara was seven, and the year she'd spent with the Mescalero Apache boys and their ponies, had given her a knowledge of horsemanship, not quite equal to Betsy's now, though Sara probably knew things her mother didn't. Sara could have managed without even the rope halter and ridden like the Indians with nothing between them and their ponies, communicating with seat, leg, and voice alone. Sara really was performing miracles considering she'd only had the black quarter horse for less than a month, and before that the horse had only known stock saddle, headstall, and a man weighing almost five times as much as Sara for years. Abraham had taken to Sara from the first day they met as if he'd been told the girl were his new master. Sara immediately rechristened him President, because she reasoned, the president was the leader of all the people and her horse was the leader of all the horses.

It was a warm afternoon and the heat of the summer was gradually giving way to the wistful cool of early autumn, though the change was more pronounced as the diminished hours of sunlight gave way to earlier and earlier evenings. Sara eased President into a slow lope, which Sara and Betsy liked best of all gaits. The lope was such a peaceful, rocking mode of riding, and Sara's seat was almost perfect, hips forward, bottom back, trunk upright, her reins collected just enough, not pressing on President's face. Maybe Sara didn't need reins at all, or even a hank of President's shaggy, black mane; though Betsy thought the reins were insurance. One never knew what a horse might take offense at, and bolt, rear, or buck.

The first time Abigail crossed paths with a sidewinder, she reared, bucked, and shy tossing Betsy into a prickly pear cactus. Still, there was precious little in the way of equitation instructions Betsy thought she could offer Sara.

Betsy thought, "As Tunstall was so fond of saying Leonardo used to say, 'poor is the student who doesn't surpass his master."

Nearly a full month had passed since that single shot boomed like a stroke of summer thunder near the Pecos ruins, and changed everything in Betsy's life except for Sara. Tunstall never countermanded his instructions to be buried in the cathedral graveyard. Betsy acted on her own instincts, and after the mayor died, she sent Gypsy to Santa Fe on Abigail, tied Tunstall to Simon Bolivar and rode back to Early on Tunstall's horse leading Enoch's Paso Fino.

Betsy made it to Early an hour before dusk and went directly to the livery stable where Ernesto was brushing down Marcie Cabot's piebald cob. He saw the mayor tied to Enoch's Paso, dropped the brush, and nearly stumbled over a tin bucket filled with iodine and liniment in his haste to reach Betsy.

"Madre de Dios," he said with an expression of horror disfiguring his handsome face. Betsy had removed Abby's headstall before coming into the stable and now she let go of the lead rope. Ernesto was clearly shaken to his core and his wiry body trembled. As mayor, the entire Mexican community in Early regarded Tunstall with affection bordering on veneration. Betsy held out her arms and Ernesto embraced her, then he broke down completely, sobbing as if the world had come to an end. After a few minutes the storm subsided and Ernesto told Betsy he considered it a great honor to see to the 'alcalde' as he referred to Tunstall.

"I'll send you a clean suit within the hour or I'll bring it myself," said Betsy. She and Ernesto agreed that because of the heat, and the beginning stages of decomposition, Ernesto would wash him, dress him, and lay him out in a pine box without delay. Betsy knew Tunstall wouldn't have wanted people staring at his corpse whether he'd died in Early of natural causes in mid-January, instead of a gunshot in Pecos in late August. Billy, the young man who was secretly in love with Gypsy, was filling the water trough near City Hal when he saw Betsy ride in leading Swank's horse. It was too far for him to see exactly what was on the Paso Fino, though it looked like it might be a body. Thinking something awful must have happened to Gypsy, he sprinted down the dusty street to the stable. When he arrived, sweating and breathless, Billy was astonished to see Mr. Aguilar in the marshal's arms, crying like a baby. Billy had seen tears on Ernesto's face when he'd had to put down a horse with a fractured foreleg, using his antiquated Spencer carbine, given to him by a veteran in exchange for boarding a horse. Ernesto was a gentle man, who understood horses in a non-verbal, intuitive way to the extent that Enoch Swank once told him he spoke horse, or caballo, a compliment that pleased Ernesto immensely. Billy liked Mayor Tunstall, he liked him very much, though sorry as he was, he was relieved to see the body on Enoch's Paso Fino wasn't Gypsy's.

Ernesto had cried himself out when he raised his head from Betsy's tear-stained shoulder and saw Billy.

"Billy," he said, heedless of the tears drying on his cheeks, "Good. Come, we have work to do."

Billy didn't know what to say to Betsy. He wanted to ask her about Gypsy, though he knew this wasn't the best time or place. Betsy saw the boy's confusion and said, "It's alright Billy. You don't have to say any-thing. There really isn't anything anyone can say," and Betsy managed a small smile and walked out of the stable.

> "First," said Ernesto, "We get the alcalde off his horse. Then I attend to him, and you see if Mr. Swank's saddle can be saved. Go to the boardinghouse and see if you can borrow a pail of milk. Milk is good for removing blood." Ernesto looked at the mayor's own horse, and was amazed to see Betsy had left the mayor's gilded, engraved, Winchester 1866 in the saddle scab-bard. The rifle was a work of art and despite it taking an obsolete rim-fire cartridge, it was still very valuable. Ernesto knew that regardless of how composed Betsy might appear, she couldn't help but be utterly undone and distracted, and the fact she'd forgotten all about the precious Winchester was proof of her parlous state of mind. Ernesto would take the rifle to Mr. Swank just as soon as he finished washing, dressing, and laying out the alcalde. The stable manager had a small number of pre-finished pine coffins in an empty stall. It would be the work of less than thirty minutes to have one ready for the mayor.

As Betsy was leaving the stable, she could see there was already a group of townspeople gathering outside and the buzz of their voices filled the air, drowning out the cicadas, crickets, and locusts. Betsy was pray-ing they'd leave her along, knowing it wasn't going to happen. Ernesto was one thing. Hard as it was to face him, she knew he really loved the mayor, and this rendered his grief palatable to her, because it was authentic. Who among those gathering, so busy talking, cared for him, or even liked him, except when he saved them, once from themselves when they were going to string up Deaf Charlie, and once from Rat Face and El Gordo? They no doubt conveniently forgot all the other less celebrated and less obvious occasions when his sense of honor and fair play saved them from committing a hundred less serious sins.

Betsy decided she couldn't face their questions or their false expressions of horror and grief, so she turned and walked back into the stable. Billy led her to a back door, out past a waist high pile of hay, fragrant with the ammoniac stink of horse-piss and a lesser pile of horse dung that hadn't made it yet to the arroyo outside of town. Not surprisingly, no one was waiting outside next to the piles. The smell of rotting hay, soaked with urine was pungent enough to sting her eyes and make her gag slightly. Betsy would have walked straight through the piles naked rather than through the townspeople, and she made it to Enoch's home without being accosted.

Enoch didn't have glass windows, though the wooden shutters were up, not that their position was any indication of the master being in residence or absent, for he closed them only in inclement weather, or when the temperature was cold enough to make him light the stove. This usually took place in late November at the earliest otherwise he'd wear a heavy coat and walk around inside seeing his breath. Betsy thought she could see an oil lamp through the open window. She knocked on the front door, which was of thin pine, nothing like Tunstall's, which would have done justice to the cathedral in Santa Fe.

Enoch was at home alone, almost as if he were waiting for Betsy. Francine was not there as she was tending the saloon. He greeted Betsy at the door and she was struck by how his almost plain, long face was beautiful in its own way, like Lincoln's was, because of the intelligence that animated it, and the wisdom rooted in adversity that dignified it. Enoch stood silently in the twilight for a long moment then he said quietly. "John is dead, isn't he?"

Once again, Betsy's heart cracked asunder there and then, her lips quivered, and large, warm, tears rolled from her eyes and down her cheeks as the emotions she'd held in check at the livery stable broke loose. Her throat swelled up like a bullfrog and her mouth was as dry as if she'd been out in the desert without water for hours. Her raspy voice retained little of her usual melodic contralto as she choked out, "Yes."

Enoch's lanky frame sagged, and his long arms seemed to reach his knees, as he let out a low, quite loud sigh that, even in the midst of her own sorrow, Betsy thought was the saddest sound she'd ever heard.

Enoch's sigh was as if he'd just been told every friend he'd ever had or ever would have, had died, and he was doomed to live all alone for a very long time. It was the sound of hopeless despair without the slightest hope of redemption, a final and infinite loss. Betsy thought she had come to a provisional acceptance of Tunstall's death, just as she'd come to temporary terms with Josiah's. She knew that at some level there would always be grief at never being able to see or talk to her father ever again, though like all but fatal wounds, scar tissue and scabs would form. Some healing inevitably takes place in the living even after the deepest lacerations to the soul as part of the necessary process of continuing with life.

Enoch's sigh threatened the uneasy truce between Betsy's emotions and her lover's death, and for a brief time, there in the doorway the outcome was in doubt. Then as if his spirit were by her side, Betsy heard Tunstall's deep bass voice quoting Shakespeare, a short speech by Caesar to his wife, Calphurnia, in reply to her fears for him should he attend the Senate after her nightmare and a night of evil signs and portents. Betsy spoke the words aloud as if it were a prayer, "Of all the wonders that I yet have heard; it seems to me most strange that men should fear; seeing that death; a necessary end; will come when it will come."

Tunstall was very fond of this quote and as Enoch heard it anew from Betsy, it made him aware, not that he didn't know it full well before that John Tunstall would always be with him. When he'd seen Betsy alone, he knew instantly that Tunstall was gone, as surely as if he saw the body, and it was the shock that elicited the animal sigh, the howl of a wolf that has lost its mate. Then Betsy quoting Tunstall's beloved Shakespeare brought him out of blackest misery like Ariadne's thread lead Perseus from the Labyrinth.

"How thoughtless of me," he said in a chastened voice and he held out his lanky arms and Betsy walked into his enveloping embrace.

Chapter 20
THE LAST LAUGH

Seated in Enoch's tiny study, surrounded by books on chemistry, physics, biology, botany, and medicine, each of them with a full glass of Napoleon brandy and a rich, dark brown cigarillo, Betsy recounted the hours at Pecos in minute detail. Enoch was intensely interested in Tunstall's every word and Betsy did her best to recall each one verbatim. Enoch's brow furrowed and his face darkened as she told him of the thunderous boom that came from the ruins of the Spanish mission.

"Cowards," he spat out, as if it were the worst curse under heaven, one that would adhere to the assassin's soul like flaming tar, and damn him to Hell.

"Sorry," he said. "Pray continue, don't mind me."

Betsy looked at Enoch, knowing exactly what he was thinking.

"Enoch, Tunstall made me swear a sacred oath not to do anything to investigate or avenge his death. I didn't want to. He insisted and I swore on my father and my daughter. He said the same injunctions applied even more strongly to you, and that you had best not flout them. That was the word he used. I've already flouted his instructions to be buried in Santa Fe. I'm not going back to Pecos to try and pick up the murderer's trail. I don't need to, because I know who killed him even if he didn't pull the trigger himself, If you want to go together with me and kill the murderer when the opportunity comes I am all for it. As Tunstall said, "Life is more like a wheel than a path." "You decide. I can't because of my oath. We come into the world naked and messing on ourselves, and we'll go out pretty much the same way if we live long enough. We bring nothing with us but our souls, and none of us is taking anything out, only I think we can lose our souls along the way."

Betsy took a luxuriant drag on her cigar and blew a well-formed smoke ring that expanded to nearly four inches in diameter as it crossed the tiny study before crashing into a finely bound, full calf, quarto volume of Newton's Principia Mathematica.

"Nice one," said Enoch. Betsy took a sip of her brandy, set down her glass, and look Enoch squarely in the eye. "The question is do we want to give up a part of our souls to do it, or do we listen to Tunstall and let it end here as he wanted it to end." Enoch took his cigar between his beautiful, long fingers and puffed twice, then blew out a smoke ring followed by two concentric rings, which telescoped together forming one very thick ring which hung in the air for quite some time before dispersing.

"What does your heart say?" he asked.

"My heart is torn in so many pieces it can't. I want him to hurt as bad as I'm hurting. Then again I've already killed at least two men that I know of because I saw the light go out of their eyes after I shot them. They would have killed me if I hadn't shot first, no questions like about Gypsy and Hal, none at all. It's a year since the last one and you know the story. I'm not proud of it, and part of me wishes I hadn't done it, but we both know I didn't have any choice."

"I have been more fortunate," said Enoch. "I haven't had to kill another man, though if you want to avenge Tunstall, I will go with you when the time comes, and if I have to pull the trigger of my Smith and Wesson, or roll a boulder down on top of him I won't hesitate at the ultimate moment."

Betsy said suddenly and decisively, "Let it end here then. That's what he wanted and I'll just have to learn to live with it and so will you."

"I agree as long as Jessup doesn't come here and brag about it," said Enoch. "If he does then all bets as they say are off."

"I don't think he'll say a word. Yes, Tunstall had his detractors in the capitol but he had some real friends and admirers there too. Jessup's gotten his revenge for all the good it'll do him. Let his soul go to Hell, or wherever such twisted, crippled spirits go."

"It runs contrary to my nature, as I'm sure it does to yours even more than mine to let this base assassination go unanswered; however your course is by far the more noble one, the more heroic one, and most importantly it's what Tunstall wanted. You did the right thing bringing him back, though we must now decide where he will rest. I don't think he'd have wanted to lie in the churchyard."

"No," said Betsy. "He tolerated Reverend Gilbert but he never forgave him for leading the lynch mob."

"That leaves his courtyard, your ranch, the reservation, or an unknown grave in the desert or the mountains. It's entirely up to you."

"I think the only reason Tunstall made arrangements in Santa Fe was in case one of his relatives came through the Territory to pay his respects."

"Well, it's not likely they'll come through Early."

"No," said Betsy considering her alternatives. "I don't know if the Apaches would want a white man buried on their land."

He smiled, "Unless I completely miss my guess, I believe in Tunstall's case they would not only make an exception, they would consider it an honor to have such a warrior rest on reservation land."

Betsy fidgeted in her chair. "I don't mean to be coarse, but with the heat and all, we uh, need." Enoch knew precisely what Betsy was talking about.

"If the chiefs and medicine men turn us down, which I think is about as unlikely as the sun rising in the West tomorrow, then we'll bury him at your ranch."

"There is one place in particular he was very fond of. It's on a little rise and has a beautiful view of the foothills. The last thing I want is to have to cart his coffin around in this heat. I'm hoping for the reservation. That way Deaf Charlie and all Tunstall's Indian friends can pay their respects. It'll keep any people from Early far away and I know he would have liked that."

"Good. If the town wants a memorial service, they can have it on their own account."
"Trust me, Tunstall would prefer the Mescalero and Pima to see to his earthly remains anyway."

"Then we should ride out to the reservation at dawn. There will probably be ceremonies in his honor. We always talked about whether we wanted to die with the rising or the setting sun."

"I know, that's pretty much all he talked about, as I told you. It was almost word for word about conversations you two had."

"You still haven't told me about his final moments. You left me with the vultures circling overhead."

Betsy took a sip of brandy, put down her glass, thought about her cigar and decided to leave it sitting on its stand in the brass ashtray.

"I've been saving it," she smiled.

Enoch took a deep drag off his cigar and blew a large tester of smoke ceiling ward. He knew a lifelong Shakespearean like Tunstall, given the amount of time he had to contemplate his approaching death, would have said something of a very profound nature. Perhaps something similar to Hamlet's dying words to Horatio, though more richly detailed.

Betsy took a deep breath and began, keenly aware that Enoch Swank, Princeton graduate, scientist, philosopher, and polyglot, was almost literally hanging on her every word.

"I was looking at him, waiting, holding my breath, afraid to move. It was like being in a dream only I knew I was awake. I couldn't even hold his hand. He was holding on to your saddle horn like it was the only thing connecting him to this life. He wasn't in pain. It must have been the shock, you'd know better than I would. He said he knew the pain was coming and he didn't want to die like that. I said those turkey vultures must think between our three horses, they're going to have themselves some feast. Tunstall looked up over his right shoulder. Mind you he'd been looking at me over his left. I could tell by the grimace before he turned, that it cost him dear, but you know him, he just had to see. Then I heard this big, wet smack. One of the buzzards must have eaten pretty well that morning, because that bird emptied his bowels and a good part of it landed on Tunstall's forehead just below the hairline. I was stunned and I could see he was too. Then he started to shake all over and all I could hear was his laugh booming like thunder over the ruins of the old mission. All I could think about was whoever fired that shot could hear Tunstall laughing. I prayed to God he could, and I believe in my heart he did. Then I knew it was Tunstall who'd won, no matter what. That laugh was so deep and so loud it echoed through that destroyed mission. It seemed to go on and on as if God, Himself, were laughing at the best joke in all Creation. I couldn't help myself and I started laughing. It was contagious. The sound of his laughter filled my ears, then my mind. When I stopped laughing I looked at him and he was gone."

Betsy drained her glass and Enoch stood up and refilled it from the squat, green glass bottle. He filled his own and raised it high.

"Here's to you Betsy Johnson. Tunstall said you were the best thing that ever happened to him, and having known you he could die content having known the greatest possible earthly joy. I flatter myself to think I knew him better than anyone and I know he meant every word, not just with his lips at that moment, but with all his heart and all his soul."

Betsy raised her glass and her green eyes shone as she said, "To John Walker Tunstall. Wherever you are, hearsed in heaven or enthroned by the River, may you know nothing but joy."

They clinked their glasses together and Enoch drained his in one draught. Betsy drank half of hers and sat back down. She asked Enoch, "What would you say to another cigar?"

Enoch said with a smile that made his long face glow with pleasurable anticipation.
"I'd say Tunstall would definitely approve."

THE END

www.ingramcontent.com/pod-product-compliance
Lightning Source LLC
Chambersburg PA
CBHW031248170626
46807CB00001B/41